STOLEN

NIGHT

Rebecca Maizel holds an undergraduate degree from Boston University and an MA in English from Rhode Island College. She is currently pursuing an MFA in Writing for Young Adults at Vermont College.

Books by Rebecca Maizel

Infinite Days
Stolen Night

Praise for Infinite Days*:*

'*Infinite Days* is a grab-you-by-the-throat, ignore-the-world-around-you, fall-completely-in-love-with kind of book, the kind I haven't really read since *Twilight*. Yep. I just used the T-word' AllThingsUrbanFantasy. blogspot.com

'*Infinite Days* builds to an exciting conclusion, and leaves the door wide open for a kick-ass sequel' www.wondrousreads.com

'There is no other vampire book like it and if you have a love for immortals but are fed up with reading more or less the same story over and over again, then *Infinite Days* is the ideal book to pick up . . . Maizel's writing is beautiful . . . Her voice is very unique and has an eloquence to it that I wish we could see more of in young adult fiction' www.yabookreads.com

'I found myself thinking about this novel long after I'd put it down . . . It plays around but still retains the haunting and tortured tone of all the best vampire stories' www.amazon.co.uk

Rebecca Maizel

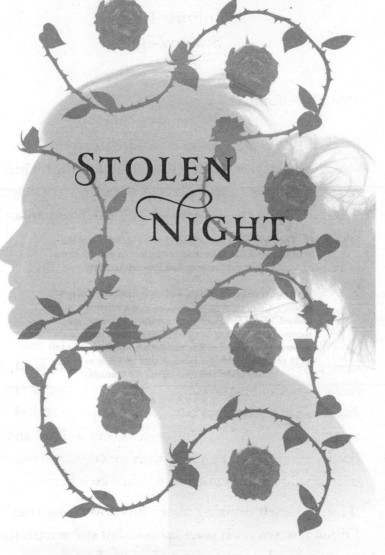

Stolen Night

MACMILLAN

For Ryan Quirk, who is brave

First published 2012 by Macmillan Children's Books
a division of Macmillan Publishers Limited
20 New Wharf Road, London N1 9RR
Basingstoke and Oxford
Associated companies throughout the world
www.panmacmillan.com

ISBN 978-0-330-52045-4

A CIP catalogue record for this book is available from
the British Library.

Printed and bound by CPI Group (UK) Ltd, Croydon CR0 4YY

An ancient parchment lies in a darkened, sacred place.
Its location unknown, its maker anonymous. It is legend.
On it is described a ritual, its words inscribed in blood.
This ritual requires the deepest love and ultimate
sacrifice – death. It will transform a vampire
into a human again. My love, Rhode, had
performed this ritual for me, and died.
I performed it only days ago.
And I survived.

CHAPTER 1

'You're home,' Justin Enos said, leading me through the great stone towers of Wickham Boarding School. I hesitated once I crossed the threshold, stopping at the main path that led past Seeker dorm and to the many halls and lanes of campus. In the distance, the tall street lamps lit up the brick buildings like tiny beacons.

Only four days ago, I was so sure that this world was no longer my own. I had performed the ritual for Vicken, my friend, my confidant, also a vampire. I performed this ritual to turn him human.

'I can walk, you know,' I said, though I stumbled and Justin had to grab on to my arm. He gave me a knowing glance. My thighs trembled, the result of lying unconscious in a hospital bed. It had been four days since my best friend, Tony, had been killed in the art tower, and since I had believed I too would die.

'It's a beautiful night,' I said, leaning into Justin's arm as we walked. He matched my baby steps, holding a bag of my possessions on his other arm.

Lovers Bay, Massachusetts, was blooming in June, hydrangeas and roses all around us. Coupled with smells from the cafe and the restaurants behind us on Main Street, scents distinct to me in my newly regained humanity filled the air: sauces, perfumes and fragrant flowers.

After everything that had happened, Wickham Boarding School campus seemed like an imaginary place. It lived somewhere locked in both dream and nightmare.

The night was quiet. The trees swayed lazily in the June air and I watched students meander across the campus, talking quietly to one another. The moon broke through the clouds and when I looked back down to the earth, far down the path towards Wickham beach, a figure leaped over the path and into the woods. Blonde tendrils of hair flew behind her in the wind.

I chuckled at first, imagining a student sneaking off campus to find something decadent to eat or to meet a boyfriend. Then something about the figure's movements caught my eye. She jumped with the ease of a dancer but with the charge of pursuit. She was lean and swift. *Too* lean . . . *too* swift.

Alarmed, I scanned the school grounds.

'What's wrong?' Justin asked.

'Want to go down to the beach?' I asked, stalling for time.

Justin took my bag to the guard at the dorm and I waited alone, staring down the pathway. If she came back out of the woods, then I would know if she was an ordinary human. Students passed by me, calling out:

Hey, Lenah!

How are you? Feeling better?

I kept my gaze forward. 'Word got around fast when you went to the hospital,' said Justin, nuzzling my neck.

We passed the union and Justin's dorm. I couldn't explain it – the *knowing* that she was strange, that the blonde might not be human. Perhaps I was just being paranoid. Of course I was being paranoid. I was an ex-592-year-old vampire. Oddities and strange creatures had been an everyday part of my life for nearly six centuries.

We walked down to Wickham beach. I took off my shoes, leaving them by the steps, and sat down on the cool sand. Sitting there, leaning against Justin's warm chest, and marvelling at the ocean stretching beyond us, I tried to forget about the wisp of blonde hair and the unnaturally agile jump.

Justin's hand wrapped around mine. We watched the bay, and I replayed the memory of the first time

I met him. During my first week reborn as a human, he had walked out of the water, glimmering and golden.

I leaned my head on his shoulder, breathed and listened to the water lap lazily on the beach.

Except . . .

A horrific knowing sent a shiver through me. I shuddered and Justin looked down at me.

'Hey . . . are you OK?'

Look left . . . my mind said.

But Justin felt it too. He looked away from me and his fingers dug into the sand and he rose up on to his knees.

Death is coming, the voice inside my mind said. The voice of the vampire queen. The hunter of hundreds.

You know this trouble, the voice slithered.

I looked slowly down the beach.

'Do you see that?' Justin asked.

I did. My heart was a cello string, vibrating as though a bow drew across it – wavering. Someone was running towards us from very far down the beach. A girl – not a child, but not a grown woman either. A student? Her slight frame swayed as she ran, zigzagging across the sand and then hitting the ground as she fell. She pushed herself up from the sand but her arm gave out and she went down again.

'I think it's . . .' Justin's voice trailed away.

She finally got to her feet and started running again. The next time she collapsed to the sand, a few moments later, she cried out. It was a scream that snaked in a long wail down the beach, hissing her terror into our ears. Goosebumps erupted over my arms.

I knew this kind of cry well.

'She needs help,' Justin said, taking a step towards her.

'Wait,' I demanded in a whisper, grabbing his arm. I narrowed my focus into the darkness.

'Are you crazy? She's hurt,' Justin said. 'What are we waiting for, Lenah?'

My terror was a heartbeat quickened. A dry mouth. Words stuck in my throat, trapped by fear. I couldn't move my eyes.

For there was someone behind her.

This someone threw her hips confidently side to side. A model's walk. A saunter of death. The woman grabbed the girl by her ponytail. There was a quick yank, animalistic and brutal.

The wind came through the trees, which shivered unnaturally in the summer breeze.

'Justin,' I said. 'We have to go. Now.'

'But, Lenah!' Justin said my name again and I pulled him to me so we could speak very close.

'Silence,' I said. 'Or we'll both be dead.'

Justin didn't reply, but an understanding passed over his eyes.

I had to be calculated, purposeful. I could not let the human inside overwhelm me. I turned and scrambled up the steps, turning into the woods that ran parallel to the beach. My legs ached from the days in the hospital and every few paces I grabbed on to trees for balance.

'Lenah! We have to call for help!' Justin whispered loudly from behind me. I spun around to face him.

'Didn't I tell you? You must be silent,' I hissed. 'And don't say my name again.'

I fell to my knees and crept to the edge of the woods where the dirt and beach storm wall met, and stared at the scene unfolding below. I gasped as I recognized the girl.

Kate Pierson, my friend. A member of the Three Piece – the group of girls at Wickham whom I'd unexpectedly grown to love over the last year. Kate was the youngest of all of us, barely sixteen. Innocent, beautiful and now in grave danger.

This changed the circumstances.

We would have to do something. I immediately ran through our options.

We didn't have a dagger or sword to pierce the vampire through the heart, so we would have to frighten her with strength, which Justin had.

'Please stop,' Kate cried to her attacker.

We lay stomach down and I clawed my fingers into the sandy grass.

The woman sauntered behind Kate, stepping over the darkened sand as though she was simply out for a night stroll. She wore all black. Thick, blonde, beautiful hair flowed and waved behind her in the wind.

She smiled, her mouth stained red with blood.

I drew in a long breath. 'I know her,' I hissed to Justin.

My home in Hathersage, England, swept into my mind along with a memory of the staircase that led to the attic.

The maid.

The friendly maid with rosy cheeks.

Now she was whiter than stone and very angry.

Below us, Kate tried to wriggle away from the vampire, but now I could see the extent of her wounds I knew Justin and I were too late, much too late.

I gulped as the blonde grabbed Kate by the front of her shirt and bit into the crook of her neck. Kate cried out, a familiar, hollow scream. This was one of finality. Her small mouth opened and she hollered into the night.

'How?' Justin whispered. 'How do you know her?'

'I –' a shiver rolled over me – 'I made her.'

Justin slowly, ever so slowly, turned his eyes back to the beach without speaking.

Congealed blood caked the sand as Kate kicked and flailed. She bled from her arms and her neck. This was a killing of strength. A vampire death can be one bite and virtually painless, but this was a death like Tony's, a ruthless killing, not done out of hunger or need but out of power. Out of joy.

Kate brought her fingers to her throat to try to stop the bleeding.

Useless. I had seen this too many times.

'I don't want to die,' begged Kate. 'Please . . .'

My heart ached, but the once powerful vampire queen inside me told me that this blonde vampire was strong. She was unyielding in her desire for blood.

Justin and I could not run. We could not help. We would die at her hands if we made a sound.

We could do nothing until the horror was over.

There was one more fading scream from the beach.

And Kate Pierson was no more.

CHAPTER 2

'We have to tell someone,' Justin said as we stepped out of the woods and on to campus.

'No. We can't,' I replied. We stood under the lamplight on the pathway. I held a hand over my stomach. 'What we have to do is get inside. I have to think this through.'

I needed help. I needed someone who understood vampires.

I wanted Rhode, but he was dead.

'We can't just leave her on that beach!' Justin said, as a girl from the sophomore class and a security officer passed by us on the pathway. Ms Tate, the science teacher, followed closely behind them.

'You said you heard screaming?' the security guard asked the sophomore.

'A couple of times, sir. Down here.'

Ms Tate hesitated next to us.

'Lenah, good to see you, dear.' She touched my shoulder lightly. 'Did you two hear anything near the beach?' she asked as we stopped next to the greenhouse. 'Someone said they heard a fight or argument.'

'No,' I said, shaking my head. 'We were just in here.' I gestured to the greenhouse.

She nodded and followed behind the security guard and the student towards the beach. It would only be moments before the sirens began.

My thoughts were at war with one another. What was a vampire doing here in Lovers Bay? A vampire I'd made. The name Vicken pulsed through my mind.

Vicken. My faithful Vicken. I'd created him in such darkness and pain. He was my compatriot. But a vampire no longer. I had performed the ritual, releasing him from the endless bloodlust and setting free the human inside.

What if the ritual had failed? What if Vicken had remained a vampire and was working with this blonde?

'Lenah, what are you thinking about?' Justin asked.

'Vicken,' I said, blinking quickly and focusing on Justin's face. 'What happened to Vicken after I performed the ritual?'

A muscle twitched in Justin's jaw and he crossed his arms over his chest.

'I left him in your apartment when I took you to

the hospital. I have no idea if he's alive or dead. I haven't been back.'

The thought of a decaying Vicken on my Wickham apartment bed wasn't an encouraging thought, but I'd have to see for myself. We walked towards Seeker, pretending we weren't shaking as we went. Just as I was about to go up to my room, a police car screamed on to campus.

It had begun.

As the car shot by, it left in its wake an unnerving feeling that wrapped around me from my head to my toes. A knowing within my bones, for the second time that night.

Someone was watching me.

The blonde? Had she been looking for me? Is that why she had killed Kate?

Dozens of students were making their way to the beach to investigate the chaos. I looked past the union and up the long slope of an enormous hill that led to the archery plateau.

Atop it stood a familiar figure, and hope immediately rushed through me. He would be able to explain everything.

Suleen. The oldest vampire.

He stood dressed all in white with a turban fitted tightly to his head. He lifted his arm and motioned for me to follow him, then turned and walked on to the archery plateau, disappearing into the shadows.

I ran, trying to ignore the weakness in my legs as I sped up the hill. Justin followed behind me.

'Lenah, wait! What's going on?' he called.

I tallied the horrors of the last day as I ran. Kate's murder, the blonde vampire and now Suleen's arrival? All of this was undeniably connected.

'Something is very wrong. He wouldn't be here otherwise,' I said.

'What's wrong? Who *is* that?' he asked.

We crested the archery plateau, the line of targets in the distance highlighted by the moonlight. Suleen was not alone. A figure stood beside him in the middle of the field, clad in black trousers, black boots and black spiky hair.

My God.

The young man turned and his eyes bored into mine – blue. Blue. Blue.

My hand flew to my chest and I stumbled back.

Rhode. My Rhode. His whole body was surrounded by a halo of silver. The light that emanated from his black hair, his blue eyes and the curve of his face was nothing compared to the beauty that radiated from within him.

How could it be? I had run my fingers through his gritty vampire remains that first day at Wickham. I'd been so sure he was dead.

Of course . . . the realization pulsed through me. If I had survived the ritual with Vicken . . . why wouldn't he survive the ritual as well?

I ran to him. He watched me, completely still. The shock of seeing Rhode coursed through me, over and over again, making my mortal heart race. I was a step from him, close enough to reach out and touch his skin.

I would touch him! Feel his skin with fingertips that were alive with nerves and pulsing with blood. Suddenly Suleen stood between us. I stepped to the left to avoid him but Suleen blocked my way. I moved to the right – blocked again. Rhode kept his eyes locked on mine, but didn't take so much as a step towards me.

My fingers shook as my hand stretched out to him. 'Rhode . . .' I whispered. 'You're not dead. You're not dead.'

He blinked sparingly, marvelling at me as if I was an unknown creature or some rare bird.

'Rhode?' I said, panic rising from my stomach to my chest.

'Lenah . . .' Suleen's slow voice broke my gaze. 'We haven't much time.'

'Damn it, Rhode, speak to me,' I commanded.

Rhode closed his eyes for a moment, seemingly gathering strength to speak. Instead he took a deep breath. When he opened his eyes to look at me, I nearly fell back from their coldness.

'Rhode?' I said. 'Do you know how long I've dreamed of this?' He didn't respond. 'I love you!'

A pressure on my arm fell away. Justin. I had almost forgotten he was there. His cheeks were streaked with dirt, and when I moved my gaze to his hands, those too were caked in mud and sand. It reminded me of our terror that night, of what we had been through in the last few hours. And Kate Pierson had died.

'This is Rhode?' he said faintly. The wonder and hurt in his tone made me want to clamp my hands over my ears.

Rhode stared at Justin with the same curiosity he had for me, as if we were some strange animals. Justin reached for me again.

'You don't want to be here, Lenah,' he said.

At this, Suleen stepped between Justin and me.

'What are you . . . ?' I started to say as Suleen opened his hand, palm facing Justin. A great gust came over us all at once. Trees swayed back and forth so their branches curled and creaked. There was a loud pop as Suleen thrust his arm forward. In a blink, a wide vertical whirlpool of water separated Justin from Suleen and me. This watery shield hovered in the air between us. I reached out, extending my fingers, and ran them through the whirlpool suspended in the air. They made lines where they broke through the water.

I had never – ever – seen a vampire with that kind of power.

'Lenah!' Suleen said from behind me. '*Rapidement.*' Quickly. He turned back to Rhode and left the swirling shield hanging in the air as though it had always been there.

'Lenah!' Justin banged a fist on to the watery barrier, then stepped back. He rose on to his tiptoes, trying to see over the water, but the barrier simply stretched upwards too. Our eyes met through the water, his face rippling strangely.

'Lenah!' He yelled my name again, and the sound of his voice breaking made a knot form in the centre of my chest. I could not go to him. Not even after everything that had happened that night.

I turned to Suleen in frustration. 'What the hell is going on?'

'Lenah,' he said gently. His touch warmed my fingers. 'When you performed the ritual for Vicken, you alerted the Aeris.'

'The Aeris?' I said with surprise. I had only heard of them in ancient vampire texts and Celtic mythology.

'What you both have done with the ritual, it

must be reckoned,' Suleen said.

'A reckoning? Like a trial?' I asked. Rhode wouldn't look at me; his arms were folded across his chest. The muscles in his forearms contracted, drawing my eyes down for a split moment. Then, he *swallowed*. I watched, just to prove to myself he was human, that he was real. His chest rose and fell in an easy rhythm. We had both performed the ritual, we had both intended to die, yet here we were together – both very much alive. Both human.

'Lenah,' Suleen said, 'you must focus right now. This will affect both of you –' he placed his warm palms on my shoulders – 'indefinitely.'

I wanted to tell Suleen and Rhode about the blonde vampire. About Kate's death and the horror unfolding down on Wickham campus.

The watery shield still hovered in the air, but Justin was gone from the other side. All that lay behind it was the rippled green of the darkened trees speckled with silver glints by the moon. The knot in my chest tightened again when Suleen spoke.

'Rhode must explain to the Aeris why he manipulated the elements to perform a ritual to turn a vampire into a human. He must explain why he passed this information on to you, so you could perform it as well.'

'Well, that's easy. I was losing my mind.

Going insane. Tell him, Rhode.'

Rhode sighed, then spoke for the first time. 'Lenah . . .' It didn't even sound like my name – it sounded like a swear word, a rotten curse spat out, wishing to be forgotten.

'You never said this ritual was elemental magic,' I said to Rhode. Elemental magic would be the only reason the Aeris were involved. For they represented the four elements of the natural world: earth, air, water and fire. Not human. Not spirit. The Aeris exist as the earth exists.

'We have to do this, Lenah,' Rhode said. His voice was calm. 'We have to clear up our own mess.'

'It's time,' Suleen said, and finally moved out from between us. Suleen looked towards the middle of the green but I kept my eyes on Rhode. The long trunks of trees behind him were a blur. The flat summer leaves were nothing but a wash of darkened emerald to me now.

'You won't even look at me?' I asked quietly. 'Did you know the Aeris were coming?' I didn't dare move closer to him. 'Why didn't you come back sooner?'

Again, his silence was his answer.

'I don't understand you,' I said.

'I didn't *want* to come back,' he snapped. 'I *had* to.' He lifted his eyes to mine. 'For this.'

His words cut into the centre of my chest.

He hadn't *wanted* to come back?

It was then I glimpsed a white light out of the corner of my eye. I knew that light – it was supernatural.

Rhode's words hung in the air, stinging me like a burn. There was a large expanse of land before me and the archery targets sat deep in the distance of the plateau. My blood pulsed in the base of my throat; I brought my fingertips to my skin to feel it. The white light in the centre of the green grew to be as long and wide as the field that stretched before me.

At first it was difficult to see anything discernible in the whiteness, but eventually the fuzzy forms took the shapes of human bodies. Four female bodies. The Aeris stepped forward.

Their dresses were flowing, and it seemed as though they were made from water. The hue of their gowns changed colour every few seconds; one moment they were blue, then a darker blue, then red. I wondered if it was a trick of the light. One of the women had impossibly white eyes and her hair drifted around her head as if she was underwater. The woman next to her had hair that fluttered around her like crackling flames, a bright red. When she looked at me, her gown flickered a poppy orange. Fire.

Behind the Aeris were hundreds, no, *thousands* of shapes that looked like regular people.

The four spoke together: 'We are the Aeris.'

Their light took over the entire sky now.

'Who are the people behind you?' I asked.

'These,' Fire replied, gesturing behind her across the field of people, 'are your victims and the victims of the vampires you made.'

My victims? I shook my head quickly. *It couldn't be.*

Yet there they stood. They were amorphous, their identities shielded by the light. Included in their masses was a bright being no more than three feet high. A horrified chill ran through me.

A child.

She was the child I had killed hundreds of years ago.

Looking from Rhode to me, Fire said, 'Your lives are destined to be intertwined. You are held together by a power that cannot be undone by the Aeris.'

'Destined?' I asked.

'Yes, Lenah Beaudonte. You and Rhode Lewin were born under the same stars. The course of your lives has brought you here – together, as soulmates.'

'You never interfered with us before,' Rhode said.

'You, Rhode, were meant to die when you performed the ritual to make Lenah human. Yet your soulmate tied you to this earth. When you went out into that sunlight, you were meant to die.

But you could not. Not without Lenah.'

'And the same for me?' I asked. 'When I was performing the ritual on Vicken?'

She nodded. 'So now we have come to undo what you have created with this ritual.'

I wracked my brain trying to understand what she was saying. Fire's hair crackled. 'You cannot manipulate the elements in order to bring life out of death. Not without consequence.'

'So you've come to punish us?' I asked.

'We have come to hold you responsible.'

Fire gestured towards the ghostly figure of the child to illustrate her point. There was nothing to say. Nothing I could possibly try to defend.

'It was our nature then,' Rhode said plainly. 'To kill.'

'We are not here to hold you accountable for your endless murders, as heinous as they might have been. The Aeris are not responsible for, nor do we police, the vampire world. Vampires are dead. Supernatural night wanderers. We cannot hold you responsible for the killings you performed in that world,' Fire said as she paced between us. 'What interests me is what you have done to become human. It is against the laws of nature to manipulate the elements. You forced yourself back into this natural world with the ritual, and once you did you became our responsibility. You will not go unpunished.'

Rhode said nothing. I was unable to keep my eyes away from the thousands of figures collecting behind the Aeris. All of those people . . .

Fire faced me and clasped her hands together at her waist, then let them hang. She moved her eyes to mine. My legs were so weak they shook and I wondered if I would fall to the ground right there.

'The choice is this: either you can go back to your natural states – Rhode will return to 1348 as a knight under Edward III. You, Lenah, will live your life in 1418 as it should have been.'

'When we were human?' I asked incredulously.

'Natural states means when you each had a white soul, a pure soul,' Fire explained.

'You'll send us back in time?' Rhode asked.

Fire glanced behind her at the crowd of our victims. A question rose in my mind.

'What about all of them?' I asked, gesturing.

'When you go back to the medieval world, these souls will return to the natural course of their lives too.'

'I don't understand,' I said.

'Every person you murdered will live again, as will those killed by the vampires you created. They will never meet you – because you won't become a vampire. It will be as though you had never met.'

She looked at both Rhode and me.

In 1348, when he became a vampire, Rhode was nineteen. I wouldn't be born for another fifty-four years. He would be dead by the time of my birth or, at best, a very old man. That was their purpose. To send us back so that we would remain apart.

'It is a balance, Lenah. All the four elements of the world create balance. You were made a vampire against your will. You are Rhode's original victim so it is your choice to decide his fate.'

'What is the other option?' I asked.

Fire stepped to the edge of the white light. Her pupils were bright red but the iris around them glowed a pearl white. I held my breath until my cheeks and whole body tingled.

'You and Rhode have unleashed a chain of reactions that cannot be undone unless you separate. You may either go back to the medieval world or you may remain here. If you choose to stay here, you and Rhode may not commit to one another.'

'Commit?' Rhode asked. 'What do you mean?'

'Commitment to love is a choice deep within the soul. If you choose to bring your lives together in this world, we will know.'

Could we touch? Talk? Kiss . . . ? All these questions popped into my mind.

'You may talk, speak, interact, but you may not

commit to be the couple you once were,' Fire said, reading my mind.

'But how will we know if we've committed to one another? If we're the couple we once were. I can't just stop loving Rhode.'

'You have always, always loved whoever you wanted, whenever you wanted. Rhode, Vicken, Heath, Gavin, Song and Justin. But who filled up your soul? How many of them have you committed to? You didn't share a life, you didn't grow with them as you did with Rhode. It's over, Lenah. You must do to Rhode what you've done with the rest of the men you've come across. Keep him at arm's length.'

'I don't understand,' I barely said, knowing deep in my soul that she was completely right. Had I used everyone except Rhode? I had, hadn't I? Fire took another step towards me and I could feel the heat emanating off her.

'Like the whitest of shores on a beach that stretches as far as the eye can see. You want that ocean. You see that ocean. But you can never go back in. Ever.'

I swallowed hard, unable to formulate the words I so desperately wanted to say. I wanted to convince her. Could I keep Rhode at arm's length? Could I pretend we didn't have the history we had? The

silver light around my victims pulsated behind
Fire's head, reminding me of all that I had done to
deserve this moment there on the archery field.

'And them,' I asked with a nod of my head. 'What
happens to them if I stay?'

'You see this light around me?' she asked.

I nodded again.

'Your victims – they have white souls. And they
will keep them.'

I imagined my soul to be black and hardened,
like a lump of coal.

'And if I return to the medieval world? If they go
back to their lives?'

'Then they will be left to their own choices. The
fate of their souls will be their own.'

I had already decided their fate. They were safe
where they were, safe in that light. How could I
release them into a past I knew nothing about? Was
I being selfish? Did I want to protect their souls or
my own? I knew more than anything else in the
world that, if I had a soul, Rhode and I were meant
to be together.

'What is your choice?' Fire asked.

I looked at Rhode. He wouldn't meet my eyes.
I wanted to kiss his mouth, even now, even with
the Aeris's decree that we would never be a couple
again. Just seeing him there, knowing I could be

near him when I had been so convinced of his death . . . I didn't want to go back. No matter what we had to face, if Rhode was by my side, even at arm's length, I could do anything.

'I choose to stay,' I said, looking into Fire's poppy-coloured eyes. 'Here and now in Lovers Bay.'

In my mind, a perfect apple orchard painted in thick swirls of colour dissolved as though left out in the rain.

'And they'll be safe?' I asked, meaning the people behind the Aeris.

Fire nodded, then said, 'You must fight her, Lenah.' She didn't need to tell me whom she meant.

She took a step back into the light and her distinct form began to blur.

The white light dimmed too and Suleen, who stood beside us, held a hand out towards the Aeris. He turned his palm left, then right, and then made a fist. He was performing some sort of communication that I did not understand. Fire mimicked these gestures. A palm left – right – then a fist. She and her sisters were almost gone, fading into the scenery as if they'd never been there.

Rhode was watching Suleen, but I couldn't stop staring at his chest rising up and down. I had stared at it for hundreds of years, wishing we were both alive, breathing and living together.

You cannot commit, Fire had said.

I jumped forward, past Suleen and towards the vanishing Aeris.

'Wait,' I yelled. 'Wait!'

I threw my arms out towards the light, but it dimmed, leaving nothing behind but misty cobwebs. The Aeris were gone. Fire was gone.

Rhode stared around the archery plateau, now shrouded in darkness. Sunset had long since fallen over Wickham campus.

'We have to do something!' I cried to Suleen.

'You did,' Rhode said. 'You chose to stay.'

There was sadness in his voice, anger too. I just couldn't part with Rhode, not when it came down to it. I couldn't go back to the medieval world without him.

The grass under my feet was grey, the sky black. I swallowed and a lump in the back of my throat hurt.

'Your hundreds of years of experience on this earth must be your conscience now. Stay away from one another,' said Suleen. His even tone broke the spell of my thoughts.

Rhode met Suleen's eyes. A tremor travelled from my shins to my knees to my thighs. I needed to grasp something hard, clench it in my fist and break it.

My mind sped up, as though coming back to the world I'd existed in before the Aeris came from their white world and lit up the archery plateau.

Justin.

I spun around to look back at the edge of the plateau, where Suleen had conjured up the water shield. But Justin had long gone. I suppose I could not blame him. I would not have wanted to linger at the scene either.

'There is no other way, Rhode,' Suleen said.

Rhode replied in Hindi – a language I had not learned. Despite the twenty-five languages I could speak fluently, Rhode chose one I could not understand.

He walked past me and descended the hill without looking back.

Was he leaving? Forever?!

'What did he say? What?! Rhode!' I yelled, and followed. Suleen caught my arm. 'No!' I screamed. I pushed against his strong grasp but he easily held me back.

I watched as Rhode ran across the meadow, then on to the pathway.

'Rhode!' I screamed. This heartache made me feel sick. 'Rhode!'

He did not look back.

I could not tell him about the blonde vampire. I

could not say, *Stay, for I love you. I've always loved you. Stay and we can do this together.*

Because without a second look, without a glance, he was gone.

CHAPTER 3

1730, Hampstead, England – the Heath

When the years of vampirism began to chain my mind to madness, I yearned for my parents' apple orchard. I ached for the succulent red apples dangling from the branches. For almost three hundred years I begged Rhode to accompany me back to Hampstead. When we finally made the trip, I wore black for the occasion. My hair fell in long tendrils over my shoulders; my ribs were constricted by a corset. The 1730s was the era of panniers, wide hoops attached to a woman's hips underneath her skirt. Women were meant to take up space, to be a spectacle, to be admired. It was a time of opulence. I loved this era most of all. I could shine when the light of the sun was no longer upon me. As for the men, many wore wigs, powdered white. But not Rhode. He always wore his hair long, black and tied at the nape of his neck. The leather of his black boots reached almost to his knees.

We were gorgeous Angels of Death.

'Three hundred and twelve years since I stepped

on this land,' I said, glancing at Rhode.

'Same for me,' he replied.

A brilliant sunset descended over the heath, washing the fields in a tangerine light. Behind him, set off by a field, was the stone monastery where I'd spent so much of my childhood. The Hampstead sunset daubed blood-red hues over the grass. As a vampire, I was relieved to know that the daylight would start to dwindle soon.

'Are you sure you want to see this?' Rhode asked.

I nodded, moving my eyes from the monastery to the lane ahead. I had often padded these fields as a child. Images of dirt caking my toes, my hair flowing behind me in the wind and the rich earth burned in my mind. The wind brushed through the branches again and a shower of leaves layered the ground. The earth seemed to shiver as though it knew something unnatural was walking its lands.

As Rhode took a step, his sword clicked against the side of his leg. I lifted my hand and gently intertwined my fingers through his. Even though almost every finger wore a jewel, he chose to rub his thumb over the onyx – the stone of death. We stepped down the long, tunnelled lane and headed towards my family's home. As we passed the monastery my eye followed the grey stone and well-kept grounds. After three hundred years, it was still a place of holy reverence.

Was it possible Henry VIII had spared it? That it had escaped the dissolution of the monasteries in the sixteenth century?

'It is a church now,' Rhode said, and when I looked properly I could see that the monastery of my childhood was no more, though the core of the building remained the same. I could hear the sounds of a service from inside, soft murmuring and chanting.

When I was nine years old, I used to hide underneath the stone-framed windows, my feet pressed into the scratchy ground. I would listen to hundreds of haunting voices. The hum of the monks' soft tones would echo out into the field, sending a vibration through my chest.

One night, my father had told me the light from the monastery was the most beautiful light in the world. 'Candlelight,' he had said, 'is a human's beacon to God. A little piece of God on earth.'

'It's just ahead,' Rhode said. There it was. I stared at the house in the orchard.

'It's the same,' I whispered. 'It's just as it is in my memory.'

The same slate roof and evenly spaced stones. The same two-storey manor overlooking manicured lanes of trees that stretched back in straight vertical lines so far that I couldn't see their end. And the trees were in bloom. Green, green everywhere, lime green, sea green, bottle green, and long grass that tickled your ankles.

I gripped the heavy fabric of my gown, lifting it up so as not to drag it along the muddy ground.

'I don't believe anyone is at home,' Rhode said, as he took in the smokeless chimney.

It didn't matter to me either way. I pressed my hands against the glass, wondering if it was cool – I could not sense its temperature. As a vampire ages, her sense of touch deadens. I leaned in closer. The wooden beams on the ceiling had been reinforced over time but it all looked the same. The familiarity sent a wave of comfort over me and that feeling overtook the anger, pain and misery that so overwhelmed me as a vampire. The comfort was a gift.

'Lenah, look,' Rhode said from behind me. 'There are—'

'Fifty acres,' I finished for him, turning from the window. A sense of calm overwhelmed me as I looked at him. I expected him to be marvelling at the acres and acres of land.

'No,' he said. 'Tombstones.'

As though I had been drenched from head to

toe in icy water, the calm vanished. It was replaced by the unrelenting familiar constant: grief. The most common feeling of the vampire. Grief. Loss. Pain.

My eyes followed the direction in which Rhode was pointing. I paused at the doorstep a few moments before walking towards the little graveyard. Rhode had squatted down on his heels and was running his index finger along a deep engraving on the front of one of the gravestones.

As I walked past the house, I glanced at my reflection in the windows. So many years before, I had seen myself as a child in the wavy lines of the glass. Now, in the same glass, I saw my long dark hair falling over my shoulders. The black of my dress stood out against the lush green of the rows of trees behind me. I took another step to the side of the house and entered the cemetery.

Rhode's finger was tracing the L in my name.

It was my gravestone.

God, it was a rotten piece of stone, but despite three hundred years out in the elements my name was still etched clearly. There was no epitaph.

LENAH BEAUDONTE
1402 – 1418

Long ago, I thought. *Long ago, I belonged to the world. I could have made a difference to my family, to my neighbours, to the monks and to myself.*

'Now you know,' Rhode said quietly, and stood back up. 'You were given a tombstone.' That had been one of my many questions about my human death.

'I wanted to see it,' I replied with a nod. 'No matter how painful.'

'Your father died not long after you,' Rhode said.

The tombstone next to mine plainly read that Aden Beaudonte died in 1420. Next to the rounded curve of his gravestone was jasmine. Jasmine flowers are dainty and white; they grow together in clusters. Grow jasmine if you need to live, someone had once told me, not just exist but *live.* Grow jasmine so you'll never be alone. I took a step, leaned forward and plucked three sprays of flowers. When I turned back to my father's grave, Rhode had stepped away and was standing at the end of a row, staring down at another tombstone.

I placed one jasmine spray on my mother's grave; she had died alone in 1451.

'Lenah . . .' Rhode whispered. I looked at him. His chin pointed towards his chest and his eyes were fixed on the stone before him. He squatted down. I walked towards him, and once I was by his side I saw the name on the tombstone. I gripped his shoulder, stumbling backwards. I had no breath to take. No heart to thud. Just the simple shock of seeing the name:

GENEVIEVE BEAUDONTE
MOTHER AND SISTER
1420–1473

'You had a sister,' said Rhode in awe. 'She was born two years after your disappearance.'

A sister. I had a sister? I stared at the name, unmoving. If I'd known she'd existed, I could have come to see her, could have watched her live. I spun from the tombstone, walked past the graves and back to the orchard. The train of my gown trailed behind me over the dirt of my father's land.

'Lenah!' Rhode called.

What had they told her? That her sister had been taken away by demons? That she was there but then gone? My sister lived to be 53, uncommonly old for her time. She outlived my mother. My mother *wasn't* alone. I stopped once I reached the orchard.

A sister.

I heard the sound of Rhode's footsteps over the grass and he stopped right behind me.

'You were right. You had to come. To find out

about your family,' he said gently.

Now that the sunset had almost fully settled over the land, I knew that if I scanned the sky I would see the beginnings of the constellation of Andromeda. I brought my eyes back to the orchard. Whoever lived in my house would return soon. They were most likely at the evening service at the church.

Rhode's hand linked through mine. When two vampires love one another, their touch will produce warmth. Without love, we feel nothing. In that moment, his touch was like the brightest sunlight on the warmest day.

'Lenah, every tombstone in that graveyard carries the name Beaudonte.' He motioned with his head towards the house. 'Your family lives there . . . even now.'

I grasped my hands around Rhode, pulling him to me. Our bodies were intertwined in the middle of that lane. We, demons of bloodlust, held one another close.

'Promise me,' I urged. 'Promise that no matter what happens, you will always be there for me.' I pulled away and looked into Rhode's vampire eyes. So glorious, they were the colour of a summer sky. My sky. 'We don't know what will come, but if I know you will always be there for me, I can bear it.'

'I promise,' he said. 'No matter what may come.'

He took my hand into his. With a glance back at the house and the graveyard beyond, the burn of tears that would never come stung my eyes. So I let the only person left in my heart take me away. As darkness swept over the long lane leading out, I could hear the singing of a few people in the meadow behind the old monastery. They were heading away from us, back towards the orchard. That was my family singing. Although they were many generations later, they were still my blood. I gripped Rhode harder, and let him take me, as he had done three hundred years before, into the night.

CHAPTER 4

Present day

Time does not tick on for the dead. After we die, we cannot keep it. It is the master of the living. For the dead, for the vampire, time is a hornets' nest. Dangerous, best to be avoided – always humming in your ear.

When Rhode had run from me after our meeting with Suleen and the Aeris, he was leaving me for the second time in our long history. The first time had been in 1740, when my mind was starting to string itself into pieces of lace. He had said, 'I will never leave you,' hundreds of times, thousands of times. Vampires like to count; they like to tally their sadness.

The last time Rhode left me, I went mad. The last time Rhode left me, I had created a very different kind of family for myself. The last time Rhode left me – I had made a coven of vampires. This time I vowed, standing on that Wickham Boarding School pathway, with the moon filtering through the lattice of branches, I would not relive that misery. I would resolve to be me . . . whoever that was.

But where had he gone this time? Back to where he was hiding during the year I believed him dead? What could possibly have been strong enough to keep him from me?

His words gnawed at my mind.

I didn't want to come back, he had said. *I had to.*

Rhode had said he would never leave me. He said that as we stood in the lanes of my father's orchard hundreds of years ago.

Security vans pulled through the campus. Guards and police officers corralled students and pointed them to their dorms. Trees swayed and the stars above twinkled in a lazy dance.

'Hey, you!'

I turned. A security guard I had never seen before walked towards me in the darkness. His badge shone under the pathway lights, which seemed brighter than usual.

'Curfew is 9 p.m. tonight, which is in fifteen minutes. Let me see your ID.'

I reached into my pocket, extended my hand with the ID held between my fingers. The guard reached for it then froze, motionless, as though he was struck dumb.

'Sir?' I said, but he stared into the distance. Unmoving.

After a moment, he shook his head quickly and then turned on the spot, heading down the pathway away from me.

I stood on the path, unsure of what had just happened.

Suleen stepped out from the shadow of a building nearby, making me jump.

'Walk with me,' he said.

'How did you do that?' I asked, breathless.

He did not answer. We went in silence down the path alongside the building, past maintenance crews working in the dark. I could not tell what they were doing but sparks flew into the air like tiny fireworks.

'They are changing the locks,' Suleen said. We were quiet again as we crossed the campus and approached the beach. Across the steps that led down to the sand was a strip of yellow tape that read: POLICE LINE – DO NOT CROSS.

Suleen lifted the tape up right beside a police officer who was reading something from a clipboard. We ducked under the tape, and the officer gave no indication that he had seen us.

When we reached the beach, they had already moved the body but Kate's blood was still soaked into the sand.

Suleen and I stood in the light of the moon.

The summer wind blew gently and I admired my silent protector. I wondered why he had involved himself in my life for so long. And how it was that he had such power. It radiated off him; it positively hummed.

I inhaled the scent of ocean and salt. When I was a vampire, I could not smell anything other than flesh and blood. My sight, on the other hand, was unlimited, needed for hunting, and resulting in countless murders. I could see the veins in my victims' skin, the flow of their blood. But touch and feeling? There was none. And taste?

'*All you shall taste is blood and it shall be the fruit of your darkness.* So say the books on vampirism,' I said aloud.

'Vampires love to record and pass on their misery. They use anything they can find to do so. Ancient documents, printed and scrawled on the oddest of paper, the bark of trees or on human skin,' Suleen replied.

I was quiet for a moment.

Then, 'I created the vampire who killed Kate Pierson,' I confessed.

He nodded. 'As you saw tonight,' he said, 'our past is not an immovable thing. It defines us; it can undo our future.'

I exhaled loudly. 'How do the Aeris have so much

power? Are they actually capable of time travel? *Could* they have sent me back in time?'

'Yes, I think so. You see, in this particular decree they are trying to repair the damage you have done.' Suleen seemed to think about his words for a moment, then said, 'The Aeris are not human. They do not have human desires or wish you any ill.'

'Yet they're hurting me in the most effective way possible – separating me from Rhode.'

Suleen drew in a deep breath, which surprised me. I watched him inhale, though he would never need the air. He drew it in, and when he breathed out he blew towards the ground, so the grains travelled in infinitesimal movements, making patterns on the sand.

When he was done, a faint outline lay at our feet. Like a silver ghost, Kate's body lay on its side, mouth gaping open exactly as Justin and I had last seen her.

The wind picked up but Kate's apparition still glowed on the sand.

'They said Rhode and I could talk and touch but we couldn't commit to one another.' The word *commit* hung in the air for a few seconds.

'Yes, this is the rejoining of soulmates. If you choose to form a life together, if you give in to your love despite their warning, you will return to the fifteenth century and Rhode to the fourteenth.'

My vision blurred, the ocean a mess of watery lines – I didn't dare meet Suleen's eyes and pressed my lips together hard. The images from my first human life swam before my eyes: a graveyard peppered with ancient stones, hazy light cast through thick glass, and monks chanting in the night.

Kate's misty body glowed underneath the bright moonlight. If I went back to the fifteenth century, as the Aeris threatened, no one I loved from this world would be there. No Vicken. No Justin. Wickham wouldn't have even been built yet – no Lovers Bay Main Street.

Kate would be alive, however. Tony too.

'Be the human you wanted to be. Revel in it,' Suleen said.

'How can I be that human when it's so dangerous here?' I met Suleen's eyes and then sighed. 'The blonde vampire has most likely returned for revenge. She seemed so delighted with herself and her murder.'

It came to me then: Suleen should stay. Suleen could help me!

'Stay,' I said simply. 'With you here, no vampire would dare attack.' Suleen's expression was one that I had seen before but not in a very long time. A kind of parental concern. Emotional pain rippled in my chest. I visualized my father and mother in the white light of the Aeris. I could only imagine what my disappearance had done to their lives.

'Your father was no victim,' Suleen said, reading my emotions and perhaps my thoughts.

I fell to my knees and Suleen joined me so we both knelt on the ground.

'You made a choice on that archery field, Lenah,' he said.

'I know.'

'Then you know you chose to stay here, in this world. That means you must deal with the repercussions, even if that means fighting this vampire.'

I didn't want to fight the vampire. Not alone.

'What about the Aeris?' I asked.

'No supernatural being has ever accomplished what you and Rhode have. Just as the Aeris did not interfere with you and Rhode, they cannot interfere with this vampire.'

Guilt spread over me. The only hope I had was that Suleen would stay.

'I cannot,' he said, reading my thoughts once again. He hesitated a moment, looking over Kate's body, then said, 'May I tell you why elemental magic is so powerful? Why your ritual called the Aeris?'

I nodded, saying nothing.

'Elemental magic is life magic,' Suleen continued. 'We, vampires, take life. It is our curse. The more powerful the magic, the more we are drawn to it.'

'Why?'

'Magic is drawn from the elements. Supernaturals have summoned it, created it with our power. That is why when a spell is performed, vampires can sense it if we are near. We crave it like we crave blood. It reminds us that we have some control in this world that ticks by without us.'

'I didn't know the consequences.'

'Of course you did,' Suleen replied, and even as I said it I knew that he was right. At the time, I didn't care about the power of the ritual. I put my selfish wishes above all else. 'And so does this vampire, who has come to Lovers Bay. She craves that magic.'

'If you can't help me, then why are you telling me this?'

'We are much more connected than perhaps you realize.'

My lips parted. 'How?' I asked.

'That is for another time,' he replied. 'Just know, when you most need me, I'll find you.'

Suleen stood above the body and held a palm above Kate. He moved his hand as if he was simply wiping the air, and the sand looked as it had before we arrived. We walked back to the pathway on to the campus and Suleen stood with me at the entrance to Seeker.

'I suggest you get inside,' he said.

'I could die,' I said to him.

He examined my face a moment, then the corners of his lips lifted, just barely. Just enough that a smile shone from behind his eyes.

'Not a girl like you . . .' he said.

I blinked. That was all it took. In that fraction of a second I stood alone. No one walked along the path. No one called to me from the meadow. All around me was the pervasive sound of silence.

CHAPTER 5

I stood outside the glass doors of Seeker dorm looking at the reflection of the sixteen-year-old girl standing there alone. Almost seventeen. How I had longed to make it here. I would age this year.

But the foyer was the same as last year and the familiar guard sat behind her desk, in her blue uniform, speaking into a walkie-talkie.

I took in my appearance. Same thin nose. Same brown hair that reached down to my ribs. Long, lanky legs, clad in black combat boots. The shadowy light illuminated my humanness. My white perfect skin used to glow in the moonlight. It healed instantly if anything or anyone dared to sully it. But now red raised scrapes marked my hands. I turned my cheek to see another, smaller scrape. These were the physical reminders that Justin and I had crawled through the brush of the Wickham woods while Kate was being murdered.

Justin.

I sighed, feeling the weight of the night's ordeals in a slouch of my shoulders. I had to enter alone and go back up to my apartment. I pushed open the door and walked inside.

'Lenah Beaudonte has checked in,' said the security guard into her walkie-talkie, and checked my name off a list. As I headed for the stairwell, from the long hallway on the first floor of rooms I could hear people speculating about the police cars on campus.

I heard Kate Pierson died.

First Tony, now Kate.

Has anyone seen Tracy?

I listened to the whispers all the way up to the top floor. When I opened the door to my apartment, I found a glass ashtray blackened by cigarette butts, dirty plates in the sink and three empty pizza boxes on my coffee table. Next to them was a familiar silver flask given to Vicken by some count in the 1890s. I picked it up and opened the top, expecting to find, as usual, a stash of blood. I sniffed for the metallic rusty scent but instead found . . . whiskey? I shook my head, unable to stop a smile.

Oh yes, Vicken Clough was now definitely a mortal.

I put the flask down and turned to my bedroom; the door was open. I walked slowly across the living room, passing messy piles of books and an empty pack of cigarettes. When I placed a hand on my bedroom door, it creaked, echoing in the silent apartment as I pushed it open. There on the bed, where I expected to see ashes and blood, were messed sheets and a couple of pairs of jeans in a heap. When I came out of the bedroom, the living-room decor was unchanged from when I'd left it four days earlier.

The longsword on the wall.

The red couch.

The thorned iron candle holders.

And then there was a bang on the door! It had to be Justin, wanting an explanation after everything that had happened on the archery field.

I walked to the door, and as I grasped the handle I noticed out of the corner of my eye something on my balcony.

'One second,' I called out. I walked slowly, heel to toe over the hardwood floor. My toes curled over the metal of the balcony doorway. On the black tiles, thousands of tiny glittering particles shimmered in the moonlight. And there, in the centre, was the clear outline of a body – my body. It must have been where I'd lain after I performed the ritual for Vicken. The golden particles were scattered unevenly near the door as though I had been lifted from the spot and then brought back inside.

There are three ways to kill a vampire: a stake

through the heart, beheading and very powerful sunlight. When a vampire is killed, she leaves behind only the dust of her supernatural form and there mine was before me, like small crystals.

Bang!

'Coming!' I spun round, quickly walked to the front door and opened it.

It was not Justin.

A young man with hair like a lion's mane and a proud chin leaned an elbow on the door jamb.

'About bloody time. You'd think I have all night to wait around,' Vicken Clough said with a smile.

'Vicken!' I cried, and threw my arms around him.

'Yes, that's my name.' His arm muscles contracted as he squeezed them around me. It sent goosebumps rippling over my arms to feel him curl around me and to hear him breathe in my ear – in and out. I pulled away.

'Vicken! My God.' I placed both hands on his cheeks. His fierce brown eyes warmed as he looked at me. '*Look* at you,' I said with an amazed sigh. My hand pressed on to his back and I waited for it, for his chest to rise and then fall. It was quick but he did, a quick inhale, a quick exhale.

The ritual had worked. He was a living, breathing human. Officially an ex-vampire.

'Hello, love,' Vicken said, pulling back with a

smile. He walked into my apartment, plopped down on my couch and rested his black leather boots on the coffee table. His shaggy hair was deliberately unkempt and he leaned back into the pillows and crossed his hands behind his head. It was so *him* I wanted to hug him again.

'You look . . .' he said, 'terrible.'

I appraised his sleek shoulders and lean frame. It seemed impossible that the Aeris could blame Rhode and me for giving someone this gift. Looking at Vicken, what we'd done seemed so easy to justify. I wondered briefly if the Aeris made an appearance to Vicken too. He had also re-entered the natural world as a human without their consent. They might have visited and threatened to send him back to the nineteenth century, before I made him a vampire.

'Vicken, have you seen the Aeris?'

'Seen the Aeris?' he asked, and his features darkened. 'You mean they exist?'

Suleen was right, then. The Aeris did not show themselves to vampires just because they were evil. They had come for Rhode and me. They had come to make an example of us.

I explained to Vicken what had happened on the archery field. That Rhode had run off and left me with no answers.

'That explains that, then,' Vicken said with a chuckle.

'Explains what?' I asked.

'I've been staying here in your room. Rhode walked in, grabbed a bag and said he had to leave.'

'Did he say where he was going?'

'No. I tried to follow, but when I went out on to campus, it was bloody chaos. Police cars, sirens, ambulances. I haven't exactly got a pass to be on campus yet – you know what I mean? What happened out there?'

I stood up straighter and clenched my hands. I did not answer him right away.

Rhode had been staying in my room the four days I had been in the hospital, while I assumed he was dead? Last year, he existed. Somewhere in the world . . . just without me.

I groaned. How strange it was to stand here now looking at his longsword and our photos without the pit of grief in my stomach. It was the same apartment, but everything was different.

'Oh!' Vicken said, interrupting my thoughts. He stood up and reached deep into the pockets of his jeans. His fingers curled around something I could not see and he opened his palm. 'This is for you.'

A ring dropped into my palm. My onyx ring.

'I found it out on the balcony after I . . . after I

awoke,' Vicken said. 'You were gone.'

The legend of onyx was that it could hold on to spirits left lingering in a world that no longer wanted them. I immediately thought of Rhode holding my hand on our long walk to my orchard so many years ago. I tried to push away the words he'd said on the archery plateau but they sifted into my mind anyway . . . *I didn't want to come back. I had to.*

'I'm sorry I wasn't here for you,' I said, clearing my throat and pushing the ring on to my finger. 'Justin took me to the hospital after the ritual was completed.'

'Typical mortal . . .' Vicken grumbled. 'All you would have needed was some simple . . .'

'Lavender water,' we said in unison, and shared a smile. I kept looking down at the onyx ring on my finger. I focused on its black smooth surface. The stone had no end, no beginning and no glint of light. Just darkness.

'Hey . . .' Vicken said. 'Your hands are shaking.'

Were they? I sat down on the couch, placing my head in my hands.

'Is it me?' he continued. 'I just got back here. You can't possibly be angry with me yet.' I met his eyes. 'Seriously – what is it?' he asked.

'The chaos on campus was caused by a murder. A student was murdered tonight. By a vampire.'

'Anyone we know?'

'Yes, I recognized her. Remember the maid from Hathersage? In 1910? I can't remember her first name.'

'Was she alone?' Vicken asked.

'As far as I could tell. I didn't see anyone else.'

I rested my elbows on my knees and looked to Vicken for answers. He would know what to do. He was once one of the leaders of my coven.

When he offered me no answer, I stood up and walked to the balcony door. Outside, I watched the moonlight shine over the sparkles of my vampire remains . . . such a strange remnant of a life so dark, so empty.

I thought of Rhode running from me and a pulse of pain rippled through me. I hoped, wherever he was, that he was safe.

Vicken joined me at the balcony door.

'We didn't tell anyone,' he said, referring to my coven and their arrival at Wickham Boarding School only a few weeks before. 'No one in the vampire world knew we were coming for you.'

'No,' I said, as Suleen's words echoed in my mind. 'It's not your fault. This vampire was drawn here by the ritual.'

Vicken turned to me, a thought forming in his mind. I could see the excitement building in his eyes.

'She'll probably wait around. Wait to see who was performing that kind of magic.'

'You can count on it,' I said.

'Let's go,' he said, walking back across the room.

'Go?' I asked. 'Do you have any idea the kind of night I've had?'

'Bollocks. Let's go find her. See what we're up against. See if there's more than one.'

'So you've gone mad. The ritual destroyed your mind,' I said.

'A simple hunt. That's all. Just to size up what we're dealing with.'

'Now? Tonight?'

I was exhausted to the core, but something in Vicken's idea made adrenaline fire up my muscles.

'Why not now? She killed that girl tonight. Should we sit around until there are more murders?'

I had to admit it was a better idea than just waiting. But I had to be logical about this.

'We don't have Song or Heath. We've got no coven. We're human, with no back-up and no supernatural abilities,' I added.

'Not true. I've still got my vampire sight and extrasensory perception. If vampires are nearby, I'll be able to feel them, sense what they're up to.'

True! Vicken still retained some of his vampire abilities because he had only recently been transformed. He would have sight like a vampire, and a sixth sense. He would be able to pick up other people's emotions and their intentions.

'Come on, then, let's go,' I said, walking out of the apartment.

'Oh, please,' Vicken said, shutting the door behind us. 'Don't act like this was your idea.'

Down near the library, a security van was pulling towards the chapel, away from Seeker.

Vicken motioned to the trees. 'Go,' he whispered.

We darted down the path into the shadows, keeping close to the buildings. We turned at the infirmary and ran down its length towards the woods beyond. I couldn't make out the stone wall but I knew it was there. Vicken's footsteps matched mine and when I caught sight of him out of the corner of my eye, a small smile was playing on his lips.

'You're enjoying this too much,' I hissed. We reached the stone wall, which was as high as Vicken was tall. He placed a motorcycle boot in between the mismatched stones and pushed himself up, then pulled me up behind him. We climbed down to the other side on to Main Street, outside the protection of the Wickham Boarding School walls.

Now that I stood there on the street, it did seem a rather stupid idea. Vicken and I hadn't taken any precautions. We could have tied rope around our necks in a knot with a protection spell. We could have tried a whole array of spells to arm ourselves.

I drew a deep breath, taking in the long view of Main Street.

'I can do this,' I said, extending my hand to Vicken. 'I'm not bad with a knife.'

'There's my girl,' Vicken said, and reached into his boot. He handed me a dagger wrapped in a leather sheath. We continued along the wall, down Main Street, away from school, away from the cafes, and in the direction of Lovers Bay Cemetery.

'Besides,' he added, 'we're here to see what she wants. To observe. We won't have to fight anyone if we stay out of sight.'

I couldn't allow myself to be afraid, even though she was more powerful than we were. Anyway we weren't helpless. By nature vampires do not have super-strength or speed. They are just hyper-aware; they can smell flesh in an instant, read thoughts and intentions, even track a person from miles away. Vicken and I could outrun a vampire over a short distance, but eventually the need for breath would weaken us. We just had to stay out of sight so she couldn't sense us or see us.

Already I was feeling better. I had been a vampire queen for almost six hundred years, and I *knew* vampires. I knew more than she did, a vampire barely a century old. Vampires by nature were loners. They usually only travelled in a maximum of five, a coven. Too many vampires together were too many vampires fighting for power. We walked past the cemetery, down towards the end of Main Street. As we walked, we could see the ocean at the end of the street.

'Do you sense anything?' I asked Vicken.

'Just how scared you are,' he said with a devilish smirk. But it vanished immediately. He inhaled deeply. I did too.

For there had been a shift in the air. A light breeze picked up, bringing with it the smell of . . .

'Musk,' we said together. Musk was a very specific fragrance, one used in many spells.

'Where's it coming from?' I asked. He pointed towards the end of the street. The wind blew again, and the smell was stronger this time.

I touched Vicken's arm. 'What are the odds?' I asked.

'Pretty good, actually. You said it yourself,' he whispered, his eyes darting down the street. 'The ritual drew her here.'

I inhaled the strong scent of musk again and looked to the sky. Right above where we stood was a constellation I knew very well.

'Pegasus,' I said. My old friend the winged horse.

Vicken and I shared a knowing gaze. Vampires looked to Pegasus for the time – you could tell how long you had until sunrise based on its position in the sky. The time now was nearing midnight, a powerful hour for vampires performing spells. Even though we were mortal, I hoped Pegasus might give us some strength.

With the musk came hints of earth and vanilla. The smell deepened; this was not traditional musk, this was different. I had smelt that combination before.

'Of course,' I said knowingly. 'This musk is being burned over a fire. Don't you smell the wood?'

I had performed this exact spell with Heath, Gavin, Song and Vicken when they first became my coven. The annunciation spell was used to cement a coven, binding their lives together. Forever.

'And it's meant to be performed before midnight at the beach. They'll need seawater,' I said, and with renewed focus I ran towards the end of Main Street.

'That's why she killed Kate. She had to be full so that she could share her blood with her coven,' I continued breathlessly.

'Yeah, I remember,' Vicken said darkly as he followed me in the direction of the beach. 'Look, if there's only one or two, we can stab them right in the heart. Get it over with quickly.' The smell of musk was nearly unbearable now. 'Get out your knife,' he commanded.

I slid the knife from my boot, and my fingers gripped around the butt of the dagger. The sidewalk ended with a gated string of houses, separated from the street by a long driveway. Vicken's fingers wrapped around my wrist and he pulled me into the shadows at the edge of a small parking lot.

His profile was serious as he looked down to the sea.

'Come on,' he whispered. I followed, crouched over as we made our way across the parking lot to a sea wall that bordered the sand.

Vicken crouched down and leaned forward.

'Stop,' I whispered. 'They'll be able to feel our presence.'

'Not if they're in the middle of their ceremony,' he said.

He inched forward so he could look around the side of the wall. His body was still as he looked down the beach.

'Well?' I asked, unable to bear the anticipation.

He sat back on his heels. In the moonlight his mouth opened and he looked at the ground before quietly saying, 'There are five. Four men and the one woman.'

Without letting him go on, I positioned myself so I could look. Without any remaining vampire sight, all I could make out were five figures, just as Vicken had said. The fire burned before the coven and tiny flickers crackled in the blackness. I inhaled musk and frankincense.

It was done. She had a coven.

As I watched, she turned her head, highlighted faintly by the moonlight so that I could see her profile. She had a small upturned nose and a pronounced collarbone, as if she hadn't eaten enough as a human. Then she spun on her heel to face me, lifted an arm and pointed up the beach directly at me.

'Run,' I said, scrambling backwards. 'Vicken, run!'

I pushed my body as hard as I could as we ran down Main Street back towards civilization. My legs, my poor legs, were shaking so badly that if it wasn't for the mental image of the vampire's arm pointing right at me, I would have collapsed to the ground. That blonde hair and the familiar slope of her nose. How could she have known I was here? Here in Lovers Bay?

Run, Lenah. Stop thinking and run.

If we could find a crowd, we would be safe. Vampires don't expose themselves to humans en masse. But she wouldn't give up. She had seen me, her maker.

Oh, what was her name?

'Here, here!' Vicken said, skidding to a halt at what seemed like a random part of the street. He started to climb over the stone wall, and only then did I realize he knew exactly where we were thanks to his lingering vampire sight.

I checked around again. Luckily the long trees curved over the wide street and it remained empty.

He extended a hand to me and together we climbed over the wall. Once my feet hit the grass of Wickham, I felt a bit better. Vicken and I crept back towards the campus through the trees, but when we were close to the pathway he stopped.

'Wait,' he said, holding out an arm.

A security car drove by, causing both Vicken and me to retreat deeper into the shadows. Once we were safe in the darkness, Vicken asked, 'What did you run like hell for? Did they see you?'

'Yes! Of course,' I said, still trying to catch my breath.

'Let's keep to the back of the buildings,' Vicken said. 'We have a better chance of staying hidden.'

We walked towards Seeker.

'Her name was Odette,' Vicken said. 'She did not linger long after you took your hibernation.'

I could see the back of Curie Building and the greenhouse as we walked.

'Odette?' I said. Her name felt odd and foreign

as I said it aloud. 'I don't remember that.' I remembered her face though. I never forgot the faces of those I killed.

'If the power of the ritual called her to Lovers Bay, then she's here to find that elemental magic,' I said. 'She'll want it to use herself.'

I didn't need to explain to Vicken that she desired power.

'Well, we won't be performing the ritual again any time soon, so maybe she'll leave when the magic doesn't present itself again.'

I hoped that was true, though I didn't know Odette's intentions. But as Vicken and I hesitated at the back of the infirmary I did know this: a vampire's number-one priority is blood. Second on that list would be power. If Odette wanted to find out the source of the magic of the ritual, she would have a plan. Vampires always have a plan.

Vicken and I ran to the media building, next to Seeker. We hesitated as two Lovers Bay police officers patrolled the pathway ahead of us. I looked all the way up to the top floor to see my balcony. The balcony where I'd performed the ritual.

I tried to ignore the voice in my head, the one that had haunted me since she'd lifted her arm and pointed at me up the darkened beach.

Odette would be back.

CHAPTER 6

I studied the longsword on the wall. I rested my face in my hands and sat on the couch with my legs tucked under me. I analysed the slim reflection of my body in the sword's metal. How many times had I stared into its silver and asked how I could possibly survive without my Rhode? How many times did I have to avert my eyes, because it was just too much?

And then I had met Justin, who brought me out of the depths of despair and back into the light.

Two days had passed since Vicken and I had discovered the vampires on the beach. We did not venture off campus after dark. No matter how hard I studied that longsword, looking into its infinite mirror for answers, I found nothing. Why had Rhode stayed away from me for so long after he'd survived that ritual? A ritual he performed so I could be human?

All I knew for certain was that our souls had linked us to earth.

For two days after Rhode left this time, I walked back and forth from the archery plateau to my apartment. I searched for answers where the Aeris had stood. But nothing came from sitting for hours on the grass. For two days, I wondered, *Where is he? Where had he hidden for the year I'd believed him dead?* I found no answers, and Rhode did not return.

Two days
    became
     two weeks
    became
     two months.

The summer passed in a blink. Up in my apartment I had whiled away the time reading and reflecting, but as we got closer to the start of school I found myself marking off the days on the calendar. On 31 August, I resolved to take a trip. Wickham students were set to return in a couple of days and I had not seen Justin or his brothers on campus all summer.

No letters. No emails.

I tried calling Justin but my phone calls went unanswered.

Three days before school was due to begin, I took a dawn drive to Rhode Island, to Justin's parents' house. I intended to give him an explanation. He deserved it. I practised my speech on the hour-long drive there. When I finally pulled on to his street, I rolled down the window. A cool breeze floated into the car, brushing against my cheeks. The big houses slept in the early summer morning. Not even the sprinklers were on yet.

I stood at the foot of Justin's family's driveway looking up at the house. The last time I had been there was Halloween. Now the trees were lush and heavy with leaves. Fresh-baked cookies, home-cooked meals, and soft hands touching my skin were associated with that house. At any moment, I expected to see a light click on in the kitchen window. Justin's mother was an early riser. Did she know we hadn't talked all summer? Would she welcome me inside?

How could I explain how sorry I was? OK, one more rehearsal.

'Justin,' I said aloud to myself, 'you don't understand. When I saw Rhode, I was . . . *surprised.*'

I heard the sound of a latch; the front door opened. I lifted my chin to see Justin, shirtless and in a pair of sweatpants with WICKHAM down the leg. He squinted.

This was it. I had to tell him.

'Lenah?' he said, and rose on to his toes to try to see me over the top of a hydrangea bush.

I shifted the weight from my left foot to my right foot. My heart was unable to find a comfortable rhythm. I couldn't scream, *I'm sorry*, across the lawn. I started up the long driveway but there was no need.

He slammed the door.

'Here's what I don't understand,' Vicken said the next evening. Careful not to venture out after dark, we had a couple of hours left before sunset. We had planned our days that way the entire summer. It was just after six and we were at Lovers Bay Herb Shop, at the end of Main Street. 'Why do we need to stay in this bloody place? Skulking about in daylight just in case we run into a vampire you might have made a hundred years ago. In case you forgot where that happened, we have a house in Hathersage. In fact, we murdered lots of people there.'

'Yes, our house that is likely to be overrun with vampires in our absence,' I replied.

'We have money,' Vicken reasoned. 'Let's go to Paris. Drink wine. Relax.'

'You know why we can't leave,' I replied, and held up a jar of dried jasmine. *Might be useful.* I scooped some into the paper bag. 'I'm not leaving now Kate's been killed. Especially when I feel so responsible.'

'Maybe it's all a coincidence. It's been ages since you performed the ritual. Those vampires probably came to town, ate your unfortunate friend and *left*. Let's go. We can find Rhode on our own. He won't be that hard to find,' Vicken groaned. 'Blue eyes, scowl, self-righteous attitude—'

'We're staying,' I replied, and piled the items on the counter. I didn't mention to Vicken that I didn't want to leave Lovers Bay because I had put down roots here. It was my home now.

'You know, just because you were queen for a few hundred years doesn't mean you still are.'

The herb-shop owner had disappeared behind the curtain to get me some newt feet. I placed a twenty-dollar bill on the counter, waiting for her to return.

Vicken examined some chanting crystals on the bottom shelf of the case, but then he slid up slowly and whispered under his breath, 'White skin, so delicate. As a human, she's truly so small, easy to break her neck.'

A tingling feeling crept over me. I shot a glance at Vicken. He stared behind the counter, his eyes wide. 'I'll siphon her blood out, slowly,' he said. His intonation was different, female and almost reptilian. He was speaking for someone else; this was what happened when using vampire extrasensory perception. 'It'll be easier to get Lenah alone,' he hissed.

He took a step back. 'Lenah,' he said in his familiar voice. 'Go. Now.'

The woman was back behind the counter. She had long, cascading ringlets of blonde hair that curled perfectly across her blouse. Her skin was abnormally polished and pale. Her eyes were glassy, their colour an unnatural jade.

Odette.

There was a screech against the glass. A white hand adorned with knife-like fingernails made a claw around the money. She ran her crimson nails along the glass of the shiny counter.

Odette wiped a tiny drop of blood from the corner of her mouth. 'Getting comfortable, were you?'

She licked her lips and grimaced from the taste. 'Blech. She was overweight. I'll be full for days,' she said, and with a sleek bend of her legs, jumped and landed on top of the counter. 'My, my . . .' she said, looking down at Vicken and me.

With my paper bag clutched in my hand, we backed towards the door.

'Lenah Beaudonte. The queen. Backing away from me?'

Blood dripped down her chin like wine running down the side of a goblet.

Vicken whipped out a dagger and stepped in

front of me. Odette jumped down to the floor just inches from Vicken's dagger and her eyes slid back and forth between us.

'Very good, Ms Beaudonte. I see your ritual works. He makes a very good human.'

My blood pounded in my ears and throat. Vicken held his arm outstretched, gripping the dagger in his hand.

From the floor behind the counter I heard a groan. The shopkeeper was still alive.

'If you want to die, then by all means come closer,' Vicken said to the vampire.

She cocked her head to the side and smiled eerily past him.

'I have always admired your greatness, Lenah,' she said, licking the blood from her chin. 'And your evil . . .'

A lump in my throat made it hard to swallow.

'Your friend Kate – was that her name? She crawled away from me. Cried and screamed. It was *such* fun,' Odette hissed.

Vicken lunged at Odette, thrusting out his hand to plunge the knife into her heart. She kicked up a leg and the dagger flew in an arc through the air and clattered on to the floor.

'Damn it!' Vicken spat, and scrambled across the floor for his weapon.

Chin dipped to her chest, the vampire's eyes bored into mine. She opened her mouth, fangs bared.

When my coven came for me all those months ago, when I killed them in the gymnasium, I never understood. It was not until this moment, as the blood pumped through my heart, that I realized what humanity meant. I was filled with it. She needed blood. I would be next. She wanted to drain me of my life force; I knew that feeling too well. How I had hungered to suck the blood from two small holes, siphon it out in rhythmic swallows as life slowly drained from my prey.

I dropped the bag of herbs to the floor and raised my hands, ready to defend myself. I turned to my side to avoid giving her a larger target than necessary. She ran at me, extending one arm and thrusting outward, slamming me in the chest. I fell backwards against the wall behind me. Small brown and black vials clanked and clattered together. Some fell on me, spilling their contents, and others broke into pieces on the floor. My chest throbbed from the force of her hand.

Odette linked her arm around Vicken, pulling him from the floor and hooking him around the neck. Vicken's eyes locked on to mine. He jerked against Odette's strong grasp. His hands were balled into fists. The dagger lay on the floor, useless.

I jumped up and grabbed on to Odette's fingers. I pulled back, jerking, but they were immovable. I was like a child pulling at a metal vice. I tried again. How was she so strong?

Odette smiled, her fangs still bared.

'What is this?' I growled.

'Such questions,' Odette mocked. She squeezed harder, and Vicken grimaced from the pain. Odette pushed me away with her right hand, but it felt like an anvil hitting me in my stomach. I fell back again into the shelves of bottles, so they popped and shattered around me. I hit the floor and shook my head to clear my vision.

The force of her hand had made my muscles tender. When I touched them with my fingertips, they seized, sending an ache through me.

'Lenah, give me the ritual. Now,' Odette ordered. Vicken's face was turning red. My eyes darted to the knife. I pushed up from the floor just as Vicken lifted a knee.

He stamped down hard on Odette's foot, and out of surprise Odette let go. Vicken jumped away and scrambled for the knife. Odette, instead of going after Vicken again, clawed through the air at me. I ducked, avoiding her knife-like nails, but slipped on the spilled oil from the aromatherapy bottles. I fell back to the floor with a smack.

Odette stepped down on my chest.

She pressed harder. Surely she would crack my ribs. My chest felt so tight. Behind her, Vicken was getting to his feet. She pressed down even harder, right below my neck. I coughed, unable to breath. I needed to breathe!

He picked up the dagger.

'I'll kill your friends one by one,' she hissed through clenched teeth. 'Kate was easy. The rest will be painful and slow.'

Vicken plunged the knife through the air but he was not as fast as the vampire.

She jumped off me and ran out of the door. Vicken scrambled after her, dagger in hand, but she was gone. I gasped for air, drawing in heaving hot breaths. I clutched my chest and rubbed at the skin where her boot had pushed against me.

Kate was easy, the rest will be painful and slow.

'Vicken!' I coughed, rolling on to my stomach and snatching my bag of herbs from the floor. I pushed up from the mess of bottles and inhaled a mix of scents such as fig and patchouli. Vicken had run as fast as he could, but he was no match for a vampire who needed no breath. By the time I stumbled out of the shop, Vicken stood in the middle of the street. All we could see was her blonde hair and lean form disappearing into the twilight over Main Street.

I walked slowly to join Vicken. He blinked, scanning the street to see if there were other vampires about. The only movement came from the fast-flying clouds sweeping by above our heads. He sniffed a couple of times and looked over at me.

'You stink.'

'Gathered that,' I replied. My blouse was slick with essential oils.

'We should go back and check on the shopkeeper,' I said. 'Though if someone comes in and catches us before she's awake, we'll be implicated.'

'I'll go,' Vicken said. 'I'm not afraid of human idiocy.' He bent down and dropped his knife into his boot. 'That vampire was quick. I couldn't get a clear shot if I threw the dagger.' He sounded like he was trying to justify it to me.

'Mind you, she didn't kill us,' I said.

'No, she didn't,' he said, and grabbed on to his shoulder. He winced. 'But she tried to take me with her.'

'She wants the ritual.'

'Gathered that too,' Vicken said, and sniffed in my direction. 'Wait here, where I can see you.' He hesitated. 'And smell you.'

*

'So, do the movement again,' Vicken demanded, sucking on a cigarette. We stood on Wickham beach and I mimicked the motion Suleen had made earlier that summer. 'He waved his hand and her body just appeared?' Vicken asked.

'Not really. It was an outline of it. Like a ghost.'

That moment seemed a thousand years ago now. Now the yellow tape and police officers had gone. Someone had combed through the sand. Combed it, cleaned it, taking away all evidence that someone had been killed there.

'I told you,' I continued, 'we were indiscernible to the people around us. Invisible.'

Vicken stood up, dropping the cigarette on to the sand as a Wickham security vehicle pulled past the entrance to the beach. The car window slid down and a security officer called out to Vicken and me in the darkness.

'Curfew in twenty minutes!' he yelled.

'Thank you!' I called back.

After a moment, I said, 'She had that *look*,' recalling Odette's saunter on the beach. 'That power-hungry look. The one where the madness has just begun to take over.'

I stopped pacing as Vicken lit another cigarette. He stood facing the ocean, his back to campus.

'Hey, kids! Fifteen minutes to curfew!'

On the path a different security guard, this one portly with a beard, pointed down at us. 'No one out past nine,' he reminded us.

When the students came back to campus in the next few days, they would find it much altered. Vicken and I had walked off campus that morning to see a construction crew erecting a heavy steel gate. It was set to connect between the two gothic entrance towers.

By the time we returned that afternoon, a twenty-four-hour guard manned a booth at the entrance. A booth which had remained empty the entire previous year.

Now, on the beach, a guard was watching.

I joined Vicken at the water's edge.

'How are we going to protect ourselves if there's five of them?' I asked. 'I'm not exactly a sunlight-wielding vampire any more.'

Vicken was quiet for a moment and then said, 'That's just it, isn't it?' He nodded to himself. 'We need to rely on sunlight.'

'That depends. She was strong enough to hold you, paralyse you. We don't know what kind of strength she has. And she was out before sunset this evening.'

'It was almost sunset. And she might just be very strong. We don't know her powers. We'll have to try to let it play out until we know what we're dealing with. I'll nose around for some more information.'

'You be careful. You sure your ESP hasn't waned at all?' I asked, hoping that some of Vicken's vampire traits had not yet faded following his transformation. He shook his head. Like Vicken, all I'd had left of my vampire powers after the ritual were my sight and my extrasensory perception. There was no telling when they would disappear for Vicken, but mine had weakened the longer I was human. The more time he had them, the more advantage we had. We walked away from the beach and back towards Seeker.

When I returned to my room and Vicken to his dorm, I lit a white candle on my coffee table. I collapsed back on to the couch and watched the candle flame flicker and dance. The light became just a golden blur. I leaned my head back on the couch, and as I watched the flame its dancing rhythm lured me to sleep. As I drifted off, visions of Justin slamming doors, and screaming at me in front of an audience of people, lingered in my mind. More nightmarish images came: Justin racing his motorboat and driving it head on into Rhode, lying helpless on the shore.

Then the images changed.

I walk down a familiar pathway. I am at Wickham.

There are brick buildings covered in dirty snow. No students. Windows are blackened, the union vacant. I walk the long path towards Wickham beach.

'What is this place?' I ask the empty campus, and suddenly I am not alone. Suleen is at my side. We walk in the snow towards the Wickham beach. As I look towards the shore, a discarded broken rowboat sits in burnt pieces on the sand.

Quartz dorm windows are dark, abandoned. No one walks in or out of the dorms or hurries with cups of coffee to their classes. Wickham is darkened, deadened. A ghost town.

'Is this the future?' I ask.

'This is Wickham if Odette achieves the ritual,' Suleen says. 'No one that wicked can pour evil intentions into a ritual this powerful without repercussions. She will destroy . . . everything.'

I stop, gasping in the bitter winter air.

I shot upright on the couch, placed my hands on my thighs and tried to catch my breath. I froze a moment – the tip of my nose was ice cold. It was as if I had been walking around outside on a snowy day.

'Suleen?' I said aloud. 'Suleen?'

I twisted about to look around the room, but it was just a dream. And I remained alone.

CHAPTER 7

A sea of black cloth. Black T-shirts. Black dresses. Black skirts. Black boots.

It was black for miles. I knew I wore everything in that closet last year but . . .

'Do I own *anything* that isn't black?' I asked the closet. Everyone already had reason to stare at me: I had left for six months at the end of last year; my best friend, Tony, had died; and I was now back at school with no explanation. *What would Tracy and Claudia say?* I wondered, holding a skirt in my hand. There were bound to be questions and talk about Kate, the third girl in the Three Piece, who was now dead. I pulled a black blouse and black jeans from the closet. My breath caught in my chest. Would Tracy and I be friends this year, without Tony around?

I sighed and tried to shake away the dream from the night before. Odette's reign if she achieved the ritual would turn Wickham into an abandoned hell. A hell without those I loved, without Justin or Rhode.

Hello, I thought, holding the blouse to me. *I am*

Lenah Beaudonte. I wear all black, all the time, and at one time was a harbinger of death.

I sighed again and made myself a cup of coffee.

When I stepped out on to the campus, I slid on a pair of sunglasses. For the briefest of moments I expected to see Tony waiting for me, as he had done so often the year before. I expected to see the gauge earrings in his ear, the charcoal on his fingertips and the backwards baseball hat. I could have seen my beautiful Japanese friend if I imagined hard enough.

But he was dead.

School, on the other hand, was lively despite the new security presence. The campus was vibrant with students from the upper schools scrambling from building to building. Some exited the union grasping mugs and cups, others held to-go boxes filled with a quick breakfast. I walked in the shade of the branches, though I no longer feared the sun. I looked down at my palms, at the lifelines I knew so well. I wondered briefly, though I knew it would never be answered, why sunlight once came out of my hands in my second life as a vampire. Who made those decisions in the world and why had that power been given to me?

As I walked towards assembly, I knew that when I could wield sunlight I harboured an enormous amount of power. I gulped my coffee and stopped short, as a realization came to me. If I had remained a vampire, I would still be one of the most powerful vampires in the world. The desire for power, the high I once felt as a vampire, throbbed deeply within me for a moment, then ebbed away.

I started walking again. Vicken stood up from a bench about ten paces down the pathway. Seeing him there, with a backpack slung over his shoulders, made me smile. Beyond, in the distance, the harbour sparkled in the morning sun.

'I'm skipping this,' Vicken said flatly.

'You can't,' I replied. 'They take attendance.'

'Attendance?'

'Roll call,' I clarified.

'I should never have let Rhode convince me to go to this sodding school.'

I stopped. A spark of surprise flickered in my chest. At the mere mention of his name, I immediately imagined scenarios about Rhode. Rhode in Hathersage walking through the empty halls, Rhode watching me from afar, protecting me. Was he wondering if I was all right?

'So,' I said, 'Rhode convinced you to go to Wickham?'

'Not convinced exactly, but you do realize I haven't been in school since there were horses and buggies?'

'When did you speak with Rhode?'

'Before he left,' he replied, though I didn't exactly believe him. I stopped short and looked straight ahead. Standing together by the entrance to Hopper were Claudia and Tracy, Justin's brother Roy and some lacrosse players I did not know. And there, standing by his brother, was Justin.

'What is it?' Vicken said, alarm colouring his tone. Perhaps he was a bit more ready to grab for his dagger than usual. 'Oh . . .' he grumbled, when he saw who I was looking at. Justin embraced Claudia with a big hug. When he pulled away, she wiped her eyes and I saw that she was crying. This unit had existed before my arrival at this school, before I'd darkened their doorstep. Now they stood together, shoulders slumped, looking smaller to me somehow. Not in numbers, but in their energy.

'I liked her perfume, the pink one with the twisted bottle,' Vicken said suddenly. He had closed his eyes for a moment in concentration. His wild hair framed his face in mane-like waves. 'She'll miss that smell,' he said, though the words he was saying were not his own.

'What?' I asked quietly.

'Your friend Tracy. She wishes Kate were here. Because . . .' He hesitated. 'Because she listens better than Claudia.'

I watched the group a moment. Tracy was looking

at Claudia, though she wasn't speaking.

'And your other blonde friend, she . . .' He hesitated again. 'She wants her friend to go shopping with, to walk with, she misses her presence. But I don't get it. It's been over two months since she died. Why haven't they calmed down by now?'

I understood mortal grieving, even if Vicken couldn't.

I would miss Kate plopping down in a seat next to us, offering us gum first thing. I would even miss her digging endlessly into my love life, asking inappropriate questions. We weren't close, I knew that, but, still, her death left a ghost in my mind.

'Two months is nothing,' I said, thinking of Tony. His death, unlike Kate's, left a hole in my heart that I was sure would never heal. 'The sorrow of death can linger for years.'

Death had been so easy to understand when we were vampires. But, as a human, the death of a loved one was a point in history always to be referenced. A fixed point in your life that you constantly measured yourself against as you grew older – a baseline.

The pin in the heart.

'Well, let's just go get attended and get to class,' Vicken said.

'Attended?' I said, tearing my eyes away from Justin and his friends.

'You know – roll.'

Vicken dug a piece of paper out of his pocket while I snuck another look at the group I once considered my friends.

'I have world literature first,' Vicken said, squinting at his schedule.

Justin walked towards us purposefully and I prepared myself with a shake of my hair over my shoulders. *You deserve this. Take it, accept it. You deserve what he is about to say to you.* He picked up speed. In fact, his feet carried him faster and *faster* in our direction. Vicken looked up from his scrap of paper only at the last moment.

When Justin's body slammed into him, Vicken was blasted into the air and hit the ground flat on his back. Justin knelt over Vicken and with devastating force punched him in the face. I reacted out of instinct. I kicked Justin directly on his hip, which disarmed him and he fell away from Vicken. A rather large crowd had formed already as I bent down to pull at Vicken's arm, helping him up. He stumbled on his feet and wiped his right eye. Blood blossomed in the skin below it. It was already swelling.

'Give me a mirror!' Vicken demanded.

'Odd time to be vain,' I replied.

'I want to see this!' he said incredulously. He shook his head as though it was preposterous that I wouldn't know this was an important moment.

He turned towards Justin. 'Nice shot, mate.'

Ms Tate, our science teacher, ran out of Hopper Building. Her eyes were wild and she pointed at Justin. She had obviously seen what happened.

'You!' she cried. Justin shook out his hand; his fingers must have been hurting. 'Come with me,' she said.

'And you,' she said to Vicken, 'go to the infirmary.' She pointed at a junior, Andrea, and ordered her to go with Vicken.

Justin stepped dangerously close to Vicken and me. He could easily have thrown another punch. I'd never seen him so calm . . . or so angry.

'That . . .' Justin said so quietly that only Vicken and I could hear. 'That,' he repeated, 'was for Tony.' He turned to follow Ms Tate but kept his eyes locked on Vicken.

My gut clenched and I waited for Vicken to react. A muscle in his jaw quivered but that was it. Ms Tate pointed again, this time towards Hopper. 'Justin!' she yelled. 'Go!'

Justin's eyes drifted over to me. They were cold and distant now, so angry, so disappointed in me. He broke our gaze when he turned around and followed Ms Tate. I watched him go with an ache in my heart. This was different from how I ached for Rhode. I wanted my old Justin back. The one smiling at me, teasing me, the one helping me to understand the human world.

Andrea stood at Vicken's side, ready to cross the meadow with him to the infirmary. She glanced back at Tracy and Claudia, as if to ask, 'Who is this guy?'

Vicken leaned towards Andrea. Tell me honestly, is it more purple? Or red?' he asked her. 'Actually, do you have a mirror, love?'

Claudia and Tracy walked directly towards me. They wore gorgeous sundresses; Claudia's was a canary yellow. I wished for a split second I could shine like them – like they always did. But when Claudia got closer I realized how truly sad she was. Her eyes were red and puffy from crying.

'Wow,' Claudia said. 'A fight over you already.' She smiled and it warmed the grief that had settled on her face.

'That wasn't over me,' I replied.

'Sure it was,' said Tracy seriously. 'Who was that?' she asked, with a nod in Vicken's direction.

'My . . . cousin,' I stuttered. 'Vicken.'

'Cute,' said Claudia, and it was a relief to see a glimpse of her old self.

'We should go in,' Tracy said. 'It's time for morning assembly.'

As I followed them, I glanced around, searching for Rhode on the virtually empty campus. It was pointless, I knew. He wasn't coming. He was taking our promise to the Aeris seriously – and I knew I should be doing the same.

Inside the hall in Hopper, a general murmur echoed through the auditorium. Students congregated together, chatting about their summers. I stepped into the doorway, then stopped. So many people. A hundred – maybe more. What I had learned with regard to human behaviour would be tested at that moment. I stepped into the spacious auditorium and a hush rolled over the crowd. The younger students didn't know any better, so they just stared. My classmates who had seen the events of the previous year stopped their conversations and turned towards me.

Tracy and Claudia had made it to the third row, their regular spot, although now Kate's seat was empty.

My hands curled nervously into fists. *Why did Justin have to pummel my only ally?*

Rhode . . . I said to myself, but it came out as a groan.

I passed by some silent juniors that I recognized from the year before. My confidence, it seemed, had disappeared along with my fangs.

I hated the human desire to gossip. Once I

was past them, they started up again.

That's Lenah. She dumped Justin Enos. Idiot, right?

Those were Kate Pierson's best friends.

Lenah was Tony Sasaki's best friend.

Yeah, she is the stupidest person alive to dump Justin.

'Sit with us,' Claudia called, and moved her backpack off the extra chair. I tucked my hair behind my ear and headed gratefully towards the two girls I hoped would still be my friends. These girls that had been on the earth a piddling sixteen years. But they had been kind to me when I needed them and were still being kind. I sat down and listened to Claudia talk about her summer at sailing camp.

'What about you, Lenah?' Tracy asked. 'Did you go home to England?'

I was about to explain I had spent my summer at school when Ms Williams, the over-controlling headmistress of Wickham, tapped the microphone.

'. . . the second you even think about signing out. You must be in twos at least,' Ms Williams dictated. 'Off campus? Twos, or lose the privilege.'

I always admired your greatness, Odette had hissed. *And your evil . . .*

'Security is more important than ever. We have lost a good third of our student enrolment because of the accidental deaths of both Tony Sasaki and

Kate Pierson,' she said with a frown. 'So it is our responsibility to reassure the Wickham Boarding School community that we remain vigilant and committed to your safety.'

Tracy looked down and wiped her eyes but I kept staring forward, pretending not to notice. Claudia reached for Tracy's hand.

'Kate Pierson,' Ms Williams continued, 'died off campus. So, while we'll miss her, please do not misconstrue the facts. These incidents are not specifically related, nor are they directed specifically at students. We will, however, maintain our new safety precautions.'

Mortals will lie about anything to protect themselves.

I sighed, tuning out her voice. I turned my onyx ring round and round so the silver band rubbed over my skin. Without Rhode, Vicken and I had no chance of fighting more than one vampire or maybe two. We needed Rhode. His years of experience could really help us now. And as much as I thought I knew about him there was clearly so much I *didn't* know. So much he could do. So much he had kept from me.

No, I thought and threw my hair back over my shoulders. *Don't go down that road – the pity road, where you dwell on Rhode. He's gone. He's gone, and all you can do is get on with your life.*

But he *was* alive. *Where was he?*

Once assembly broke for the day, the chatter immediately started up again. Most people were discussing the new sign-out policy and pointing at the security guards that stood at the auditorium entrance.

'I'm so glad you're back,' Claudia cried, grabbing me into an embrace. I inhaled fresh soap and a spicy perfume. I couldn't help looking over Claudia's shoulder at Tracy, who watched us with the remnant of a tear in her eye. Claudia pulled away and her eyes too were wet. 'Especially with the whole Kate thing, you know? Now promise us – you're not going anywhere, right? No running off like last year?'

'No,' I said to Claudia, who had now taken both of my hands into hers. 'I'm staying.' Her hands were warm and tight around mine. If I'd still been a vampire, we would have been in perfect proximity for me to snap her forward and bite her neck.

I glanced at her wrists. To *investigate* her veins. It was so shocking that I would still feel the urge to do this, a silent horror overtook me. Immediately I pulled my hands from hers. *Must get away from her,* I thought.

It seemed that old habits die hard. Wasn't that the expression?

The feeling passed and I bent forward to grab my backpack. I was mortal. Not a vampire. Not like Odette. I started after Tracy and Claudia to the front door of the auditorium.

Turn around, a voice in my mind whispered. Perhaps it was intuition, or the vampire queen deep inside me. *Turn around, Lenah. Look behind you.*

Slowly I turned, and I froze. Standing at the top of the stairwell at the back of the auditorium was . . . Rhode.

A deep gash, scabbed and blackened ran horizontally across the top of his head. Running down the top of his beautiful lips was another scab, so dark in colour I wasn't entirely sure whether there was fresh blood oozing out of it. His right eye and right cheek were puckered and swollen.

My jaw dropped.

'Come on, Lenah,' Claudia called from the auditorium door.

But I couldn't look away. A couple of seconds passed, then Rhode did the honours for me, walking down the back stairwell and out of sight.

'Rhode!' I called, running for the back door.

'Lenah!' Claudia called after me, but I ignored

her and sprinted out into the quad after Rhode.

'Rhode!' This time I screamed it. He spun around; sunglasses hid his eyes. I could see my horrified expression reflected in the shiny glass.

That close to him, I was able to *really* see the damage. A purple bruise ran over the thick ridge of his nose. The black tinge on his skin made him look ill. Beneath the ridge of his forehead was a deep cut, which probably needed stitches but it was much too late for that. The skin had scabbed and puckered and would most likely scar. His lips, his beautiful lips, were split down the middle and brown with scabs.

I lifted a hand to touch his forehead, but he backed away from me. Pain ripped down the middle of my chest and I lowered my hand. In the reflection in Rhode's sunglasses, I could see my downturned mouth and the squint of my eyes from the sun.

'What happened to you?' I asked.

'Nothing,' he replied. 'I told the headmistress I was in a car accident.'

His right eye was so purple I couldn't help but lift my fingers to touch the mutilated skin. He stepped back again.

'What happened isn't really any of your concern,' he said. 'I have to go to class.'

He walked past me towards the science building where, if I was lucky, we were headed to the same room.

CHAPTER 8

A line of students snaked out of the classroom and down the hall. Geology was a popular course for the senior year – there were three sections full of seniors and a few select juniors. I rose up on my toes to try to see Rhode at the front of the line, but all I could make out was the short crop of his black hair. My heart fluttered as I remembered how his hair used to fall past his shoulders like black silk. Oh, how I had loved his top hat and the angle of his fangs. Back then, fangs were a part of our physical being. The thought of the sharp point of Odette's fangs made me press my fingertips to my neck as though to protect it.

'Ah, good, Lenah,' Ms Tate said.

I dropped my hand. *Oh.* Apparently I had made it to the science-room doorway.

Rhode sat in the front row, chin down, writing something in a notebook. Ms Tate looked over her roster, pointed a pen at Rhode and said, 'Rhode Lewin, you stay there. You'll sit with . . . Justin Enos.' Ms Tate was planning the seating charts for the year. 'He'll be able to get you up to speed.' She was mostly talking to herself.

Very, very bad idea.

Ms Tate handed Rhode a sheet of paper. 'I heard about your car accident. How are you feeling?'

'Better, thanks.' He placed his pen down and with trembling fingers picked up the sheet. His hands, both of them, were wrapped in thick gauze: one around the wrist and one over the knuckles. I froze when he looked up. Beneath those purple and black bruises were the blue eyes I'd known and loved for half a millennium. My stomach knotted and I took a shallow breath. We did not break our stare and his gaze lingering on mine was enough to make my head spin. Much to my confusion he sighed, closed his eyes and broke the spell.

'Lenah,' Ms Tate said, 'you're in your old seat. We have a junior who placed for this class and once she comes you'll sit together.' I nodded and tried to keep my eyes away from Rhode as I walked towards my desk.

I loathed that empty chair next to mine. Tony's. I was about to sit down when Ms Tate spoke again. 'Oh. Hmm.'

Justin and two other students had walked into the class. Ms Tate looked down at her list. 'On second thoughts, Justin, you sit with Lenah. And, Margot –

actually, we'll put the two newbies together; you sit with Rhode here. Caroline . . .' Ms Tate continued to the other new girl who had just walked in. 'You sit at the back with . . .'

I stopped listening to the jumble of names. Avoiding my eyes, Justin sat down, and when he placed his books on the table I noticed his knuckles were wrapped in white gauze. He gripped his textbook and his knee bounced up and down, trembling from either excitement, rage or possibly too much caffeine.

I swallowed, unnerved by his silence. I twisted the onyx ring again, round and round, and finally, as I opened my mouth to talk to him, Ms Tate called the class to order.

'Let's get to today's plan. We'll review some basics.'

Justin stared forward purposefully. The aching in my gut surprised me. Why wouldn't he talk to me or even look at me? For a moment I expected the familiar touch, his warm hand on my knee or my lower back.

'OK, today we'll be analysing the pH levels of local water samples from Lovers Bay. I know it's very elementary, but I think we need to revisit some basic skills before we go forward in our experimentation process.'

I looked over at Justin again and he pressed his lips together.

'What?' he said coldly, and blinked a couple of times, keeping his gaze forward. It took me a moment to realize he was speaking to me.

'Oh. Nothing,' I replied, and looked back down at my notebook. 'I just . . .'

'What?' he said again, this time with a slow turn of his head. The green of his eyes was hard, cold. 'Want to humiliate me some more?'

'Humiliate you?' I whispered, and glanced at Ms Tate, who was writing on the board.

'Your boyfriend is up there. You should be sitting with him,' Justin hissed.

'I just want to—'

'If you talk to me again, Lenah, about anything other than this assignment, I'm leaving the room.'

'Hand me the litmus paper.' Justin's tone was icy. Silently I handed it over.

'Seven,' he said. 'What's yours say?'

I checked the colouration of the paper and then recorded our results. As soon as we finished, he scooped up the papers, dropped our classwork on Ms Tate's desk and swiftly left. At the front of the class Rhode gathered up his pens and notebook. His jaw was clenched and he winced as he placed his bag on his shoulder. I followed him out of the room.

'Rhode,' I called quietly once he was out the door and a few paces down the hall. 'Rhode!' I called again, a little louder. He walked quickly down the hallway. I'd had enough of being treated like the Invisible Woman. 'If you don't turn around, *right now*, I'll scream bloody murder.'

He turned on his heel and looked at me.

'There was a vampire in a herb shop,' I began. 'Here in Lover's Bay. I recognized her from Hathersage. The maid I killed before my hibernation. And she knows,' I added, 'about the ritual.' I stood a foot or so away from Rhode and watched for his reaction. 'Vicken and I wanted to tell you earlier, but you were unreachable.'

'Were you hurt?' he asked, keeping his stance the same, arms folded, back straight.

'She's already killed one friend of mine,' I said simply. 'She said she'd be back for the ritual.'

It was as though Rhode was having the conversation with me against his better judgement. He was respecting the Aeris's demand that we stay apart, but surely he was allowed to speak to me?

'She's fashioned her nails to points.' I gulped, imagining my flesh splitting in two from the strike of her fingers. Rhode brought a gauze-wrapped hand to his chin, nodded once and kept his eyes on my feet. 'She created a coven. Vicken and I saw the ceremony ourselves.'

'Five?' Rhode asked.

I nodded, but couldn't help myself. I had to know. 'What happened to you?' I asked. 'You look terrible. What kind of fight did this? Was it because of the ritual?'

'No, and I already told you it was nothing.'

'You're lying,' I said in disgust.

'I have to go,' Rhode said, but before he turned completely away from me, he added, 'We should meet tonight. About this coven. I'll have Vicken alert you when and where.' He walked a few steps and I listened to the echo of his heels on the floor. Anger bubbled up inside me.

'You know,' I called after him, just a little louder than my natural speaking voice, 'it was always this way.'

He stopped, keeping his back to me. We were alone again now that the next period had started.

'For hundreds of years, you were in control and I knew nothing.'

Rhode turned to me now, our eyes locked in a stare.

'It's true,' I said, my voice faint. 'I had other distractions, but it was always you who held the power. I loved you, so it didn't matter.'

Rhode walked towards me until we were inches apart. This close, I could see the tiny hairs growing on his chin and the faint bruising along his jawline – bruises I hadn't noticed before.

'I don't care about power,' he whispered. He seemed to catch himself in a moment of real anger. He took a deep breath. 'Always, always my thoughts were with you,' he said in an angry hiss.

'You kept me in the dark,' I challenged. 'Perhaps if I had known about the particulars of the ritual, I could have helped you. We wouldn't be stuck, cursed by the Aeris with no possible way to be together.'

At the back of my mind I wondered why Rhode had said he would never have come back to Wickham, and where he was for the year he was gone. It kept nagging at me. What could possibly be a strong enough reason for him to stay away? Another secret, another truth he was keeping from me.

'I told you, I didn't know we would face these kinds of repercussions from the ritual,' Rhode said.

'You said a lot of things, Rhode. Made promises, which you have since broken.' An image of my sister's grave laced with jasmine flowers flashed into my mind.

'Such as?'

'I do not need to remind you. The point is that if I had helped you with the ritual, if you had told me what you were doing, we might have found another way. Maybe we'd have done things differently. You wouldn't have had to fake your death,' I dared to say.

'I really do have to go,' Rhode said. He looked at my lips and my anger dispersed. How quickly it evaporated into the air and away from me. We were *so* close. Close enough that our lips were just a kiss away. My body wanted it so badly that my muscles ached. His eyes, surrounded by those bloody bruises, gazed at me.

We'd never touched before. Not as mortals.

If he just leaned forward, he'd kiss me, lip to lip, skin to skin, and we'd know what it was like to touch. With human feeling. What we'd craved for hundreds of years. The Aeris wouldn't mind. *Would they?* Just a simple kiss . . .

'Can't you feel that?' I asked.

I looked up at him, peering into his eyes. I stared at the purple bruising, wondering if it still hurt.

'Can't you?' I repeated.

In the pit of my stomach was a tornado of feeling, churning and spinning, pulling me towards him. I continued to stare at him, drinking him in. My feet were rooted to the ground, but I swayed just slightly. My body was on fire, the glorious feeling of blood racing through my veins and my heart. I extended my hand and watched him do the same. His hand, so different from the cool, smooth skin of a vampire, was now the weathered hand of a human. We stood like that for a moment, almost touching, enjoying the electricity between us. I let every pore, every cell, feel the sensation of heat.

'Yes,' he answered at last, and dropped his hand.

It can't be like this for everyone, I thought. *Not everyone feels love like this.*

Finally I took a tiny step towards him, but he stopped me.

'We can't,' he said.

I didn't want to come back. I had to. His words echoed inside me. I ripped my eyes away, and the space between us opened up.

'You should leave. Permanently,' I replied, looking at the ground. I took a step back. 'If it's such a torment to be near me. If you didn't even *want to come back,* as you said, then go.' Even as I said it, I knew I didn't mean it. And Rhode was not so easily fooled.

He blinked slowly. 'You know I couldn't leave. Not now.'

My anger bubbled again. I swallowed hard.

Rhode inched closer. I could breathe him in: soap, deodorant and his skin too. He smelt sweet, of humanity. He clenched his jaw as though he was fighting tears, and when our gaze met I saw that his eyes . . . were *glassy*.

'Lenah,' he said, drawing my eyes to his, 'I stay because there is an extraordinary difference between thinking of you and seeing you in the mortal flesh. I stay for the one moment you smile throughout the day. Or to watch you run your hand through your hair. Because I must, must –' his breath was short – '*must* be near you, in any way I can.'

I was speechless. I wanted to say something – anything. Tell him I felt exactly the same way, but I couldn't stop him before he turned from me.

And then . . .

I was engulfed by the pungent smell of ripe apples. Apples everywhere. As though I was standing above a wooden crate holding dozens of shiny red apples from the September harvest. I shook my head to clear it, but the scent was so strong I was compelled to close my eyes to escape from it for just a moment. Images flooded my mind. A scrapbook of memories from my life ran through my brain, unstoppable.

Rhode and I are vampires. We kiss on the great hill at the foot of our stone manor. I wear a great black gown with a long train. It is moments before sunset. His hands press against my back, drawing me near. My skin has a porcelain sheen. My lips are rose coloured and I can see the points of my fangs. Why can I see myself? A hand holds a cane. I know that cane and its owl-head handle made of onyx.

I opened my eyes, shook my head and focused on my breath. *In and out, Lenah,* I thought. *In and out.* Slowly the images dissipated along with the scent of apples. The sound of Rhode walking away brought me back to the world of the present.

I must be near you.

My breath couldn't catch up with me fast enough.

Rhode walked down the hallway, his words ringing in my mind and the smell of apples lingering on the air.

CHAPTER 9

'It's September third. We have twenty-seven days before the start of the month of Nuit Rouge,' Rhode explained that evening.

As promised, Vicken had summoned me to the library after dinner. I stood at the glass window of a study atrium. From the back of the library we faced the great hill that led to the archery plateau. I tried not to follow the slope of the hill, especially since I intended never to go up there again. I doubted a vampire would watch from there, so exposed. There were no trees to hide behind and no cover of shadow. Vampires liked to watch and study their victims. By knowing their weaknesses, they could kill them with ease. I pressed my body weight against the glass, letting it cool my skin. I used to do that as a vampire to make sure I still retained some vestiges of my sense of touch.

I turned from the window to the two men of my past. Vicken leaned against the wall, arms crossed over his chest. His brow creased and he kept his gaze on Rhode. Rhode sat at the table and rested his bandaged elbow on the study desk.

'Why does Nuit Rouge matter?' Vicken asked.

'It's when the connection between the super-natural world and the mortal world is at its weakest,' I said. I could feel Rhode's gaze upon me. 'It's why our Nuit Rouge party was always particularly bloody. Ever notice you felt stronger on those nights? More . . . animal-like?'

Vicken considered this with a frown. 'Yes. I guess you're right.'

'Until October first, it's unlikely Odette will be able to attack on the campus,' Rhode said.

'She attacked on the beach,' Vicken said.

'Technically it's not within the grounds,' Rhode replied. 'The ritual was performed on campus more than once. It might be what called Odette initially, but it may offer us protection as well. The energy may be lingering, as a shield. At least until October first, when Nuit Rouge will endow her with extra powers.'

'Brilliant. So in the meantime we're prisoners in this loony bin,' Vicken replied.

I ran a hand through my hair, massaging my scalp to relieve some tension. I finally met Rhode's eyes. There was a zing in my chest as though he was touching something within me, very near my heart.

I wanted to tell him about Tony's death and

Justin's defence of me. I wanted to explain how it felt when I was able to wield sunlight. But Rhode had not asked about the coven. He had not asked how they'd died. Again I reminded myself I still had no clue to his whereabouts the year before. He had revealed nothing.

'Let's go, shall we?' he said. 'I think we've covered everything.'

Vicken turned off the lights to the study atrium, bringing our meeting to a close. Rhode glanced at me just as we walked on to the courtyard in front of the library.

As his bruised eyes locked on to mine, I stopped short, inhaling the smell of apples again. But it was different this time. Now the scent was just like when I was a child. I brought my hand to my eyes and rubbed at them and brought with it the smell of cider in winter. In the black of my mind, I saw the geology classroom from that morning.

I am sitting at Rhode's desk at the front of the room. I look up to the doorway and my chest clenches. I see myself walk into the classroom. I am wearing all black, my brown hair falling over my shoulders.

How can I walk into the classroom and sit at the desk at the same time? This is someone else's vision. Someone else's mind!

Beautiful, a voice says. A deep voice, a man's voice.

Someone is looking at me. I am aware of the pain in my hands, the cracking sensation whenever I move my lips. I have been in a battle.

It was all worth it, *the person thinks. His whole body aches. But there is something else too. As I walk by, the person inhales deeply, hoping to smell something familiar. He grips on to his notebook so as not to lift a hand to touch me. Just looking at me hurts. This is painful. This love, he thinks, is so deep it cannot be undone.*

A realization overwhelms me: I'm in Rhode's mind. These are Rhode's thoughts!

I blinked, breathing in the familiar smell of campus: the union, the cut lawns and of course the ocean. The sweet smell of apples had vanished as if it had never been. I took a moment to replay what I had just seen. I could see myself in geology exactly as Rhode saw me. I smiled at the green grass at my feet. *He thought I was beautiful. This love is so deep it cannot be undone.*

With the mechanical click of a lighter, and a plume of cigarette smoke, Vicken tugged at my elbow. Vicken did not fear my touch but Rhode did. With that realization, another burst of happiness pumped through me. Rhode *wanted* to touch me, but was resisting. I could feel the conflict within him during the vision. Hope rippled through me again as it had in the hallway that morning.

I stay because there is an extraordinary difference between thinking of you and seeing you in the mortal flesh . . . Because I must, must, must be near you, in any way I can.

'We will always be in love,' I said aloud.

'Oh Lord. Let's go,' Vicken growled.

We headed across the courtyard and on to the main pathway.

'Where are we going?' I asked.

'The star tower at the top of Curie.' He called the science building by its official name.

Vicken puffed at his cigarette as a collection of junior girls passed by.

'Hey . . . Vicken,' one of the girls said, with a curl of her lip and a breathy tone to her voice. 'You shouldn't smoke,' she added with a giggle. He walked backwards for a moment to maintain eye contact.

'I heard it could kill me,' he said, with his Cheshire Cat grin.

Another round of giggles and I rolled my eyes as we approached Curie.

'One of them is jealous. She thinks I have a *huge* crush on you,' Vicken said, and I rolled my eyes a second time.

'Are you ever going to finish that cigarette?' I asked.

He drew another puff. 'I like to fully experience things that are bad for me.'

'You know,' I said, as he blew out the last breath of smoke, 'contrary to when you were living your old life, those will actually kill you.'

Vicken exhaled angrily and stubbed his cigarette out on the brick of the building.

'So will your friend Justin. This actually hurts,' he said, and pointed at the yellow and purple bruise beneath his right eye. 'I keep touching it to check. You know, it's easy to forget physical pain when you haven't felt it for more than a hundred years. Glorious.' He brought his cheek towards me. 'You touch it. I wonder if it feels different if someone else presses on it.'

'You're sick,' I said, and ran my student ID through the scanner – just one of the many precautions introduced at Wickham Boarding School since Tony and Kate's deaths.

'*I'm* sick?' Vicken said, following me into the building. 'Need I remind you of the time you killed an entire beach party by yourself?' He paused and we climbed the six flights up. 'Don't get me wrong,' he said between breaths. 'It was brilliant.'

After an hour, the bright moon cast a milky light through the glass ceiling on to the observatory floor.

We opened the roof windows, and instead of using the enormous telescope, Vicken and I admired the passing constellations with our naked eyes, lying on our backs on the floor. Even though the sun had descended only a couple of hours earlier, with every moment the sky darkened and more stars twinkled in the night sky.

'You know, as a point of conversation, Rhode may have got into a fight here,' Vicken said. 'Not in Hathersage, like you think.'

'All right,' I replied. 'Then why didn't Odette mention Rhode at the herb shop. She clearly doesn't know he survived.'

'You're speculating.'

'How do you know she has anything to do with Rhode? Wouldn't she have said something? Wouldn't she have mentioned Rhode?'

A shooting star raced across the sky. I pointed straight up to the sky and so did Vicken. In unison, we counted in Latin . . .

'*Unus, duo, tres* . . .'

Waiting . . . waiting . . . Another shooting star flew across the sky. The exhilaration of seeing that bright light streaking over our heads faded quickly and the Aeris's words echoed in my head.

You are soulmates. Your lives are destined to be intertwined.

'Leave it with me,' Vicken said. 'I'll figure out what happened. I was a soldier, for Pete's sake. Snooping around won't be too hard. Difficult to miss Ol' Bludgeoned Face these days.'

I laughed. 'Old Bludgeoned Face?'

'Spot on.'

'You're funnier as a human,' I said.

Vicken waited a moment and then asked with a wide smile, 'Do you want to touch my bruise?'

'Still no.'

He turned on to his side and inched forward like a seal out of water.

'Come on, Lenah. Touch my bruise.'

'No!' I cried. He was so close I could smell the tobacco on his skin.

'Just do it. Are you afraid of it?'

I smacked him hard.

'A little tiny blood mark!' he exclaimed, and we were hysterical until I heard another kind of laughter echoing up the stairs. I froze. A squeal of girlish giggles followed by a voice I recognized. We sat up and I twisted around to look to the doorway. Justin walked into the observatory with a junior I recognized: Andrea.

'If it isn't my escort,' Vicken said with a devilish grin. Andrea smiled.

Justin's eyes shifted from Vicken to me.

'Let's go, Andrea. This room is *occupied*,' he said.

'It's not,' I cried, and scrambled to my feet.

Vicken scooted back against the wall and lit another cigarette. 'Oh, let them go. He's a twit,' he said from behind me, and crossed one ankle over the other. 'By the way, he came in here to take her clothes off.'

I glared at him.

'ESP,' he said with a shrug.

'Put out that cigarette,' I hissed.

I clambered down the stairwell after them. Justin already hated me, and now he thought I was with Vicken!

'Wait!' I called, and burst out on to the quad.

Andrea and Justin stood by the door; her expression was murderous.

'This will just take a second,' I said to her. 'Will you excuse us?'

She looked to Justin, eyes wide, waiting for him to say no. When he didn't, she scoffed.

'You're pathetic,' she said with a dramatic turn, and stalked off.

'Andrea!' He called after her again, but she was already on the pathway joining other students. It would be curfew soon.

Justin moved to follow after her.

'Can you please give me a moment?' I asked. He

turned back to me with a huge sigh.

'I'm not with Vicken,' I said emphatically.

'Did I say that you were?' Justin replied, his tone stinging me like a smack against my cheek.

'No,' I said quietly. 'You didn't.'

'On the archery field you left me for Rhode,' he said. 'But I guess I wouldn't be surprised if you were with Vicken now. It's tough keeping up.'

I didn't have the heart to tell him the actual order was: Rhode, Vicken and then him.

'Vicken and I are really just friends,' I said.

'So you're friends with a murderer. He helped your coven kill Tony!'

'It's more complicated than that,' I said.

'Yeah, well, it doesn't seem too complicated to me,' said Justin. 'I have to go.'

That seemed to be a common phrase these days.

But Justin didn't go. He looked down at the ground and then at me.

'What do you want from me? What about Rhode?' he asked. 'Aren't you guys soulmates? Ritual mates? Whatever.'

'I'm not with Rhode,' I said after a pause. 'I'm not with Vicken. I'm with no one.'

His nostrils flared and his cheeks reddened. He blinked a few times and I struggled to read his expression. 'Don't you love him?' he asked. 'Rhode?'

'Things just changed,' I said with a shake of my head, and it was the truth. As much as Rhode consumed me, as much as I would love him forever, everything was different now. I had to move on.

'Kind of seems like a hard thing to change,' Justin said.

We let the sounds of the campus resonate around us. People were talking and laughing. Cell phones chimed, and somewhere close cars whooshed by on a street.

'Look,' I said. 'I don't want you to hate me. I know I deserve it . . .'

'I don't hate you,' he said, and shifted his gaze from the ground to my eyes. 'I just don't want to know you any more. I want to live my life without rituals, and covens of murderous vampires killing my friends. I like dating girls who, you know, stay alive.'

His words cut though me. It seemed to me then that I'd never again feel the joy and comfort of lying in his arms. I remembered how powerful his warmth had felt after being cold for hundreds of years. Warmth, touch, tenderness – that was Justin. He was a reminder that I could truly be alive and feel love. He had helped me move on last year; I wanted him to help me now. Help me in the way only he could.

But he turned and walked down the pathway after Andrea.

'Wait,' I called. 'Please.'

He stopped next to the pathway light. 'What?' He kept his back to me.

'I'm sorry,' I said, then hesitated. I chose my words in my head, but none of them sounded right. 'About all of it,' I finished.

He shook his head but faced me again.

'Sorry, Lenah, but it's not enough.'

'I just want you to know . . .' I took a step to him and raised my palms to say *stay*. 'No, let me rephrase. I want you to try to imagine someone in your life that you've known forever. Let's say, Roy, your younger brother.'

Justin frowned but nodded once.

'And then, one day, he's gone. How he held a cup of coffee, or laughed, or touched his face is left only in your memory. Gone forever. I want you to try and imagine that grief.'

'Tony died, Lenah. Kate died. I know what grief is like.'

I dared to take another step.

'Humans can learn to live again after grieving, but for the vampire, that grief is constant. It's what makes us so dangerous. And when Rhode died, or I thought he did, you were there, at the moment when I was human for the first time. You brought me out of that curse. You healed me.'

Justin avoided my eyes by looking across the campus. I waited for him to respond, to say that he was touched, that he understood. But he just exhaled and put his hands in his pockets.

'I know you heard me talking to Rhode that day, on the archery field. I was surprised to see him,' I tried to explain.

'I bet,' he said, still looking away.

'It's not that I don't love . . .'

Justin's eyes snapped up.

'. . . love you,' I finished.

He kept my gaze but didn't reply. Didn't say *I still love you too.* I gave it a few more seconds.

'Fine,' I said, and turned on the spot. I hurried down the path.

'Wait!' Justin called from behind me. 'Lenah, wait!'

But I did not wait. I kept walking down the path, embarrassment rolling over me in waves. *I can't believe I told him how I felt and got no reaction. No reaction!* It was so unlike him. I walked and walked until I found myself almost back at Seeker.

I stopped on the path, directly next to the library, when a desire to go inside swept over me. There was another hour until curfew. I wanted to go inside the listening room, where I could sit and listen to music at the push of a button. Where I could be alone. Perhaps I would play Mozart. I saw him play in person several times, four to be exact.

I had walked away from Justin's words. I hoped the listening room would help me forget the look in his eyes. I entered the library and walked down the main aisle and towards the tiny rooms at the back. I had worked in that library the year before. I knew its contents well. I checked through the small rectangular window into the listening room. It was empty. I opened the door and stepped inside.

There were no CDs any more. Instead a computer sat on top of a small desk. I had spent the last year learning to navigate computers. I sat down and clicked on a small icon that said: NEW SONGS. Someone had classified them as well: Romance, Classical, New Age, Death Metal. *Death Metal?*

I searched through the songs for a few moments, marvelling at the thousands of choices. A hand reached over my shoulder. I jumped a little as it then gently grazed the top of my fingers and rested on the mouse. I hadn't even heard the door click! The hand was warm and golden bronze.

'Pick this one,' said Justin quietly. He double-clicked and a ballad, a very soft song with a woman singing, echoed in the small room.

'What are you doing?' I asked quietly, as he pulled me up from the chair.

'Dancing with you.'

The image of him shoving his hands in his pockets came to mind.

'But I thought you were angry with me,' I said.

His strong arms pulled me to him gently and his grasp was firm around my shoulders. His palm rested on the centre of my back and I lifted my chin to him. Underneath his shirt collar was a black leather strap. A glint of a silver pendant peeked out from his shirt when he moved, but Justin drew me closer. I wondered what kind of pendant it was and what else could have changed over the summer. The sound of a guitar filled the room and the melancholy piano swirled through me. Our eyes met and Justin's gentle gaze compelled me to speak.

'I really am sorry. About Rhode, about . . .' I hesitated. It felt odd to apologize for almost dying when I performed the ritual. 'Well, like I said, I'm sorry. About all of it.'

He hushed me gently and nuzzled his nose to my shoulder. He grabbed on tighter and we started to revolve.

'About Tony . . .'

'Shhh,' he said again, and this time I closed my eyes. I was back at winter prom with Justin, dancing under the sparkling lights. In this modern world, people danced so intimately. Body to body, chest to chest. I could sense Justin's desire in the heat between us. This close, the music made me aware of his wanting. The vampire in me longed to feel Justin's heartbeat. And when I closed my eyes and listened to the song . . . I did.

Imagine if this was Rhode. What would he say about modern dancing? There were no choreographed steps like we had in the medieval era. Just two bodies, together, moving. If this was Rhode, his hands would come up my back, landing at the base of my neck. Justin's hands slipped under my arms. Goosebumps swept over me. Justin pulled me even closer so my lips kissed the crook of his neck.

Yes, he's here. Rhode's here. This is not Justin, but Rhode.

Rhode squeezed me closer as the musical serenade echoed in the room. I swallowed nervously and let myself give in to my fantasy. Rhode and I spun in that room, his graceful hands flowing up and down my body. His warmth, his human warmth, overwhelmed me. Rhode pulled me closer so there was no space between us. He kissed my neck, sending chills through me.

Love. What a strange word. How endless. How it had defined my beliefs for so long. Because we had run through decades of time, hands held, always, always waking with the moon. We revelled in every colour of sunset.

'I love you so much,' I whispered.

'I love you too,' a strange voice replied.

The American accent startled me from my reverie. I blinked a few times, holding on to the wisps of the fantasy, but knowing as I lifted my chin that I would look into Justin's eyes and not Rhode's.

We kept dancing even though my spell had broken into a thousand pieces.

'I thought when you saw Rhode it would be over between us,' Justin said.

I can't have Rhode. I'll never touch his hand again. It's over.

I refocused on Justin.

'I thought it would be easier to be mad at you,' he continued.

'I'm not used to the angry version of you,' I replied.

'I can't stop loving you, Lenah. I can't,' he replied softly. 'I keep trying. But I can't.'

I looked into his eyes as the song slowed to its last bars.

I can make this happen. Can't I? Justin and me?

This was so much easier than the endless rejection from Rhode. Nothing supernatural was telling us we couldn't be together. Nothing was stopping us.

Justin held my cheek with his hand and ran his thumb across my cheekbone. I searched his eyes. What was love anyway? Love was warmth and comfort. Love was for the living. Justin could help me feel alive again. I knew he could. I had felt it last year.

I didn't want to come back. I had to. Rhode's words reverberated in my mind.

Justin leaned forward and kissed the top of my nose.

'Want to walk back?' he asked. 'Thirty minutes until Williams's stupid curfew.'

We shut off the lights in the listening room. Justin stole one more kiss before extending his hand and leading me home.

CHAPTER 10

Late-night rain had left the grass glistening. It tickled the tops of my toes as I walked the path next morning and turned the corner to Curie. Ms Tate came flying around the corner into the courtyard.

'Lenah,' she said, stopping in front of me. 'I'm glad I found you. We need to discuss your semester project.' She rambled on for a moment about Justin and me and the importance of teamwork. I took some papers from her load of files and held them for her.

'Oh, thank you,' she added, continuing her diatribe. I listened for a few moments but the wind distracted me. It was stronger than a breeze. It had intention. The air snaked through the trees and lifted my hair from my ears as though acting of its own accord. I smoothed it down as quickly as I could. Ms Tate's voice floated off and I turned my attention away from her.

The leaves above us shivered again. The water from the fountain fell away in an unnatural hush. I needed no vampire ESP to know. I would always harbour the knowledge. I could feel it in the air.

I was being watched.

I searched the shadows. Any clue would do. The lift of a sly smile or eyes still as death.

'OK, Lenah?' Ms Tate said.

'Right. Of course,' I said.

Ms Tate smiled, though I had no idea what I had just agreed to. I scanned the grounds in front of me, but without my vampire sight it was impossible to see as far as the other side of campus. When I turned to follow her into Curie, I realized I had forgotten that behind us were the woods that circled the school. They were a perfect place for someone to hide to watch an unsuspecting victim.

'Lenah, I'll need those papers in class today,' Ms Tate said from the darkened entrance to Curie.

My eyes lingered on the trees and on the morning sunlight shining through the breaks in the branches. I did not have time to search for eyes watching me.

I walked into the building with an absolute certainty in my gut.

I was being hunted.

I slid into my seat next to Justin, trying to shake off the goosebumps still lingering on my skin. Justin's hand was wrapped in gauze and momentarily I thought of his arms around me in the listening room.

'I can't get last night out of my head,' he said.

He reached under the table, placed his hand on my knee and squeezed. I smiled at him. Perhaps this wouldn't be so hard. Being with Justin. He knew how to calm me. Perhaps the girl from last year still existed, the girl who wanted to be human, the girl who needed Justin to help her feel that way. Not like Rhode. Rhode, who was much better at following the Aeris's decree than I would ever be.

'Guess she's just jumping right into this,' Justin said. 'Yesterday pH tests, today sediment something or other. I can't even pronounce whatever that other word is.'

The experiment *was* complicated – very complicated. Justin and I stood up to gather our assignment tools from the storage chest. I made sure to avoid catching Rhode's eye or even looking in his general direction. That was all I needed, to look at him and have another strange connection that I couldn't control. I wasn't sure what had spurred the overwhelming smell of apples, the memories and the window into his mind.

'Maybe we can have dinner tonight,' Justin said quietly.

'Oh,' I said, hating that I wished it was Rhode

asking me to dinner. In my mind was a dark room lit by candles. Rhode and I sat at a long oak table and raised goblets filled with blood. I'd never eaten a meal with him. I wondered what he liked to eat in the modern world.

'Lenah?' Justin said. 'Pizza?'

'Sure,' I replied, replacing my fantasy with linoleum tables and plastic cutlery. Greasy food from the union and paper napkins, just like we had had the year before, dozens of times.

I felt the empty space between my seat and Rhode's. I knew very well that the candles, the ones in the darkened dining room in Hathersage, were long burned out.

I bet Rhode hated modern-day pizza. Too messy.

Justin grabbed a box of slides. When he reached up I saw the leather necklace again. I rose up on my tiptoes to try to get a better look at the silver pendant.

'Andrea's not speaking to me,' he said with the slightest of smiles.

'Sorry about that,' I replied, and we moved back to the desk.

Justin handed me a dropper and some iodine. With a wink he commented, 'I'm not.'

I attempted to nap later that afternoon, only to

be awoken by sirens screaming on to campus. I threw off my covers and ran to the window, looking down at the scene below. Security guards directed students to the sides of the pathways. Across the quad teachers were corralling students into the union and away from Hopper.

The sound of another police siren travelled in a wave, swelling loudly as the car curved along the pathway and stopped in front of Hopper. I tried not to think about Tony's death in that very building. I caught sight of Vicken and Rhode standing just to the side of the building. Rhode's blue eyes locked on mine.

With a casual nod of his head he requested I come down. In a heartbeat, I followed his orders. As if I could ever say no.

'What happened?' I asked. There were hundreds of students on the green. People inside the union stood against the circular windows pressing their hands against the glass.

'I need to get into the art studio,' a student said to a police officer. She held a portfolio under her arm. 'My portrait is due tomorrow.'

'Hopper Building is going to be off limits for a couple of hours,' the officer said, moving out of the way for a security guard.

'Did someone else die?' a student asked.

'Just go back to your dorm, please,' the officer ordered.

'Someone else totally died!' the student cried. People were already taking out their cell phones.

A third police car pulled on up. Its siren was off, but the blue lights swirled around and around. Vicken pulled on my shirtsleeve and we walked down the side of Hopper, away from the fray.

'One of the gymnasium windows at the back is open,' Vicken said with a nod. The back of the building met the bottom of the large hill that led up to the archery plateau.

'Let's go,' Rhode said.

'Casual,' Vicken said, always thinking like the soldier he had once been. 'Slow.'

One by one, we walked around to the back of Hopper. Once we stood together at the gym windows, I said, 'Odette. It's got to be. She warned us in the herb shop. She said she'd be back. And I sensed her this morning.'

'You sensed her?' Rhode asked.

'I felt someone watching me. I can only assume it was Odette.'

'Well, there's just one way to tell for sure,' Rhode said. 'We need evidence. Clues.'

'Clues,' I parroted. I ran my hand along the

windowsill. The pane was horizontal and at least three feet tall, but narrow. I could easily fit through, but Vicken and Rhode would have to wait for me to open a door to let them in. I reached the handle on the inside, opened the window wider and slid into the gymnasium.

I landed on the floor in the darkened room. I took a few steps and then looked back through the window.

'Go,' Rhode whispered.

'She shouldn't go alone,' Vicken said.

'I'll be fine,' I replied, and tiptoed towards the double doors. I pushed them ever so slightly, just enough to peer both ways down the hallway. Once I turned the corner of the first floor, I would be in the administrative section of Hopper building. The headmaster's office was there along with the admissions. I hurried quietly, finally turning the corner. Voices echoed from the offices.

As a vampire, it is of the utmost importance to remain confident. As the years go by, you gain more and more confidence. It was hard to find that confidence now as a mere human. I hunched over, careful to tiptoe in my heavy boots. I crept towards the voices at the end of the hall. My body wasn't as agile as it had once been, now my organs were filled with blood that *moved*. I kept tiptoeing forward and stopped near the office door.

'She's dead. We're absolutely sure?' Ms Williams's questioning voice echoed out of the room.

'I'm afraid so. Been dead for at least a half-hour,' a voice replied.

'What do I tell the students?' Ms Williams asked weakly.

'Our team is going to have to do a thorough investigation, ma'am. It would be best if you arranged to have Ms Tate's classes covered and temporarily moved these offices to another building.'

My hand fell away from the wall. I hadn't realized that I had been clenching my fist.

Ms Tate? My science teacher!

'I don't understand,' Ms Williams said, and her voice cracked. There was a moment of silence and then the sound of someone blowing their nose. Footsteps collected near the door and Ms Williams spoke again, her voice nasal and closer now. 'Why leave that note with the body? What does it mean?'

'It's like a riddle,' said a voice I did not recognize. 'It'll be taken with the rest of the evidence.'

'What evidence? You said there were no fingerprints.'

'It looks as if she was murdered just like the other two. Puncture wounds. Depletion of blood. We'll need to photograph the body and have our forensic team investigate.'

'You make it sound like a gothic horror movie, officer.'

'We get these from time to time. Some psycho who has watched *Dracula* one too many times.'

The footsteps echoed again. *Oh no.* They were going to come out of the office. I looked across the hall. A door. I ran, opened the door and jumped inside a tiny janitorial closet. I sank to the floor, pressing my back against the cement wall and drawing my knees to my chest. I held my breath, my heart thudding in my ears.

'Ms Williams, we're going to need you to keep this area off limits. We'll mark it off with police tape and have it manned overnight.'

'And she really drove herself on to campus? Bleeding?' Ms Williams pressed.

'There's blood all over the car but we don't know the specifics yet, ma'am.'

I had to see the body to be sure. I hoped they wouldn't take it away just yet.

The voices trailed off as the group of people walked down the hall and out of the building. I kept my arm tucked close to me, to avoid a precariously positioned broom and bucket. I cracked open the door, just barely, and peered back into the hallway.

One officer had been left on guard inside the office, I presumed, to guard the body. I would have to sneak into the room through the connecting door from a neighbouring office.

The officer stood, legs slightly apart, hands held behind his back. I just needed him to look away for a few moments. Be distracted by something, *anything*. I waited. As the moments ticked by, I knew Rhode and Vicken would become impatient and come looking for me.

Oh just look away, you idiot.

A girl screamed from outside and the officer spun to look out of the window. Perfect! Her scream trailed away into laughter just as I crawled out of the janitor's closet. I had to leave the door open behind me. I scrambled across the hallway and into the office next door. I stood up, waited a moment and pressed my back against the connecting door. I tried to breathe quietly, and waited to see if the officer heard me. Unlike Odette, I *would* leave fingerprints so, again, I kept my hands close to my sides. I knew how to be quiet. If I applied pressure to the whole foot instead of the ball of my foot, I would make less noise. I had to go in. I had to see if it was Odette who'd killed Ms Tate.

I took off my boot and removed my sock. I used it to twist the doorknob as quietly as I could. I placed

my boot back on and, on my hands and knees, crawled into the room. The officer stood in the office, but near the hallway.

I would never fear the dead. Never. It was Ms Tate's heels I saw first. She was on the floor, on her side. *She had driven back to campus and died here, in this office.*

A vampire's bite mark will ooze for hours, even after a person is dead. As I knelt beside the body, I could sense it was cold without needing to touch it. Body heat emanates from a live body. This body was still, hard. And there they were, two puncture wounds in her neck, still thickly oozing, following the depletion of the vampire's bite. The last of Ms Tate's blood. It would stop soon. The thicker the blood, the longer it had been oozing from the victim.

Her eyes were closed; someone must have closed them. There, on the floor next to the body, was a small piece of white paper. The note Ms Williams had mentioned.

In curly old-fashioned handwriting, it read:

Like the lick of a flame, death can be quick.
Or drawn with a knife slowly.
Endlessly.
Over skin.

I gulped away a scream. At the bottom of the note was one more line.

You know what I want.

*

'It sounds like a little poem!' Vicken said. 'How lovely. You know – if you enjoy threatening poems about murder and death.'

'She's doing it on purpose,' Rhode said.

'Of course she is. It's exactly what I would have done. It's sick.'

'One by one, she'll take out anyone that she knows is close to you, Lenah,' Rhode said. 'She must have been watching for days now,' he explained.

I paced back and forth at the gymnasium window.

'The second line of the poem is threatening more deaths. Prolonged torture. She'll never quit,' Rhode said.

Vicken crossed his arms over his chest. 'So what do we do? We can't give her the ritual.'

'Of course not,' I replied. 'Think of the consequences.' I had seen the consequences in my dream with Suleen.

'We have to join the rest of the school. Ms Williams has called an assembly in the union,' Rhode said.

Another death would bring the school one step

closer to closing. They would surely have to if there were any more deaths. The only place we could go was Hathersage, and that would mean leaving Lovers Bay.

We walked around to the front of the building, passing by Ms Tate's car. A scene-of-crime officer was taking photographs of it. Security officers were already leading students towards the union, to the assembly. Tracy and Claudia walked together at the front of a mass of students.

'Here's something,' Vicken said, stopping near the car. 'Ms Tate wasn't killed on campus. You said –' he looked at me – 'that she drove back here. She drove herself, bleeding. She got away.'

'Or was set loose,' Rhode replied.

'Either way, the power of the ritual is still working. Odette can't come on to campus. Not yet,' Vicken said.

'This way, please,' a security officer said, and we walked into the union and into pure mayhem.

CHAPTER 11

'I repeat, this accident occurred off campus. *Off* campus. There is no connection between Ms Tate's accident and the safety of your school. Now, let me continue . . .'

There was uproar again, but Ms Williams yelled into the microphone, 'Silence! Now, only seniors are to be allowed off-campus privileges at this time and must sign in and out. If you go off campus, you must go in groups of at least two. Ms Tate's accident was off campus, so it appears to be unrelated to Wickham or the other unfortunate accidents. Regardless, we must insist on a buddy system no matter where you go. Wickham continues to be the safest environment for our students.'

The union exploded in voices and questions.

'Why did she drive back on to campus?' someone yelled.

'Please, please . . . I don't know.' Ms Williams put up her palms and the room quietened. The canteen serving windows were closed due to the emergency meeting. Metal grates and empty counters surrounded us. 'Lovers Bay, Massachusetts, has never before seen this level of violence, and I am sure this will be the final incident.'

'If it was an accident, why do we have to walk in twos?' someone called from the crowd, and the union erupted in jeers and questions again.

'I want some answers!' a sophomore girl cried, and broke into tears.

'Quiet!' Ms Williams yelled into the microphone. Some people put their hands over their ears. 'A buddy system is best for student safety on or off any campus, and Wickham is no different.'

As I looked around, I finally spotted Justin. He sat with the lacrosse team across the room. 'This school remains the safest place for all of you,' Ms Williams exclaimed.

'Guess not!' someone called from the audience.

'I understand some of you would like to go home and we cannot stop you. As we will be assuring your families, Ms Tate's car accident *off* campus was surely that – *an accident.*'

'She's lying,' I whispered to Vicken.

'Everyone in this room can sense that,' Vicken replied. 'The disbelief is actually overwhelming.'

'What else?' Rhode asked.

'Well, they can tell she's upset. Most of them are angry. They know something connects these incidents. Their trust has been broken.'

'Wouldn't you feel the same?' Rhode whispered.

The assembly ended with most of the students staying in the union to talk about Ms Tate. Some people were crying, some were asking what they should do about their homework. Some wanted to know who would teach science.

I couldn't cry.

I didn't want to cry. I had seen the mark of death.

I sat there waiting to feel *something*, some sorrow. But all I could muster up was anger. Anger and rage at myself. At Odette. At Rhode and the memories between us that I didn't understand.

'Lenah!'

My head shot up. I looked at Rhode. 'What?'

He motioned to Claudia and Tracy who stood above me. Clearly they had been trying to get my attention.

'How are you?' Claudia asked.

I shrugged. 'All right, I suppose.'

I scooted over for them to sit down next to me, but Claudia sat next to Vicken and I wondered if she did it on purpose. I smelt something sweet from her, like vanilla. 'You smell nice,' I said. 'I know that scent.'

'It's Kate's old perfume.'

I immediately focused on the Formica tabletop.

'Oh,' was all I could say.

'Weren't you sort of close to Ms Tate?' asked Tracy. She raised an eyebrow and I realized she was talking to me.

'Not really,' I said, and considered last year. I wasn't *close* with Ms Tate, though she was the first adult I had spent any time with since my parents. And that was 592 years before.

'She's the third person to die,' Claudia said.

'What? Are we keeping count?' Tracy asked, taking a sip of soda.

'Maybe we should,' Claudia replied.

'Coincidence,' Rhode said, and stood up and walked off. Tracy followed him with her eyes all the way to the union door until he was out of sight.

'You're not saying much,' Claudia said to Vicken.

'I don't worry about much,' Vicken replied.

Claudia exhaled heavily. She shook her head. 'I don't want to see Ms Tate when they . . .' Her voice trailed off and she shivered. 'When they take her out of the building.'

'Me neither,' I said, remembering the sight of her lifeless body and the heels of her shoes.

'Want to go off campus with us?' Tracy asked. She got up from the table and smoothed out the front of her blue shirt. I admired the colour against her skin.

'Now?' I asked.

'Yeah, now,' Claudia replied earnestly. 'I want to go somewhere where there's a lot of people. The movies or something.'

Bad idea. Dark.

'Or maybe for a drive?' Tracy suggested.

Claudia stood up too and crossed her arms over her chest. 'I can't believe you're being so calm about this,' she said to Vicken.

Vicken stood up from the table.

'What should I do, blondie?' He threw his hands in the air and pretended to run around. 'Scream?' He dropped his hands by his side, then stuck a cigarette in his mouth. 'Death happens to all of us. Some just get it earlier than others.' He walked out of the union leaving the smell of his cigarette wafting behind him.

'Lenah,' said Justin, joining us. He immediately took my hand. I exhaled into the familiar cotton of his shirt and hugged him tightly. I lingered in his embrace for a moment, allowing his strength to overwhelm me.

'Want to come with us?' Claudia asked Justin. 'For a drive. Get off campus.'

Justin frowned. 'I can't. Coach wants to have a meeting with the team.'

I pulled away and he met my eyes. I could sense

the question in his mind. Because Claudia and Tracy were here he couldn't ask me what I knew he wanted to. *Was Odette behind this?*

A group of cheerleaders passed by. They held their arms linked over each other's shoulders and held hands. One of them, in the middle, was wailing.

Claudia tugged on my shirtsleeve. 'Let's get out of here. I can't handle this,' she said.

'Be careful,' said Justin, and kissed me quickly.

'I'll be all right,' I said. 'I've got the light of day.'

I knew Rhode wouldn't like the idea of my leaving campus after Ms Tate's murder, but going out to a public place seemed safe. Even if we were just going for a drive, we'd be in Claudia's car, and I could suggest somewhere people would be if they wanted to stop.

'I just need my wallet,' I said, and we walked back to Seeker.

As I walked up the stairs with the girls, it occurred to me they had never been in my room before. Not even during the previous year when Tony was still alive. Tracy was directly behind me. She stood so close I heard her breathing.

'I'll be right out,' I said.

'We can't come inside?' Tracy asked. 'You're Super-Secret Girl or something, Lenah.'

Right. Should have thought of that.

'Of course you can come in,' I said.

I stood at the door unlocking it; the rosemary and lavender dangled in their usual spot.

'Cute,' Claudia said, and lightly grazed the flowers with her fingertips. 'Dried flowers. I always dry out my corsages or a flower whenever I get a bouquet.'

I opened the door and the girls stepped inside. They oohed and ahhed over the longsword, my furnishings and all the space I had. It was Tracy who lifted a finger to touch the sword.

'I wouldn't do that if I were you,' I said. 'It's remarkably sharp.'

'Why do you have a sword?' she asked.

'Passed down through my family,' I replied. *We really do have to get out of here*, I thought.

'What is this? *Ita fert . . .*'

'*Ita fert corde voluntas.* It's Latin,' I said. 'It means *the heart wills it.*'

'The heart wills it,' echoed Tracy after a moment. 'I like that.'

Together, we looked at the longsword I had got so used to. I supposed, standing there next to someone who had never seen it before, it was quite magnificent.

'What's all over your balcony?' Claudia asked,

and I turned. She had her hands pressed against the glass of the balcony door. She lifted her chin to get a better view.

And there, still stubbornly sticking to the tiles, were my vampire remains. Most had washed away in summer rainstorms, but a few glimmers shone under the midday sun.

'Were you doing an art project?' Claudia asked.

'I'm not sure what they are.' I decided that playing dumb was my best bet. 'Let's go, shall we?'

Before I knew it, we were on our way. I opened the window of Claudia's BMW, feeling the late summer air whip through the back seat and toss my hair about my face.

'Happy. Happy. Happy. Not thinking about Ms Tate. I am haaaaappy,' Claudia said, and turned up the music. A loud explosion of guitars, pianos and multiple voices echoed near my ears. The singer crooned about love and bubblegum. This was definitely not Mozart. Tracy, I noticed, was exceptionally quiet, looking out of the passenger window.

After a few moments Claudia said, 'What about the mall? We can walk around or whatever.'

Yes. Smart. Bright. Loads of people.

As silly as it may have seemed in the moment, it was good to get off campus in September, while

I still could go to the mall like a normal teenager. Before Nuit Rouge began.

Claudia ripped around a corner and the engine revved as we climbed on to the highway. I had to hold on to the armrest or I would have slammed against the door of the car.

'So,' Claudia said, 'tell me about Vicken.' I gripped the armrest as hard as I could as she peeled around another corner.

'Nice black eye,' Tracy said sarcastically. It was the first time she had spoken the whole car ride.

'He kept wanting to touch it,' Claudia said, but the tone in her voice was not disgust. It was, dare I say it, excitement.

'We're talking about Vicken?' I said, surprised. *Murderer. Excellent swordsman. You would have made a lovely meal for him.*

'He's from Scotland?' Claudia asked.

'Girvan, in Scotland, near the coast,' I clarified.

'Isn't he your first cousin or something?'

'Right. He's my mother's brother's son,' I lied.

'Just ask her already,' Tracy interjected, and flipped her hair. 'Is he seeing anyone?'

'I . . . don't think so,' I said, slightly horrified at the thought of Claudia and Vicken dating. We pulled into the mall parking lot. Claudia whipped the car into an empty spot so fast I was sure we were going to have an accident. But miraculously we didn't smash into the wall. In fact, the girls were getting out of the car before I even exhaled.

They seemed to be speaking another language. They were talking about types of trends I clearly knew nothing about.

Cardigans. Peplums.

Platform shoes, are they in?

What about a wooden heel?

Rhode had provided most of my clothing last year. I just wore it, accepted it. I hadn't paid attention to fashion since the Victorian era. I was a bit more knowledgeable now, but still kind of useless when it came to making choices.

'Lenah!' Claudia said, and pulled me by the arm into a store. 'You have to try this. That colour would be gorgeous on you.'

She pointed at a mannequin in the window. On it, a tangerine blouse flowed out over a pair of blue jeans. The material was gauzy and soft; the colour brought a memory to my mind. A night in an opera house, a glorious orange gown. As vampire queen, the easiest way to draw victims in had been to taunt them with exquisite things. When they approached to compliment me on my clothing or my jewels – well . . .

Claudia snatched an orange blouse from the

racks and thrust it at me. Soon after, laden with clothes, we each stepped into our own private dressing room. Claudia and Tracy ran through items, stepping out and modelling their ensembles. I had never displayed myself to anyone in modern clothes. Asking for approval seemed silly but apparently this was the thing to do.

'Lenah! I want to see that top!' Claudia called.

Feeling foolish, I stepped out wearing the blouse and turned to show the girls.

'Oh!' Claudia's jaw dropped. 'You look amazing,' she said. 'You should so get that!'

'Colour looks good on you,' Tracy agreed.

There, in the mall, I could almost forget Odette's note. Ms Tate's death and Kate's too. I could be distracted with the possibility of wearing these clothes. I even considered going back to school and wearing them in front of Rhode.

Next, I slipped on a pink skintight dress, which was contemporary and revealing, with thin shoulder straps. I loved it. I hoped the girls did too. I wished the ladies of the nineteenth century, with their corsets and bustles, could see me now. I stepped out and looked down the dressing-room aisle. The girls were admiring black dresses similar to the pink one I wore. Justin would like this dress because it was tight. He would notice I was wearing a colour that wasn't black and say *you're beautiful*. He reminded me it was important that I was participating in this modern world, just like Suleen had told me to.

Rhode hadn't seen me in contemporary clothes before. I wondered if he even noticed my body, now that it wasn't hugged tight by a corset or pushed out by a bustle.

A tall woman was admiring her reflection in the three-way mirror at the end of the hall. Long blonde hair tumbled perfectly down her back. She smirked at herself and ran a hand down her abdomen to smooth the material of the dress.

Oh no.

The skin was perfect. Too perfect. That blonde hair. Red fingernails. Sharpened to dangerous, horrific points.

Odette.

Immediately I stepped back into my dressing room.

I held a hand over my mouth to stifle my scream. I trembled, unsure how to stop my body from shaking so badly. How was it possible? How could she stand the bright lights of the middle of the day? I looked down and took an involuntary step back towards the mirror on the wall. One long leg slid beneath the separating panel. Cat-like, she flattened herself and crawled from the next dressing room into mine. In a shot, she stood up in front of me. My back pressed against the mirror, I could hear myself breathing rapid, shallow breaths.

Her mouth curled into a red, lipstick-stained sneer.

'Come out, Lenah!' Claudia called from the aisle.

My friends . . .

'In a minute,' I called back.

Odette took two steps towards me. I could see the marble-like sheen of her skin under the fluorescent lights. She looked like a moving statue. She cocked her head to one side.

'Surprised to see me, Lenah?' she hissed. 'Thought you'd be safe in the middle of the day? Thought you'd be with lots of people? Daylight doesn't frighten me. Not even a little.'

She slammed a hand against the wall just next to the mirror.

'What was that?' Tracy called.

'Do you think this makes my butt look weird?' Claudia asked.

'No way,' Tracy replied.

I continued to keep my back against the wall. The only way to escape would be to get the dressing-room door open and run. But then Odette could kill both Tracy and Claudia instantly.

'I'm not afraid of you,' I lied, keeping my voice low.

Odette smiled, but the smile quickly turned. Her white teeth flashed under the light, her fangs sliding down, pointed and sharp. The vampire hunger that made the fangs descend was overtaking her. She pretended to lunge at me and then laughed quietly, pulling back. Her laugh was stifled by the dressing-room music and Tracy and Claudia cooing over a blouse.

'The great Lenah Beaudonte. How I have waited. How I hoped it would be me to bleed you first. Did you know I danced with Heath? That big Latin-speaking member of your coven? Yes . . . in the 1920s.' She leaned forward so her mouth was next to my ear. 'While you slept six feet under the ground,' she hissed.

I shivered.

Like an animal she lunged at me again, this time slamming her palms on either side of my head. She took a deep breath, running her nose across the base of my throat. 'You smell like your blood would light me up.'

I took a short breath. Light her up?

'Don't play dumb. The ritual endows you with the weapon of sunlight. It's how you killed your coven.'

'That's not true,' I said. 'That's not what happened.'

'Shhh,' Odette said, so I could see the pointed tips of her fangs again. 'Your lies are not welcome here. But you were once a powerful vampire, weren't you?' she whispered. She raised one pointed fingernail towards the sky. 'Guess who is now?'

She left her razor-like nail pointed at the ceiling and looked at me out of the corner of her eye.

'Of course, I didn't go by Odette when I was human. Do you remember me? You killed my mother, my father and my love.'

Images of the mass of victims hovering behind the Aeris bombarded me. Her mother, her father and her lover were in that mass. I wanted to tell her they were safe and would be forever – never again victims, never again subjected to fear and terror. They had white souls now.

She slammed her hands against the wall again just as Claudia laughed loudly on the other side of the door. I loved her laugh. I had to protect her.

I had to make a plan. I focused on the knife-like fingernail. If I screamed for help, I would risk Claudia and Tracy being hurt by Odette. If I kicked out the dressing-room door, I could run, but she was faster.

'Lenah!' Claudia said. 'Seriously, you're taking forever in there!'

Odette gave a flick of her wrist and I heard

a ripping sound. My flesh. Odette had cut me so the blood seeped down my shoulder. It was not a deep cut, but the skin split open cleanly. It burned and the blood trickled down my arm. She leaned forward to whisper in my ear, so close that I could feel her cold lips on my skin.

'The blonde idiot. Then the teacher. You know what I want,' she sneered again. She gripped me around the neck and lifted me from the floor, holding me against the mirror. I could barely breathe. I coughed and she loosened her grip a little.

'I want that ritual,' she said through clenched teeth. The flesh over my collarbone burned as it bled.

'It won't make you human,' I croaked.

A sneer spread across her face, making her look like a strange circus clown. Her nostrils flared and she whispered, 'Is that what you think I want? Didn't you hear me? I'm your replacement.' Her eyes hardened. At that moment I could see the truth deep within them.

It was a kind of familiarity that I could not describe, a view I knew well: an ocean view or a field I once knew. I saw a terrified young woman who had been ripped from her life too soon.

I spluttered out the words as I dared to meet

her unnatural green eyes.

'It's the torment, isn't it? The endless torment.'

She flinched. 'What?'

'If you pour your intentions into that spell, you will bring ruin. Release black magic you never intended. I see your heart. I see your need for power. Power relieves the pain, doesn't it?'

Claudia's voice echoed from over the door.

'Let's see if they have it in your size, Lenah. What size are you?'

'Answer them,' Odette ordered, and with one hand she held me to the mirror. With the other, she scooped a tiny river of blood off my shoulder and licked it away.

'Medium,' I called with a lurch of my stomach as I watched Odette swallow my blood.

'I'll get you one,' Claudia said, and two pairs of feet travelled away out of the dressing room. Odette threw me against the mirror again. My head smacked against the glass and white spots of light exploded before my eyes.

'Give it to me now, or by the time your friends walk into this room you will be dead.'

I tried to swallow but hacked a cough. I was going to die. I had died before.

As another white pop of light exploded before my eyes, an image came to me. Rhode and me on my parents' orchard. Not as we were but as we appeared now, in the modern world. Hand in hand, walking towards the house. The chimney was smoking. An apple in Rhode's other hand. Was this possible? Was this the future?

My breath rattled in my ears and I tried to breathe, but an eerie hush began to drown out the rest of the world.

'OK!' I croaked. She released me immediately and I fell to the ground in a heap. My hands hit the carpeted floor of the dressing room and sound whooshed into my ears. Just then, as though choreographed, I heard Tracy and Claudia come back into the dressing-room area.

'Write it down,' Odette commanded. I found a scrap of paper in my wallet and started writing. *I am giving you the ritual. I am giving it to you.* I kept repeating it to myself so she would read my intentions. *This is the ritual. I don't want to give it to you, but I am anyway.*

I tried to hide the lie deep beneath my heart as I wrote. Ingredients. Method. She had to be convinced.

'Lenah, here,' Claudia called, and a blue top came over the dressing-room door. Odette caught it and held it against herself, admiringly.

I finished and handed over the piece of paper.

This is real, real, real. Real. I wouldn't think anything else.

Before she slid back to her dressing room under the separating wall, she threw me a knowing, haunting smile.

'I can see why he likes you,' she said with an animalistic cock of her head. 'So fragile.'

With that, Odette returned to her dressing room. I watched her feet move as she gathered her things. Listened to her light footsteps as she opened the door and walked away down the aisle. Exhausted, I slid my back down the mirror and sat on the floor.

'Did you die in there?' Claudia joked.

'No,' I barely said. 'Just getting back into my clothes.'

My reflection was a sad sight. My hair stuck to my forehead from sweat and the horizontal cut that ran over my collarbone was raw and red. It had stopped bleeding, but the blood was sticky at the opening. However, it would be easy to cover with my shirt.

She was bloody brilliant, as Vicken would say. I had to admire her style. Truly Odette would have been decent competition, had I still been a vampire. I had to get up. Had to get dressed. The girls couldn't see me like this. My hands shook as I pressed against the carpet to stand up.

I didn't know how long I would have until she

figured out that I'd given her a fake ritual. Weeks? Days?

I got dressed, smoothed my hair as best I could and shakily stepped out of the dressing room. I avoided the three-way mirror. But there was no need to look – Odette was gone.

'I'm hungry,' Claudia said.

'Let's eat here,' Tracy replied. 'I don't want to go back yet.'

We paid for our items and I followed them out of the store silently. I tried not to move my right arm because the cut throbbed. Once we were back in the brightly lit mall my trembling subsided, but only slightly.

I went through the motions of ordering my lunch but I kept reliving that moment in the dressing room. Odette could be out in the sunlight, which meant she was powerful. *But how?* How could she have gained power so quickly when it took me one hundred and eighty years to withstand full midday sunlight? How did she acquire the strength so fast? Odette said I had killed her family, but I had killed many people. Technically I had even killed her, breaking the contract of her human life. The Aeris had reminded me of that.

We sat and ate our lunch, but I kept looking at every face that passed. Anyone with blonde hair.

156

This vampire would not be alone. She was powerful. She fancied herself my replacement.

'What happened to Rhode?' Claudia said. At Rhode's name, I slammed to attention, back into my seat. I refocused on my lunch and nibbled a piece of lettuce. 'Whose fault was the car accident? His face looks awful.'

'He must be the most secretive person alive,' Tracy said. 'I tried talking to him about it in maths, but he brushed me off.'

'He wouldn't tell me either,' I said, hating how true this was. I was used to knowing everything about Rhode, but not now. 'Rhode and I aren't as close as Vicken and me.'

'Bet he told Vicken,' Claudia said. 'They're always sitting together at dinner.'

'I'm surprised he survived it,' Tracy said, still talking about Rhode's accident. She delicately ate a forkful of her Greek salad. 'He's *still* got bruises.'

'His eyes are amazing,' Claudia said.

I stared at a girl with her blonde hair in a ponytail for a moment but then relaxed. She was just a girl shopping.

Tracy nudged me.

'Sorry,' I said, and took another bite of my sandwich. 'Yes, they're quite blue.' It felt ridiculous as I said it.

'. . . you're very quiet,' Tracy said.

'Sorry,' I said again. 'I'm just a bit tired.'

'So what's going on with you and Justin?' Tracy asked.

I opened my mouth to join the conversation and . . .

There she was.

Odette walked the long length of the mall running parallel to the food court. My hand holding the sandwich hung at my eyeline. I stared, unable to help myself. Though she wore a man's baseball hat over her eyes, her long blonde hair fell down her back. She was stunning. Her beauty would sway most humans, but I knew why she shielded her face from the fluorescent lighting. It would highlight the unnatural hue of her skin and the dilated pupils.

She turned her face towards me.

Her eyes slid over the people in the food court directly, purposefully – to mine. Her jaw dropped, her eyes fell to my sandwich filled with lettuce, chicken and tomato. And then, with a horrible curl of her mouth, Odette smirked. And . . .

Winked.

CHAPTER 12

'Vicken!' I banged on his door three times. When I banged a fourth time Vicken's hall advisor stuck his head out of his room; he was a tall assistant professor who taught photography.

'Some of us are preparing lessons, Lenah,' he said, and slammed his door.

The door in front of me creaked open and Vicken appeared, scratching his head and yawning.

'It's six in the afternoon,' I said. 'You're sleeping?'

'I have a few hundred years of sleep to catch up on, if you don't mind.'

I stepped inside and Vicken grabbed a towel from his desk and stuffed it in the crack under the door. He opened a window, clicked on a fan and lit a cigarette. I paced back and forth across his carpeted dorm room.

'Odette attacked me,' I said.

Vicken's head snapped up so his hair fell into his eyes. 'Where?'

'The mall. I was there with the girls shopping and there she was, trying on a cocktail dress.

Vicken . . .' I ran a hand through my hair and grabbed at the roots. 'I gave her a fake ritual.'

'You did *what*?'

'I had to. She was going to kill me.'

Vicken took a drag from the cigarette, considered me through the smoke as he breathed out, then stubbed the barely smoked cigarette out on the windowsill. He dropped it into an empty soda can.

'Let's go,' he said.

Together we walked to the end of the hall. I expected to descend the stairs, perhaps to another dorm besides Quartz. I had not considered which room Rhode would be living in on campus. At the end of the hallway was room 429, a single like Vicken's. This was Rhode's room. There was something strangely comical about Rhode living in a dorm after serving as a knight under Edward III.

Vicken knocked and as we waited he looked down at me, meeting my eyes with an encouraging wink. We heard footsteps from behind the door and then Rhode opened up. His eyes travelled back and forth between us. The bruising made his right eye tighter and smaller than the other.

'What happened?' he asked.

'Not something we can really talk about with the general brouhaha, my friend,' Vicken answered, motioning towards the other dorm rooms.

Rhode opened the door and we walked in. I guess I expected opulence. I expected his life at Wickham to mimic our life at Hathersage. But how could it? There would be no apothecary tables, no fine furniture. We were in hiding now. With the exception of a telescope pointing out of the window and his clothes in the closet, Rhode's room was nothing more than a place to lay his head. When Vicken shut the door behind us, out of the corner of my eye I saw rosemary and lavender tacked on the inside.

Of course. Those would remain.

Rhode sat down at his desk.

'Odette attacked me. I gave her a fake ritual. Really convoluted items. It'll take her days just to find them. Ignacious plant. Rattletail wood.'

'Good choices. Innocuous ingredients. Even with the worst of intentions they won't produce much of an effect.'

Love surged through me at Rhode's support. It made my chest tingle. He lifted his eyes to mine and crisp apples and the rich earth of my father's house were on the tip of my tongue. I stumbled back a couple of steps, trying to break the connection. If I looked away, perhaps it would stop the memory from engulfing me. I inhaled but there were *more* apples, a fireplace too. The wood crackling, smoking, and the scent of rain. I stepped back, on to Vicken's feet.

'Hey! Watch it!' he cried.

A vampire's mouth. Lips parted, going for the kill. Where the two fangs would descend are two black, gaping holes. A vampire with no fangs? I want to run but I know I can't.

'Lenah?' Vicken's hand curled around my arm. 'Are you all right?'

'She had me by the throat!' I said, shaking my head. 'And she cut me.' I moved the collar of my shirt aside to show them the wound.

'You'll need to clean that,' Rhode said. He gripped his hands on the chair even tighter.

'Well, I imagine when she finds out the ingredients are fake her retaliation will be swift,' I said. 'But she did say one other thing . . .' I hesitated as the memory of Odette sent a rush of shivers over me. 'She said she could see why *he* likes me.'

Rhode turned towards the desk and brought a bandaged hand to his chin.

'He?' Rhode asked.

'A member of her coven?' Vicken offered, leaning against the wall, one booted foot against it.

'You've bought us time but no resolution,' Rhode said.

I tried not to be stung but his words hurt. 'In case

you missed it the first time I told you, she tried to kill me,' I replied, as the gaping, fangless mouths from Rhode's memory sifted into my head again. Before he could respond, I added. 'She wants power. It's the only relief from the madness. It's her only goal.'

Rhode leaned his arm on the back of the chair; a bruised circle marked his wrist. It didn't look like a vampire bite – those would be punctures. When he realized my gaze had shifted from his eyes, he lowered his arm.

'She's not after humanity. She wants to *perform* the ritual in the hope it will give her power. Power to reign over the elements. With elemental power, she can draw beasts to her, control weaker beings. She can . . .' I remembered my dream again. I saw the abandoned Wickham in my mind, the dishevelled stone of the buildings, the vacant beach. 'She can do whatever she wants.'

'There's nothing we can do until she shows herself again,' Rhode said. 'And she will. In the meantime,' Rhode said, looking at Vicken, 'you and I could be a target. Anyone close to Lenah is. I would keep your dagger on you.'

Vicken raised his leg, placing his boot on top of the desk, and Rhode peered inside. I assumed he was looking at the dagger.

'You do the same,' Rhode said to me.

'And why do you think a simple dagger will work?' I raised my chin. He was so in control, telling me what to do, telling me he loved me, but then keeping his distance. It was enraging.

'We can't carry a sword around all day, can we?' Rhode replied. 'And you don't have sunlight coming out of your hands any more.'

Anger stirred within me. Sunlight. So he did know something about last year.

'OK, I'll carry a dagger too,' I said, placing my hand on the doorknob. My heart started to pound. 'And I'm going to take that bloody sword off its holder so I can behead the next vampire that sets foot near me.'

'That's the spirit!' Vicken said, and his eyes shifted back and forth between Rhode and me. 'Given the circumstances,' he muttered under his breath.

I glared at Rhode.

'Why are you so angry?' Rhode asked.

'Because you keep all your knowledge tucked away inside. Tell me, Rhode – were you here last year, or weren't you? Did you stand in the shadows and watch me fight for my life? Did you watch my best friend, Tony, die at the hands of a coven I created when you left? You know all about leaving, don't you?'

His lips parted slightly.

I started to walk away. I almost couldn't believe how good it felt to say those words out loud. He was businesslike and battered, with all his secrets and his bruises. But I still wanted to know exactly who or what had beaten him to a bloody pulp.

'Lenah, wait,' Rhode said.

I turned to face him, crossing my arms over my chest. 'You act like it doesn't matter. Like it's just some inconvenience that I had to fight for my life in a dressing room and couldn't run without endangering my friends. But don't worry, Rhode, I'll keep an eye out,' I said, mocking his instructive tone. 'I'll be a good girl and carry a dagger.'

Rhode's expression hardened. 'I don't understand you,' he said with a shake of his head.

I wanted him to hold me, as he had for hundreds of years. In my mind, for one moment, we sat in an opera house in the 1700s. His mouth grazed the nape of my neck, his hands travelled slowly up my stomach. But I couldn't say any of that out loud.

I blinked the memory away.

'I know what I have to do,' I said, turning away and leaving his room. My fury continued to build as I raced down the stairs of Quartz dorm. I did not need a dagger. I would not be afraid in a dressing room again. No one would tell me how to live or

165

what weapons to carry, least of all Rhode.

You are soulmates. No one can change that.

I didn't want to be soulmates if it had to be like this. I needed to take control of something. Anything. Anything to keep Odette away from me. So I was going to do a barrier spell and protect myself in my own way.

'Wait!' I heard from behind me. 'Wait!'

I stopped at the entrance to my dorm and turned.

Vicken ran to catch up with me. 'Don't . . .' he said puffing hard, 'perform any magic.' He rested his palms on his thighs.

'If you stopped smoking,' I jibed, 'you might find it easier to catch your breath.'

He stood up, seeing something in the reflection behind him. 'Damn it!' he said, and walked towards the glass front windows. 'It's fading.'

'What's fading?'

He turned to me and said with complete disgust, 'My bruise!' He whipped open the door, and after showing our IDs we climbed up the stairs to my room.

I shook my head. 'Since when are you Rhode's messenger boy? Why no magic?'

'If you do any spells,' he said, turning his body to avoid a couple of students coming down the stairs, 'I mean, SPELLING,' he yelled to cover. We climbed up further. 'If you do any spells,' he whispered, 'it could release enough magic to draw in energy, even *more* vampires. They can sense it, remember?'

I remembered Suleen's words about performing magic, but if Rhode was right and we had some protection until the start of Nuit Rouge, then we might be safe on campus. I told Vicken as much.

'Either way,' I said, 'I am doing a little something special tonight. A barrier spell.'

We walked into the apartment and the first thing I did was enter the kitchen. My fingers lingered on the black tins of herbs and spices that Rhode had left me when I was first human and came to Wickham. It seemed impossible that he was the same person. But so far he'd stayed away from me. He'd done as he was told.

Back in the living area I knelt before my old travelling trunk, and there was a click from the latches as I lifted the lid. Inside, hidden, were some things I would need for the spell. My fingers fluttered over a small sheet of satin. I moved it out of the way along with old crystal spheres, daggers with engraved sheaths and other trinkets from my life as a vampire. From the depths of the trunk I pulled out one of the few books Rhode had left for me. The book was bound in 1808 and entitled simply: *Incantato*.

I opened it and flipped through the thick pages until I found the correct one.

'Barrier spell,' I said aloud, and walking through I placed the book down on the kitchen counter.

I snatched the sage and an old scallop shell big enough to hold the combination of herbs. After checking the book, I organized dried dandelion, thyme, sage, lavender and an apple. I held the book in the crook of my arm and sprinkled the dried herbs around the perimeter of the room.

Vicken stood in the doorway of the kitchen with his arms crossed over his broad chest, watching me.

'Do you know . . .' I asked, continuing to lace the room with herbs, 'the origins of the Invitation Myth?'

'What? That vampires need to be invited into a house?' Vicken asked, and sat down on the couch. 'It's bollocks.'

The aroma of the herbs came to my nose in waves of sweet thyme and soft lavender. Remnants of herbs landed on the open pages of the book.

'Hand me your dagger,' I said, and he did. I sliced the apple through the middle and left it face up. When cut in half, the core is a pentacle, a five-pointed star, a form known in the supernatural world to bring power to those performing incantations. It could also represent all four elements: earth, water, fire and air; the fifth point is for all of the elements combined – sometimes called spirit. The thought of the pentacle reminded me of the Aeris, of their power. I turned it out to face the room. 'Vampires created the Invitation Myth,' I continued, 'to keep out the truly horrible beasts. The shape-shifters, the half-men/half-animals, the reprehensible of all kinds. Drink a little blood and suddenly you're the worst sort!' I met his eyes and gave him a knowing smirk. 'But we knew there were worse creatures than vampires. Creatures that came into your room through an open window, robbing you of your breath. Creatures that broke bones . . . for pleasure.'

I found a grey candle in the trunk and lit it. Grey is used on only very specific occasions – a colour between evil and good. A middle colour. *Do not trifle with grey candles.*

The candle flickered, and with the book open before me I read the enchantment soberly. I poured all my intentions into that moment. I wanted to protect us.

'I am safe and protected here in this space.' I intoned the incantation and placed the book down on the table. I took the grey candle between the palms of my hands and circled the room again. 'I am safe and protected here, with the blood in my veins, with these herbs. Let no vampire or supernatural beast walk through this door. I am safe and protected here.'

I walked five times around the perimeter of the room. When I had finished, I placed the candle down on the coffee table. I tried to ignore a throb from my collarbone.

'We need to let the candle burn,' I said. 'And you can't leave until it's out. We can't disturb the energy.'

'We aren't vampires any more. How do we know if we can even summon this kind of magic?'

I watched the candle smoke flicker into the air.

'I guess we'll have to wait and see,' I said. 'If this works . . . well . . .' I hesitated, and Vicken waited for me to continue. 'Well, if it works we can try other things.'

'Other things?'

I shot a glance at my book. How many times had I used it in Hathersage? Thousands? Granted, it was usually used to draw an enemy to me.

'You know what I mean. We could try stronger spells,' I said.

'Why would we be trying stronger spells?' Vicken asked. I thought of Suleen's warning on the beach. The longer I was a mortal, the weaker my connection to the supernatural world.

'We won't know if it works unless vampires try to

come in here and murder you.'

'Only one way to find out,' I said, and reached for the television remote.

Slow. Skin against skin. The low glow of a lantern. Two bodies together. A thigh rests against mine – lips whisper in my ear.

Vampires love with their whole souls. Not just with their bodies. They cannot feel as vampires. Their sense of touch wanes, leaving nothing behind but the human shell. Inside, the tortured soul is driven mad from numbness. When two vampires come together, two vampires that love, they can touch souls.

But not in this dream.

Rhode and I are on a bed made of straw. The windowpanes are old, the candle flame reflects in thick glass. The wood is so dark it is almost black.

Rhode's hand is behind my head, his lips graze mine. In this dream . . . I can feel him as a mortal would.

Our bodies make heat in this old room. A fire blazes and it makes my skin sweat. 'Rhode,' I whisper, and he pulls back from my ear. He looks into my eyes – the blue of his is captivating. I forget for just a split second how close we are. 'I wish I could feel you,' I say.

'Can't you?' he whispers, and brings his face to mine. 'Never,' he says. 'Never again can I be parted from you.'

The word you *echoes. Just one small syllable.*

You. You. You . . . and the image fades to darkness.

The straw bed shifts and the warmth of Rhode's body against mine is gone. Suddenly, the space opens up and I'm floating in mid-air – maybe I'm hovering, flying above the bed below me.

'You don't understand.'

Rhode's voice. I drift back towards the ground, the air supporting my body as though I'm a bird. I hover even lower and I'm below a black ceiling. I am on my feet, standing in a room. This is not the bedroom – I am somewhere else. Rhode kneels on the floor, his head bowed.

'You don't see,' Rhode is saying to someone in the room. 'I can't do it. I can't. What you ask is too much. Your demands are too great.'

I turn to see who he is speaking to, but it is all shadow.

'It's too much,' Rhode says again.

I am aware of my mortal body lying in a bed. The straw bed? No. It's softer. I am sleeping in my bed at Wickham Boarding School.

I want to wake up. Wake up, Lenah. The white light of the Aeris that has been haunting me flashes before my eyes. There – there is that vampire mouth again, the one where there are no fangs. Gaping black holes are where his fangs should be. Wake up, Lenah!

Wake up!

My eyes flew open.

I gasped and cool air rushed down my throat.

Through the open door of my bedroom, the television showed the early-morning news. The grey candle had long burned out. Vicken had fallen asleep and all I could see of him were his motorcycle boots dangling off the end of the couch. He snored in a rhythmic pattern.

I breathed out and sat up. A small line of sweat ran down my forehead. I wiped it away and ran a hand over my hair, my pulse racing. The cut on my collarbone burned so I hunched a bit and touched at the sensitive wound. *Rhode*, my heart said. *Rhode*.

But Rhode was across campus without me.

I got out of bed because I wanted to find Rhode; I wanted his eyes burning into mine. But what I wanted and what I needed had now become two drastically different things. I stopped, holding a blouse in my hand. Despite the heat and closeness I'd felt to Rhode in that dream, he would reject me if I surprised him at his room. What I needed was someone who would comfort me. Someone who would accept my touch when I gave it.

I needed Justin.

CHAPTER 13

When I stepped out of the newly broken side door (thanks to Vicken earlier that week), dark blue and black clouds swarmed across the grey sky. It was just before sunrise, an hour at most. I knew I wasn't supposed to travel on campus alone. The cut on my collarbone pulsed as I stepped down the path, a reminder that I was breaking the rules. I brought my fingers to it and the crackled blood and scab were rough under my fingers.

I checked to see if anyone was on the pathway that ran from Seeker to the bay, then checked behind me at the parking lot. Besides the security guards' booth, only one van was parked near Hopper. With another scan of the campus ahead of me, I darted down the side of the pathway, making sure to keep to the sides of the buildings and the darkness that still lingered.

I knew Justin's single room had been moved for his senior year and was now on the first floor of Quartz, facing the woods and the ocean beyond. The wind whispered through the trees, shaking their orange and gold leaves. A shiver rolled over me and I looked down the path to the beach, momentarily expecting Suleen to be standing there, waiting for me. But it was empty.

When *did* Suleen think it was important to show himself? Before or after I was almost murdered by a hungering vampire? He said he would come when I most needed him. How about now?

A car pulled past the school on Main Street, making a whooshing sound. My hair lifted from my ears as a gust of wind breezed through the campus. No. It couldn't be. No one would be watching me now. Surely my fake ritual was keeping Odette and her coven busy.

Run, Lenah . . .

I didn't want to look behind me at the alleyway of Seeker. What if one of the members of her coven was in those shadows? Someone she had sent to watch me. I told myself to walk faster. If someone was behind me, they would grab me by the shoulders. *A little faster now.* I took short breaths; the union was just ahead.

Faster, Lenah. They could come at any moment.

I skirted by the greenhouse and the science building and then looked back at the path. If a guard caught me, I would lose privileges, and I needed as much freedom as possible, given

175

the situation with Odette.

I ran towards Quartz dorm, ducked around the back of the building and pressed my back against the stone. In the woods, a yellow light fell in long vertical lines down the bark of the trees.

The first-floor windows stretched along the building. They were long windows, like those in the gymnasium, and opened by turning a metal handle.

Justin's room. Justin's room . . . which one? Yes. There it was. Even though all the windows were the same, his curtains were pulled back. Beyond the windows I could see various lacrosse sticks, and a foot dangled off the end of the bed.

I knocked on the glass twice, standing to the side of the window so as not to scare him. There was movement inside and a small grunt. I knocked again.

'Jesus!' I heard footsteps. The window squeaked open. I stepped in front of it. Justin's hair was messy from sleep. He wore no shirt, just sweatpants. Even at that time in the morning, he looked incredible.

Absolutely incredible.

'Um,' I said, taking a step back on to the strip of grass that separated the back of the dorm from the woods. He leaned on the window frame.

'Lenah? What are you doing here?' His voice sounded gentle, happy.

I stood in the morning sunrise and pulled the neck of my thin T-shirt to one side, exposing the long cut that ran along my collarbone.

'Holy crap!' he said. 'Get in here.'

I leaned into the room, grasping the ledge. When I pulled myself up, the wound throbbed and I nearly fell back on to the ground outside. Justin grabbed me and hauled me inside.

'Sit, sit,' he said, and led me to his bed. Flashes popped into my mind of our bodies tangled under the covers of his bed last year. He knelt before me for a moment. He pulled my shirt down again to examine the cut.

'Ouch,' he whispered. He met my eyes. 'You should probably take that off and let me clean it up,' he said.

'My shirt?'

He stood up and my gaze rested on his defined stomach. I looked all the way up his chest to his eyes, passing over the necklace he wore. I saw then, in the morning light, the pendant. It was a silver disc that fell at the base of his throat. I knew that symbol.

'A knowledge rune,' I said, and stood up. I touched the pendant with my fingertips.

'Yeah, I just got it the other day,' he replied.

'Why?' I asked.

'I got it in town,' he said. 'Supposed to help make sense of everything. When that guy with the turban did the water barrier – I just . . . I don't know. I had to try to make sense of everything. Make sense of you.'

'Me?'

'You, the ritual, Rhode. Why you're still alive.' He got up and walked to the back of the room. 'Anyway, I have a first-aid kit in my lacrosse bag.'

I was touched by the gesture and let the topic drop. Justin had purposefully sought out an object that would connect him to my dark, unearthly world. I was sure then that I had made the right choice in coming to him that morning. He was doing his best to understand me.

He rummaged in the corner of the room and I looked out through the window to the woods. In between the darkness of the trees, I could see myself as a vampire. Sauntering from the back of the woods towards the dormitory in an enormous red gown, my hair long and flowing over my shoulders. My fangs dripping with blood.

'Lenah,' Justin said, kneeling before me again. When I looked back at the woods, the ghost from my past was gone and the woods empty. 'Your shirt,' Justin said.

'Oh!' I said, and lifted it from my body, exposing

my bra. Justin leaned forward so he was kneeling before me and dabbed something on a white cloth along the line of my collarbone. I winced at the stinging feeling. Justin blew on the skin and dabbed at the cut. He lifted his face to mine.

'Should I stop?' he asked.

'No. It just burns a bit,' I whispered.

We hovered there for a moment. Then Justin lifted himself higher on his knees. His lips came closer and closer until they were on mine and our lips traced each other's movements. My heartbeat sped up and I wanted him to keep kissing me. So I could pretend that I was never that beast in the woods. He started to crawl on to the bed and I lay down. Just as his body pressure was on top of mine, he pulled away suddenly. I brought my fingers to my lips in surprise and swallowed.

The passion humming between us evaporated.

'Your cut,' he said. 'It still looks bad. Let me try something else.'

He dug in the bag. I came down to the floor so we sat opposite one another. He opened a different bottle and a most familiar smell overwhelmed me. I placed my hand on Justin's wrist and he lowered it for me to look at the bottle.

'My mom makes it,' he said.

'This . . .' I said, taking the bottle from him

and sniffing it, 'is lavender and aloe. A medieval combination.'

'Well, it should work,' he said, dabbing at my skin again. I could see the rust-like particles of my blood on the tiny cloth. He dropped it into a bin. 'We would get hurt all the time as kids. Mom made this up. I brought it with me to school for lacrosse injuries.'

Next Justin lifted two fingers covered in a gooey ointment and rubbed them along the cut.

'Anti-bacterial. This way you won't get an infection.'

After a few more minutes, he had covered various parts of the wound in gauze held on with tape.

'I won't ask how you got that cut,' he said, pulling me back up on to the bed and joining me there.

'You already know,' I whispered. 'You saw her murder Kate on the beach. I couldn't tell you in the union, but she killed Ms Tate too – not long after she spoke with me outside Curie.'

The tears rushed to my eyes and I blinked them away. My voice cracked as I said, 'She's probably seen you with me, which makes you a target, and I—'

'I'm not afraid of her,' he declared, and looked me straight in the eye. 'I'm not. I've seen what a vampire can do.'

'I just had to see you. I knew you would understand,' I said, as I blinked away the threat of more tears. He pulled me to him and I rested my cheek against his chest.

A large crack of thunder exploded outside and we both jumped. He hurried to close the window.

'What does she want? Has she been watching you this whole time? I should stay close to you in case she comes around again . . .'

Justin kept talking but I lay down on the bed and closed my eyes. I meant to tell him all about the strange feeling I'd had talking to Ms Tate, but I must have been so tired. I lost myself in his warmth as he lay beside me. He held me close, and when I just barely opened my eyes sometime later, my nose was nuzzled into his chest. His breathing was slow, steady. I listened to him breathe in and breathe out until I was moments from sleep again. Then I dreamed . . .

A field of lavender, and the smell is so wonderful, calming and cool. I hold the black fabric of a gown in my hands. The image changes. This is not the lavender field. I am somewhere else. A masculine hand with a bruised thumb grips a ceramic sink. It grips it harder, the forearm shaking. What happened to the field?

The hands shake and reach up, and in the reflection of the familiar bathroom mirror the hands cradle a face – Rhode's face.

'Do you love her?' Rhode asks the sink.

This is a Wickham bathroom; I recognize the blue-checked tiled floor.

'You don't need her,' Rhode says, looking up at his reflection and quickly tearing his eyes away. In this connection I can feel his distaste as though I am experiencing it myself. I can feel the misery and hate ripping through the centre of his stomach. It is not hate for me. It is hate . . . for himself.

Rhode lifts his right hand. He has taken off the bandage and long scabs are visible across the knuckles.

'You don't need her,' he says again, this time stressing the word need. 'You can do what they ask.' He surveys his reflection. With a downward cast of his eyes he says softly, 'No, you cannot. What they ask of you is too much.'

Like a bolt, he punches the mirror, cracking it into a kaleidoscope of lines. Fresh blood speckles the reflection. His blue eyes are spattered with crimson blots. Rhode repeats, 'I can't, I can't,' again and again and again.

I shot up in bed, my chest heaving. The spot next to me was empty. Across the room was a closet filled with lacrosse helmets, men's shirts and a football. That's right. I was in Justin's bed. On his night table, a note read: Practise, even in the rain!

I threw off the covers, pulled on my T-shirt and slipped on my shoes. When I reached down to do them up, the bandage from Justin's handiwork the night before pulled on my skin. I touched it out of instinct. I hesitated before the window and watched the rain pelt the grass and the woods beyond. These dreams of Rhode were becoming so realistic. This one even had the Wickham bathroom tiles! I unhooked the window clasps, and just as my fingers curled over the slick edge the reality hit me as a punch to my gut. I took a step back because I *knew*. Maybe it was because we were, as the Aeris said, soulmates, but I knew.

My dream wasn't a dream at all. It was reality. It was a Wickham dorm bathroom and Rhode was standing before the sink. So it wasn't just memories but his present-day thoughts I was accessing too. I ran a hand through my hair and stared at the tiny raindrops smacking the windowsill. So we were soulmates that could no longer be together but I was privy to Rhode's thoughts? This was *unnecessarily* cruel. There was nothing I could do about it either. This was what the Aeris decreed. No matter how connected we were, our lives had to remain separate. *Unnecessarily cruel* echoed in my mind again. I stepped on to the window ledge and out into the storm.

The rain picked up as the day went on. A few hours later, I sat alone at one of the long dining tables in the union where I was making yet another list.

Memories from the past.
Rhode's present-day thoughts.
Why am I receiving them, and more frequently with
every day that passes?

Outside, the rain lashed against the glass roof and massive windows. In front of me, a piece of iced lemon cake sat untouched on a plate. I crossed out another theory about Rhode and our *connection* when there was a scratch of ceramic against lino, and a drenched umbrella leaned against the table. I placed the book down gently and raised an eyebrow as Vicken took a bite of my cake and pushed a newspaper cutting across the table. It was from the British newspaper *The Times*.

HATHERSAGE, DERBYSHIRE
MASSIVE FIRE DEVASTATES HISTORIC MANSION

There it was: a photo of my glorious home. The great lawn was crawling with dozens of men and women. A moving company was carrying out a large bureau I recognized as being from my bedroom. The first-floor windows were blackened, blown out. Jagged remnants of glass pointed up from the window frames. A couple of curtains hung out of the windows as though trying to escape.

Vicken took another bite of the cake.

'Where did you get this?' I asked, resting my fingertips on the thin paper.

'I told you I was going to do some nosing around. I've been getting *The Times* for the last few weeks. And by the way, despite my moaning and groaning about this school, I've been in the library.' He turned the piece of paper back towards himself.

'On August thirty-first,' he read, 'a devastating fire engulfed the historic Hathersage mansion which dates back to the early seventeenth century. Thousands of items of extreme rarity have been recovered from the house. No bodies have been found, and it's believed the house, reputed by locals to be haunted, was empty when the fire occurred. The fire consumed the entire first floor and destroyed a tapestry that once belonged to Elizabeth I.'

'Her mother actually, Anne Boleyn. I had it restored and preserved several times,' I said. The sinking feeling in my chest was something else. The paper said the house had been empty. That house wasn't empty. It was filled with my history, my past, and it had almost burned to the ground.

Vicken kept reading. 'Local historians have

uncovered rare daggers, unusual herbs and strange amulets. Some believe the items are occult in nature. Many of the objects on the upper floors were spared, such as a four-poster bed from the 1800s, as well as anonymous portraiture also dating from the 19th century.

'Expert David Gilford of the Occult Group of London,' Vicken continued, 'was most impressed by the weapons room, which contained ninja stars, countless daggers and some of the rarest longswords he had ever seen. One had a handle made of human bone. Gilford also commented on some of the oddities found there. He was particularly struck by the apothecary equipment and by various strange devices that looked as if they were for torture.'

'They were,' I agreed.

Vicken continued, 'The house appears to have been in the same family since Elizabethan times. Strenuous efforts are being made to contact the current owners, whose identities have not been revealed. The recovered items will be catalogued under the management of the British Museum which is coordinating the salvage operation together with English Heritage.'

Vicken lit up, his whole face brightened and he smiled.

'Did you hear that? The *British Museum*!'

The date on the newspaper cutting was 31 August.

Today was 5 September.

Wait – 31 August? Rhode hadn't been seen back at Wickham until 3 September, which meant he could have been at Hathersage when the fire occurred.

I swiped my books into a bag, stuffed the cutting into my pocket and stood up.

'Where is he?' I demanded.

Vicken didn't respond.

'*Where?*' I screamed and slapped tabletop with my palm. Other students studying and eating their lunches looked over with wide eyes.

'He's in his dorm,' Vicken said with a sigh.

I tossed my bag of books into Vicken's lap and glanced at the rain pelting the windows. With an angry curl of my lip, I asked, 'Whose side are you on?' I swept out of the union and into the rain.

Rhode wasn't in his room. After banging on his door, I stepped back outside Quartz and within minutes my T-shirt was soaked from the rain and my jeans were sticking to my thighs. I intended to walk to my dorm when I saw Rhode, clad in all black, cut across the pathway some distance away from me. He kept his face down and held a large duffel bag over his shoulder. This was odd. I stepped off the path, attempting to conceal myself behind a statue of the school founder, Thomas Wickham, as Rhode disappeared behind the greenhouse. Where was he going? Hadn't we agreed that it wasn't safe to travel alone?

I ran down the path and stopped at a large oak tree next to the greenhouse. By the time I reached the end of the building, he had entered the woods that circled the school. I caught sight of a fresh bandage wrapped around his fingers. The white gauze stood out brightly against his black shirt and jeans. Back in our history, he had taught me how to follow someone without being seen, predator and prey.

Perhaps he was sneaking out for a good reason. Perhaps he was going somewhere that would clue me in to where he had been the year before. He wasn't going to tell me, no matter how many times I asked – that was clear. Either way, he was deliberately sneaking out of school without Vicken and me – and I wanted to know why.

I wiped the rain out of my eyes and hesitated at a nagging thought: he *knows* he shouldn't be going anywhere by himself. But he's going anyway. As the cut on my collarbone proved, Odette wasn't afraid of the daylight. Granted, the morning hours were more dangerous than the afternoon, but she had shown herself well able to withstand the sun's rays.

I took a step, watching him weave in and out of the trees, and rested a hand against the glass of the warm greenhouse. Rhode was making his way towards the stone wall that circled the perimeter of the school. If he jumped over, I'd have no idea where he went unless I kept up and followed him.

Go, Lenah. Go!

So I did. I made sure to keep my distance as I followed. Once, he glanced back to the campus. I jumped behind the cover of a stand of three maple trees and pressed my back against the hard bark. I was being careless, following too close. Just a few seconds. I could wait a few seconds. I bounced on my toes. What if he was outside the wall already? I peeked around the trees just as Rhode disappeared over the wall, on to Main Street.

I climbed over, and when my boots touched Main Street I stayed in the shadow of the wall, as though somehow the shade would protect me from Rhode's gaze. Rhode kept walking, duffel bag swinging in his hand, past the Lovers Bay public library, past the herb shop, past the last store on Main Street before it turned into a suburban neighbourhood.

At the entrance to Lovers Bay Cemetery Rhode hesitated. I pulled back into the shadows, listening to the rain patter on the sidewalk. I waited until he walked through the entrance. He was going into the cemetery. Why? Was this a hint? A clue to what had happened last year?

I followed behind Rhode, keeping pace just enough so I wouldn't lose him among the granite tombstones and trees. He navigated the pathways so easily. He didn't stop and refer to a map. He didn't need one. He knew exactly where he was going.

Ahead of me, I found a place to pause and regroup. There was an enormous grey stone mausoleum in the centre of the cemetery. Nearby was Rhode's tombstone, the one I had put up the previous year in his honour, thinking him dead. But he passed right by that. I pressed my back even harder against the cold stone of the mausoleum.

He turned at the row where Tony was buried.

I hadn't been to Tony's burial. I couldn't bear to see his parents' sorrow, knowing the part I had played in his death. But I had known the location of his grave. Of course I had known.

Curiosity churned in my stomach. 'Oh, go home, Lenah,' I whispered, but I could not make myself turn around. My boots squelched in the soggy ground as I padded quickly over the grass. I had to fall back to avoid him hearing me.

Rhode stood, his back to me, and looked down at what I assumed was Tony's tombstone. A couple of rows behind him, I got down on to my knees and crawled forward. The earth was wet and smelt of cut grass. I stayed close to the ground – I didn't see any other way. If I stood, he would catch sight of me out of the corner of his eye.

I stretched my arms forward and crawled down the wet row. I peeked up to see Rhode unzip the duffel bag. Out of it he pulled his longsword. I drew shallow breaths. What he did next was very calculated. He dragged the tip of the sword through the earth in a circle around Tony's tombstone. As he did so, he cut into the earth so it made a deep groove in the muddy soil.

Rhode was almost done drawing a complete circle around Tony's grave. This was no spell, at least not one I knew. Then he lifted the sword high in the air and plunged the sword into earth. Imbibed with magic, imbibed with his intention, for whatever reason, the sword slid easily into the soaked ground. In the dark of my mind, I imagined the metal slicing through the soil, the blade breaking the jagged clumps of earth protecting my friend and pointing at his wooden casket.

Rhode fell to his knees and wrapped one hand around the hilt of the sword, then rested his other palm flat against the tombstone. He dipped his chin to his chest and closed his eyes in a silent meditation. Silent until he began to whisper quick words.

'*Honi soit qui mal y pense,*' he said, over and over like a chant.

I recognized this as the official motto of the Order of the Garter. 'Shamed be he who thinks evil of it,' was the English translation. Rhode was performing a ceremony from back when he was a knight. I had never seen him do anything like this before. I stayed frozen to the ground, unable to look away.

Rhode sat back on his heels and brought both his hands to his face.

Why? Why Tony's grave?

This made no sense to me. I wanted to call out to him but I knew better. I shouldn't interrupt him during something so sacred.

Rhode then fell forward, extending an arm so his fingers curled over the top of the wet headstone. The gauze wrapping his injured fingers was soaked through. My eyes locked on a bright red blood spot that had seeped through the dressing. It was so bright in that grey rainstorm. He had punched the mirror, just as I'd seen in my dream.

Wait. He was speaking again. What was it? I held my breath so I could make out the words. I drew a tiny gasp, for all I could hear, all that travelled through the air to me, lying with my cheek on the soft grass was, 'Forgive me.'

I could not bear witness to this in secret. It was a betrayal. I stood up in the aisle behind Rhode. I needed to make a sound. Just the movement of my body was enough for him to realize I was there.

He lifted the sword from the ground, swung it through the air and pointed it directly at me. The ferocity in his eyes stunned me. I watched the recognition pass over his face and he dropped the sword to his side.

'I taught you well,' he said.

'Lovely day for a visit to the cemetery,' I said. 'What are you doing here?'

'Paying respects,' he said, and squatted down, placing the sword in a leather wrapping and then back into the duffel bag.

'To my friend?'

Rhode started walking out of the cemetery. I followed behind.

He went quickly down the soaked paths, back into the less wooded, more open part of the cemetery. We passed the mausoleum.

'You said we shouldn't be alone, but yet here you are,' I said, trying to provoke him into having a conversation with me.

He stopped and looked at me. He said simply and definitively, 'I am not without a weapon.'

'Do you want to explain this?' I asked, pulling the newspaper cutting from my pocket. I blinked the rain out of my eyes. 'It's in the bloody newspaper. The Hathersage house burned down. Now it's overrun with historians! It's gone!' Just saying it aloud sent a stab of pain through me.

He glanced at the newspaper but did not respond.

I threw the soggy shred to the ground. 'Enough games. Explain yourself. The date on that is August thirty-first.'

'Why are you doing this?' Rhode asked. The rain continued to cloud the air between us – I could barely see him.

'Did you see it burn?'

Rhode placed the duffel bag on the ground and let the rain drench us both.

'Yes,' he said finally. 'I saw it burn.'

Sorrow laced through my chest.

'How could you? Just let it?'

Rhode maintained his infuriating silence.

'Fine,' I continued. 'So you're not just lying to everyone else about a blasted car accident. You're lying to me. I asked you if you were in Hathersage. You never answered.'

'Should I tell everyone that I was beaten within

an inch of my life? That the only way out of that house was to set the place on fire?'

'*You* set it on fire?' I asked, horrified.

The rain pelted so hard the cold drops were actually hurting my nose and cheeks.

After a few moments he said, 'Vampires came looking for us. I had to torch the place to kill them and burn any evidence of my survival. So I did.'

I ran my hand through my soaked hair, my fingers catching in the wet tangles.

'Who attacked you? It was Odette, wasn't it?'

Rhode bent over, snatched up the bag and started walking out of the cemetery again.

'When the vampires saw me and realized I was mortal, they attacked. I ran for my life.' Rhode, my fearless Rhode, shuddered in that horrible, drenching downpour. 'I didn't think I would make it out.'

'You could have died,' I said.

'What's it to you? You thought I was dead for a whole year,' he said.

'And you think I could survive it again? That I don't worry whether you are all right every day? Every minute?' It took me a couple of tries but finally I got the words out. 'Tell me. Did you watch me last year? Did you know what I was doing?'

Rhode dipped his chin to his chest. He seemed

to think it over a moment, then said, 'Yes, I saw you. After your friend Tony's death, I could not come to you. At the time, it seemed . . . fruitless.'

An explosion of relief flooded through me. *Finally*, something.

'But you knew the coven were after me. Yet you did nothing?'

Rhode's eyes were focused on my neck; he didn't answer.

'Rhode?' I asked again.

He took a step to me and lifted his hand. Was he actually going to touch me? My stomach jumped. But no. He took the collar of my cold, wet T-shirt between his thumb and index finger and pulled the fabric down a bit. The bandage had slipped in the rain, exposing the cut. He examined it for a few moments, then let go, all the while careful not to touch my skin.

'That day when we discovered that I had had a sister, you swore we would always be together,' I whispered.

I took a step towards him, intending to take his hand into mine.

Rhode jumped away from me and I saw fear, actual fear, pass over his eyes. I drew my hand back, hurt and embarrassed that he had rejected me yet again.

'I can't!' he cried, and I froze. 'I will never leave

you, Lenah.' He met my eyes but the look in them was pained, struggling. 'But I cannot love you any more. Not like this.'

After a moment of silence, when the only sound was the rain pelting on the grass, Rhode said, 'Our circumstance is absolute.'

Our circumstance.

'*Our* house. *Our* portraits. *Our* library,' I dared to reply, 'are all gone. It's like they're erasing our history.' I brought my hand to my chest. The water drenched my shirt and slicked my fingers. 'And all those beautiful books,' I said.

'You're worried about *the books we left behind*?!' he said, and his blue eyes cut through the misty grey air. 'You should be worried about the skeletons we left buried in the walls or the goblets of blood we left sitting on tables, forgotten. They'll test the contents of old goblets. But we don't have to care any more. It's over, Lenah. Aren't you relieved? Glad you can leave it all behind?'

I pulled back from him. All my belongings. All the old photographs and jewellery. The great halls where we took life so willingly were now empty and ruined.

What Fire had said to Rhode and me on the archery field replayed in my mind.

Vampires are dead. Supernatural night wanderers. We

cannot hold you responsible for the killings you performed in that world.

Rhode was right. I was glad the years of destruction and sadness were over.

And then . . . the rain came down even harder. It pummelled the grass and I had to wipe the water away from my eyes with both hands.

'Everything was destroyed. It's irrelevant now,' he said, his words clipped. 'We're human.' He picked up the duffel bag and took a few steps towards the cemetery exit.

'Isn't this what you wanted?' I asked.

'For you,' he said gently. But my wonderful Rhode was hiding something more. I could tell from the curve of his back and the gaze of his eyes to the ground.

'If the Aeris had not interfered, would *you* be happy with mortality? Wherever you were?' I asked, hoping this would lead to him to continue opening up about his whereabouts the year before.

Rhode turned back to me, a black-clad figure in that drenching rainstorm. 'I'm not really mortal. I may be flesh and blood but I'm something else. Stuck.'

'What are you then?'

'Something forgotten. Archaic. Put me in a glass case and shut the door.'

'You don't really believe that, do you?' I asked.

'I believe I met a girl in the rain. Who had lost her mother's earrings. And I killed her. Now I stand here in a time I know nothing about. I watched the death of kings far greater than any man living now. And I am *still here,*' Rhode said, his face soaked with rain and his blue eyes piercing me through the grey of the storm.

The image of a pair of ancient golden hoop earrings came to my mind.

Rhode held my gaze through the curtain of rain. I understood him – we understood each other completely.

'My mother's earrings,' I said, 'were in the house.'

Rhode considered his answer, then said, 'And so were the ghosts of all our pasts.' The rain pelted the bag housing the longsword. Rhode looked at me. '*Est-ce que tout ça valait la peine?*' he asked in French. 'Was it all worth it? For the sense of touch?'

He turned from me then and left the cemetery. He did not need to say that I should follow; we both knew that neither of us should be alone.

When we got back on to campus, I stopped at Seeker. Rhode disappeared into the crowds of students. As I watched him go, I finally understood why the knight of Edward III had visited the grave of my best friend, Tony Sasaki.

He felt responsible.

CHAPTER 14

Later that afternoon I walked out of Seeker dorm.
The sun broke through the grey clouds and I was
barely able to focus my eyes when Vicken screeched,
'I was just coming upstairs to get you!' He grabbed
my hand. 'Let's go.'

'What are you doing?' I asked as his strong grip
led me down the pathway. 'What's wrong with you?'

'We need a lot of people. We'll go to the union,
that's it. A lot of people are there usually.'

'Have you gone mad?'

'There!' Vicken pointed at the lacrosse field
behind Hopper. 'Throngs of people.' We had
managed to walk into a crowd of middle- and
upper-school students watching a Wickham lacrosse
scrimmage. Half the team wore white jerseys, the
rest were in dark blue. Vicken didn't care; he led
me to the sides of the crowded bleachers where he
finally let go of my hand.

'You! You there,' he cried.

He pointed at a tiny ninth-grader who clutched
a backpack to her chest. She quivered under his

pointed index finger. 'Look at me. Look in my eyes.' He waited a moment then spat out, 'Damn it!'

I grabbed him by the back of his T-shirt. 'Stop it!'

The girl turned away. Her little feet seemed to explode with speed and she ran off towards Hopper. Vicken continued. Every few seconds he stopped people. 'You! Hey, you! What are you thinking! Get back here! Don't you run from me!'

'What are you doing? You've gone mad,' I hissed at him.

'Have I? I've lost my sodding ESP. Spend over a hundred years with something and then, *poof*, it's gone.'

'Gone?' I parroted dumbly. This was not in our favour.

'ESP – gone!' he yelled, and slapped his hands against his thighs.

'Shhh!' I said, and motioned to the crowded bleachers behind us. Claudia and Tracy were sitting way up high watching the game. Claudia waved at me and I smiled back. I could feel Tracy's eyes on me even though they were hidden behind her sunglasses.

'Oh, you think anyone knows what I'm talking about?' He extended his arms. 'ESP! ESP!!' he yelled to the sky.

I slapped his arms down.

It was as though Vicken suddenly realized where he was. He turned to face the field, his back to the bleachers.

'What the hell is this?' he asked with disgust, raising both arms from his sides.

'It's a sporting event.'

'I realize that. What the hell are they doing?' he asked.

'It's called lacrosse.'

A pause, then, 'Well, I'm not staying for this shite. Let's go.'

As he turned to leave the field, cheers erupted around us and I could hear Tracy and Claudia's voices chanting, 'Justin! Justin!'

On the field Justin, in his full lacrosse gear, ripped off his helmet, threw it to the ground and marched up close to another player. He jabbed his finger to the other guy's face and was yelling something I couldn't make out.

I placed my hand on Vicken's arm. He stopped and we stood at the base of the bleachers looking out at the scrimmage. Vicken stepped close to me and said in a low tone, 'You're a human for two minutes and already you're a sports fan?'

'No . . .' I said. I couldn't remove my eyes from Justin on the field. 'Wait.'

Vicken sighed.

'Cut it out, Enos!' the referee yelled, and Justin picked up his helmet as the players reassembled.

I sat down on the bleachers. Vicken groaned, sat beside me and crossed one motorcycle-booted leg over the other. He leaned his elbows on the row behind.

On the field one of the players slapped his stick against Justin's and the white ball flew in the air. Once Justin realized who had the ball, he smacked his stick against the other player's so hard that the player stumbled backwards. Then he whacked the player's stick again and again, until the referee blew the whistle.

'What?' Justin yelled at the referee. He lifted his shoulders and arms out to the side. 'What's your problem?'

'I'm not telling you again, Enos. One more and you're out!' the referee shouted back.

The whistle blew, signalling the scrimmage was beginning again. The players assembled and immediately Justin slapped his opponent's stick, sending the ball into the air and down into his own net.

Justin ran down the field so fast that no one could catch him. He slammed into other players so hard it was as though he wanted to throw them to the ground. When a defenceman from the other side smacked the ball out of his net, Justin threw off his helmet again and punched the player in the stomach.

'I've never seen him play like this,' I said.

'Like what?' Vicken asked.

'Like he's out for revenge or something.'

Cheers and raucous rounds of 'Justin! Justin!' echoed about us again.

Another whistle.

The referee pointed to the bench. Justin bowed to the crowd walked off the field. When he passed by the defenceman who had got the ball out of his net, Justin lunged at him, pretending he was going to punch him. When the other player recoiled, Justin threw back his head and laughed. He then plopped down on the bench and shook the sweat away from his face. As the crowd continued to call his name, Justin turned back to the bleachers and laid eyes on me.

He licked his lips and the twinkle in his eye reminded me of the first time we met. It was right after Rhode had performed the ritual and I was human for the first time. I saw him on a beach walking hand in hand with Tracy Sutton, long before he broke up with her and dated me. There on the lacrosse field, he broke our gaze and turned back to the game.

*

'He's the one who's gone mad,' Vicken said when the scrimmage was over. We walked with the rest of the students down the bleachers back on to the field.

'Hi, Vicken,' a group of girls said, almost in complete unison, as we walked by. He nodded his head, his eyebrows creased and hands in his pockets. He had no time for girls at the moment, apparently.

'Even without my ESP I can tell you something is wrong with that nutter.'

Justin lingered on the field, surrounded by his teammates and also a few girls, including Andrea, the junior from the other night at the observatory. Most were wearing early fall attire entirely too warm for a day like today. As I approached, I looked at the shorts I wore. My pale legs seemed long and too white compared with the unnaturally darkened tans of the girls surrounding Justin. I stopped and anger burned my cheeks. I hated this. This mortal embarrassment. If only . . . No. I stopped myself. I would not wish it. I would not let myself even consider wanting my vampire powers back.

'What?' Vicken asked. 'You don't want to go over and talk to Monsieur Aggressive?'

Not when he was acting like that I didn't. Last night, he had been so tender. So open, as he used to be. Last night, as I lay next to him dreaming of Rhode, it could have been last year. We had been together like we were then, lying next to one another, and Rhode, as always, was unavailable to me.

Justin caught my eye over someone's shoulder and manoeuvred around people to get to me. He stopped before he reached me, his eyes shifting to Vicken.

Roy joined Justin at his side and squinted at Vicken. Soon another couple of lacrosse players, pads under their jerseys, stood on either side of Justin. Vicken placed a cigarette between his lips. If Justin and his boys were coming over, it would probably not be cordial.

'Did I mention he punched me in the eye?' Vicken said. He overdramatized his blinking to highlight the slight yellow bruise still lingering there. Then he turned and headed out on to the campus with the rest of the crowd, leaving a plume of smoke behind.

Justin broke from the group and I waited as he approached me.

A flurry of goosebumps ran over me.

I drew a small breath, swallowed and looked at the ground. Someone was watching me again. I knew it. The feeling mesmerized me. Where were they? I turned my head ever so slightly to the right, following the feeling that was crawling all over me. Odette. Surely it was Odette. I kept turning until I faced the quad in front of Quartz dorm.

Students there walked together towards the union or the library. They passed security guards and maintenance crews erecting violently yellow emergency telephones at virtually every intersection of the pathways on campus. My eyes were drawn to a shadow by Quartz Building and my breath caught in my chest.

Rhode stood in the shadows, watching me. I would love those blue eyes forever. How they had looked at me when I first awoke as a human the year before. I wanted to go to him, be with him. And I knew, as all vampires know, when you are the watched, you are the wanted.

He could not love me any more, that's what he had said. *Not like this.* I didn't know what *this* meant. It could have been many things: we couldn't love under the Aeris's decree, we couldn't love as humans. All I knew was that I couldn't answer for him. It was done. Love for me would be Justin Enos and a lifetime of reminding myself that I was human. Not a girl of the medieval world. Of stained-glass windows and candlelight.

'Lenah,' Justin said. I jumped and turned. He

stood alone before me, wiping sweat from his forehead. The definition of his biceps kept my attention.

'Sorry,' he said. 'Didn't mean to scare you.'

'You didn't,' I lied.

'You're beautiful.' Justin smiled at me again. 'Have I mentioned that?'

'Oh,' I didn't know what to say. 'Well, no,' I said, my cheeks suddenly hot. A thrill rushed to my stomach. I looked back over to Quartz and examined the darkened shadow made by the building. Rhode was gone. To my surprise, I was glad Justin and I were alone.

'That was an . . . interesting scrimmage,' I said, looking into Justin's eyes, not entirely sure what to say next.

'You liked that?'

I flinched, not understanding what he meant.

'Liked what?' I asked.

Justin held his shoulders back and casually licked the sweat from his lips. He smirked at me, raising an eyebrow. 'Lenah, come on. You like me.'

He took a step closer, so close that I could smell the sunblock and sweat on his skin. I did like him. It was no act. His mannerisms were so thoroughly twenty-first century. Even the casual flick of his head to rid himself of the sweat rolling down his face was a gesture that would have been alien to Rhode. Gentlemen of past eras would wipe their brows with a handkerchief. Justin's movements were quick, abbreviated. This world was one of instant messages, instant communication and interaction. People spoke to one another with a casual cadence and clipped colloquial words. Even though I had been born in the medieval era, I had come back to life in the twenty-first century. Justin's world was my world now.

'You know how I feel about you,' he said softly before I could think any more. The way he spoke sent a shiver down my spine. Tiny beads of sweat lined his upper lip. He glowed and always would to me. He emanated a life force which I had loved when I was first human and even now I wanted a piece of it.

He lifted his hand, running his fingers lightly across the cut on my collarbone. It made me tremble.

'Your bandage came off,' he said.

'You may have to re-dress it,' I said, with sudden heat to my cheeks.

'I will.' He took a step closer, his expression suddenly serious. 'Any more sightings of the blonde?'

I shook my head. No.

'Enos!' someone called from behind us.

Justin backed away, dropping his fingers. My skin cooled where the warmth of his touch had been. Suddenly he stopped walking backwards and gestured by lifting his helmet towards me.

'Hey! I almost forgot,' he said. 'Happy birthday!'

My jaw dropped. It *was* 6 September, wasn't it?

'Of course,' I said. 'It is my birthday, isn't it?'

'You forgot your own birthday?' Justin asked, incredulous.

Ah, well, my soulmate of six hundred years is living here at school, but I can't be with him because a supernatural force ordered us to stay apart. You're beautiful in every way, shape and form, but I probably blew my chances with you. My best friend, Tony, was murdered and my friend Vicken killed him.

'A lot on my mind,' I replied.

'Well, I'm having a party tonight,' said Justin. 'I've asked the guys. Down at the camping ground. I tried to find you earlier to tell you.'

The moment in the listening room replayed in my mind. His arms travelling over my back and shoulders as we danced.

'So does that smile say you'll come?' Justin asked.

Was I smiling? It seemed impossible after everything that had happened over the last two days.

'Look – meet us at seven. Site 404. Lovers Bay

camping ground. You can bring Vicken – you know, because we have to keep in twos. It's a couple of miles up Main Street,' he said. 'There'll be a lot of us,' he added before I could say no. 'We couldn't book it unless there were at least ten of us.' Once he said that a part of me, the foolish part, didn't want to refuse, no matter how bad an idea I knew it was. Justin gathered up his kitbag, and when he threw it over his shoulder the pendant around his neck caught the sunlight.

He turned away to join the rest of his team, walking towards the gymnasium. As I was about to turn away, he glanced back at me with a bright smile.

He always lured me in this way. He so easily commanded a room when he walked into it. Everyone wanted to see the tiny lines appear around his mouth when he smiled. The casual mess of his sandy hair. I couldn't help but want to go. I couldn't help but want to be happy, even just for an evening.

CHAPTER 15

As far as Ms Williams was concerned, as long as the campus was safe, it didn't matter what happened off campus. This particular point enraged Vicken endlessly, who thought off campus was definitely *not* safe.

Either way, I thought we should go to the party, and I wanted to. As long as we all signed out together, we could go. Odette had shown no sign of coming back yet. Presumably the fake ritual was still occupying her, and I doubted she would make an appearance in front of so many people.

I guessed if Rhode knew I'd decided to go off campus without his supervision, he would have been furious.

That evening, I looked at my reflection in the mirror next to my bureau. My eyes seemed a darker blue than usual, as though I could not hide the anxiety brewing and churning inside me. I smoothed down some flyaway strands of hair and then looked over at the photo of Rhode and me on the bureau. It was back in its rightful place after

Tony stole it last year, trying to uncover the history of my vampire life.

In the mirror I could see the scabbard that had held Rhode's sword for the last two hundred years.

The sword was gone, the scabbard empty, as I expected it to be.

I got down on the floor and checked the herbs from the barrier spell, as I did every day since I had first performed the spell. If a barrier spell works, the herbs ignite, leaving nothing behind of the intruder but charred ash. As long as whoever came into the room was accepted, the herbs were not dangerous.

I turned back to my reflection and started to put on a pair of gold ear studs I had bought in the early 1900s. They had been in my jewellery box, almost forgotten, but now that my mother's earrings were lost, gone in the Hathersage fire, I decided to wear the studs. I pushed one into my lobe.

An overwhelming stench of apples *exploded* in the room.

I slammed my hands against the wall and dropped forward, my body engulfed in the stink of apples. I grabbed at my gut because it twisted and turned. Fake apples. How could someone manufacture such a beautiful smell and make it so ugly? So sickly sweet? Its force knocked me to the ground. I fell to my knees, the gold studs skidding across the wooden floor, and just when my palms hit the ground . . .

'She must be isolated so no one can find her.'

It is Suleen's voice I hear first. I am in Rhode's mind again.

Together, Suleen and Rhode stand by a tombstone in the cemetery directly next to my mansion in Hathersage. Four or five headstones are together in a small plot surrounded by a wrought-iron fence.

There is my tombstone. No epitaph, no name. Just an L carved into the stone.

Rhode buried me in 1910 and uncovered me one hundred years later to perform the humanizing ritual. Based on Rhode's appearance, he is the modern-day Rhode, the Rhode I saw when I first awoke at Wickham Boarding School. He uncovered me in secret, without the coven's knowledge, without Vicken's knowledge. I recognize Suleen's appearance from modern times as well. He wears white and his traditional turban.

'You are sure of this, Rhode,' he asks. Rhode nods but Suleen's expression is dark. Rhode turns, looking at himself in the reflection of a house window. In this memory, Rhode's marble-like eyes are colder than in his human self. It's hard to believe I am now accustomed to his mortal face.

'It'll be easier this way. I don't trust her coven. Have you noticed how strong they are? Vicken, Heath, Song and Gavin. They're all hand-picked for their strength and

cunning. We need to do it while they are not here.'

'That's not what I mean. This ritual? Sacrificing yourself?' Suleen asks. The sun is almost fully descended, a full moon above brightens the evening sky. 'Your death offers me no comfort, Rhode.'

'This ritual is the only way for Lenah to live. The Hollow Ones will protect her. They'll make sure nothing happens to Lenah after I am gone.'

'The Hollow Ones will keep their end of the bargain only if you die. There is no telling what will happen if you survive. They cannot be trusted, Rhode.'

Rhode stares into the hills as the sunset washes them in gold.

'What about her soul?' he asks Suleen.

'What about it?'

'How do we know?' Rhode's eyes flick to Suleen's and then back out to the field. 'How do we know Lenah's soul isn't damaged. That as a human she won't fall back into her desire for power. Even I . . .' He stops and considers what he is about to say. 'She killed a child, Suleen.'

'Do you question your forgiveness? It is key to the sacrifice,' Suleen reminds him.

'I question her human self. Can she love after being capable of such evil?'

'I cannot answer this for you,' Suleen says. He looks to the sky. 'If you want to unearth her, you must do it now.'

'Tell me, Suleen — can someone who has done such

evil really come back? Her evil has surpassed that of any vampire I have ever seen.'

'Now, Rhode! You must start before the sun fully descends.'

'What if I can never forgive her?'

The truth finally comes out. He has not forgiven me for killing a child. For falling into madness as a vampire.

'Now!' Suleen yells.

Rhode lifts a shovel and stabs the earth.

'Stop him! Stop him!' I screamed. Someone was holding my shoulders and trying to shake me awake. The hardwood of the floor cooled my back and I blinked.

'Lenah! Hey. Lenah!' Vicken was calling my name. I looked up at the ceiling. Vicken leaned over me so his shaggy hair fell into his eyes. He raised an eyebrow. 'You fell asleep on the floor. You have a couch, a lounge chair and a bed. But, hey – don't let me criticize your choice of napping locale.'

I sat up, swallowing hard, and ran a hand through my hair. I sat there for a moment staring at the base of the bureau, gazing at its carved legs and intricate woodwork.

Vicken squatted down beside me. 'Does this need immediate attention? Should I be calling someone to help you?'

'I . . .' I concentrated on the floor, following the

grain in the wood. 'I don't know.'

It's not that Rhode *couldn't* love me any more, as he had said in the woods after visiting Tony's grave. It was that, at one point, he didn't *want* to. Because I didn't deserve it. Perhaps that's why he didn't come back last year. He didn't want to return to someone with a heart like mine.

'Who or what are the Hollow Ones?' I asked.

Vicken frowned. 'Hollow Ones?' He shook his head. 'Never heard of them.'

'Help me stand,' I said, and lifted a hand. Vicken's warm fingers grasped mine and he pulled me up. I walked to the wall and leaned my back against it. Vicken stood looking at me, his arms crossed over his chest. Rhode's memory swirled in my mind.

'I'm seeing Rhode's thoughts,' I said, and it came out in a rush. Vicken's eyes narrowed. 'I see his thoughts, sometimes his memories.'

Vicken dug in his pocket for a pack of cigarettes. He lit one, then said, 'What do you mean? Thoughts . . .'

I slid to the floor and wrapped my arms around my knees. 'I see him in my mind, but it's as if *I'm* in *his* mind. I verified it. I dreamed that I saw him punch a mirror. And then when I saw him in person there was fresh gauze wrapped around his injured fingers.'

'Why on earth would he punch a mirror?'

'He couldn't stand to look at himself. So he punched it.'

Vicken shook his head. 'Odd.'

I exhaled, looking out of the balcony door at the dark void. From above, the moon lit up the tiles and my vampire remains still sparkled. It felt good to tell someone the truth.

'Why would I see his thoughts now? I'm completely mortal. I don't have my ESP or my vampire sight. And it never happened at any other time in our history. When he left before . . . before I met . . .' I hesitated and chose my words carefully. 'When I met you.'

Vicken thought it over for a moment, then shot up. 'Remember that story Rhode used to tell?' Vicken said. 'The one about the vampire who loved the human girl. The one during the Plague. The—'

'Anam Cara?' I said, remembering Rhode telling the story by firelight. I had forgotten the phrase until now.

'Yes. The vampire had a deeper connection to her than any other. So much so that he could sense her thoughts, not just her intentions. He hid his vampirism from her, and when she got the plague—'

'He let her die,' I said.

'Yes!' Vicken said, and went over to the trunk pushed against the wall below the iron candle holders. He sifted around inside.

'Uncommon for vampires, who are inherently selfish,' Vicken said, and the smoke from his cigarette wafted and hung over his head. He pulled out one of the few leather-bound books Rhode had left me when I was first human: *A Book of Celtic Magic*. 'It would have been easy. Cure her – make her a vampire forever. Instead, he let her go to her death as she should have. Not a pleasant death, but she got sick. And she died as humans do.'

I liked that story and I remembered it well. It reminded me of how I felt for Rhode. Except, he didn't let me go . . .

Vicken opened the book.

'Here it is – "Anam Cara. A soul-friend. When one finds one's Anam Cara, the connection is undeniable. Unyielding. It is a white string of light connecting two souls through space and time. Some believe the Anam Cara share a mind. A mind of a past so deep, so interconnected, that they can share thoughts."'

He looked up at me and took a last drag from his cigarette, which was down to the nub.

'So, soulmates can share thoughts?' I said. And then it hit me again. I had temporarily forgotten, but there it was: Rhode's voice wondering whether he could forgive me for killing that child and for making the coven. Disappointment flooded through me again. I picked up my gold studs from the floor and stood up, facing my reflection. I smoothed my hair, fixing it after my tumble to the floor. What was the use of sharing thoughts if Rhode couldn't love me any more? If I had a damaged soul.

'So that's it?' complained Vicken. 'You ignore my moment of brilliance and go back to getting ready for your party?'

He placed the book back in the trunk, shut the lid and sat down on top of it.

What if I can never forgive her?

I put on the earrings and surveyed my reflection again. My hair fell down my back over the thin gauze of the tangerine blouse I had bought at the mall. I wanted the studs to be my mother's earrings, the hoops that were lost in the fire. Sadly that was not possible. I watched as my nostrils flared and I clenched my jaw again.

'Anam Cara,' I said aloud, letting the expression roll around on my tongue.

'Well,' Vicken said, pressing his hands on his thighs and standing up, 'I guess you're still going to go to this party despite the news of the mind meld.'

'You're damn right I'm going.'

'All righty,' said Vicken, and dropped two daggers, one into each boot. He then slid another into a leather strap hidden up his shirtsleeve.

'Preparing, are we?' I asked.

'Your life has been threatened twice and you're willing to risk it for a little campfire? I have an idea. I'll light a fire on the balcony and sing you "Happy Birthday".'

'I know it's strange,' I said.

'No, it's bloody ridiculous,' Vicken replied. 'But I'm not letting you go alone. I'd chain you to the wall if it wasn't against school policy.'

I opened the door. Vicken was following directly behind me.

'You don't *have* to come to the party,' I said, knowing that Vicken would, of course, come.

'You got that right. With those screaming loons? Knowing them, they'll get lost and we'll have to search the woods to find them – it'll be a mortal mess.'

'So where are you going to be?' I asked.

'Watching the perimeter of the woods. Making sure no one with fangs crosses into the park.'

'There'll be too many people surrounding me. Don't you think they'll be less likely to attack when they're outnumbered? I wouldn't have attacked in those circumstances.'

'Maybe . . .' Vicken said as we descended the stairs.

'Also, it's my birthday! You realize this means I'm actually ageing.'

'Really? How old are you?' Vicken asked as we walked down the stairwell. His smile was a sly one.

'Seventeen,' I replied.

'*Really?* You look *so* much older.' I could have slapped him if it wasn't so . . . well, *Vicken* to say something like that.

A few moments later, we were heading down Main Street towards the camping ground. I listened to the chatter of people around us. We parted as a woman walking her dog stepped between us.

'Maybe Rhode is connected to your mind too,' Vicken offered.

'There's no way to know. He refuses to touch me and is barely speaking to me,' I said as the smell of coffee wafted over us from the Lovers Bay Cafe. 'You know, there's other things, stranger things that I've seen outside of his memories. I see his thoughts too.'

I turned my head as we walked past the busy cafe. To be honest, I wouldn't have minded an evening sipping a cup of coffee and chatting to Vicken. One evening to forget about Odette and Rhode and all that lay before me. We kept on walking up

Main Street and I explained about Rhode's odd behaviour when he punched the mirror. But when I opened my mouth to mention Tony I glanced at Vicken keeping pace beside me and said something else instead.

'I'm telling you,' I said, 'he punched the mirror and said, *I can't*, over and over.'

'Rhode? Going insane? It doesn't make sense,' Vicken said. His gaze did not pause scanning the road, back and forth.

'I think it's deep-rooted. That he doesn't think he deserves his humanity or something. I told you, he kept saying, *I can't*.'

Vicken let this hang in the air between us, then said, 'Can't what?'

'I don't know. I just want to make it better,' I replied. And I knew a way to alleviate Rhode's pain. I had wanted to do it for days now: call on Suleen. Or perhaps the Aeris. Call on someone, *anyone*, who could help him. Perhaps Rhode hurt because we couldn't be together. Or, and I didn't want to admit this because I didn't want it to be truc, perhaps Rhode did not believe he deserved to survive the ritual and be human. He had meant to die – we both had. It was our connection as soulmates that linked us to this world.

My head hurt.

'Don't worry about Rhode,' Vicken said as we walked in the crisp air of the late summer night. We entered the camping ground. 'Try to have fun with the . . . screaming loons, was it?' He placed a cigarette between his lips.

'Precisely,' I replied.

I heard the music first. Something with electric guitars and a light melody. I remembered the hundreds of times over hundreds of years when I had stepped over branches, parted leaves and walked through woods. Never, not once, had electronic instruments echoed through the trees and undergrowth.

Ahead of me was the orange glow of the fire. When I came upon two or three cars parked facing the campsite, I knew this was the place. Music played out of Justin's silver SUV. Claudia and Tracy sat by the fire with a few others, drinking out of big red cups. Tracy was talking very closely with a guy from the lacrosse team whom I didn't know. Justin looked up at me from unpacking some hamburger buns and a small charcoal grill.

Claudia jumped up when she saw me.

'Happy birthday!' she cried, and wrapped her arms around me. She had to rise on to her tiptoes to hug me, but when she came back down she reached into a pocket of her light jacket and pulled out a small card in a purple envelope.

'For you,' she said.

'Claudia . . .' I said. 'You didn't . . .'

'Yes, I did.' She nodded.

'Thank you,' I said, genuinely touched. I held the card in my hand.

'This party was *my* idea. Don't let Justin fool you – I suggested it.' She glanced back at him and gave a playful smile.

I opened my present. I couldn't remember the last time I had been given an actual gift. One that didn't involve its immediate murder, anyway. I opened the flap and inside the envelope was a small plastic card, like a credit card, but on it were the words *Cape Cod Mall*.

'A gift card,' Claudia said. 'It seemed like you had a good time when we went to the mall. And you're wearing the shirt!'

A gift? For me? I turned the card over and over, marvelling at the small present in the flickering light from the campfire.

'Thank you,' I said to Claudia, whose eyes were warm.

Tracy looked up and gave me a half-smile, as if she didn't really mean it. She was roasting a marshmallow on a long stick. It looked wonderful and gooey. Her hair glimmered with the flicker of the fire and her angular features looked more pronounced to me than they had a few days before. Perhaps I was only just noticing it now, but she looked as if she had lost a lot of weight in a short time.

I slid the gift card into my back pocket. As I watched the marshmallow melt away in the heat of the fire, another bunch of Wickham students walked on to the camping ground. They were the normal variety – athletes, academics, just kids looking for a party. But when I really looked I pulled back and blinked a few times to make sure I was in my right mind. Had I just . . . ? Had I really mistaken one of these high-school students . . . for Rhode?

But no. There he was, trailing behind everyone.

'Hey! Hey!' Someone at the front of the group called out and hoisted some paper bags in the air.

'My peach schnapps is here!' Claudia cried.

Rhode was all in black and I couldn't look away. How did he know where I was? For a moment, I felt like I was a disobedient child. Then I lifted my chin in defiance.

Claudia spun around and gave a tiny gasp. 'There's Rhode,' she murmured to me. 'Have fun . . .' and she went to join Tracy.

I stood up. Rhode walked in long strides and stopped directly in front of me. When he breathed out, he dug a hand into his pocket. With the image of vampire Rhode still in my mind, I noticed the small, human things, the pouted mouth, the need to inhale and the band of sweat across his brow. He reached deeper into his pocket and pulled out a tiny black bag. He nodded his head towards the woods. 'Could you come talk to me for a moment?'

'Sure,' I replied, as casually as possible.

He wasn't here because he'd changed his mind; I knew that much. He had made that plain when he told me he *couldn't love me any more*. I followed him into the woods down a worn path, until the fire and campsite chatter were far enough away that no one would overhear us. He looked up through a break in the branches. There were long stringy clouds over the moon.

'Lace on the moon,' he said before I could. And when the wind moved the clouds out of the way he added, 'You remember the first time we saw that?'

I nodded and smiled. 'Of course. You showed me in 1604, during *carnevale* in Venice.'

We both knew lace on the moon was a harbinger of change – something was coming.

Rhode took a step towards me but this time I stepped back, unsure of his intentions. 'Now you fear me?' he asked.

'I could never fear you,' I whispered.

What if I can never forgive her? Rhode had said.

The hurt from his words churned in my stomach again. I wanted to ask if he had, in fact, forgiven me. If he had found a way to see past my horrible actions and manipulations as a vampire.

'If you don't fear me,' he said, drawing my eyes to his, 'then open your hand.' And I held up my palm as though for his heart.

The contents of a tiny black velvet bag spilled out.

Anam Cara.

I didn't look up at Rhode – not yet. My heart pounded deep inside my chest. My fingers curled around two small objects. Gold. They felt cool to the touch. I looked down. My mother's earrings. He had saved them from the fire.

'Lenah?' Justin's voice interrupted, echoing towards us. 'Come back! Food's ready!'

I looked back up at Rhode. 'Happy birthday,' he murmured. His quiet, forlorn expression drew me in, but he couldn't look at me for more than a few seconds.

'Rhode . . .' I said, and reached out towards him. He backed up a couple of steps.

I drew in a breath as tears stung my eyes. I so badly wanted to touch him it made my teeth ache. The pain of wanting him ran down through my arms, into my fingers – it radiated deep into my soul.

'They were all I could bring back. I only had a few moments. I jumped out of your bedroom window. Punched out the glass.'

I recalled my dream, remembering his fist propelling into the mirror, sending it into a thousand fragments of light.

'I used a chair first,' he clarified.

His eyes searched my face. His brow furrowed so a line settled deep between his eyes. Blue. The ocean. The sky. The love of my life.

'Happy seventeenth birthday,' he said quickly, and turned on his heel.

He set off quickly through the wood back in the direction of Main Street.

'Wait,' I called quietly after him.

He turned, highlighted only by the faint moonlight filtering through the clouds, before he moved on further into the woods. Pain stabbed in my chest deeper than I ever thought it could.

'Rhode, you'll get lost,' I called after him, my voice cracking. 'It's dangerous.' He looked up at the sky, at the stars and the lace on the moon.

'Who taught you how to use the movement of the constellations to find your way?' he asked, but by now he was just a black silhouette. I wanted to walk by his side, go home with him, talk and touch him – skin on skin.

I wanted someone to hold me and tell me it would be all right. To assure me that the sun, moon and stars were not governed by invisible forces. I wanted to believe that I was free and had a will of my own. But in the depths of these thoughts I knew the truth – Rhode and I were not free and never would be.

And he could not love me any more.

I watched him weave his way through the shadowy forest until he was indistinguishable from the trees. I knew Vicken would patrol all night. Rhode might too. And maybe it was selfish of me, but I stood in those woods with the ghosts of my past resting in two earrings lying in the palm of my hand.

With a heavy sigh I walked back towards the party, listening to the leaves crunching under my feet. I saw that most of the senior class had come to the camping ground. There were a lot more red cups and many more people milling about.

I stood at the entrance to the path where Rhode had led me into the woods. I looked back, knowing he was gone – but knowing that the spot where he placed the earrings in my hands would always be ours.

'Happy birthday to you . . .' a group of people sang together.

A tiny candle bobbed in the darkness towards me. Justin handed it to Claudia, who walked towards me with Tracy. They were carrying an extravagantly decorated cupcake. Chocolate frosting twisted and turned in a decadent swirl and in the centre of it a small candle flamed.

Justin sang the loudest of them all, and I wished – oh how I wished – that Tony was there.

The candle flickered and I met Justin's eyes above the little flame.

'Well,' he said, leaning close to my ear, 'make a wish.'

'A wish?' I said, looking into his eyes. 'What do I wish?'

'Anything you want,' he said, nuzzling close to my neck. My body reacted with goosebumps rippling over my skin. 'Any wish for your birthday.'

I closed my eyes, blew out the candle and made a wish.

I wish first for our safety. All of us – Vicken, Rhode, Justin and me. And for Wickham. But my heart wants the hurt to go away. I wish for someone to tell me I am all right. That who I am and what I did is forgiven.

As I opened my eyes, the wish still swirling in my mind, Justin's happy expression shone back at me from behind the flickering candle. He really did throw this party just for me.

'Happy birthday,' he said. He took my hand, running his fingers over my skin.

Someone placed a cup in my other hand. I took a sip and the slick tangy peach liquor slipped down my throat. Still holding my hand, Justin drew me around the side of his car. He had set up a small tent next to it. He took my drink and placed it on the ground, then brought his hands up and cupped my face. With thoughts of Rhode and the earrings still pulsating in my mind, I wasn't sure what to do. And if Vicken was walking the perimeter, he could see us.

'I know you love Rhode. You've loved him for six hundred years,' Justin said. His body heat warmed me. 'I can't compete with that.'

'What?' I barely whispered. His words were so true that they took my breath away.

In the dark, Justin's expression was ferocious. He leaned forward and whispered in my ear, in a low growl, 'But he has no idea who you are as a human. Not like me.'

'Justin . . .' I said, surprise rolling over me, down my back to my toes.

'No,' he said, and he cupped a hand behind my head. 'I want to be the one to show you what it's like to survive a ritual, Lenah. What it means to live. He doesn't know you like I do.' His sincerity pierced me. He meant it and I could feel it in the locked gaze. 'Let me in, Lenah,' he said, and the intensity was in the rush of his words and the tightness of his jaw. 'Let me in,' he said, his voice husky.

He brought my face close to his and leaned in for a kiss. He groaned as though he was hungry. My shoulders relaxed. My chest released. Because I wanted touch, I wanted warmth, I wanted what I could not have when I was a vampire. He pulled away and we both took a breath. *Wow – I did love his kiss.* As he pulled away, I saw the silver rune at the base of his throat.

I had to try to make sense of everything. Make sense of you.

I relived that moment in Justin's bedroom when he had delicately cleaned my collarbone wound. I touched the pendant lightly with my fingertips.

He put an arm around me, pulling me close. I could feel passion emanating from him. 'I need you,' Justin said. His eyes were fierce and he didn't move. 'So whatever you did with that ritual doesn't matter to me. I want . . .'

Claudia appeared around the side of the tent. She wasn't alone, I realized. Tracy stood behind her, looking unamused. As if she had been forced to be there.

'Come on, Justin, you can't keep Lenah all to yourself tonight.' She grabbed my hand, and with a tug I was back at the party around the campfire. Throughout the rest of the night I danced, drank peach schnapps and melted into the warmth of Justin's embrace.

Justin kept my arm in his, parading us around the party as though we were royalty. I didn't fear the woods. I didn't fear the vampires. The presence of so many other Wickham students helped to ensure my safety. They were grieving for Tony and Kate and Ms Tate and trying to forget the violence. I was revelling in the humanness of it all. I let Justin's hold ground me. When we were touching, skin on skin, I knew which version of Lenah Beaudonte I was meant to be. I could smile. I could be human.

There were no strange smells of apples. I was not a crazed vampire who could not be forgiven. I had already been forgiven. I was just a seventeen-year-old girl celebrating her birthday. We leaned our backs against a large oak tree and watched as a small circle formed. Claudia danced in the middle of it, shaking her body and laughing with some of the other senior girls. Tracy stood on the outside, watching. She did not smile, at least not

234

like everyone else. Her smile was just a lazy lift of the left side of her mouth.

As the night went on, Rhode's gesture in giving me the earrings was easier to forget. They sat deep in my pocket where I need not touch them. I could wrap my fingers around Justin's skin instead.

Hour by hour.

Sip by sip.

It didn't really matter at all . . . did it? So easy to forget on a warm night with friends. With Justin and his soft touch. He whispered words in my ear.

I missed you so much.

Don't go back to campus.

Words like this led to . . .

Justin's arms around me.

A sleeping bag . . .

Inside a tent.

In the darkness of my closed eyes were blue hydrangeas, whose petals were the symbols of love and hope. Love and hope. Love and hope.

'I love you,' the deep voice said. As in the listening room, this voice had no British accent. Justin whispered my name again and again . . . until we slept.

CHAPTER 16

My head was filled with sand. *What an odd sensation.* I was aware it was on a pillow. I squinted an eye open – too bright. *That hurt!* Was this a demon light to cause so much pain? I'd heard that a demon hell was so bright it left a normal creature blinded.

Birds don't chirp in demon hells.

I would just sleep; I was warm. Was I in my bed? I inhaled deeply: the woody ash of a campfire. Oh, right. I was at Lovers Bay camping ground. I dared to peep out.

The sun filtered through a blue vinyl ceiling, making the sleeping bag I lay in very warm.

I was in Justin's tent.

He lay asleep next to me, on his back and his face angled towards me. I looked at his beautiful pouted lips and narrow nose. He had a slight stubble on his chin. He adjusted his position in his sleep, moving his arms above his head.

'Lenah . . .' he groaned.

The night's events slammed back into place.

Oh, Lenah, you fool. Worse than a fool. Idiot girl.

Foolish idiot girl. I had to figure out how to get out of the tent without waking him up. Oh *no* – what if Rhode had seen me with Justin? What if Rhode had never left the woods? He was bound to have been watching me, with those vampires milling about.

Calm down, Lenah. Get up slowly. Where is your shirt?

The weight of my blood made my head throb as I tried to get up. *Slowly,* I thought as my backside edged over the cloth of the sleeping bag. I grabbed my clothes that were lying next to the sleeping bag. A wave of nausea overwhelmed me. Not because I regretted spending the night in Justin's tent.

Because a part of me *didn't* regret it.

I watched him sleep for a moment. The silver rune necklace lay around his neck, shining in the early-morning light.

I don't know, he had said about the necklace. *I had to try to make sense of everything. Make sense of you.*

He had sought out that knowledge rune so he could understand me and supernatural power. But what had happened last night was not supernatural. I needed him to touch me, to remind me what it felt like to be mortal. To know that even I could be forgiven. Forgiven by Justin, who had been so angry with me. Who had found a way to let me in.

I scooted out of the tent as quietly as I could. I peered around, but a large bush hid me from the rest of the camping ground. I quickly slipped into my clothes.

We were far back in the woods, but I could see Justin's SUV near the remains of the campfire. Small silent tents dotted the campsite in a circle and remnants of marshmallow bags and party cups littered the ground.

I had to get back to Wickham campus, and it looked as if I would have to do it alone. Somehow I would have to explain to the security guards why I didn't have a buddy to sign on to campus. I knew I shouldn't be walking alone, but I would have to risk it.

Fully dressed, with a tip-tap of my toes on the crunchy grass, I headed for the woods, hesitating when I heard rustling in the tent. Justin must have been waking up.

I set off towards the pathway that led out of the camping ground, surveying my options. I did not dare walk across the camping ground, where Claudia and Tracy slept. I took a few steps towards the campsite exit but stopped.

A figure clad in black stepped out of the woods and on to the pathway in front of me. My heart stopped. I drew in a shallow breath. And another. The figure had dark hair and a tall frame, but he stood in the shadows of a large tree and I could not

238

make out more. The morning light only touched the treetops. He took another step and my throat constricted at the sight. A vampire? I could run into the woods, perhaps lose him that way. I could make a ruckus in the camping ground, wake everyone up.

Wait.

This vampire was smoking a cigarette.

Vicken.

I stuck my hands deep into my pockets as I finally crossed out of the camping ground and into Main Street.

'You are monstrously stupid. Do you know that?' Vicken said. 'I don't need my ESP. I was told by that Claudia girl not to disturb you. I slept with my back against a bloody tree just to get away from her.'

'Vicken . . .' I said. My tone was an apology; as we walked back to school our strides matched.

In the warmth of the pocket of my jeans, my mother's earrings, in their little black bag, bit at my fingertips. My peach-schnapps headache ebbed as I kept walking. The sunrise kissed the buildings on Main Street.

'I was supposed to protect you,' Vicken said in a low voice.

'Spare me,' I said as a tingle of guilt spread from the pit of my stomach to my face. We kept walking, faster and faster, in that early-morning light. Up Main Street, past the shops and market until we were at the campus gates.

'Names?' the security guard demanded.

Vicken and I showed our IDs and the pedestrian gate opened.

'Vicken,' I said as we walked back on to campus, 'you have to promise me you won't say anything to Rhode.'

'Promise you? He was walking the perimeter too!'

I didn't know what this meant, so I bit at the inside of my cheek. Vicken's dark expression softened.

'Why'd you do it?' he asked.

I didn't answer.

'Never mind, let's just get upstairs. I'm dying for a coffee,' he said.

Step by step, we walked past the security guard of my building and up the staircase. We were almost at my floor when –

Apples again, coming up the stairwell in a nauseating stench. Apples rotting. Apples fermenting in a broken wooden barrel. I could see them in my mind. An image from my past: apples sitting out in the sun too long, brown and leathery.

'No!' I shouted, throwing a palm against the nautical-themed wallpaper of the hallway.

240

Rhode stands in the centre of his room. He lifts the sword from the floor. I see his chest – he breathes rapidly. He then hits the sword on the telescope, sending pieces of black metal into the air. He slams his lamp, and glass shards fly in all directions. His rage . . .

'No!' I yelled, and fell to my knees. Below me a few doors opened with metallic clicks.

'Everything OK up there?' someone yelled.

'We're fine. Fine!' Vicken called back, and I opened my eyes, trying to focus on him. But his wild hair kept coming in and out of my vision of Rhode destroying his room.

I held back a scream of horror. Rhode's anger pulsed through me in a series of heartbeats. I tried to recall the images of Rhode, close my eyes and see him. His anger rushed through me as tiny sparks exploded in my body.

He *knew* I had been with Justin in that tent.

'What did you see?' Vicken asked, and it was only then that I realized he was holding my hand. 'That was another vision of Rhode, wasn't it?'

'He's angry,' I said. 'He definitely saw me last night.'

Vicken pulled me up. I could smell pine on his clothes and tobacco on his skin and his breath. No apples . . . luckily.

Somehow, the last set of stairs seemed impossibly

hard to climb. But I managed them. Once in my apartment, I would shut the door, go into my bedroom and crawl under the covers.

Do you forgive me? I had asked Justin. He had said yes. But now I realized I was asking the wrong person.

I'd hoped as Justin touched my salty tears that he hadn't realized I was crying because I wished he had been Rhode. Shouldn't I have been happy to be touching someone who cared so much for me? Exhilarated, just like last year, when we were together and I was overjoyed and happy to feel loved?

'If you keep gasping without telling me what's going on, I'll lock you up until you do,' said Vicken.

'It's just about last night,' I replied, and reached out to grasp the doorknob. My fingers gripped the metal.

Searing pain radiated up and down my body. My gut wrenched in a knot so tight that I doubled over. My knees hit the cheap carpeting and the hard fabric raked my skin through my jeans. I placed a palm on the floor, saliva whooshing into my mouth.

The barrier spell *worked*!

'You used to be able to drink pints and pints of blood. You were a powerful vampire queen. This is ridiculous,' Vicken said.

He lifted a hand to open the door.

'No! No!' I cried, and raised my hand. It felt like a dead weight and I pressed it back on to the floor. 'The barrier spell has ignited,' I said. This sickness was the mortal reaction to powerful magic.

It meant that a vampire had tried to break into my room. If it was Odette, she would be a pile of ash on the floor. The spell would have killed any supernatural intruder instantly.

Vicken sat back on his heels and stared at the door, his eyes wide in shock. 'Guess she found out the ritual you gave her's a fake,' he said.

The magic of the barrier spell meant all the herbs I scattered had ignited, sending energy about the room. That energy made us, now mere mortals, ill. I reached a palm up and hesitated in front of the door. I had to see if it was hot or cold. If it was hot, the spell was recent; cold and it had occurred some hours earlier.

Almost simultaneously, Vicken and placed our palms against the door. His knuckles whitened and then his hand dropped, hitting his thigh.

'Hot,' he said, and his tone was grave. 'They must have just tried.'

My fingertips zinged as I also dropped my hand from the door. The energy of the spell sent shocks of electricity up my arms. Vicken clenched and unclenched his hands. I grabbed on to him to help me stand. He stood up too. I hesitated, holding the key before the door. Then I slid the key in the lock, turned it and the doorknob, and the latch clicked.

'*Hunc locum bonis ominibus prosequi,*' I said, *Bless this space* in Latin. My hands still tingled as though they had fallen asleep. I kept squeezing them into fists.

'Let's go in,' Vicken said. The door creaked open slowly. We stood there a moment – waiting. A weird white noise echoed, as though hundreds of people were screaming from the end of a long tunnel. These were the reverberations of the vampire's screams.

Tiny specks of grey ash now lined the perimeter of the living room where the herbs had been.

In the centre of the room was a collection of sooty grey ash.

I walked towards it but something caught my eye. The door to the balcony was open. Someone was moving out there. It took me a moment to recognize her. Odette rolled on to her side so her blonde curls fell over her face. She appeared to be struggling to her feet.

I jumped over the pile of ash to the balcony door, but Odette was already standing. Vicken pushed past me and shoved Odette so she fell. She sat down abruptly, and I saw she was hurt. Her arm was covered in blood, her fingers raw and nails cracked. Perfect – she was injured. Perhaps we could beat her while her guard was down. Vicken reached into his boot for a dagger, but Odette rocked on to her back and kicked out, sending him backwards.

Why, now of all times, had Rhode taken the sword?

Odette ran to the edge of my balcony.

'Go!' I yelled, and pushed Vicken towards her.

But she was much too fast. Like her strength, Odette's speed outmatched that of any normal vampire. I made it to the stone ledge of the balcony, threw out my hands and tried to grasp on to a leg of her trousers. The fabric grazed my fingers as she shot into the air.

She landed on the roof of the building next to mine. I expected her to fall cat-like, on her feet, as I had seen her do every other time. But she stumbled, her arms windmilling to keep her balance until she dropped to her knees.

Vicken lifted a leg to step on to the ledge of the balcony. He was going to try to jump!

As a human, there was no way Vicken would make it without serious injury. I grasped on to his arm, heaving him back on to the balcony. We fell together on to the tiles.

'No,' I said breathlessly. Our eyes met. 'I will not lose you again.'

He held my gaze for a moment, and the fight in his eyes softened. He sighed and pulled me up. We stood together by the ledge for a moment.

'Let's go down,' I said, pulling Vicken by his shirtsleeve. I intended to meet Odette at ground level. Two against one, we maybe had a chance. If she didn't outrun us first.

'Wait . . .' said Vicken darkly.

Odette pressed herself up from the roof, but her arms gave out and her elbows hit the ground.

'What the . . . ?' Vicken said. 'Look!'

She heaved again and this time got upright. She went over to the edge of the building and raised her arms above her head. I gripped Vicken's forearm in anticipation as Odette jumped off the roof and ran away into the darkness.

'Wow! How the hell did she do that?' asked Vicken.

'And her arms,' I whispered. 'She healed instantly. Did you see them when she lifted them above her head? They weren't bloody any more.'

'I'm more concerned that she can get on campus,' Vicken replied. 'She did it before October too. The protection of the ritual is over.'

The ash of the vampire who did not make it out

of my apartment sat in a small pile, directly in the centre of the room.

But, for Odette, her cracked and bloody wounds had healed in minutes. No vampire I had ever known could heal that quickly. But, then again, everything I knew about vampires was being tested by Odette.

We went back inside my apartment and Vicken bent over the ash of the dead vampire. He squatted down and pulled out a thick silver watch from the centre of the pile. It dangled on the end of his finger.

'A man's watch,' Vicken said. 'Odette's ruthless,' he continued. 'She sacrificed a member of her coven. She knew you would raise a barrier.'

As I surveyed the charred herbs around the perimeter of the room, I could sense that the energy in that room had changed. Any supernatural creature who entered would know that the barrier spell had protected me. That was why Odette had been injured. The first vampire had probably been incinerated by walking into the space. Only Odette's fingers and forearm had made it into my apartment before she'd realized what was happening.

Either way, it was now my space, sacred and holy. Just like Rhode always said . . . energy leaves an indelible mark. With the smell of the campfire in my hair, and the pulsating images of Rhode smashing his room, I knew what I must do. We needed help. We needed protection. I couldn't let Odette and her minions dominate us any more.

I turned from the doorway.

'I'm going to perform a summoning spell,' I said to Vicken. 'I'm not going to wait and let her control me.'

'Oh, *really*,' he said, his tone laced with sarcasm.

'Despite what you may think, Rhode is losing his mind and I need your help. Especially now that Odette can come on campus.'

'Do you want me to bow, or will an *all right* suffice?' He lifted an eyebrow and leaned a shoulder on the wall.

'We're calling Suleen, and we're doing it at sunrise.'

Vicken didn't respond, but he kept looking at me with that same smug expression: one eyebrow raised and an unlit cigarette dangling from his mouth.

'You're not going to fight me on this?' I said, disbelieving.

'I'm not going to win, am I? You did the barrier spell. I didn't think *that* would work and it did.'

'Let's try it at sunrise. When the moon and the sun share the same sky. It's the most spiritual time of the day.'

'Should I call you *ma'am?*'

'Stop it,' I said.

'How about *mistress?* Or *goddess?*'

'She's lost a member of her coven; there are only four now,' I said. 'And we know she heals quickly. At least we know those things.'

'That's not all we know, love,' Vicken added, and lit the cigarette. He inhaled deeply then on his exhale said, 'We uncovered something else of the utmost importance this morning.'

'What's that?' I asked.

'She fell when she hit that roof. She's weakened when she bleeds.'

If Odette was weakened when she bled, then we would have to bleed her to fight her, eventually stabbing her in the heart. It would be the only way to kill her. In the meantime, we needed help.

We wasted no time.

Before dawn the next morning, I was resting my head against the passenger seat of my tiny blue car, my eyes closed, my hair whipping back and forth from the breeze. If it wasn't for the sound of the motor, we could have been in a fast-moving carriage – but we weren't. Vicken was driving, and with a sharp turn and another rev I was thrown against the door. I clutched on to the armrest and opened my eyes. When we pulled on to Lovers Bay beach, the moon hung over the harbour, creating wavy lines of grey-blue light. Soon the sun would rise. I could feel it in my heart, in my bones. Perhaps, like a sixth sense, I would always be able to perceive the sun and its power. Its danger.

We sat in the quiet and looked out at the water.

'She's getting her strength from somewhere,' I said, staring out at the ocean. 'A spell or something. That's the only way her skin can regenerate so fast.'

'Let's not worry about that,' Vicken said. 'Just focus on the spell.'

'We need all four elements represented.' Even as I said it, the Aeris came to my mind. Especially Fire and her crackling hair.

I reached into the back seat for our supplies and the spell book, which were all in my special spell bag. We got out of the car, and when I stepped on to the small beach, my boots sunk into the soft sand. Stars twinkled above us in the hazy light. This time of the morning was called *the Line*. Vampires consider it holy. A time for spells, when the world is unsure of itself; no longer night, not quite morning . . .

I checked the area immediately in front of the parking lot.

'Let's go down there, out of sight,' I said, wanting to be far away from any common human's eye. 'We need that driftwood over there. We can stack it by the shore.' I pointed to a stand of three trees at whose base was stacked a pile old wood, weathered from the seasons.

'You sure are bossy for someone who's most likely going to kill us both with this spell,' muttered Vicken.

As I walked to the shore to acquire what else we would need, Vicken got some of the wood. I stood at the water's edge and watched the tiny ripples lap on to the rocky sand. This spell would act as a beacon – a calling. A vampire as powerful as Suleen, if he did not want to be contacted, could avoid it. But if this wasn't a time of need, then I didn't know what was. I reached into the warmth of my spell bag and unearthed a small empty jar. I scooped up some of the bay water and walked back to Vicken, standing above the driftwood pile.

Jasmine was crucial for the success of a summoning spell. From the bag I took out a tiny box of amber resin, some jasmine and matches, then handed the jar of bay water to Vicken. As his fingertips touched mine, I smiled slightly, looking at my old friend. Our love, the one between Vicken and me, whatever it had been a hundred and sixty years ago, was over now, replaced by the love of friendship.

'Let's just do this before Odette decides to show up,' Vicken said with a sigh. 'I'm all itchy. I hate anticipation – it's thoroughly human.'

'You should begin the spell. You were the last one connected to the supernatural world,' I said to Vicken. I meant that he was the last to be turned human by the ritual.

I reached into the bag and pulled out the heavy leather-covered book of spells. My boots sank deeper into the sand as I stepped forward and handed it to Vicken. The gold print of its title, *Incantato*, glinted as the morning sunrise crested the horizon, out at sea. He opened the book to the page marked with a small red ribbon, looked from the spell to me and said, 'Ready?'

Draw a door in the sand . . . said a voice from my memory. *I had almost forgotten.* Once, long ago, Rhode told me he had performed a summoning spell. I surveyed the stack of driftwood and the area around it. When I stepped back from the pile, I placed my finger in the cool sand and drew the distinct outline of a door around the firewood. I met Vicken's gaze for reassurance and said what Rhode told me all those years ago.

'As long as there have been doors, there have

been summoning spells – entryways, passages,' I said, backing away from the door.

'So we summon Suleen and he helps us with these vampires?' Vicken said.

And Rhode.

'That's the plan,' I said, and lit a match so it flared between my fingers.

I flicked the match and it flew in a wide arc through the air and on to the driftwood pile. Sparked by the flame and the supernatural ingredients, the wood hissed and smoke rose up to the sky. I opened the resin box and took a pinch of amber between my thumb and index finger and sprinkled it over the fire. Tiny orange flames flickered and hissed.

'Begin,' I commanded gently.

Vicken looked down at the book.

In Latin he announced, *I call on you, Suleen. I summon you to appear before me in this sacred space.*

I bent down, took the jar and unscrewed the top. I sprinkled the saltwater so the fire hissed and crackled. The water slid over my hands, dropping in tiny pearls to the flames. There was an unnatural crackle and the flames burst up. I pulled back in surprise.

'Wow,' I said. 'That was powerful.'

Were the flames meant to jump in the air like that?

I knelt down and with my arm fully extended

took a handful of sand in my fist. I sprinkled the sand over the burning driftwood.

Vicken didn't need to hand me the book. I remembered this spell.

'I give you the earth and the water. I call to you, Suleen.'

'Lenah . . .' Vicken started to say in a warning tone. He too had noticed the growing flames. I ignored him, keeping my energy and my intentions constant.

'I summon you, Suleen, to come to us in a time of need.' I dropped the jasmine flowers into the orange flames. The outline of the door I drew in the sand glowed a bright blue like the morning sky. Was it working? I needed to help Rhode. Needed to stop him smashing mirrors and performing ceremonial rituals of the Order of the Garter at my best friend's grave. I wanted to stop him feeling the pain of seeing me with Justin. I felt a surge of need – someone *had* to come and help us.

'I summon you!' I screamed. 'I call on you, Suleen!'

A blast of orange flames!

The driftwood exploded with a surge of energy like an inferno. It threw me into the air and I flew back, landing on the sand. And then . . .

My arm.

Red-hot flames crawled up to my elbow.

'Damn it,' Vicken cried, and scooped handfuls of sand on to the flames. I rolled on to my back and sat up just as the flames extinguished. Swaying back and forth, only then did I realize that my wrist was badly burned and I was screaming. I hadn't heard my own terror. I drew in a deep breath. Those flames had come from nowhere. They shouldn't have grown to that height. Vicken grabbed the spell book, then dragged me up the slope towards the car, though my feet kept slipping in the sand. I glanced back at the door that I had drawn in the sand and at the now barely smoking driftwood.

The door. The door was gone!

'What happened?' I grimaced as my arm throbbed. 'Has it failed?' I groaned in pain. Vicken opened the passenger door and I slid on to the seat.

We were soon out on the road but the bumps made my stomach churn.

'Where's the hospital?!' Vicken yelled, panic rising in his voice.

'Infirmary. Go to the infirmary at Wickham. I need to be near my room. The barrier spell,' I yelled, not daring to touch my forearm. 'If we called anyone with the spell, we need to be in a safe place.'

My skin seared – I wanted to plunge it into ice. I leaned my forehead on the glass, hoping to cool the pain. We ripped around corners, but Vicken was driving fast and every time he turned a corner it made my arm throb.

'It's best you don't look at it, love,' he said. 'It's not having its best moment.'

We turned a corner quickly and my shoulder hit the glass, sending pain down my arm.

'This was your great idea!' Vicken yelled. 'Summoning Suleen. Using elemental magic to call him too. Who told you not to meddle? Fire, the element herself, told you not to meddle. But no! Lenah Beaudonte won't listen to the bloody Aeris!'

'Can you keep your criticisms to yourself, please?' I hissed, gripping my hands together even tighter to support my burnt wrist. I shouldn't have looked but I did and my stomach lurched. The skin had bubbled – a red raw blistering mess. Just when I thought I couldn't take the movement any more, we pulled through the Wickham gates, waved through by the security guard, who recognized us. It was busy for a Saturday morning. Even with the weekday students gone, dozens of people were out in the grounds, studying or relaxing. We screeched to a halt. Vicken ran to the side of the car, opened the door and the pressure of his arm around my shoulder comforted me as he helped me to stand. Voices. Pain in my arm . . . so many voices.

Lenah!

Are you OK?

Someone get Justin!

In a messy shuffle, Vicken and I made it to the infirmary door. I was sure my legs would give out. I wanted to scream, I wanted to cry. I hated pain. This pain was so intense that I was sure my arm was going to be scarred for life.

Vicken threw the infirmary door open. We stumbled inside even though I could barely stand. A nurse popped up from behind her counter; she yelled for the doctor. I leaned on Vicken, grasping my arm. I couldn't help it; tears bit at my eyes. The burning of my arm and the waves of pain overtook me. I finally understood the human relief at seeing a doctor as a woman in a white coat ran into the foyer and towards me.

I fell into the doctor's arms and vomited on the floor.

CHAPTER 17

'How did you manage to do this?' Nurse Warner asked about an hour later. Thick white gauze was wrapped around my arm from my wrist almost to my elbow.

'I was cooking on a campfire,' I replied. A blatant but necessary lie.

Why had the spell failed? I wondered again.

'Well, you were lucky, young lady,' said the nurse. 'An open flame can result in third-degree burns. These are bad second degree. From now on, eat at the union.'

'Look at it this way . . .' Vicken said as he leaned against the wall across from my bed. He had not left my side. 'Now you're in the club.' He pointed to his eye, which had almost healed, the skin now tinged just faintly yellow. Rhode's battered face flickered through my mind.

'Lenah?' Justin's voice reached me from around the corner. He burst into the room and came to the side of the bed. 'What the hell happened to you?' he asked. 'You left this morning before I could—'

'Only a few minutes, Justin . . .' Nurse Warner said with a lift of her eyebrows. 'We can't have a zoo in here.'

'Yes, ma'am,' he replied. He took my good hand into his own and kissed my fingers.

'This is making me sick,' Vicken said, rolling his eyes.

Justin shot Vicken a murderous look just before the nurse walked out. 'I'll be right back with some pain meds, Lenah,' she said.

Once she was gone, Justin asked, 'Was it Odette?'

Vicken frowned but didn't say anything.

'Not Odette. Vicken and I attempted a summoning spell,' I said.

'Summoning?'

'To call Suleen,' I explained.

'Guess it didn't go too well, then?' he asked.

'Yeah, guess not, mate,' Vicken said, pushing away from the wall. I slid off the bed, and when my feet touched the ground Vicken held the fingers of my burnt arm and Justin held my other arm. I sighed, just wanting to lie down. Nurse Warner came back in, examining the label on the small brown bottle she held between her fingers.

'Vicken, you should take Lenah back to her room,' she said, and looked up. Her eyes travelled back and forth between Justin and Vicken. 'Or

Justin should. You guys figure it out.'

'Justin needs to hurry back to his lacrosse practice,' Vicken said with a smirk.

'Stop it,' I hissed at him.

Nurse Warner handed the pill bottle to Vicken. 'The instructions are on the bottle, Lenah. I suggest you follow them.'

'How about I bring you some dinner tonight?' Justin asked, letting go of me as Vicken led me to the door.

'Great,' I said. 'That sounds perfect.'

As the three of us walked out of the treatment room, I kept glancing at the door of the infirmary, waiting for Rhode to walk through.

No, Lenah. This is how it's supposed to be. Justin is here for you. Not Rhode.

'You must keep this covered. Come back on Friday and we'll unwrap it and see how the burn is doing,' said Nurse Warner, following us through the door.

'I'll bring her,' Justin said, glaring at Vicken.

They made me take a pain pill before leaving the infirmary. They said it would make me sleepy. Justin kissed me again before Vicken led me down the pathway towards Seeker.

Sleep would be good, I thought as Vicken prattled on and on about how much he loathed Justin.

Sleep, I thought again.

Sleep would keep me from wondering why Suleen had not come to save us. Sleep might lead to dreams that might explain why the spell had backfired. Why, after all this, Suleen had not come to save Rhode.

'Now, remember, when you shower you have to wrap that gauze, cover it with a plastic bag to keep it dry. Are you even listening to me?' Vicken asked.

I lay back on the couch, looking up at the ceiling fan. Round and round it went. The blades. What happened to them? The spinning made them smear across the ceiling.

'Who painted the ceiling?' I asked in a daze.

Vicken looked up at the ceiling and then down at me. He raised an eyebrow.

'Why didn't he come? Why didn't Suleen come to me?' I asked. 'Is it because Rhode doesn't forgive me? Did I tell you that? He thinks after all my unspeakable evil acts, my soul is black.'

'He said this to you?' Vicken asked.

'No, not exactly.' My eyelids kept slipping over my eyes, again and again. *My, they were heavy.*

'OK . . . time for you to sleep,' said Vicken. 'I think those painkillers are finally taking effect.'

'I love sleeping,' I replied dozily. 'Do you think

we'll die? That Odette will kill us?'

'Oh, good,' Vicken said with a sigh. He pulled a blanket over me, tucking it around my body, a familiar gesture now. 'Let's discuss this now, or maybe we should wait till you're in your right mind.'

'Right mind?'

'I have to run,' he said. 'But I'll come check on you later. Don't perform any more spells.'

Spells, I thought as I watched the ceiling fan again. *Spells that don't work. Spells where I am hurt.* Slowly . . . I fell asleep.

I stand in the centre of the gymnasium, alone. It's decorated with shining white stars and snowflakes covered in glittering sparkles. This is familiar. The room is decorated just like at the winter ball last year. I look down and touch the silk of a long gown. I'm wearing my gown from the dance! Above me, the ceiling lights flash blue and red, over and over, reflected on the floor. The DJ plays a slow song, but no one mans the booth. The music is loud here, vibrating on the empty wooden floor.

Where is everyone? I go to take a step but I pull my foot back – what is that? I almost stepped on something. A necklace? I look down and pick up a leather strap. Hanging on it is Justin's rune pendant. I look around. He wouldn't have lost it so easily. Not after everything he told me. He has to have this back.

'Justin!?' I call out to the empty room, yelling and straining my voice over the music. 'Justin!' I yell again.

'I always loved that dress,' a familiar voice says.

I spin to face the gymnasium doorway.

Tony walks up to me dressed in a tux, looking exactly as he did at the winter prom. Alive and well.

'The girls picked it out,' I say, referring to my dress. Tony stands before me, his hands in his pockets. The familiar gauge earrings and sunny smile are just as the last time I saw him.

'I lost Justin. I can't find him,' I say, looking around the empty gymnasium.

'He'll turn up,' Tony says calmly. 'Do you want to dance with me?'

'Yes,' I smile, and wrap my arms around him.

We spin in that gymnasium, my best friend and me.

'I would give anything to see you again,' I say, taking in the handsome features of his face.

'You will.'

'When?'

He spins me again so my dress twirls out around me. But when I face Tony again Odette is standing before me; we're dressed identically. I gasp, backing away from her. Her hair falls long and straight over her shoulders.

She wipes blood from her mouth and says, 'He tasted the best.'

*

The next morning, dressing, I noticed the scent of tobacco in the air. Vicken must have checked on me during the night. Thinking of him, I dropped a dagger in my boot.

He tasted the best.

Odette's words kept ringing in my ears as I walked out of Seeker and across campus. Yes, Odette could be out in the daylight. But so could I. I had people on this campus who loved me, and people who, if I needed them to, would help me. And after that dream I had to see Tony's portrait. I hadn't wanted to until now. I hadn't been in the art tower since his death, but now it was time.

I walked across campus, inhaling the warm morning air, trying to clear my head. Students called out to me.

Hey, Lenah – how's your arm?

Lenah, what happened?

I tried to shake the haunting memory of the dream away in the bright sunshine, among the crowds of students on campus. Tingles swept up and down my arms, down my legs to my toes. I hated those white pills that made me feel as though I had taken double opiates and absinthe combined, something I remembered from my vampire days. I kept walking, though it was difficult not to grab at my burnt arm; my heart pumped blood into that arm, every pulse sending a throb to my fingers. I squinted into the sun and shielded my eyes with my damaged hand. I continued past the union and the crowded meadow in front of Quartz dorm. For a moment last night my best friend had been alive. How cruel to have him near me again, then taken away in the morning, but I would find comfort from him even in his death. I was going somewhere I could feel close to him and have him around me.

Now that Hopper had finally been reopened, students pressed out of the building holding art easels and thick black portfolios. I looked at their hands, at the paint on their fingers and clothes, and the charcoal under their nails. They reminded me of Tony, with his paint-smeared face and bright smile. I was so absorbed in my thoughts I almost slammed straight into Justin.

'Heads up,' he said, and smiled that lazy, cocky smile. 'I was just coming to your room to check on you. I knocked twice last night but you never answered.'

'Oh,' I said, stalling. 'Those pills really knocked me out. I didn't hear you.'

He took a step towards me. 'I've been worried about you. First with Odette cutting you, then Ms Tate dying, now this summoning spell and you getting burned.'

The intensity of his gaze made me pause. An uncomfortable beat passed between us. It reminded me of the night of my birthday.

'I think I've been cool with this whole thing,' he continued. 'I want to help you. On your birthday, I thought we were . . . I thought you were *with* me.'

'We are,' I said. 'I mean, I am.'

'Good,' Justin said, and caressed my shoulder with one hand.

'Look, can we talk later? I'm just going to go upstairs, to the art tower. And if I don't go now I'll never go. You know what I mean?' I said.

Justin's back stiffened. 'You're going to see the portrait?' he asked.

I nodded in reply.

His eyes widened. With his free hand he reached up to the pendant around his neck and rubbed at it nervously.

'I can't go up there,' he said, and dropped his hand from my shoulder. I could see the twitch of his mouth as he tried to formulate the words. He shook his head and frowned, then met my eyes. Without blinking he said, 'I'm not ready. I didn't think Tony and me were friends, but when he died – and I saw what I saw . . .' His voice trailed off. It was clear he was still wounded by witnessing the horror of Tony's death. Justin and I had got there too late.

'I understand, but I need to do it now,' I said as students continued to file past us out of the door. He took a few steps on to the quad but didn't remove his eyes from mine.

'Come to my room after,' he said. As he walked away, he slung his schoolbag over his shoulder.

'OK,' I said with a small smile. 'I will.'

I glanced around the campus again, surveying the students out enjoying the beautiful day. But I wanted to be in the art tower, even if people were in there working. They didn't have to know what I was doing. There was a quiet thud from the glass door as it closed behind me. Step by step, as I climbed the circling stairs, I breathed deeply, relieved. I actually felt better instead of worse. This *was* what I needed.

As I climbed, I passed a few students coming down the stairs towards the ground floor. They had to turn to the side to avoid hitting me with their portfolios. I climbed higher and higher and stopped at the window I had looked through when I first came to Wickham. My fingers grazed over the familiar stones and I hesitated when I caught sight of Justin walking into Quartz.

I reached the last step and I walked through the doorway – and there it was. There *I* was. Tony had wanted to paint that portrait the whole time I had known him. It was based on a photograph he had taken of me during a snorkelling trip. I looked at myself in paint: a back view from my waist up, my head turned to the side, in profile. My hair was pulled to the side to reveal the tattoo on the back of my shoulder – the motto of my coven: *Evil Be He Who Thinketh Evil.*

I didn't notice her at first, but standing below the painting was Claudia. She was leaning down to zip up a portfolio, and when she stood up she glanced at the portrait and then at me.

'No one's been able to take it down. We just keep putting up our paintings around it.'

'I didn't know you were an artist,' I said.

She pulled her blonde hair back into a ponytail. 'Oh, I'm not,' she said. 'Drawing's my elective.'

Together, she and I looked at my portrait for a moment, at my profile and the curve of my smile.

'I feel like I'm looking at myself in a different time. A different life.'

'Lenah, you're seventeen. You don't have to be so dramatic,' she said.

'You're right,' I said, just as there was the thud of a heavy door slamming.

'Did the . . . ?' Claudia started to ask but there was no need. I knew immediately.

The door to the art tower was ancient and wooden. It was *always* open. Now someone had closed it. Claudia and I turned to look.

Odette.

A flood of horror flashed through me, but then it was immediately replaced by something else. My cheeks burned. Anger exploded within my stomach, along with the familiar determination I had once felt as a vampire queen.

Odette's perfectly coifed hair fell in delicate ringlets. Her dark green eyes locked on me as a wide smile stretched across her face. How dare she stand before me? Here. I could almost feel the vampire queen within me baring her fangs.

'Claudia, get behind me,' I commanded, and Claudia hid behind my back. I could feel small breaths on my neck.

'You see, I do not fear humans any more,' Odette said. 'I could outrun any of them now.'

'You should fear me,' I replied.

Her eyes floated up to my portrait. 'It's lovely, isn't it?' she smiled. 'Such a shame about the boy.'

Claudia let out a tiny cry.

'Did you think I wouldn't know?' Odette said. Her tone was clipped. She meant the ritual.

'Actually, yes,' I said. 'I don't think you're very smart.'

Odette looked like a statue. She stood with her

legs slightly apart. She was stunning in her jeans and red top.

'Lenah . . .' Claudia whispered. 'Who is this?'

'Shhh,' I said, not removing my eyes from Odette's.

'You don't think I actually tried that ridiculous fake spell, do you?' Odette asked.

'Yes,' I answered. 'I think you did try it. I think you believed me to be so stupid as to give you the real one.'

Stay strong, Lenah.

Odette walked around the circumference of the room and stopped directly below my portrait. I grasped Claudia's wrist, keeping her behind me as I turned to watch Odette. Her thin fingers pressed against mine.

If I could made Odette bleed, we would have time to try to pull the door open. I just had to weaken her and stall for time.

Keep talking.

'You tried that spell days after you received it, didn't you?' I smirked. 'You sent your men on errands to find the ridiculously rare items I placed on that list. Black crystal from the African coast!'

Odette stepped on to a small stool near the wall. She raised one hand and made a claw. She rose on her tiptoes so her hand now hovered in front of my image.

There was a horrible ripping sound as Odette scratched her talons down the centre of my portrait. It felt as though she was ripping me in half as I watched shreds of Tony's painting fall like feathers to the floor.

'What's happening?' shrieked Claudia.

I clenched my teeth.

Odette climbed down and started to walk again. I kept hold of Claudia's wrist and moved us away from her. We circled each other for a few moments.

We had no choice but to keep our distance. My fingertips grazed the wood of the door as we passed by. Claudia was trembling and her body vibrated against mine every time she shuddered. There, beneath the painting, were cubbies and I could see a box of craft knives. Perfect! Stabbing her in the heart with so small a blade probably wouldn't kill her but maybe it would buy me some time. And if we could get the door open we could get out of the art tower.

'Claudia,' I hissed, 'try to open the door.'

Odette stopped her slow pursuit and instead marched directly across the room. In a blink, she had wrapped her fingers around my neck and lifted me. The back of my head hit the wall of wooden

271

cubbies. Odette's nails dug into my throat and a hot pain erupted where she had pierced the skin.

My hands clawed behind me for the cubbies, raking through the air for one of the knives I could see. I couldn't grab one. I wanted to open my mouth, croak to Claudia to hand them to me, but Claudia had backed away to the door, her mouth hanging open. Odette held me up by my throat even tighter than she had in the dressing room. I raised my knees towards my chest and kicked my feet out, directly into Odette's stomach. She stumbled backwards and threw her arms out. She quickly regained her balance but the look of surprise on her face was a small victory.

My knees hit the ground as I fell forward. I was no fool – I had learned self-defence; I had had my coven member Song teach me defence tactics. Odette would retaliate, and fast. When I tried to lean my body weight on my arm to get up, I collapsed from the pain of the burn.

'Do you know what will happen when I have that ritual? I'll have the most powerful coven in the world,' Odette said, and walked slowly across the room. She was not coming towards me.

Oh no . . .

Claudia was pulling at the door handle and screeching as she heaved and yanked. Her blonde ponytail waved in the air as she tugged on the door, but it was fruitless.

'I wanted to get you without Vicken or Rhode. And I have, but I can't kill you! Doesn't irony enrage you?' Odette shrieked, and slapped her hands against her sides. 'Rhode is *never* alone without a weapon. Stupid mortal. Always travelling with other people or talking to teachers. But you – arrogant Lenah. Choosing to be alone with a human girl.'

Odette grabbed Claudia by yanking on her ponytail, just as she had done to Kate. She then positioned herself so her right arm was clutching Claudia's neck. It reminded me of what she had attempted to do to Vicken at the herb shop. She couldn't kidnap Claudia in the light of day, but she could kill her.

'Lenah . . .' Claudia's chin trembled. Her tear-stained face and confused eyes would haunt me forever. Odette pulled back on Claudia's ponytail, exposing her neck. 'Please, don't,' Claudia's voice warbled.

Please don't. I have a family. I love my life. I don't want to die. I could say those phrases in dozens of languages. They had been said to me so many times.

As Odette bit into Claudia's neck my mouth salivated and a wave of nausea swept over me.

Somewhere deep within me, I desired that metallic taste of blood.

Claudia's knees buckled.

I grabbed on to the shelves on the wall and at last curled my fingers around a bunch of craft knives. I threw myself towards Odette and plunged the blades into her thigh.

There was a sucking sound. Odette lifted her head. Claudia, barely conscious, hung limply in Odette's arms. Odette laughed manically as a trickle of blood dripped from Claudia's neck on to her blouse.

'You think those tiny knives would hurt me?'

Odette moved her hands over Claudia's ears, met my eyes with a smirk and snapped Claudia's neck, sending her to the floor. Her body crumpled instantly. Her limbs hit the floor with a horrible crack.

She lay motionless. Dead.

The knives in my other hand dropped to the floor. My stomach plummeted.

No. She wasn't dead. I wouldn't let it happen. I crawled to Claudia and took her small hand into mine. It lay limp and unmoving, still warm. Her hair fanned out on the floor, feather-like and soft.

'Get up,' Odette said, pulling me by my hair, yanking at my scalp. The knives remained in her leg.

I stood up, Claudia's fingers falling away from mine. Odette held on to a fistful of my hair and snarled in my ear, 'Every day that passes, I'll get stronger and stronger.' She brought her face to mine and I could smell rotting blood. 'I can't wait for Nuit Rouge.' She let go of my head, releasing the tension in my scalp, and walked to a bookcase across from Claudia. 'And because I can't have you if I'm in jail . . .' With a horrific sneer she used both hands to rip the bookcase from the wall and send it crashing to the floor, crushing Claudia's lifeless body.

I shot up, jumping across the room, away from Claudia's body and into the opposite wall.

'You better run,' she said.

With a knowing smile, she pulled the door open as though it weighed no more than a leaf. She cackled at me, drew out the knives from her leg and threw them to the floor.

'Vampire queen,' she scoffed, and descended.

The sand of the Wickham beach made my knees cold. With a shudder, I released my fingers, and the clean knives clinked as they fell in a tiny pile on to the sand. I had to bring them with me. With Claudia dead, I couldn't leave any evidence behind.

I stared at the tiny ridges of sand, knowing that once, not that long ago, I could see their infinitesimal specifics. But I didn't focus, not really. My back shuddered as I drew in breaths. I expected to cry; that would have been a normal human reaction. But there, as I sat on that beach, I could not find the capacity. I just stared at the sand, my whole body shaking.

There was a jingle of keys behind me, then a shuffling of sand as someone walked towards me.

Let it be Odette.

Let her take me away. Let us be done with it.

Out of the corner of my right eye I saw a pair of black combat boots stop next to me. On my left another set of boots, worn down, the front lip of the toe separated from the leather. I looked up at Rhode.

These boots were another small clue that he had lived the year before. That he had been mortal and walked through the world. He fell to his knees but did not touch me.

'Claudia Hawthorne is dead,' Rhode said.

'I ran down the stairs just minutes . . . No.' I said breathlessly. I couldn't stop the air from coming in and out so quickly. I looked at the waves rolling ahead of me. '. . . I ran away mere *seconds* before security ran upstairs.'

'You're better off,' Vicken said. 'It would have been an ugly mess of questioning and the human legal system.' He knelt down on the other side of me. 'The police are already deeming it an accident.'

I shook my head, disbelief rolling over me. It trickled over my shoulders, down my back, all the way to my feet. Vicken held the knives in his hand and inspected them.

'She has unbelievable strength. I don't know how. Not like us,' I said, looking into Rhode's eyes. His eyebrows furrowed, his eyes jumped back and forth between the gauze on my arm and the sand. 'Our strength was never heightened because we were vampires. And she can be out in the light of day with droves of people. She doesn't fear crowds.'

'Come on,' Vicken said, pulling me up by my elbow. 'We should talk about this. But not here, not outside in the open.'

'I agree,' Rhode said, and glanced behind him at the stretch of trees that lined the beach. Anyone could have been hiding in the shadows.

CHAPTER 18

That night the whole school was abuzz with the news of Claudia's death. I was not sure which rumour was more ridiculous: she was killed by a gang that came in to steal tech equipment; the art tower was haunted and a poltergeist killed Claudia; or someone had purposely unbolted the bookcase from its metal fixings so it would fall on her. None of it made sense, though I suppose to a normal human it wouldn't. Extra maintenance had been called in and classes were cancelled for the next two days.

After yet another emergency school meeting, Rhode, Vicken, Justin and I stood in my apartment. Rhode and Vicken stood by the balcony door, arms folded across their chests. Justin sat near me on the couch.

'So someone's gonna tell me what really happened, right?' Justin said, and looked to me for an answer. He rested his elbows on his knees and leaned forward, folding his hands. 'Because I saw

Lenah right before Claudia . . .' He dropped his head for a second. 'Right before I heard.'

'One by one. That's how it's going to go. The moment our guard is down,' I said, looking at Rhode and Vicken with guilt running over me. 'I can't figure out where she's getting this power. Without bleeding her, we have no defence. Especially if she can suck blood so quickly. How *can* she suck blood so quickly?'

My skin was too tight. I wanted to spit. It had been so selfish of me to go to the art tower. No, selfish *and* stupid. She far outpowered me even when I was at the pinnacle of my strength as a vampire. She came to the mall, yes, but she could have snuck inside through a basement, or stayed undercover in a car. There were ways to avoid direct sunlight, but she didn't need to. And she had purposefully sought me out alone. This time she had walked on to a crowded campus. With hundreds of people. She was powerful and becoming more so.

'We need a strategy,' Vicken said.

'We have each other,' I replied.

'We've got shite,' Vicken said flatly. 'Tell him what we did, Lenah.'

'Thank you, Vicken,' I said, hoping he'd caught the sarcasm in my tone.

'Tell me what?' Rhode asked.

I stood up from the couch and crossed my arms over my chest.

'I tried to call Suleen. For help. But it was unsuccessful,' I admitted.

'What do you mean, you tried to call Suleen?' Rhode asked quietly, leaning forward.

Vicken cleared his throat. 'See, we did this summoning spell.'

'You *what*?' Rhode said, pushing off the wall and throwing his hands into the air. 'Vicken – you didn't think it necessary to tell me this?'

'What, he's your spy?' I asked.

'It seemed like it might be useful!' Vicken replied, but he was talking to Rhode.

'Have you no sense at all? It's as if you two were never immortal. I'm surprised she didn't find you while you were performing the bloody spell and stab you both through the heart.'

'Some things are worth trying,' I replied. I kept my arms crossed but leaned against the closed door to my bedroom.

'Like hurting your arm? That's when it happened, isn't it?' Rhode asked. I didn't reply. 'You let her do this?' Rhode said, turning to Vicken.

'Like I could stop her, mate.'

'Suleen can offer us protection,' I explained.

'Don't discuss these things in front of him!'

Rhode said, motioning to Justin. 'He doesn't understand.'

Justin sneered. 'I understand fine.'

Rhode ignored Justin and continued, 'Don't you think I tried myself? I called Suleen after you told me you saw Odette at the herb shop. He did not respond. You made that choice on the archery . . .' He stopped himself and considered what he would say next. He drew a shallow breath. 'No one is coming to help us.'

I had always believed that, out of any of us, Rhode would be able to reach Suleen. After the memories I'd seen, I'd been sure he would come.

'What does Odette want?' Justin asked.

'To be Lenah,' Vicken replied.

'The ritual,' Rhode said to Justin.

'Can't we just give it to her?' Justin asked. 'To avoid any more deaths?'

Vicken laughed cruelly, the sound cutting the air.

'What's the big deal?' Justin asked, looking back and forth from Vicken to me.

'What's the big deal?' Vicken mocked.

Rhode sighed. 'If supernatural creatures pour their intentions into a spell that powerful, it will backfire. The ritual could anoint Odette with unimaginable powers. Could release real evil and

draw entities to Lovers Bay that don't drink blood –
but drink souls,' he explained.

My dream from earlier that month of an
abandoned Wickham and a ruined Lovers Bay
resurfaced in my mind.

There was a palpable silence, then Vicken said,
'It's not like we can barrier spell the entire campus.'

Rhode sighed. 'What shall we do?' he asked, but
it was rhetorical. 'Wear garlic in our hair? Crosses
around our necks?'

'We need Suleen,' I said again. 'Or we could call
the Aeris. They're more powerful than any vampire.'

'We can't call on them,' Rhode growled. 'You
just failed to summon Suleen. Now you wish to call
entities even more powerful?'

'Why not? We have time. Nuit Rouge begins in
just a few weeks. The barrier between our world and
the supernatural world is weakening already.'

'Lenah, you barely got out of that art tower alive,'
Rhode replied.

'So, what, then?' I said. 'Stay locked in our rooms
for the rest of eternity?'

'We need to prepare ourselves,' Rhode replied.
'We know Odette's weakened when she bleeds. We
have to find the right moment to attack in the only
way we have left.'

The only way. Of course . . .

There was a pause, and then I said what I knew was on Vicken and Rhode's minds. 'Weapons.' I met Justin's eyes.

Rhode nodded once.

There it was – our last and only hope. For our human bodies were no match for Odette and her unnatural powers.

'This is how it should go,' Rhode offered. 'We're *never* alone.' He looked at me. 'We're *never* unarmed. It's very simple. We remain at the ready at all times. Carry a dagger everywhere, stay in full public view.' His eyes scanned the room, finally resting on Justin. 'This is what it's like to be the hunted.'

Claudia Hawthorne's funeral was held on the night of the harvest moon, the start of the month of Nuit Rouge, 1 October. The tide was higher than ever in recorded history, with waves over twelve-feet high crashing on to Lovers Bay shore. It was a short service, one where I kept my eyes to the cemetery ground. When the students boarded the buses back to campus, Rhode left a jasmine flower on Claudia's coffin. If only they knew why. If only they realized why we felt so responsible.

When we returned to school, Tracy walked quickly away. She darted, with quick steps, her heels clicking on the pavement as she crossed the quad towards her dorm.

I watched her go. With Claudia's and Kate's deaths, all that remained of the Three Piece was Tracy Sutton. I expected her to leave this cursed place, to run home to the comfort of her parents. About a dozen members of the sophomore and junior classes had now left the school permanently.

As the days went on, some students continued to wear black, but slowly colour came back into the mix, as well as enthusiasm for the upcoming Halloween dance. It seemed to be the only thing we had to look forward to on campus. In between discussions of the various carnival booths and the costumes people were wearing for the dance, the school announced that a pine tree would be planted near Hopper in Claudia's memory. Didn't these mortals know pines planted unnaturally would bring sadness to whoever sat beneath? Didn't they know that oaks are the trees to bring peace? Yet they wanted to plant a pine, and I couldn't exactly make my objections openly.

I wondered if Claudia had already joined the white light of the Aeris. The thought of her there dead because of me, victim of a vampire made by me, killed because she was close to me, made me drop my dagger into my boot every morning after brushing my teeth. Any time I thought to leave it at home, I remembered Claudia's fine blonde hair fluttering around her lifeless body.

A few days after Claudia's funeral, Vicken and I made our way to the union to have breakfast. We watched members of the senior class bring streamers and cardboard skeletons to decorate the gymnasium where we were to have our Halloween dance at the end of the month, 31 October, the last and most powerful night of Nuit Rouge.

Across the green, behind Quartz, Tracy emerged from the small dorm for senior girls. I had to look twice to make sure it was actually her. She had dyed her hair a dark brown, and her cheekbones were so pronounced she didn't look like the same person. She was gaunt and sallow, so unlike the vibrant glowing girl from the year before. The girl who matched her outfits and paraded around the campus. The girl who wore make-up even to exercise, and had matched her pyjamas with those of her friends. Friends who were now both gone. A strength emanated from her now, the steely hardness of someone who has held the hand of death. I would not have wished that for her so soon in life. She had a backpack over one shoulder and was dressed as she had been for weeks, in all black. She was heading towards the section of the woods that remained unguarded.

'Where do you think she's going?' Vicken asked.

Tracy glanced back on to the campus to see if anyone was behind her and tugged the backpack more tightly to her shoulder.

'I'm following her,' I said.

'No, Lenah.' Vicken tried to hold me back by my arm. I wrenched it out of his grasp.

'You know what will happen the moment she's alone,' I said.

Vicken considered my words, then said, 'Well, you're not going by yourself.'

'Let me get a head start,' I said, and jogged across the grass towards Tracy, who was just passing behind the library.

'Tracy,' I called, catching up with her. 'Hey! Wait up.'

She turned, and I was expecting her to smile at me, but instead she pushed me away roughly.

'No, Lenah. Stay away from me.'

I found myself blinking stupidly. The blue of her eyes really popped next to the contrast of her darkened hair.

'Me?' I asked. 'You want me to stay away from you?'

Tracy adjusted her backpack and something in there jangled. A clinking metal sound. 'Where are you going, Tracy?' I asked.

'Nowhere.' She scowled and crossed her arms over her chest. Another clunk.

'This is ridiculous,' I replied. Behind Tracy, down the side of the library, Vicken inched towards us. He lit a cigarette and pretended, with a leg resting against the wall, that he had simply popped out for a smoke.

'I have to go now,' Tracy said. She turned and took two steps away from me.

'No, Tracy. It's not safe,' I said, and almost as it came out of my mouth I knew I had said too much.

But she didn't listen to me. She ran.

After a few moments, Vicken joined me at my side.

'She's carrying weapons,' I said.

'What kind?' he asked, and we started to jog along behind Tracy. She was already on Main Street.

'I don't know.'

'Did she say where she was going?' Vicken asked.

'No, but I have a good idea.'

Vicken and I made sure, as always, to keep to the shadows. The late-afternoon sun shone through the bare branches, and my black boots crunched over the jewelled coloured leaves that carpeted the ground.

'I only have one dagger,' I whispered as we turned into the cemetery.

'I have two,' Vicken replied.

'How long until Odette arrives, do you think?' I asked.

'Minutes,' he said gravely.

I kept having to remind myself it was Tracy as we followed behind. Her hair now fell in long waves of chocolate brown. She grasped the straps of her bag and turned, as I expected, down the row containing Tony's gravestone.

'What the hell is she doing?' Vicken asked.

'Come on,' I whispered, and we inched our way up the path to join her. I stopped, gasping a bit when we reached Tony's row. Tracy had dropped her backpack and was kneeling on the grass. She ran her fingers over the strange circle of turned earth Rhode's sword had made around the grave.

I wrapped a hand around Vicken's arm. We stepped back into the shadows of a nearby oak and I did what I had been trained to do for hundreds of years. I watched. She knelt down, lowered to her hip and leaned on one hand with her other arm outstretched in front of her on the grave. She leaned her weight on that one arm and peered down at the even soil.

Tracy's hand gripped the dirt tight, her head fell

limp and she broke into cries. Her supporting arm gave way and she fell on to the grave, hiding her face in the crook of her arm. I watched her back heave. Her sobs were uneven, the kind of crying a person does when she thinks she is alone.

Daylight clung to the sky but this was Nuit Rouge, so the light provided no protection. The attack could happen at any moment. I bent forward, eyes scouring the woods beyond the cemetery. The birds chirped as they settled down for the evening. The wind was light, bringing with it the musky smell of soil. As a former hunter, I paused and took the time to listen. A hunter listens for unnatural movement. Even air moves. It can leave an echo. For now, it seemed we were alone.

I walked down the row from the cemetery path, Vicken behind me. Tracy snapped her head up, her eyes streaked with tears. She reached into her backpack and pulled out a crucifix.

'Stay away from me!' she screamed.

Vicken jumped back and pulled out a dagger. His arm dropped when he realized she wasn't holding something dangerous.

'You're kidding me, right?' Vicken asked. 'First of all, those don't work and, second, we're not vampires.'

'You know who did this!' Tracy shrieked at me.

'Who?' Vicken asked. 'Did what?'

'Who killed Claudia!' she yelled, but looked at me. 'Justin told me you were in there with her. In the art tower.'

'I didn't touch Claudia,' I said.

'Or is it you?' she spat, now looking at Vicken. 'We all know what you're capable of. The art tower is your favourite place.'

Tracy stood atop Tony's rounded grave. All I could see carved into the granite headstone was the word *Artist*. Her body blocked the rest of the epitaph.

'Tracy, calm down. It wasn't us,' I said.

'*I* was the one who went into your room with Tony last year. *I* saw the picture of you and Rhode on your bureau from, like, a hundred years ago. You come to this school, and guess who dies? Tony. Then both my best friends, Kate and Claudia. Am I next, Lenah? Am I?' She finally broke down, her face collapsing, and she sobbed, dropping the crucifix on to the grass.

Vicken and I shared a look. I went over to Tracy and wrapped my arms around her. She wept into my shoulder.

There was a clapping sound.

Someone was clapping.

Someone was clapping?

'So, the mortal knows you're ex-vampires?' Odette said, appearing through the trees on the edge of the cemetery. 'If only she knew how you used to murder children for pleasure.'

This time I was ready.

'Get behind me, Tracy,' I ordered, and a memory of the art tower flashed through my mind.

I reached down into my boot and whipped out the dagger. I held it outstretched in front of me.

The heart. The heart. Aim for the heart.

Odette sneered, fangs bared. Tracy's fingers gripped my shoulders. Odette came towards us and Vicken, my wonderful Vicken, ran at her, a dagger raised in the air. Odette got to him first. She wrapped her fingers around his wrist and tossed him aside, as though he weighed nothing. Vicken's body flew ten feet high through the air and crumpled at the base of a tree.

He lay unmoving. My gut clenched but I had to stay focused. I had to do this.

I would not fail Tracy as I had failed Claudia. Not this time.

I stood my ground and extended my dagger in front of me.

'Have you learned nothing? Why would you leave campus without your precious Rhode?' Odette said, and clawed through the air at me. Tracy and I jumped back; Odette only just missed my chest.

'Tracy, run,' I commanded.

Odette moved so quickly she was a blur of honey and black. But I knew that was what she would do. I grabbed Tracy by her shoulders and threw her to the ground. Odette clawed at my chest – her nails ripped through my shirt and scraped my skin. I screamed out, pain searing my chest.

Odette laughed and then threw a malevolent glance down at Tracy. I knew what I must do to protect her; I went for it. While she laughed at my pain, I stabbed Odette in the forearm. The blade plunged into the hardened vampire skin. No measly craft knife this time. This knife stopped her. Odette stared at the wound as though she couldn't believe I had done it.

'That's a perfectly good fisherman oozing out of my arm,' she spat.

Down at her feet, Tracy pulled a long silver blade from her bag. It flickered in the rays of the setting sun, but Odette didn't seem to notice. She sneered and took a step towards me, intending to retaliate. I raised my dagger, poised to plunge again.

Odette hadn't considered the human at her feet. Why would she? Hope slid through me as Tracy stabbed Odette hard right through the leather of her shoe. Odette screamed and fell back on to the grass.

'Go!' I yelled, meeting Tracy's watery blue eyes. This time, she followed orders.

She fled through the maze of tombstones and trees. Suddenly I was flying through the air. Odette had swept her good foot under me, making me fall to the ground.

I landed with a thud, hitting the ground with my back, sending more pain through the cuts on my chest. Winded, I tried to draw in air but I couldn't. *Breathe, Lenah.* A kick slammed on to the right side of me. Another kick on the left. Odette's dandelion-coloured curls dangled before me. Her devilish smile faded as tears flooded my eyes and washed out my sight.

'Did your little friend think stabbing my foot was going to stop me? Haven't you seen how powerful I am?' I struggled for breath. 'I am only to get more powerful as the days go on. Oh, darling, are you having trouble breathing?'

She squatted above me and lifted an index finger, showing me her knife-like nails again. Slowly I was able to draw a shallow breath, my frozen lungs finally thawing. She pointed to my bandaged arm.

No . . . don't stab me.

'*Of course* I'm going to stab you,' she said, reading my emotional plea with her ESP. 'I thought I'd warned you, but I guess you don't listen. Being a queen and all, you think you still call the shots. But not any more.' Her long red fingernails hovered over the gauze of my burnt forearm. 'Give. Me. The. Ritual.'

'Never,' I said, gulping in air.

She sneered and then stabbed my injured forearm. Her fingernails sliced through the gauze to my still raw skin. A ripping sound, then hot pain seared my burnt flesh. I screamed so loudly that it scratched my throat. The pain was so intense that acrid bile made its way to my mouth. Where was Vicken?

'Why, queen of all vampires? *Why* do you insist on making this so difficult for yourself?'

Queen of all vampires.

As she looked down at me, with her porcelain skin and bloody mouth, time seemed to slow. Our eyes connected. Mine blue – hers green. Together. Yes. Within her eyes I could *see* myself as a vampire, throwing my head back, mouth agape, laughing into the night.

How familiar was the overwhelming desire to *feel* once again. All we wanted to do was feel. *So numb. No feeling in my fingers or hands. Release the pain. Need the blood running down my throat and the power to surge through my body.* I could sense the duality within myself.

I *was* the vampire queen again.

Catch them by surprise. A public spectacle. On Halloween.

These were Odette's thoughts. I knew her plan because in that moment, as her unnatural jade eyes bored into mine, I could see her plan. It was just as I would have formulated it.

She was going to try to kill me at the Halloween dance, when I would be too busy trying to protect the humans around me. I could see the decorations, and Vicken's and Rhode's bodies, bloody and dead on the gymnasium floor.

And with this remembrance of my vampire evil came some of the memories I had forgotten in my human state.

Odette's murder, when she was made a vampire.

'I remember the day you changed,' I whispered shakily. 'It was only hours before my hibernation. I told Vicken to make you a vampire. But he did not. And I desired the rush, the high of bringing another night wanderer into the world.'

She pulled back and I saw her fingers curl over for the barest of seconds. My arm throbbed again, sending tears of pain to my eyes. It was easier to say this when I couldn't see her clearly.

'I'm sorry,' I said. 'I'm sorry for what I did.'

She gripped her hands over my shoulders. She

lifted me just slightly and then with a push threw me back to the ground.

'Don't distract me!' she yelled. Pain pulsated at the front of my head.

'I attacked Rhode in Hathersage in order to get the ritual, but all he could do was set the bloody place on fire. You're both cowards. I am going to take you with me tonight. I'm going to take you with me and then –' she grimaced – 'when Rhode comes for you, and you are dead, drained, chained to the wall, he'll tell me all about this ritual.'

'It will be useless to you,' I spat. 'You're not powerful enough to bring forth the darkness you seek.' I tried to stare into her eyes again, to call back our connection, but it didn't work.

'You don't know anything about my power,' Odette said, raising her hands, ready to strike again.

I flinched in anticipation.

Suddenly she hunched over. There was an awful thud and the sound of ripping flesh. Vicken's dagger was pinned through her neck. She fell forward, grasping at her neck, and rolled on to her side, grabbing for the hilt of the dagger.

Vicken appeared next to me with his wild hair and a bloody scrape on his cheek. He lifted his boot and stepped lightly on her stomach. She bared her fangs and hissed.

'Now, now, play nice,' he said.

'She's very strong,' I warned.

'That's why I stabbed her, love,' Vicken said out of one corner of his mouth. 'Now, tell us, where did you get your super-strength?' he asked, his boot still on her stomach.

'I've performed spells you've never dreamed of,' she sneered. 'Each time I grow faster, stronger, more cunning.'

But now I could see fear in her eyes. Blood from her neck trickled over her shoulder and on to the dirt. She tried to push herself up but collapsed with a thud back on to the ground, still under Vicken's boot.

'Lenah, I need another dagger,' Vicken said, gesturing at Tracy's knife, which lay near Tony's grave.

Odette struggled against his boot, baring her fangs like an animal.

Yes, I had made her a vampire, though I did not make her a vampire in the attic as I had originally planned. I had moved the misery downstairs. She'd hidden behind my ancient furniture. Her eyes then had been beautiful and green, desperate for salvation. The first night I had tried to kill her she outsmarted me, ran from the attic and found her family by the stables out in the back gardens.

'Lenah! The knife,' Vicken cried.

Her father had begged. Naturally I killed him first.

I stared at the ground. Ella had been her given name.

I have a life to lead, she'd said, pleading with me.

'Do you?' I'd said with a merciless laugh.

Through my reverie I heard Vicken's voice: 'The dagger – now! She's healing!'

'No, you pathetic child,' I'd continued. 'I have a life to lead and I can't take my hibernation unless I am full. You are young and healthy.'

I hated the sound of my vampire self.

'Please . . .' Odette's human voice echoed in my head.

Followed by the same dead laugh. How I had laughed and laughed as she cried for mercy and begged me to spare her life.

'Lenah!' Vicken shouted again.

I refocused on Odette grasping for the knife protruding from her neck.

I couldn't move. A sickening feeling overwhelmed me. Unmistakable and undeniable.

Odette pulled the bloody knife from her neck. She jumped up and kicked out at Vicken, who fell. In the time it took for him to get back on to his feet, she had run into the woods.

'What the hell are you doing?' he yelled at me.

Tracy appeared from nowhere, snatched her

knife from Tony's grave and set off towards the woods.

'Hey!' Vicken yelled after Tracy. 'Crazy girl, get back here! Now!'

Tracy stopped at the edge of the wood, the knife in her hand hanging by her side.

Odette had vanished.

Vicken walked down the long lane of gravestones and stopped by Tracy.

He offered her his hand. She went to hand him the knife but he shook his head. She lifted her eyes to meet his and then considered his palm again. It was enough to make my heart break. She dropped the knife to the grass and wrapped fingers with his.

CHAPTER 19

'Where did you come from?' Vicken asked Tracy. 'I thought you ran out of the cemetery.'

'I hid by the mausoleum. When I saw her run away, I don't know, I got brave for a moment,' Tracy replied.

I held Tracy's sweatshirt to my injured arm as we walked back through the campus towers and past the security guard. The sweatshirt soaked up some of the blood that had seeped through the cut on my arm, but aside from a mild throbbing, the pain wasn't bad.

'I'm sorry,' I said, 'that I didn't . . .'

'It's all right,' Vicken replied.

'It's not all right,' I said. 'I froze.'

Tracy's expression was pensive. 'It took me all summer to accept Tony's death.'

Vicken bowed his head a bit.

She looked at him. 'Did you kill him because you were a vampire?'

'We did many things as vampires which we would never dream of doing in human form,' he replied gently.

'*She* killed Kate and Claudia, didn't she?'

Her eyes shone in the ghostly blue of the early-evening light. I nodded.

'I've spent all summer looking up how to kill vampires. I know why you have a sword on your wall. Why you keep herbs on your door. Lavender is supposed to protect your home. And rosemary.' She ran a hand through her hair. 'Rosemary is for remembrance.' She pulled a chain out from beneath her shirt. It was a silver locket. When she opened it, there was a tiny sprig of dried rosemary.

My breath was short. I couldn't help staring.

'Tony researched you too,' she said. 'It's why you wore those sparkly ashes around your neck last year. Like the ones I saw on your balcony. Then Justin confirmed it,' she said. 'That you were . . .' She paused and her eyes met mine. 'That you were a vampire.'

I had never believed Tracy to be that astute. It seemed I had underestimated her.

'I loved Tony,' I said. The centre of my chest ached, taking the pain away from my arm. 'He was my best friend.'

'I'm not going to say anything,' she said. 'About either of you. It took me all summer just to accept that the rumours could be true. And then Justin confirmed it.' She ran her fingers through her hair again. 'Well, he didn't so much confirm it as I forced him to tell me.'

'How?' I asked. The prickly feeling of betrayal dissolved as she spoke.

'I threatened to smash the lights of his car. When that didn't work, I showed him all my research. Everything I'd found. I told him about the pictures. He finally told me the truth.'

'You and Tony are more alike than I thought,' I said. Her tenacity reminded me of how he too had unearthed my secret all on his own.

'I want to know. Someday. Not today, but I want to know exactly what happened to Tony.' She looked at Vicken as she said it. 'That's all. Can you promise me?'

'Yes,' he said. 'I promise.'

We set off across the campus into the busy student body, all walking in twos and threes to the union or the library or their dorms.

'What do we do about the Halloween dance?' Tracy asked.

'You stay out of the way, love,' Vicken said, lighting a cigarette.

'If you need me, I'll help you,' Tracy said, and pulled her bag tighter over her shoulder. 'Any way I can.'

*

That night, I stood at my balcony door looking out at the tiles. Only when I moved did I occasionally see the flicker of my vampire remains. I reached into my pocket and felt the gift card Claudia bought me for my birthday.

'So it felt like your extrasensory perception was back?' Rhode said.

'Yes,' I replied. 'It was very clear to me what Odette wanted. I could sense her deepest desires. I saw images from her plans for Halloween night.'

'What could have caused it to come back?' Justin asked.

The only explanation I could fathom was that the bond created between Odette and me on that dark day a hundred years ago linked me eternally to her mind.

'I was her maker,' I whispered. 'It's the only explanation. I understood her motivations, as much as I didn't want to.'

'Why didn't you kill her when you had the chance?' Rhode asked.

I locked my gaze with his and kept my jaw tight. My heart thudded. I hated thinking of myself in that moment, with the dagger by my side, Vicken at the ready, waiting, needing my help. I didn't know how to answer this. I *knew* this woman. She had been alone and afraid and I had sucked the very life from her. I had killed her. Worse, I had created the monster she became. Her death played in my mind – the memory of how warm she'd been, how her body trembled with fear, and my joy at taking both her warmth and her life.

I met Rhode's eyes.

'Because I already have killed her. I'm sorry, but it's the truth, and it paralysed me.'

Silence. Then Vicken said, 'On that note, it's time for dinner.'

There was a clink from Vicken's boots as he stood up, and the shuffle of papers being moved. I turned my back on the living room and faced the balcony again. I knew what was coming in a few days' time and I would have only an old sword and a couple of daggers with which to take down Odette. I didn't know if I could make myself do it.

'You OK?' Justin asked me, placing a hand on my shoulder. His voice was close to my ear.

The door closed and I realized that Vicken and Rhode had left without saying goodbye. It meant that Justin and I were alone together for the first time since the night of my birthday.

I leaned my back against the glass balcony door and looked at the knowledge rune on Justin's neck. I focused on it. He had put it on backwards and it hung in reverse.

I met Justin's eyes. He kissed my forehead, and when he pulled back he smiled at me. His eyes lingered on mine. I thought of him that day, the day I turned Vicken human again with the ritual. How Justin had fallen to his knees when I walked out on to my balcony. I had been so ready to leave it all behind.

'That's the most difficult part,' I said. 'The ingredients and the words are important, of course, but the sacrifice, the intent, it's always the most important part of any ritual.'

The intent . . .

Images from the summoning spell floated into my mind: the jump of the flames and the door glowing in the sand. Had I been channelling my intentions into the spell so that it would bring me what I desired? Were my intentions pure?

'Of course,' I said aloud. 'Of course.' The spell backfired because my intentions hadn't been pure. In order for the spell to work I needed to channel my intentions in one direction only, but mine were split. I wanted protection from Odette, but really I was calling Suleen for Rhode's benefit.

I knew what I had to do!

My spirits lifted considerably.

'I need your help,' I said to Justin.

'OK . . .' he said.

The bright spark in his eyes glowed at me. It reminded me why I had slept in his tent the night of my birthday. Why I let his touch take me back to last year when I thought that being a human was going to be simple. That I could be a seventeen-year-old girl in love, with no repercussions from her past.

But there will always be payment for your past atrocities. That's why the intent behind all spells matters.

'Lenah?' Justin said.

'I'm going to perform it again,' I said.

'What? The summoning spell?' Justin asked.

'Yes.' The fire in my belly was back. *Yes. Yes.* I would call Suleen again, and this time my intentions would be pure. This time he would come!

'Let's go.'

After grabbing Rhode's spell book, *Incantato*, a jar for the water and all the ingredients I would need, I raced down the stairs of Seeker, ignoring the twinges of pain from the burn on my arm. I ran past students sitting in the hallway putting together Halloween costumes.

'Wait. Hey!' Justin called.

'Keep up!' I said, and stepped outside the dorm. I found Vicken sitting on the bench in front of Seeker, a cigarette in his hand.

'Hold on,' Vicken said, when he realized I wasn't

going to stop. 'Where are you going?'

'I'm going to perform the summoning spell again.'

'Oh, right,' he said, following me. 'So, you've officially gone mad.'

I kept going, not caring what he thought.

Justin joined us in the parking lot.

'What's he doing here? Where are we going?' Justin asked.

'We're going back to Lovers Bay beach,' I said, throwing a glance at Vicken as I unlocked the car.

'You're bloody mad, you know that? I can't even smoke I'm so angry,' Vicken said.

I opened the door and tossed the bag filled with the spell ingredients and the book into the car.

'Then I consider this trip a success already,' I said.

I was about to slide into the driver's seat when Vicken stopped me again by grabbing my shoulder and forcing me to face him.

'Lenah. You could die. You're barely healed now.' He glanced at my bandaged arm. 'Didn't we learn our lesson last time we left campus?'

'If Lenah wants to do it, she'll do it without you,' Justin said, from the passenger side door.

'Pretty boy, you've got no idea what you're talking about. So get away from the car, and shut it.'

Justin came around the side of the car so fast that I stumbled to get between them.

'You could die too,' Vicken said to Justin through clenched teeth.

'I'm doing this,' I said, my hands pressed against Vicken's heaving chest, 'and we agreed not to leave campus *alone*. I'm not alone.' I indicated Justin.

'Then I'm coming too. Three is stronger,' Vicken sneered. He met my eyes and took a step back. 'Triangles are symbols of infinity. It could work . . . better.'

'Good,' I said, and Justin also backed away. 'If you promise me you won't fight. I have to stay focused.'

'I will,' Justin replied, 'if he promises not to get close to me. I'm not a fan of murderers.'

I spun round, anger swirling in my chest. 'Then you're not a fan of me.'

Justin's expression was stunned. His jaw dropped. 'I didn't . . . I mean . . .'

'Just get in the car,' I said. 'Both of you.'

As I drew the outline of a door, the sand was cool on my finger. The moon hung over the horizon. This time we were doing the spell at dusk.

'You're ready? You're sure?' Vicken asked.

Justin's eyes were wide as he stared down at the door. And, strangely, he was almost smiling.

When he caught my eye, he quickly dropped his expression, his mouth becoming a thin line.

'Sorry, just – you know – never seen a ritual before,' he said.

I unscrewed the jar with the harbour water and sprinkled it over the flames.

'I summon you, Suleen, to this sacred place.' My eyes lifted to the moon still hanging low in the sky. 'I call you here to protect us from the impending danger.' And I meant it. I wanted to protect our souls, our lives.

The amber came next, and when the oily resin hit the flames, the door frame, just like last time, burned a bright gold. All three of us stared at the fiery outline.

'I summon you,' I repeated. The fire crackled again, the flames lower than the last time. Good! Yes! This time it seemed it would work!

A wind whipped through my hair and a great blast came up from the fire.

I jumped back. I expected a ten-foot flame to jump into the sky. But no. The fire was completely out, leaving behind charred and blackened wood.

A tiny blue ball of light sat in the centre of the wood where the flame had been. The blue orb hovered directly over the embers of the fire, glowing and expanding into a vertical oblong shape as the seconds passed.

'What . . . ?' Justin said.

'Shhh . . .' I replied.

The blue orb grew to the size of the door I had drawn in the sand. It glowed for a few more moments and I expected Suleen, the man I had grown to love, to step through. I expected to see his white clothing and familiar turban.

The door did not open. Like an old-fashioned film it flickered, playing a scene in a ballroom in a familiar mansion. The blue light from the orb grew brighter and larger.

'Oh no,' Vicken said.

Heartbeat – a pulse.

The blue orb took over almost the whole sky. So big – a portal to another world? No . . .

A blast of blue light and then . . .

Vicken, Justin and I were part of the scene before us, standing on the edge of the ballroom.

'We're in Hathersage,' Vicken said in awe.

'Shhh,' I said, waving a hand across myself as though to wipe away his voice.

Justin said nothing. He watched the scene play out before him, with his jaw dropping in either disbelief or fear, or both.

Glasses filled with blood clinked together. A small orchestra of vampires played in one corner of the room. Chatter from dozens of vampires echoed throughout my banquet hall.

'Lenah, what is this?' Vicken asked. 'I don't recognize these people.'

'This was before your time.'

I knew what this was. This was the horrific night that secured my infamy throughout the world.

This was the night I killed a child.

We three mortals stood invisible to the partying vampires.

I gasped as I caught sight of my vampire self spinning around, a goblet in hand. My gown was black and corseted. The 1740s was a colourful era but I had worn black . . . on purpose. My silk dress was encrusted with roses of jet and black pearls.

'Did you know,' my vampire self said, 'that Nuit

Rouge is the month in which you can access black magic?' The corset pressed into her ribs as she laughed, leaping over the body of a man in a white tunic and black breeches. A local farmer drained of all his blood. 'Tonight is All Hallows' Eve!'

The vampires around her lifted their goblets in the air and drank.

Bright torches threw the hall into an orange dreamy light.

A vampiric Rhode appeared at the doorway of the banquet hall in his finest silk. He too wore his traditional black, his hair slicked back so his turquoise eyes glowed out from the darkness of the hallway behind him. He slid his palm over his mouth and ran across the room to the body of the child he'd buried only hours before. Now she lay in a corner of the room, where I had wanted her placed. Just for the evening.

'I unburied her! With my bare hands!' my vampire self called to him, laughing and taking a deep swig from a goblet of her blood. The dancing intensified in the middle of the room, the vampires jumping to a lively drum.

'Isn't she lovely?' she called to Rhode, who was on his knees by the dead child. 'She sort of looks like me, don't you think? She could be my little sister.'

The flowers bounced with the vibration from the dozens of feet striking the floor, up and down and up and down. Roses, lavender, daisies, orchids, all in fragrant abundance. Vampire Lenah picked up some daisies and roses and brought them to Rhode, who still remained on his knees, staring down at the child.

My vampire self covered the child's eyes with daisy heads. The petals reached her eyebrows.

'I'm going to give her a proper burial,' said my vampire self happily. 'I've invited all our friends in Derbyshire,' she continued, dancing a circle around Rhode, holding her gown in so she could scoot around him and the dead girl. She scattered roses and daisies over the body. 'And this young lady! Here's a daisy! I would give you some violets, but they all withered when my father died: they say he made a good end.'

Rhode stood up. As I watched, I knew what was coming next.

'Oh, come now, don't you enjoy Master Shakespeare?' asked vampire Lenah.

He looked to the other bodies scattered about the floor. His eyes met vampire Lenah's. She held his gaze for a few moments.

'Why . . . ?' he asked.

'Why? Her blood is the purest!' My vampire self

walked to the feet of the body of the young girl, still in her white dress, and merrily scattered even more flowers over her.

'No more!' Rhode yelled. He gripped my shoulders, sending me back against the wall with a thud. 'Lenah, what have you become?'

Lenah laughed at his earnest gaze. 'Oh, come on, I'll have someone bury her again when the party is over.'

He growled and it was almost a scream. His eyebrows furrowed together in a pinch. This was the pain of a vampire who wanted to cry. Rhode gripped vampire Lenah again and shook her so hard that her shoulders vibrated and her teeth chattered. I hated watching myself like this.

'Why can't you just let me love you?' Rhode said, his teeth clenched together.

'Because I am unravelling,' my vampire self said. 'And only power can relieve the pain. Not love.'

He let go and swept away from her then, leaving down the darkened hallway. I watched my vampire self run after him into the distance. I followed, Justin and Vicken in my wake.

'What are you doing?' she cried. 'Rhode!'

But he did not answer. He kept walking until he reached the hall in the front of the house. By the door was a small black leather bag; he grabbed the handle and whipped open the door. The sunset, a burning orange, scorched my eyes. Vampire Lenah instinctively threw her hands across her face, but this was 1740, and after three hundred and twenty-two years she did not need to fear the sun.

'Rhode!' she called.

'You are reckless,' Rhode hissed, whipping around. 'Power will not save you. It will only further the deterioration of your mind.' He walked out of the door and away from the house towards the endless sweeping hills. Vampire Lenah took a few steps after him.

'I know what I am doing,' she said, bringing her feet together and raising her chin defiantly.

Vicken, Justin and I watched from the doorway. Rhode stopped and turned to face vampire Lenah again.

'Do you?' Rhode moved closer until he was an inch from her face. His fangs showed as he whispered, 'Do you? You murdered a child. A child, Lenah.'

'You always said that infant blood was the sweetest. The most pure.'

Rhode looked horror-stricken. He backed away from her.

'I said it as a fact, not as an invitation to sample it. You have changed. You are no longer the girl in the white nightgown I loved in your father's orchard.'

His eyes had a misty look and, even as a memory, I could tell he was formulating his thoughts. 'I told you to concentrate on me tonight. That if you can focus on the love you feel for me . . . you can break free. But you can't do that; I see that now,' he said. I watched myself try to speak, but Rhode continued before Lenah could find the words. 'You've seen it yourself. Vampires your age begin to lose their minds. Most choose fire or a stake through the heart to bring them to their deaths, to avoid a slow descent into insanity. The prospect of forever is too much. And for you the life you lost has made you insane. Living on this earth for all eternity has brought your mind to a place where I can no longer reach you.'

'I'm not insane, Rhode. I'm a vampire.'

'You make me regret what I did in that orchard,' he said sadly, turning back to the path to the hills.

'You regret *me*?'

'Find yourself, Lenah. When you do, I will return.'

My human self remembered this moment so clearly. Back then, I could have watched him leave. I could have followed his frame with my gaze until he was out of my sight, but this time the pain was too much. I wanted out of that blue light, out of that memory. Instead, I watched my vampire self turn and walk back into the brightly lit hall. Music echoed from the ballroom but it was another world to me. My vampire self placed a hand on the stone wall. I remembered that the stones had no temperature, nor could I feel the thick ridges beneath my fingers.

Nothing . . . nothing . . . nothing.

'I want out!' I yelled, falling to my knees. The house was gone. My life was Wickham now. 'Out!' I screamed.

A blast of blue light and the cold sand of Lovers Bay beach hit my knees. I held my face in my hands. A kind of cry ripped through me. A huge surge of sadness. I had to draw in a breath; I could smell the salt of the sea and amber resin on my hands. I wept, a horrible wailing kind of sobbing. The tears slicked my hands, and as I drew in ragged breaths of salty air I let the horror of that memory wash over me in waves of embarrassment and shame.

Justin and Vicken were silent.

I had not brought Suleen to me. I had summoned the truth, a reminder of my nature. I was a killer.

And I deserved no help.

CHAPTER 20

I ran as fast as I could, sprinting down the long street away from the beach.

Come and get me, Odette. My chest ached from how hard my lungs had to work as I ran, but I kept going. The sound of feet slamming the pavement again and again and again echoed behind me.

'Lenah!' *Justin's voice.* 'Lenah, it's not safe!'

I didn't reply. The biting wind nipped at my cheeks. A car engine revved and then screamed to a stop ahead of me. The headlights of my blue car swung around and the car cut me off from running any further. I backed away and brought the heels of my hands to my eyes.

I heard the slam of a door. Vicken's boots walked to me on the concrete. The sound of Justin's feet hitting the pavement caught up behind me, then stopped.

'Don't touch me!' I screamed. The words burned my throat.

I looked to my palms.

'How much blood did we shed, Vicken?' I asked.

My back shuddered as tears pushed their way through me and down my cheeks. 'Answer me.'

I shoved him on the chest so he fell back a few steps.

'I can't do this. I can't kill her. I've tried and I can't.'

Vicken came to me and silently wrapped his arms around me. I cried into his chest until his shirt was wet through.

'You *can* do this. We'll help you,' Vicken said.

His eyes stabbed to Justin and they shared a look, one that said, *Yes, we're in this together.*

Somehow I walked back to the car; somehow I climbed in; and I knew that somehow I would have to find the killer within myself once more, and finish Odette.

I was silent in the passenger seat, my hand resting on the car window as we made our way back to Wickham. The sky still held a blue twinge, like the blue of the orb that had showed us my past. *My horrible past.* As Vicken drove, I could only guess what he was thinking. I had explained it to him so many times but now, finally, he had seen a glimpse of my life before 1850, before he joined my madness.

Justin sat in the back throwing questions at Vicken. 'What the hell was that?'

He avoided answering. 'I don't know.'

'But why did we see it?'

'I don't *know*,' Vicken said again.

'But we . . .'

'Look, mate. Just shut it, all right?'

When we pulled on to Wickham campus, everyone was in full preparation mode for the Halloween carnival and dance. I got out of the car and inhaled cider and cinnamon coming from the union. I started down the main path. *How strange*, I thought as I walked out of the parking lot and on to the grass. Vicken and Justin's footsteps echoed behind me. But they were like drumbeats to me. *How strange*, I thought, as orange pumpkins and black streamers blurred into October colours. *Like a Monet painting*. It was all just a mess of colour I couldn't understand.

Students wound black lines of ribbon around lamp posts. A crew far out on the lacrosse field was putting up tents and booths. They didn't seem like students. Or maybe I didn't. Maybe I didn't know what I was any more.

'Wait,' Justin called softly. I kept walking.

'Let her go,' I heard Vicken say.

I walked past Seeker, past the Curie Building, where once I couldn't dissect a frog because I couldn't destroy another creature.

I continued past Hopper Building. A hallowed place where I could not even glance up at the great stone tower because two of my friends had died within those walls.

'Lenah!' Tracy called to me as I walked by Quartz dorm. She sat out front on a blanket alone, reading a book. I could not explain what had happened so I ignored her. I went to the greenhouse and opened the door. The misty, humid air engulfed me, and I hurried down the aisle, snatching roses, sage and lavender from various pots. I held them in my fists and clenched hard. The petals crumpled under the pressure of my fingers. I sank to the floor.

That child . . .

There was a creak from the door behind me. Sneakers squeaked on the wet concrete. The sudden gust of fresh air brought with it the humid smell of the greenhouse mixed with the smoke of a summoning spell gone wrong. Justin sank to his knees next to me. His warm hand slid over my palm and curled over the petals in my hands and between my fingers.

'I'm sorry you had to see that,' I whispered. It was all I could say.

'You were . . .' Justin started to say. 'You were really powerful.'

I lifted my eyes to him slowly. He leaned towards me and kept my gaze.

'Is that what you saw?' I asked. 'Power?'

He opened his mouth to speak. All he was able to get out was a *no*, then he immediately dropped his hand from mine. 'I don't mean it like that. Just that . . . you didn't fear anything back then. You were . . .'

'Pure madness. Nothing more. Nothing less.'

'True, it was. But . . .'

When I met his eyes, even the green colour looked different. I was not reminded of the trees swaying on his parents' street. I did not see the evergreen leaves of the woods that surrounded Wickham Boarding School. Despite his best efforts, he would never understand me. He could not possibly know what it meant to be alive after being dead for so long. To have kissed death and lived to tell the tale.

Justin grasped my hand. The warmth of his grip grounded me in the greenhouse. I blinked away the image of the little girl. Instead I focused on the sounds of the plant misters and the glimpses of the orange and black streamers outside. In this space, with the flowers and herbs, I was quiet, my mind able to soften the atrocity of what I had done. Justin rubbed his hand over mine. Last year, with all its beauty and happiness and its horrors, had made me a different person. I wasn't supposed to survive that ritual, but I had. And so had Rhode. Things between Justin and me were never going to be like they had been. Too much had changed. *I* had changed.

I would never love Justin.

I could go through every motion, wear the clothes, wear the perfume and say all there was to say, but I was never meant to live in this modern world. I was never meant to be here.

I would live my life for Rhode even if it meant I had to live without him. He was the only person. My soulmate. My love.

Even if he could never forgive me.

Even if it was over.

CHAPTER 21

Once, long ago, I ran through an apple orchard dusted with snow. The wind bit at the tip of my nose. Arms out, I ran and ran, wind flying through my fingers and through my hair.

'Lenah! Lenah!' my mother called from the doorway of our house. She smiled at me as I turned and ran into the depths of the orchard. It was the fifteenth century, which meant we would burn the fires at all hours. Without it, we would die in the cold.

I stopped at the end of a long lane formed by two rows of apple trees. The chill licked at my nose and I could feel it in the air, not as a vampire would, but as a child of the medieval world. Spring was upon us; the falling snow was wet, almost rain. I stood at the edge of my father's land and looked out at the great world beyond it. The woods were my favourite place at that time of year, the beautiful trees laced with silver and diamonds of ice. I drew in breaths of cool fresh air. I stared into those woods, absolutely unafraid of the world beyond.

'So you'll get the costumes?' Justin asked Rhode, who nodded. 'We can hide the weapons that way.'

I stood in the study atrium with my back to the window on the night before Halloween. Justin, Rhode and Vicken sat at a table looking over a drawing Rhode had made of the gymnasium.

'Everyone know your positions?' Rhode asked, looking up from his drawing. 'Lenah?'

I had looked at that sketch ten times now. I knew exactly what I would have to do; I just hoped I could do it.

'Let's go over it one more time,' Rhode said.

I sighed and recited the plan for what seemed like the millionth time.

'We'll isolate the members of her coven so I can get a clean shot. One stab,' I said, finally meeting his eyes as I tried to convince myself. 'One stab to the heart.'

That night, I dreamed of vampires with no fangs. They were faceless demons: no eyes, no nose, just mouths with gaping holes in the gums. Blood rolled from their smirking lips and on to their chins.

It was hard to shake the image when I awoke on Halloween morning. What helped was that the campus had gone through a complete metamorphosis. Banners read *Happy Halloween*; pumpkins lined the pathways and decorated entrances to many buildings. Classes were cancelled. After Rhode returned from buying costumes, we decided that it would be best if we stayed among other students all day. I had knocked on Justin's door twice, but he had not answered. He was, I guessed, already out and about with friends. I wondered why he hadn't checked in with me, after everything that had happened the day before.

I stood staring at a carnival booth displaying dozens of bowls of goldfish.

'Oh, just play the game,' Vicken said. 'One game in honour of Nuit Rouge. And this one won't involve you murdering someone for sport.' He rolled his eyes at me. 'You're not abandoning the school if you win a fish.'

If I tossed a small ball into a bowl, I would take the tank home and keep that fish for a pet. I scoffed. Me? Keep something . . . alive?

As Vicken leaned his back against the booth of the Goldfish Toss, there was a boom-boom, boom-boom of bass drums.

'Oh no, here they come . . . again,' he groaned. For the fourth time that afternoon, the school band banged on their drums and marched across the football field towards the carnival. They wore funny hats with what looked like a bright gold quill pen on the top; one of the Wickham School colours. Many of the students around us abandoned carnival games mid-turn and ran towards the football field. Vicken motioned with a disgusted wave of his arm.

'Look at them all! Abandoning their games. If I was in the middle of the ring toss, I would most certainly not quit!'

'You *would* take it so seriously,' I said, eyeing the dozens of fishbowls, each with a graceful goldfish swishing its tail.

Vicken reached into his jacket pocket for a cigarette, then patted down each pocket of his trousers in search of a lighter. There was a mechanical click and then a plume of smoke as Vicken took a sharp drag of his cigarette and exhaled.

'Look, all I'm saying is, if you're going to do something, do it right.'

'Vicken Clough! You put that out right now!'

Ms Warner, the school nurse, blazed towards Vicken, her finger pointed directly at his chest. Vicken dropped the cigarette and stamped it out with his boot.

'My dear Ms Warner! You're looking lovely today.'

'How many times do I need to tell you, Vicken?

Smoking is not allowed on campus. And you're not eighteen – it's *illegal*. Hand it over.'

'Hand what over?'

'The pack.'

Vicken scoffed.

'Do not scoff at me, Vicken. Hand them over.'

I abandoned my potential fish to a more capable owner and put the ball down.

'Not gonna throw?' the man operating the booth asked.

'Not today,' I said.

As I walked away from Vicken and Ms Warner, I thought about those goldfish. How they would live their whole life in that tiny bubble. They would swim, swish, roll up and around in their tiny world.

Ahead of me, I saw that the rowing crew had changed the boat cabin into a haunted house. Wispy strands of fake cobwebs hung in lazy designs across the windows. Someone had hung a black curtain so people couldn't see inside. The door burst open and a student dressed in a white sheet pushed out two Wickham underclassmen. The couple grinned at each other and ran back towards the football field.

The girl giggled. 'That was actually kind of scary!'

The ghost looked at me from two cut-out eyeholes.

'Come in! If you dare . . .'

I glanced back to see if Vicken was following but there was too much of a crowd. Students ran from booth to booth; the band gathered far down at the end of the field and launched into a synchronized march. Suddenly Rhode appeared around a corner and I froze. He smiled at me just a little, so that one corner of his mouth raised.

We shared that small moment, but it was over too soon.

'Come in! Come in!' Ms Williams said, gesturing towards the haunted house.

'In a minute,' I said to the headmistress, who was dressed as a cat, with black fuzzy ears, tail and all. Rhode stopped next to me and I waited for a moment to try to talk to him. Vicken emerged from the crowd with what seemed like every single candy and sweet at the carnival.

A candy apple in his mouth, he said, 'What?'

'I can see you're just frightened to death about tonight,' Rhode said.

'If you don't mind, I'd like something sweet before I have to fight for my life.'

'Lenah! Vicken,' Tracy called to us. Her tone was off kilter, a line creasing between her eyebrows. She seemed even more porcelain-skinned with her hair so dark.

'Are you all right?' Vicken asked, as more students ran by us into the haunted house.

'It's Justin. He never checked in with the resident advisor last night. Hasn't been seen today either. The school has called the police.'

Rhode, Vicken and I exchanged glances. My heart gave a little twinge. I wouldn't panic. Not yet. It wasn't completely unlike Justin to wander off with friends or his brother for a bit.

'When was the last time you saw him?' Tracy asked me.

'Yesterday afternoon,' I said.

'Did anything happen? Anything where he could have been hurt?' she asked, and I could tell from her tone she was talking about Odette.

'No, we were in the greenhouse. Safely on campus.'

'What time?' Her eyes lit up. It seemed I had given her a new piece of information.

'Evening. Six? Seven?' I guessed.

'OK, thanks,' she said, backing away, a smile appearing on her face. 'That's something. That's great.' She turned and ran off down the lane of booths back out into the campus.

'Justin? Missing?' I said. I hadn't seen him at all that day. It also explained why he hadn't answered when I knocked on his door after breakfast.

'If Justin was *truly* missing, wouldn't they have called an assembly? Cancelled the carnival?' Vicken asked. We both avoided the obvious. We both knew Odette could be to blame. 'I'll have a look around,' he said. 'Let you know what I find.' He dumped his half-eaten candy apple and disappeared back into the crowd.

'We should look for him too,' Rhode said.

I didn't get it. Why would Justin have gone off? After everything that had happened? Had he had second thoughts after what he had seen during the summoning spell?

Rhode and I passed a shooting game and a ring toss. Interspersed between the student carnival tents were professional ones belonging to a company that the school had hired. A large rented white tent read *House of Mirrors* in white light.

'Shall we check in here?' Rhode said.

Without replying, I walked inside.

I knew Justin wouldn't be in there, but I wanted to go in the tent anyway. I wanted to keep pushing away the thought that Justin could be in real trouble. Or, worse, dead.

No, Lenah. Stop.

I turned around the first corner. Trick mirrors had been hung from screens. Some of them made me look long and stringy. Another brought my face together in a squish.

Rhode followed behind me, his strides matching mine.

'I thought you would want to search with Vicken,' I said.

Rhode shook his head. 'I just want this battle over.'

We stopped and stood before the same mirror, which made our reflections bleed into one another. My arm was Rhode's arm. His chest, my chest.

'Your lies are overwhelming,' I said, turning to Rhode. 'Odette told me that she was the one who attacked the Hathersage house.'

He stood, appearing to ponder for a moment.

'Yes, Odette arrived at the house first,' he admitted eventually. 'To begin with, I didn't know what she was looking for. She seemed generally cordial, but things quickly turned ugly. I tried to fight her, but as you saw she is extremely skilled. Though she was not unnaturally fast at the time, so I was able to get away. That particular gift is a recent one,' he said.

'Why wouldn't you just tell me?' I asked. 'You don't have to hide everything from me.'

He leaned towards me. 'Because I thought I could protect you – that I could call Suleen or take care of it myself.'

'And did you?' I asked.

'I could not do it alone,' he said eventually. 'As always, I am better with you. Stronger.'

And we were close again, standing side by side, only inches apart. No longer battered and bruised, his skin was smooth again, like that of a young man with his whole life before him.

'Why do you fear my touch?' I whispered.

'I don't fear your touch,' he said with a deep sigh. 'It's never been about that.'

I wasn't sure how to respond except to say, 'You haven't let me near you for months.'

'Lenah,' he said gently, 'I only fear what I am capable of with a beating heart. What the Aeris warned of. I can't promise to stay away from you.'

'By touching me?'

Please, I begged silently, *don't let anyone disturb us now*. He raised his hand so I could see his palm. He looked at me, his eyes twinkling but his mouth a thin line, serious. He reached forward, palm out, and placed it on the centre of my chest, right below my neck, right where Odette had stepped on me in the herb shop.

His skin, the smoothness of it, I never wanted anything more in my life than his touch in that second. Our world had been thronged by hunger for blood. We had been perpetrators of pain and here we were touching properly for the first time, as humans. I reached up to his cheek and could feel my heart thumping against his skin. I wanted to breathe him, the way he smelt, to see every pore of his skin, to feel his heart beating.

I shivered. Rhode continued staring down at his hand pressing against my flesh.

'You . . .' I whispered, 'are worth every moment I have left on this earth. Even if I have to love you from afar for the rest of my days.'

Rhode's bottom lip trembled and mine did too. I swallowed hard.

Tears spilled over his cheeks as he watched his hand rising and falling as I breathed. I couldn't look into his eyes while he cried tears for me.

Apples! No! Not now. Apples. Everywhere. The scent overwhelmed me. A white light blinded me.

Rhode stands in the centre of a great library. I have never seen a room like this in my life. Huge wooden bookcases stretch to a ceiling decorated with an Italian-style fresco. But I cannot focus on the cherubs or the white billowing clouds of the painting.

Rhode has short hair. He stands with his hands behind his back and wears a black three-piece suit. It must be 1910 or close to it.

'She is in hibernation,' Rhode explains to people I cannot see. 'Below the ground in Hathersage.'

'You wish to bring her here?' a deep voice asks from across the room.

'I wish to make a bargain,' Rhode says.

'Lenah Beaudonte in Lovers Bay?' the voice says with a hoarse laughter. *'The vampire queen herself.'*

'She will live as a mortal, sir,' Rhode says.

'Fascinating! Let us discuss this bargain,' the deep voice says again.

A white wash of light wipes over my sight and the library disappears. Where did Rhode go? Rhode? Now I am back in that foyer I have been seeing for months. Even though it is dark, he comes into focus . . . slowly. A modern-day Rhode, a human Rhode, falls to his knees.

'I can't do it!' Rhode yells. *'I understand the consequences. I know the risk.'*

Images come in bullets.

A beach road lined by tall cliffs.

The ocean, stretching far into the distance.

A large house, a Gothic mansion, set far back from the ocean.

Number forty-two chiselled in a stone plaque outside the mansion.

I knew instantly that this house was a terrible place. A place of dark power. I had to find it.

Back in the House of Mirrors Rhode touched me. I drew in great heaving breaths and stumbled back into the mirror behind me. It swung on its hinges. I blinked hard, trying to recall the images.

'What? What was that?' I asked. 'That house.'

Rhode wiped his eyes quickly and looked down at the floor. My skin still pulsed where his hand had been.

'That house. What did you do?' I hissed.

'Did you have a vision?' Rhode asked, and stepped forward, his arm outstretched.

Rhode had bargained with someone at that mansion. Someone powerful who knew me and exactly what I had done in my past. And I was going to find them.

I stalked quickly out of the Hall of Mirrors back into the sunlight.

'Lenah,' Rhode said, coming after me.

Students all around us were talking about their costumes for the dance that night.

'I have to go,' I said, matter-of-factly.

'Lenah!' Rhode ran after me but I was quick down the lane, past the many booths until I stopped short. Roy Enos and some lacrosse players held a very close and intimate court. Roy's expression was dark, his posture hunched, crumpled.

Nothing is wrong, I told myself. *Nothing is wrong with Justin. I am going to fix this.* Something within me told me that house was of critical importance. I had to go there. It would help us to fight Odette.

'Lenah!' Rhode's voice echoed. 'Lenah!' He was right behind me.

I spun around. 'No, Rhode. Whatever it is – I know that road. That house. And I am going.'

'Don't,' he said, and we stood at the edge of the field. 'For once don't follow your impulses.'

'You can't stop me,' I said. Rhode lifted a foot to take a step towards me when . . .

With a crash of cymbals, the band happily charged on to the field for the fifth time that afternoon. The white wool outfits and silly hats separated us. I watched Rhode try to duck through an open spot but the band was relentless. I took that as my opportunity to turn and run.

CHAPTER 22

That house was the key. I knew it. Someone would help me. Help us. We could fight Odette and we could win. I found Vicken by the boat house watching Roy and his buddies in their huddle.

'I need you to come somewhere with me,' I said. 'While there's still daylight.'

'No.'

'I had another vision. I saw a place in Rhode's mind.'

'What place? What are you doing trusting his visions?'

'I can't explain it now. I need you to come with me. To a house.'

'I seem to recall already saying no. No more spells, no more summonings.'

He tossed his cigarette into the grass and sighed, meeting my eyes again.

'What will it cost, going to this house? More burns? Your skin? Your soul?' Vicken asked.

'Fine,' I said, and crossed over the grass towards the pathway, leaving the Halloween carnival behind me. I would just get in my car and go alone. I knew that road. It went past the town beach and led to Nickerson Summit, where I had bungee jumped the year before.

I had to be quick, before Rhode could find me and stop me.

'Damn it, Lenah!' sighed Vicken. 'You know I'm going to help you. But this house, this vision, it could be any house.'

'No, it can't. It was a stone house and I've been on the road that leads there – I recognized it,' I said as we approached the car.

'It's not good for us to go alone,' Vicken said.

I opened the car door and slid inside. 'Where we're going, we're not going to be alone. We're going there to get help.'

I knew we were close. The road grew steeper and steeper, rising higher and higher. Just as in Rhode's memory, to the east there was a drop of hundreds of feet of cliffs and sand dunes to the water below.

'We have to get back in time for the dance, Lenah,' Vicken said. 'She's going to start wreaking havoc.'

'We will. We're going to get help.'

'So you keep saying.'

'There it is!' I cried. I slammed on the brakes,

making the tyres squeal. On a small stone plaque on a tree next to a long driveway leading deep into the woods, away from the ocean, was the number forty-two.

We turned off the road and followed the curves and bends of the driveway. We must have driven a mile, maybe more. When we finally came upon the house, we had to stop because a mechanically controlled gate protected the entrance to the grounds of an enormous grey stone building. There were tall towers on the left and back of the house. There were only two windows on the front of the house; they were utterly black.

Vicken exhaled heavily then said, 'I don't know about you, but this house says to me: *Come inside if you want to die.*'

I rolled down my window. On an intercom on the gatepost a sign read: PRESS FOR ENTRY.

As my finger hovered over the button, a deep voice with an indistinguishable accent said through the receiver, 'You are welcome here, Lenah Beaudonte.'

'Well, that's comforting,' Vicken said.

I gulped away fear. We had to keep going.

I backed into a space just next to the front door. The front of the car faced the woods, but in my wing mirror I could see the stone monstrosity. Just like my house in Hathersage, this mansion had barely any windows.

Vicken sat beside me. I loved his mane-like hair and pensive eyes. He looked at me from the passenger seat, waiting for me to say what we would be doing and why we had come.

'I'm glad you're here,' I said.

'Wouldn't miss it for the world,' he replied as he undid his seatbelt. He stopped me as I motioned to get out of the car. 'We really might die in there,' he said, his brown eyes serious.

I considered him again, his wild hair and the strong point of his chin. He was the soldier of my life.

'I won't hold it against you if you decide to stay in the car. This is for me to do,' I said.

He got out without another word.

Our feet crunched over the tiny shells of the drive. Once I was out of the car, I realized just how well cared for these grounds were. Stone statues hid among flowers. At the end of the long length of the house was the glass of a greenhouse. This was not just a house. This was a compound.

We walked to the front door and stood together before the thick black oak. Hand poised over the door knocker, for a moment I imagined that Vicken and I were going to a dinner party at a friend's house.

We were normal people, not former vampires. Just people. Teenagers who wanted to live their lives. I was about to knock, when the door opened.

With a little skip of my heart I recognized the man behind the door. He was the man from my vision, but he did not wear a robe as he did in my dreams. He wore a cotton sweater and conservative brown slacks. He could have been a professor, from the looks of his spectacles and outfit. His eyes moved back and forth from Vicken to me.

'Oh, good,' he said with a relieved sigh. 'You're both unforsaken.'

With a swipe of his hands, his entire outfit morphed into a mist of colour as though it was made of nothing but coloured dust. The man was suddenly clad in black dress trousers and a set of black academic robes. *This* was the ensemble I had seen before.

'Unforsaken?' Vicken asked.

'You are both the damned. Once vampires. You are welcome here,' he said, and opened the door wide. As our feet stepped over the threshold into a foyer, I snuck a last glance behind me out of the door. With a heavy thud it closed – leaving us momentarily in complete darkness.

Vicken held his breath. He was primed to defend me.

'No need to consider tactics of speed and strength, Vicken Clough. They would be quite useless here,' the man said.

With a snap of his fingers, candles flickered and their brightness bloomed. There were glass wall sconces in the four corners of the room. Above us was a small chandelier. Five sconces, five candles – a pentacle star. This room held power.

'I am Rayken, Lenah Beaudonte,' he said, and extended a hand. When I took it in mine, my suspicion that he was most definitely a vampire was confirmed, for his hands were icy cold and the pupils of his brown eyes were wide and black. Rayken held my gaze and a small smile played on the edges of his pressed lips. 'You are warm,' he said, letting go of my hand. 'Fascinating.' He took a step back. 'You may wait here and I will alert my brothers to your arrival.'

He walked down the long hallway and turned to the right. Vicken and I stood alone in the foyer. Vicken turned around and placed his hand on the door. There was no doorknob.

'We're locked in . . .' he whispered, looking around and up. 'Whoa! The ceiling is onyx!' he marvelled.

The blackness of onyx will show the original soul. And there, glowing above me, was the true reflection of mine. In my reflection, hanging above my heart was a smoky orb. When I moved about the foyer, it followed. I looked down, trying to reach out in front of my chest to touch it, but I could not see it except in the onyx ceiling, where it hung just in front of the place where my heart beat inside my chest. Vicken had one too.

'What is that?' Vicken asked, pointing.

'I . . .' I stuttered. 'I think they're our souls. I've never seen myself in onyx before so I can't be sure.' I was in awe of this strange orb, a silvery grey cloud hanging over my heart.

'We couldn't,' Vicken replied, 'as vampires.'

Now we were both mortals we could see ourselves in the onyx ceiling; vampires cannot see themselves because there is no soul to reflect. Onyx, as a stone, harbours enormous power. Dark power. The darker the soul, the darker onyx will appear. It sucks up the negative energy.

'This way, please,' a voice said from the darkness of the hallway. Vicken and I stole one more glance at ourselves in the onyx ceiling and went down the hall behind Rayken. We twisted and turned through a labyrinth of passageways until we reached a wooden archway. Two doors were decorated with sculptures of hundreds of twisted and pained bodies with long serpentine tongues and bulging eyes. I looked away.

The grotesqueness made me uncomfortable.

The vampire reached for a doorknob shaped like a dagger. I had had similar ones in my own house in Hathersage. Crafted by the Linaldi vampires in Italy. Master craftsmen – I remembered as I had killed many of them in 1500.

'Good luck,' the vampire said, and opened the door.

I glanced back at Vicken, who took my hand in his. We entered a huge library. The one from Rhode's vision! As my eyes scanned the circumference of the room I saw that every wall was lined from floor to ceiling with books. Above me, the familiar fresco recreated the brightest sky of the loveliest summer day.

A crackle of flames drew my eyes from the ceiling. An enormous fireplace was set at the back of the room, taking up half the length of one wall. The fire flickered, casting an orange light about the room. Before it sat three vampires in comfortable chairs, each with a book in their hands.

In the middle was Rayken, who seconds before had been standing in the hallway.

I swallowed, trying to remain calm.

'Welcome, Lenah Beaudonte and Vicken Clough. It is with great pleasure that I see Rhode's ritual has worked – twice,' said Rayken.

'You have impressive power. Your speed,' I observed.

'I do not aim to impress, Ms Beaudonte. My power is in my knowledge. Vampires cannot move any faster than the natural human being.'

He hasn't met Odette, I thought. It was obvious Rayken had reached his seat long before Vicken and I had even stepped over the threshold. Either way, I didn't believe him. I had seen what Suleen and Odette had been able to do.

'You know our names. I believe we should know all of yours. It is only fair,' I said.

Rayken looked his left.

'Laertes,' that vampire said with a nod of greeting.

'Like in *Hamlet*,' Vicken piped up from behind me, and for a moment he sounded pleased with himself. He cleared his throat. 'If you read that kind of thing.'

Laertes the vampire smiled, and it was warm enough to make him seem human.

'Fascinating,' said the third vampire. He smiled as well, an open-mouthed smile, and it was then I saw he had no fangs. Just two gaping holes where fangs would normally be. Just like in my nightmare!

'She sees we are different,' Laertes said, and placed a hand on Rayken's knee.

I saw they were different, but I also saw their

power. I wanted them to help me fight Odette, but first I wanted answers.

'Ms Beaudonte, you've already met Rayken,' Laertes said. 'And to our right is Levi. We are—'

'The Hollow Ones,' I said. The men from Rhode's vision.

The three bowed their heads in unison.

'The Hollow Ones?' repeated Vicken.

'I know very little of you,' I admitted awkwardly, 'but I have heard of you.'

'Your friend Rhode has not told you of our expertise?' Levi asked. He had great folds of skin and deep wrinkles around his eyes, indicating that he was likely to have been made a vampire very late in life.

'He has come here, I know. I have seen it in my mind,' I said, and dared to take a step towards them. 'I had a vision in which you met with Rhode. He begged you to spare his life. He pleaded.'

'Spare his life?' Rayken said. 'Rhode Lewin never asked us to spare his life.'

He didn't?

'Hmm. Hmm . . .' The Hollow Ones exchanged glances and their tone was one of concern.

'You say you saw it in your mind?' Laertes asked.

I nodded.

'Interesting. How was it you were privy to his

thoughts?' Rayken asked, folding his hands in his lap.

'We are soulmates. Once the Aeris decreed we couldn't be together, he refused to touch me. Yet I seemed to become connected to his thoughts. Sometimes his memories.'

Laertes, Rayken and Levi shared a glance and spoke in a strange hushed language. I heard the phrase *Anam Cara*. Then the name Suleen.

'True soulmates, those whose essences of life are intertwined, will find a way to connect even when they cannot physically be together,' Laertes explained.

These vampires knew me, they knew of my atrocities. I needed no summoning spell this time. I needed their strength to help me deal with Odette. I didn't need to solve the mystery of Rhode just yet. I had to stay focused on the task at hand.

'I have come to ask of you a different favour than Rhode,' I said.

'We do not partake in favours,' Rayken replied.

'It's true,' Laertes said with a sigh. 'Knowledge, and knowledge only. Rhode sought our protection, which could only be achieved for a trade.'

I knew this trade, whatever it was, would be dangerous. Perhaps kill me.

'What did Rhode bargain with?' I asked.

'Love,' Laertes replied.

'What?' I whispered. This didn't make sense.

'That's what Rhode was here for. If he gave us his capacity to love, for us to study, we would protect you for the rest of your mortal life.'

'How can you do that?' Vicken asked.

'We can do many things,' Rayken replied.

'We cannot love, Ms Beaudonte,' Laertes said.

'Vampires *can* love,' I countered.

'We removed that ability from ourselves long ago – it diminished our power to learn,' Laertes said.

'So you would take away his love for me?' My voice wavered as horror raced through me. 'Did he do it?' My voice cracked. I thought back on all the visions. Today in the Hall of Mirrors, Rhode had touched me. He had wept.

I tried to draw in breath as this realization rolled over me. I had been so foolish! I thought Rhode couldn't handle his mortality. But it was so much more than that. He had considered giving up his love for me in exchange for keeping me safe? That was the source of his torment?

'He failed,' Rayken said. 'He could not.'

'What is it you desire, Ms Beaudonte?'

'Rhode could not give up his love for me?' I asked. I wanted this confirmed before I asked for protection from Odette.

'No,' Rayken said again. 'He would not part with his ability to love you, despite your circumstances with the Aeris.'

It had to be true. How else would they know about the Aeris?

Rhode could not give up his love. He had said it in his vision: *What you ask is too much.* And in the Hall of Mirrors he had finally given in to the torment. No matter what, we would never be able to stay away from one another. We would keep coming back to this moment again and again. I could call it any number of names: Anam Cara, soulmates, the love of my life; he was my Rhode.

Forever.

But it wasn't just about Rhode.

Images swam into my mind and a different understanding of love overwhelmed me. It wasn't just my love for Rhode . . . it was something else.

Tracy telling me she would help me – no matter what.

Tony's portrait in shreds.

Ms Tate's closed eyes, almost sleeping. A note resting on her chest.

Claudia's tear-streaked face moments before her death.

Was this life? Is this what I begged for during the days I spent in utter madness in Hathersage? My heart burned in my chest when I thought of myself scattering daises like a madwoman over the floor of the mansion.

I looked up at the Hollow Ones. I knew what I wanted and it wasn't protection any more. What I had to do, I should have done months ago. It was the only way to finally let go of Odette and the life I had led in Hathersage. If I was truly no longer the monster I had been, the one capable of killing for no reason, then I had to let go of my human life at Wickham. I knew what I had to do and why all of the events of this year had brought me to this moment with the Hollow Ones.

'I am willing to trade,' I said. 'I don't know what you could possibly want from me. But I am willing to give it.'

'Lenah!' Vicken said, shocked.

I dipped my head. I had to get this out. 'I came here to ask you to help me fight a vampire who is coming for me. But that's not what I want any more. I want something far more important.'

The desire within me shifted as I spoke.

'I want you to call the Aeris for me,' I said. I wanted to go back to the medieval world, just as Fire had proposed all those months ago.

Laertes considered me for a moment. 'You are a very curious creature, Ms Beaudonte . . .'

'And foolish perhaps,' I said. 'I know I cannot

give up my ability to love. Rhode and I are the same in that way.'

Laertes waited a moment and then said, 'Your blood will suffice as a trade.'

'My blood?' I lifted my chin.

Vicken stepped to my side.

'No,' he said, and his tone was hard.

'We will help you. Your ritual is very intriguing, as is the story of your ability to wield sunlight. We have never seen the blood of anyone who has this capacity. Not even your Rhode.'

Agreement echoed from other two Hollow Ones.

'No,' Vicken said again. 'This is some silly ploy to murder you.'

'Your bodyguard must remain silent or he will have to wait outside,' Laertes said as he rummaged in a small box. There was a clinking of metal and glass.

'Lenah, no,' Vicken said, putting his hands on my shoulders. 'I beg you to see reason.'

As I looked into Vicken's earnest gaze, I knew what I was doing was right. I looked at my old friend, knowing I never should have taken him from his father's house. Just as Rhode would never give up his love for me, I knew I could never live a life where all the people I loved could die at the hands of vampires. Or be hurt. All so I could be human. It was clear to me now. For Rhode and me too. We would keep damaging each other, keep trying to find ways to be together without breaking the impossible decree.

That was no life.

I needed to go back to the medieval world, just as Fire had proposed to me all those weeks earlier.

Laertes took long strides towards me, his robe billowing behind him, sending waves of air that made the flames flicker. The other two Hollow Ones remained seated. Vicken backed away as the vampire came closer to me.

'I am going to drain you of nearly all your blood, Ms Beaudonte. When you awake you will be in a small room. Just there.' Laertes pointed to an archway that materialized next to the fireplace. A heavy door of dark brown wood was decorated with silver curling designs that looked like strange alien flowers. 'You will be in a bare room. Do not come back in here until your meeting with the Aeris is over.'

'You could kill me and I'll never get to have my meeting,' I said, feeling my heart thump in my throat.

Laertes held a small knife in his hand – a tiny blade. Now that I was close, I could see the gaping holes in his mouth where he had removed his fangs too.

'She must go alone,' Laertes said, looking at Vicken. I turned to look at him and our eyes lingered on one another's. Vicken's hands hung limp by his sides. He swallowed hard but said nothing. I did not know if I should leave him like this. But I had to take the risk.

'I find it interesting, Ms Beaudonte, that at precisely ten o' clock this evening, you will fight a coven of vampires. The newest vampire queen and her coven in fact. Yet you choose no protection. Instead, you call for a meeting with the Aeris. Why?' Laertes cocked his head with an ever so slight smile.

'Because I think I can win that fight.'

'Then if you die from this blood removal, it is no matter.'

'Oh yes, it is,' I replied, and bared my wrist to him. 'I have to take her down with me.'

Laertes replied only with a gummy, fangless smile.

CHAPTER 23

Vicken had to be held back by two silent men in black who came in through the door from the hallway. I did not watch as my blood flowed into the large glass vessel. I tried to ignore the pulsing of my heart through the cut on my wrist. Just when I felt woozy, just when my legs gave out, everything went black.

I tried to blink once or twice but my eyelids were sticky. I wanted to lift my arms. *So do it. Lift your arms, Lenah.* I tried, but could not. I tried again, groaning, but my hands were too heavy. I tried to focus, but all was swimming blackness. Laertes' face loomed over me. His eyes travelled over my features.

Oh God. He was going to kill me. He did it. He tricked me.

'Can't,' I whispered, but it was all I could say.

The Hollow One produced a small vial from within the folds of his robes. A tiny glass tube with a blue liquid inside. He lifted my arm from the floor and it seemed to float there in the air in his hand. A dark line of blood ran from my wrist and down my forearm. Laertes dropped two small spots of blue liquid on it. It sizzled as though on fire, but it did not hurt. The skin tightened as though being sewn back together.

Within seconds, the blood on my arm seemed to melt into my skin, becoming part of the flesh tone of my arm. Soon after, my hands and fingers began to tingle with pins and needles.

'Your blood will regenerate very quickly. Do not get up until you can move your toes. Good luck,' he said, and with the sound of a few footsteps he was gone.

I lay paralysed on the floor. The temperature was cool against the back of my head. The weight of my body seemed to sink into the icy floor beneath me.

Wait . . .

I could sense temperature. I tried to press down on the floor with my palms. I could. My fingertips gripped at the floor as I tried to push up. I fell back to the ground with a smack of my head against the floor. I groaned and tried again. *Push up!* My stomach muscles shook. *Keep pressing, Lenah!* I sat up, exhaling, and looked ahead of me. There was nothing but a stone wall. No windows. I stared upward, my feet still numb. The ceiling here too was black onyx and there were no windows or candles,

356

yet somehow I could see. With my legs extended straight out in front of me, I surveyed the back of the room with a heavy twist of my neck. Behind me was a wooden door with a black dagger handle. Along the bottom was a piping of golden light. The only way out. But I could not leave, Laertes had said. Not until I had finished speaking with the Aeris.

The door started to glow as if a spotlight was being shone on it. I used my hands, which were stronger with every moment that passed, to pull myself around to face the light. Like a fishtail, my legs tingled.

As on the archery field, there was a tiny speck of white light, in the centre of the room. It grew and grew until the whole room was dazzling. Within that light were the outlines of hundreds of bodies, including that one small childish shape.

The four figures of the Aeris materialized in front of the sea of bodies, stepping forward in unison just as they had up on the plateau. Fire stepped forward, ahead of the other three elements.

She looked down at my legs. The pins and needles were travelling down my thighs. It wouldn't be long now.

'Forgive me,' I said. 'I would stand but I cannot.'

Fire bent low so that her dress hung over her knees and flowed out over the floor. The other three members of the Aeris joined her at my feet. Together, they stacked their hands one on top of the other and placed them on top of my ankles. The pressure of their hands was like soft petals on me; they were so light even though they leaned their body weight on top of me.

They sent something through me, a surge of light, of love, or life – I didn't know. I heaved in a great gust of air. I caught it quickly and clenched my hands. I ran my palms over my thighs and could feel the smoothness of my skin beneath my clothes.

I got to my feet as the other elements retreated and stood behind Fire.

'Thank you,' I said. I looked at the Aeris, each one in turn, and said, 'Thank you,' again.

Each bowed her head.

'You are very brave,' Fire said.

I hesitated, then said, 'I wish I could have worked it out sooner.'

'Why have you called us?' she asked gently.

'I admit, part of me wishes to plead with you. To beg to break the decree that keeps Rhode and me apart. There's nothing I want more.'

'But . . . ?' she said, leading me. She wore her red gown and her hair crackled, a curl of red flames that spat and sparked tangerine and gold light.

'I've burned myself, thrown myself in harm's

way to fend off a vampire attack.'

I lifted my wrist to show Fire the gauze still protecting my burn, but it had disappeared when they'd healed me. I dropped my arm.

'The Hollow Ones wanted to study my blood. They asked Rhode to give up love,' I said, meeting the spooky red eyes of Fire.

She smiled at me with understanding, almost proud.

'And after all that, do you know what I wish?' I asked.

'Tell me,' Fire said, and her skin seemed to glow, as if tiny lightning storms flickered under the surface. I conjured the words from deep in my brain and deep within my human soul. I whispered my truest confession, one that I had only uttered once before, to Tony before he died.

'I wish I had never walked out into the orchard that night. I wish I had died in the fifteenth century as I was meant to.' As I spoke, my voice cracked and my eyes burned from tears.

Fire kept my gaze and nodded once, slowly. She then stepped aside and invited me to look into the white light behind her. One shape came forward from the indistinct mass. The form of a young man stood next to Fire and took on substance. Focusing again, forming, until I could make out who he was.

Gauges in his ears, a warm smile, and he held his hands in his pockets.

Tony. Tony in colour – unmistakable in colour and life. Warmth exploded in the centre of my chest, radiating down to my hands.

He met my eyes but did not speak.

'I miss you,' I whispered in a rush. He backed away with a smile on his lips and disappeared back into the light. The last clear, distinguishable feature I saw were the apples of his cheeks as he smiled.

Fire bowed her head. 'Sometimes, making the difficult decision is what sets us free,' she said.

I tried to find Tony again but the shape of his shoulders and his artist's hands were a wash of light now.

I drew a deep breath.

'I want . . .' I said, and looked into her eyes. I meant every word that came out of my mouth. 'I want what you offered me on the archery field. To go back to the fifteenth century. But alone.' I took a breath. 'I know Rhode is a vampire in the fifteenth century and the only way for us to be together is if I join him there. That is too tempting. So I ask you that he will remain here in the present day.'

'Remain?' Fire asked.

'He died for me, or at least he tried to. I want him to live. If he remembers his past, he'll go mad.

So I also ask that he retains no memory. That he is with a family, free.'

'And Vicken? If you go, if you return,' Fire explained, 'Vicken returns to the nineteenth century. He never becomes a vampire.'

A memory engulfed me momentarily. *Vicken in a blue soldier's uniform. He dances on a table, kicking out his legs, smiling. He is sweating. He is human . . . and he is happy.*

'This is a time in which he was never meant to live.'

Fire walked to me, out of the light and into the darkness of the room. She stood directly on the line separating us. The line that divided her world of white light and mine of darkness and colour – the mortal world. She looked at me, cocked her head and smiled another tight-lipped smile.

'All cycles must complete. The sun that begins the day must set. The spark that lights the world must go out. Finish what you started. Break the cycle of the ritual and it will be done.'

'I defeat Odette and you'll send me back, as I wish?'

Fire nodded.

'And my victims, they'll be free? And those killed by the vampires I made?'

The white mass of souls behind the Aeris swayed

and fluttered as though a light breeze had blown through the room.

'They will all be free,' Fire said.

'But they will not be white souls?' I asked.

'They must make their own way, as it should always have been.'

As on the archery field, Fire started to fade; I could already make out the wall behind her.

'When it's over, you must go to the archery field. When the new sun rises, you will be sent back.'

'And the battle?' I asked, knowing she would understand. 'If I die?'

Water, Earth and Air faded with the light, yet Fire was as bright as ever. She came to me and lifted my hand to hers. Her skin felt like satin on mine.

'I have faith you can do this, Lenah.'

'I keep none for myself,' I replied.

In a grave whisper she said, 'Knowledge is your key.'

'Knowledge? What does . . . ?' I stopped as she glanced back at the fading mass of people behind her.

Then with purpose she said, 'The dead do not show themselves to the living. Not unless they deserve it, unless they have a white soul.'

'My soul was not white. I saw it in the onyx ceiling. It was grey.'

She retreated towards the wispy strands of white light. She too began to fade away.

'You do now.' She looked up and my gaze followed hers. In my reflection I saw an orb as before, but this time it was white, clean, pure.

My mouth parted and for the first time in what seemed like an eternity, I smiled.

'Wait!' I called, taking a step towards her. Fire flickered before me as a candle burning out. 'Rhode – will he be happy?'

Fire smiled and disappeared into nothingness.

I turned back to the door and twisted the knob. I expected to step back into the library. Instead, I found myself on the front stoop, back out in the late-afternoon sun facing the shelled driveway. I shielded my eyes from the light. Vicken shot up; he had been sitting on the bottom step facing the long drive and smoking a cigarette.

He spun around and grabbed me into an embrace. I held on to his lean frame. He smelt of tobacco. I lingered there for a moment, taking him in.

'I actually feel sick,' he said, and I felt his deep voice vibrate within his chest. 'Now I know why bloody idiot mortals say they're worried sick.'

'I'm all right,' I said, and pulled away.

'Ten o' clock is six hours from now, Lenah. We have to go,' Vicken said. I dug in my pocket for the car keys and I handed them to him. But he didn't run to the car. Instead he asked, 'Well? Do we fight?'

'Fire said, no matter what, we must succeed in beating Odette. It breaks the cycle of the ritual.'

'Breaks the cycle?'

'The ritual will be gone from the world if we defeat her,' I explained.

'Excellent. Did Señor No Fangs or the Fiery Lady say what happens if we win?'

I couldn't tell him what would happen if we won. He would try to convince me to stay in this world, stay together, because that's all he had known for the last hundred and sixty years. But I needed to send him back where he belonged.

I shook my head and managed to smile as a strange sense of calm washed over me. We got back into the car. As he drove, I leaned my head against the seat, listening to the sound of the engine. I listened to the motor, to the radio and the gearshift. I watched the street lamps go by. I took in everything and anything. Anything that did not exist – that would not exist – in 1418.

The door creaked as I walked into my apartment. I expected to be alone, but someone was sitting on my couch: tall body, hunched posture, spiky black hair. Rhode held his head in his hands. When I was first made human again and Rhode walked out on to that porch to die, he was so sure, so absolutely sure of his death. He looked up at the click of the door.

'What have you done?' he demanded. I sat down next to him. He looked at me, eyes wide.

'For months, I thought you were trying to hurt yourself. That you thought you didn't deserve your humanity or something,' I admitted.

'Why would you think that?' he asked.

'Since you came back from Hathersage, I have been connected with you. I could see your thoughts. Sometimes memories. And I misread your pain. That's what happened in the Hall of Mirrors.'

'Connected?' Rhode asked, not understanding.

'What I thought was your mind unravelling was your struggle with the Hollow Ones. That you could not give up your love for me.'

Rhode frowned and stood up from the couch.

'I see. So you've uncovered my relationship with the Hollow Ones,' he said, and walked to the bureau. He placed his hands on it and dipped his chin to his chest. I watched his strong back muscles contract through his thin T-shirt as he spoke.

'When I awoke after the ritual, you lay on the

couch, asleep. I just kept watching you. A human finally, *finally*, after you had wanted it so badly.'

He turned to me and leaned his back against the bureau. I was too afraid to speak. As if interrupting his thoughts would stop him telling me what I had waited so long to hear.

'I could not help my reverence. I was proud,' he said with a quick shake of his head. 'Of what we had been able to accomplish with the ritual. It was unheard of. A simple combination of spells and herbs. But the intention – the crucial, most variable ingredient – was the most difficult to find. For we both had to find it within ourselves.'

Now Rhode paced before me.

'So, I had two choices. Either I could wake you and we could begin our human life together, or I could let you live a life without me. I had so many debts to pay. A large one to Suleen . . . I owed him.' He met my eyes, and although I didn't understand all of it I felt we were there, on the verge of it, on the brink of truth.

'I owed *you*,' he continued, 'the chance to be human without me interfering. So I chose to pay off my debts, believing you could acclimatize to your human life and, if you and I were going to come back together, surely I could explain it to you over time. So I went to the Hollow Ones. They pledged your protection for the entirety of your mortal life if I could . . .' He hesitated and I listened rapt. 'They sent me on an impossible task, Lenah. They expected me to deliver love. Actual love. If I could capture it, if I could find incantations or spells that might steal love away so that I could give it to the Hollow Ones, they would protect you. You would be free from the darkness that had engulfed you for centuries.'

Rhode picked up a photo of me from the bureau and I wondered momentarily if he would throw it across the room. 'I failed,' he said, and his voice was barely audible. 'And then I found myself in the debt of the Hollow Ones. The protection for you was lifted. Vicken arrived and I was too late to get you out of Lovers Bay.'

I was silent and looked down at my hands. I couldn't imagine Rhode failing at anything.

'Where did you go?' I asked hoarsely.

'Back out to search. To the furthest corners of the earth. I failed again.' He dropped to his knees in front of me and placed his hands on my thighs. 'Once you take love from someone through magic, they can never love again. They are not evil, they are not angry; they are hollow and empty, which is almost worse. I couldn't siphon life away from anyone else. I had done that for hundreds of years by taking their blood.'

The thought of Rhode doing this sent goose-bumps over me.

'I could not and do not understand that kind of evil. When I returned . . .' He gulped and took a moment to finish. 'When I came back to Lovers Bay to tell the Hollow Ones, I heard that you were a vampire again.'

He gripped my knees and I wanted to hold him to me. I wanted to say it was all right.

'I saw your life as a golden orb hanging before me. Drawing me like the brightest of suns. I did not fear your light.'

'You couldn't give up your love for me,' I said.

'I could not,' Rhode replied quietly. 'Would not.'

It was time for me to tell the truth in return.

'I bargained with the Hollow Ones, Rhode. I asked them to call the Aeris.'

Rhode's eyes snapped up to meet mine. He dropped his hands from my legs and the mood in the room changed considerably.

'They never do anything willingly – what did . . . ?'

'In exchange for my blood, the blood of a vampire who could wield sunlight and who had survived the ritual twice, they called the Aeris for me.' I swallowed hard, trying to stay in control of my emotions.

Rhode stood up and kicked at the coffee table, sending books and pens flying into the air. I flinched and looked away from the falling debris.

'How could you? They can't be trusted, Lenah. You don't know what that transaction could mean for you years from now. They'll have that blood. Have that magic.' He ran his hand through his hair. 'You could have died.'

'I did not die, Rhode.' Exhaustion laced my tone.

I stared at the curve of his neck, the line of flesh between his hair and his black T-shirt. I wanted to touch his skin while I still could.

'And what did you ask the Aeris for? For protection tonight from Odette? Lenah, there will always be more vampires. Did you ask to break the decree?'

'No!' I yelled, and Rhode sighed. His silence was his response. 'You expect so little of me, always the selfish girl. Do you remember what the Aeris said? That we were soulmates and there was nothing they could do about that?'

Rhode nodded.

'All this time I've been thinking about myself. About you, about me, about what we can't have. I was never worried about the people who *really* deserved justice.'

'Lenah—'

'No,' I said, and cut him off. 'No more formalities. We have to beat Odette. Fire said so specifically. Once we do, once we kill Odette, the following morning, at sunrise, I will return to the fifteenth century and Fire will undo all of our atrocities. Erase our murders, and the ones committeed by the vampires we created.'

'*What?*'

'Why weren't we worried about the people in the white light behind the Aeris? About Tony or Kate, or Chloe? Even Justin? Who knows where he is now, if he's even alive.'

'The medieval world . . .' Rhode started to say with a shake of his head.

'My life will be short. I'll marry young, die young. But I'll get to live, Rhode. And we'll spare the lives of everyone we killed.'

He seemed to consider something, and then he spoke.

'But I can't live not being able to love you,' Rhode said, and my heart ached at his words. 'I'll be a vampire in the fifteenth century, watching you. Waiting for you.'

I swallowed. Gathering strength. I couldn't look at him when I said it. 'I worked that bit out too. When I go back to the fifteenth century, you will remain here with no memory of your past. You will be seventeen-year-old Rhode, with a family. A young man with your whole life ahead of you.'

'No, Lenah. This isn't fair. I've had no choice in this.'

I lunged at him, pointing my finger into his chest so he stumbled back against the bureau.

'No!' I said with a shout. 'No. *I* never had a choice. *You* walked into my orchard and made *me* a vampire. Everything that has transpired since that event will be undone by this choice *of mine.*'

I caught my breath in the silent moment that passed between us.

'Did you ever forgive me?' he asked quietly.

'Did you?' I asked. 'I saw you. You told Suleen you were unsure if you could ever forgive me. That perhaps I was unlovable after . . .' I hesitated, 'after what I had done.' My voice cracked. I was unable to help it.

Rhode and I were only a foot apart. I watched the realization of this pass over his face. 'That was a thought I had a few months ago. It never happened, and I regretted it '

'So your memory was . . . ?'

'Just a thought I was having in the moment. You *were* connected to my thoughts.'

I allowed this to settle over me.

'You forgave me?' I said quietly.

I leaned to him and brought my lips within millimetres of his. He looked down at me, and we could so easily have kissed. His breath was so soft on my mouth.

'Didn't I always tell you, Lenah? You're my only hope.'

He bent forward just a hair, our lips grazed each other's. I was about to kiss Rhode as a mortal for the first time.

'I love you, Lenah,' he whispered.

I was lost in the possibility of Rhode's lips caressing mine. My heart sang, and every pore in my body craved his touch. I wanted to be one with his soul.

Bam!

Someone pounded on the door to my room.

We jumped apart.

'I'll get it,' Rhode said, and when he backed away the air between us felt strange and spoiled.

Vicken stood in the hallway dressed all in black, his hair slicked back so his features were more prominent. He smiled with his lips closed as though he was hiding something. Then his grin widened and two very fine and very white pointed fangs gleamed.

'Wow!' Rhode said, stepping back, and my spirits lifted when he chuckled.

'You're dressed as a *vampire*?' I asked.

Rhode shook his head in disbelief and chuckled again.

'What?' Vicken said with a shrug, as though it was the most normal thing in the world. 'It'th *ironic*,' he said with a lisp. The fake fangs made it difficult for him to close his mouth. He came in and shut the door behind him.

'Lovely . . .' Rhode said. He unzipped his duffel bag and pulled out his longsword. The silver blade caught the light and reflected tiny beams over the floor.

'Vicken took a couple of steps into the room. 'Look at the two of you. Pathetic,' he said. 'Where are you cothtumes? You can't juth walk into a danthe with a thord on your back.'

Rhode motioned at the bag lying open on the floor. 'I took care of that.' He turned over the duffel bag and five daggers spilled out. 'Now, help.'

CHAPTER 24

White ruffles hanging off cheap fabric . . . faces painted to look like demons or angels . . . These were the snippets of costumes that I could see around me on Wickham campus the night of the Halloween dance, the final night of Nuit Rouge.

The decorations were coupled with orange flashing lights. Security vehicles lit up the pathways.

This was a new Wickham.

A frightened Wickham.

A Wickham tainted by vampire bloodlust.

I scanned the crowds for Justin's tall frame but I did not see him.

Rhode, Vicken and I stood in the alleyway next to Seeker and watched our classmates cross the green towards Hopper and go into the gymnasium. I tightened the baldric on my back, a leather strap that held the sword close to my body. It pulled on my back whenever I moved.

'So tell me what Fire said,' Vicken asked for the tenth time.

'She said knowledge was the key.'

'We can't worry about cryptic messages from the Aeris. We have to stay focused,' Rhode commented, keeping his gaze on the dark campus.

'Laertes said ten,' I reminded Rhode.

'Well, that's easy then,' Vicken said. 'We wait here until ten, then we strike.'

'We can't leave those people in there,' Rhode said. 'We go to the dance. The first intimation that something's out of the ordinary, we fight. Remember, we need to get Odette away from her coven so Lenah can pierce her heart. It's crucial she succeeds.'

'Yeah,' Vicken said, trying to push his fake fangs tighter into his mouth. 'But you're forgetting one important thing about this fight.'

'Yes?' Rhode said.

'There will be hundreds of people in the room. We're going to have to reveal ourselves in front of them.'

Rhode shot me a meaningful look. We both knew the changes coming at dawn. We *had* to succeed. Succeed, or we would both be stuck here – with the Aeris's decree and vampires seeking the ritual.

'Let's go,' Rhode said, and we stepped out from the alley on to the pathway. I hadn't told Vicken about my choice to go back to the medieval world. He deserved to know, yes, but I didn't know how to explain to him the choice I had made.

'Did I mention this is a smashing look for you?' Vicken said, looking Rhode and me up and down.

'They were the only costumes that would make sense with Lenah's sword and my arrows,' Rhode replied.

We were dressed as Vikings. I would have laughed or perhaps suggested we took photographs, but in the situation that was not appropriate. The only costume events we had ever attended were masked balls in the seventeenth and eighteenth centuries. This was different. My costume was a tank top, a pair of shorts, and boots with fake fur trim, good for concealing a spare dagger. Rhode's was a kilt and a black tank top. I tried not to notice the curve of his biceps or the ripped muscles of his back.

Matching my baldric, attached to Rhode's back was a quiver holding arrows. All anyone could see were the feathers poking out of the top. Rhode held on to his bow, a sleek black modern-looking weapon.

'You carry it,' Rhode had said, when he fastened the sword behind me at the apartment earlier that night.

'But it's your sword,' I had said, feeling the weight of the metal as the straps tightened over my chest.

'I only borrowed it,' he'd said, referring to the

afternoon he visited Tony's grave. 'I left it in your possession for a reason.' Our eyes met and he raised one side of his mouth, giving me a sad, uneven smile. I had never asked him about the ceremony at Tony's grave.

As we walked, it was hard not to appreciate the efforts Wickham Boarding School had made to decorate for Halloween. Finally we were able to see it complete. Black streamers wrapped the trees that lined the pathways, orange twinkling lights blinked like lightning bugs from all imaginable scaffolding. Wickham was trying to bring its students together . . . Tony would have loved it.

Everyone was wrapped in their fall coats, so as they walked towards the gymnasium I could only see glimpses of costumes. I felt warm, but it could have been the adrenaline running through my body.

Vicken, Rhode and I walked together, like a team, like soldiers, carrying our weapons. We turned on to the pathway that led to Hopper, and next to it was the hill that led up to the archery plateau. It reminded me of Suleen, who had not shown himself in months. Even when I had really needed him, he had not come. The only remains of the carnival were the students' booths. It seemed that the professional company had taken the House of Mirrors away with them.

With Rhode and Vicken by my side, we kept walking behind the other students. I took some deep breaths of fresh air; the smells of Wickham campus cleared my head. Wet grass, clean air, and the scent of the ocean somewhere close by. I tried not to say goodbye as I breathed out, but I knew that in some way I was already letting it go. Straight ahead of us was a good view of the campus including a stretch of woods beyond Hopper.

There were gasps and screams of happiness when the door to Hopper opened just ahead of us. Booming music from the gymnasium sent ripples of sound out into the night. I told myself to remember the way electricity lit up the darkness. That coffee could be brewed instantly into a cup. That music, the kind playing in the gymnasium, would have to hide deep within my heart, where I would always hear it.

'Lenah!' Tracy called from the pathway. I turned and saw her in a black overcoat and jeans. She jogged towards Vicken, Rhode and me. When she caught up with us, her eyes were red and she folded her arms across her chest.

'I tried to find you earlier,' she said.

'What is it?' I asked.

'Justin,' she replied.

'Is there any news?' I asked, the panic in my voice apparent.

'He's still missing. Officially now,' Tracy said, 'but they're keeping it quiet because they don't want people to panic.'

'Are you all right?' I asked Tracy.

'I don't know,' she croaked. 'Just hoping he's OK.' Her eyes told me that she hoped he was not already Odette's next victim. 'They sent Roy home,' she added.

She was almost shaking as she went on. 'The police have nothing. No note. No sign of distress,' she said. 'What about you guys?' she asked, and finally looked at us properly. I couldn't help but notice her eyes move from my sword to Rhode's bow and arrows. She finished by looking at Vicken.

'Are you . . . ? Are you dressed as a *vampire*?' Tracy asked, taken aback.

I gulped nervously. *Oh, Vicken, you nitwit.*

A creeping smile inched its way across Tracy's face. 'You're kinda sick.'

Vicken opened his mouth to reply but Ms Williams interrupted.

'Hey! Come on, you guys,' she said, appearing at the door to the gymnasium. She wore her mouse outfit again and had drawn whiskers on her face. Music echoed out over the campus once more. As we went inside, Ms Williams stopped and put a hand gently on my shoulder. She said quietly, 'They're looking, honey.'

I would have been more worried, but something deep within me told me what was going to happen. Perhaps it was a sixth sense, coming from the vampire inside me who once was so powerful she commanded not hundreds but thousands of the undead. That powerful part of me felt that Odette *had* Justin and that he was going to be part of her power play. I couldn't say this aloud because it meant Justin wasn't just off somewhere being his typical mischievous self. That he hadn't gone back to being the boy who loved to race boats and was going to show up at the dance, brother Roy in tow, smiling and laughing. Somehow saying any of this would make it all too real and too much.

Saying it to Tracy would be too much.

'Lenah,' Tracy said, stopping in the gymnasium doorway. 'I love him. Not like before. He's my friend.'

I placed a hand on her shoulder. 'I know,' I replied. 'I'll do whatever I have to.'

Odette was going to use him as bait. Bait to bring us to her and make us fight. I was prepared for that. Even if I no longer loved Justin, I would save him.

As we walked, our boots joined the high heels and costume shoes. Tracy looked at me as we crossed into the gymnasium and I could see the strength beneath her worry. Only a very special human could run through a cemetery prepared to fight a vampire.

Rhode and I were silent as we joined the line of students.

Tracy turned to meet up with some of the other seniors who sat on the back ledge of the room.

I had plaited my hair so that it hung in a long braid down my back. I wanted it out of the way when I rammed the sword through Odette's heart.

'OK,' Rhode said. 'We have twenty minutes.'

'Should we circle the perimeter?' Vicken asked.

Rhode shook his head. 'We should each go to a corner of the room and watch out for anyone or anything out of the ordinary.'

I agreed. By standing in different corners of the room, we would be able see if these vampires came into the gymnasium from any entrance. Next to where I stood were three tables of food, which made my stomach grumble.

If I was right that Odette had Justin as bait, there was no telling how she was intending to use him in this scenario. Lead me out alone into the hallway? Make a spectacle? I adjusted the baldric on my back, drawing Rhode's sword closer to me.

Vicken and I stood against the back of the room

in opposite corners, the bleachers stacked between us. His main blade was concealed in his boot, though I knew he had two more daggers hidden elsewhere on his body. We pretended to have a good time. When I'd first arrived at Wickham, I had hoped I would be able to be a normal girl, a girl who could forget the years she'd spent manipulating people and living off the joy of their pain. I had stood on the outside and Justin had made me feel like I could be on the inside.

I would never be on the inside again.

I tried to pay attention the best I could. Everyone's costumes would have been entertaining had we actually been able to enjoy them: bunnies, superheroes, cats and Knights of the Round Table. There was plenty of skin showing, so I didn't feel out of place in my skimpy Viking outfit.

The gymnasium was overrun with people dancing chest-to-chest, so close that their hips touched. Tiny drops of sweat collected on foreheads and slid off cheeks. Vicken and I were at either end of the bleachers, keeping watch. Rhode stood across from us, watching the entrance. Every once in a while I would see him talk to a teacher. He was always quick to make an excuse and go back to the shadows to keep watch again.

I glanced at the large clock on the wall. If Laertes

was right, then Odette was two minutes behind schedule. Rhode stood against the wall, his arms across his chest. He met my eyes and kept my gaze. I would always be lost in that blue. Like the many thousands of night skies I had seen when I was a vampire.

With the scent of tobacco Vicken appeared next to me. His eyes stared unmoving across the room. He said simply and gravely, 'Well, this is an interesting twist.'

I followed his gaze to the front of the room. What I saw would shock me for the rest of my mortal days. I couldn't move. I knew I was supposed to protect everyone in that room, but my feet and hands seemed not to be attached to the rest of my body. My breath caught and I blinked hard, trying to focus.

Then the screams began.

For Justin was here, and his costume was no costume. The youthful dew to his skin was gone, and the pores buffed away. The eyes that had softened for me, that had told me how much he loved me, were now glassy. Hardened. I could not mistake the madness.

Justin Enos was a vampire.

CHAPTER 25

Two security guards lay lifeless on the floor, their necks held at odd disjointed angles. Dead. Immediate. Had they had time to call for back-up? Had they reached for their modern-day technology to save them? If so, it had failed them.

Justin stopped in the doorway, extended a hand into the hallway and pulled Odette into the gymnasium. He linked an arm around her waist, dipped her so her back arched and kissed her deeply. My lips parted in disbelief. Together they stalked into the room flanked by three other vampires. Justin wore the bright blue polo shirt that I had seen him in hundreds of times.

With a small bend of his knees, he jumped on top of a food table and kicked the chips and treats so they went flying into the air.

'Welcome,' Justin yelled, and pointed at the DJ, who lowered the music, 'to the Halloween Ball. You know, I was looking forward to tonight.' He squatted down on the table and extended a hand so Odette could climb up next to him.

Justin was a vampire. The horror rolled over me. *She had won.* Odette had won. She had stolen Justin away from humanity, taken all his beautiful warmth and life and made him into an icy, soulless vampire.

Odette and Justin stood on top of the table revelling in the terror they'd created. Most people stood in small huddles, while others leaned against the walls, frozen. A junior I recognized from my science class last year slowly inched a hand towards a knife on the cake table. Before he could reach it, Odette walked along the table to him, snatched the knife out of the cake, leaned down and stabbed the student in the side of the neck. More screams echoed throughout the gym, and a herd of people ran for the exit.

Blood spurted out of the young man's neck in a wide arc and he grabbed at the knife, trying unsuccessfully to remove it. Odette stood back up as though she had simply brushed away a fly. I had to turn my eyes away. I did not want to watch his death; his cries made me sick to my stomach. The student fell, lifeless, to the floor.

'The next person who even thinks of fighting me, dies.' She turned to me with a sick smile. 'Except for you, my dear.'

I couldn't remove my eyes from Justin. How strange he looked as a vampire. How frighteningly regal and *strong*. How hard and statuesque. The morning I'd gone to his window, he was so soft. So gentle. So Justin. And now he was nothing. Just a shell harbouring anger and death.

I swallowed hard. I had to move – the rage inside me pulsed throughout my soul. I had to kill Odette. Then I could make things right. Justin wouldn't be a vampire. My friends would be alive and safe. Everything would be reversed come morning.

'We've come here tonight for a very special request,' Odette announced.

Two vampires stood below Justin, standing guard. Another one was by the entrance. My stomach lurched as I remembered the vampire I had killed with the barrier spell. Justin was the fifth, the vampire that completed her coven.

Odette turned suddenly from Justin, jumped to the ground and walked quickly towards the gymnasium entrance. The sea of students parted before her, but Tracy stood firm against bleachers that were stacked by the wall. She sneered at Odette. She was planning something. She took a step forward, wielding something in her hand but I couldn't see what.

Odette snatched at Tracy by grabbing and yanking her ponytail. A flash of silver, and I realized Tracy had been holding a knife. It clattered to the floor. I wouldn't let her suffer. I had to get to her.

As I took a step, Justin jumped from the table in front of me, drawing my eyes away from Tracy.

'I'll take the two below Justin,' Vicken yelled, and he ran past me. I could not watch because my gaze was locked on Justin's unnatural marble-like eyes. I looked for any sign of the human boy I had loved.

There was a crash near the door. I glanced at the shadows where Rhode had been but I couldn't see him. Odette had thrown a boy wearing a football-player costume against the bleachers, while still keeping a hand locked around Tracy's hair. He lay in a crumpled heap on the floor.

'The famous Rhode Lewin,' I heard her say, and it ripped me in half. I wanted to run across the room but Justin was walking towards me in slow, long steps.

Instinct kept me backing away, despite the fact that only twenty-four hours earlier Justin had been holding my hand. I found my composure and comfort by pulling the baldric close to me. Ms Williams and the other teachers were opening windows at the back of the room.

Come on, Fire. I thought to myself. *What is my knowledge? What's the key?*

Justin broke into a sneer and I took this as my cue.

I slid the sword out of the baldric and held it before me.

'Lenah!' Rhode yelled from somewhere.

'I'm all right!' I yelled back.

'I always admired that sword,' Justin said, stopping a few feet in front of me.

My body reacted but my mind still couldn't believe it. A vampire behind Justin corralled a group of students into a corner. They huddled together, black make-up running down their cheeks in streaks.

'You're going to give me the ritual,' he said as students ran for the open windows. He reached out and grabbed a girl from the group by the back of her costume. Justin held her in front of him and smiled at me through his cold dead eyes. His fangs slid down.

Maybe it was the connection between us, but I could feel Rhode's presence. I could feel his power, his concentration. I didn't need to look. All the times I had been unnaturally privy to his thoughts showed me now that he was lifting an elbow ready to fire an arrow into Justin's heart. In my mind, I could see the sharp tip of the arrow pointed directly at Justin.

I could see Rhode's face, spotted by specks of blood and sweat. *No*, I said in my mind. *Rhode, you cannot kill Justin.* I sidestepped so I stood directly before Justin, making it impossible for Rhode to kill him without first hitting me.

Rhode dropped the bow and arrow to his side.

'Give me the ritual, Lenah,' Justin said, and he adjusted his grip on the student even tighter. 'Or I kill her. No, wait. Better yet, I'll make her a vampire.'

I held my sword out in front of me. It only struck me then that the student he had ensnared was Andrea, the girl he had romanced earlier that year. Tears ran down her face.

'Let her go,' I said evenly.

I made myself forget the boy that had made me feel so warm and human. I concentrated on the hardness of his eyes.

'Let. Her. Go,' I said again.

I wasn't sure what to do. Around us there was the sound of glass breaking, and an alarm wailing somewhere in Hopper. What had happened to Tracy? Justin threw Andrea forward so she fell to her knees. She scrambled away behind me.

'Justin, I know this isn't you. Sometimes the human within can remember.'

'I remember your power, Lenah. From that day on the beach. I remember your power as a vampire. And I've always wanted it for myself.'

He was going to lunge forward, I knew that. His

green eyes, now so alien, so strange, bored into mine.

I was smaller than Justin but I only had to choose one body part, one small body part, to disarm him. I could do any number of things to break his concentration, and then I would have to stab him directly in the heart or behead him.

The thought of that was impossible. He swiped, a dagger suddenly in his hand trying to stab me, but I jumped aside.

'Go! Go!' Vicken yelled, and the sound of his voice comforted me. He was still alive. But where was Odette? Where was Rhode?

Justin and I did not falter in our stare. I was ready, and as I raised my sword I lurched forward, lunging with all my body weight on to my left leg. I thrust the sword through the air but missed, and the blade arced through the air, the tip driving into the floor. A hard vibration rattled up the sword to my hand. I wanted to scream from the pressure on my fingers.

'I could have just brought a gun,' Justin said as he neatly sidestepped my attack. I kept my feet firmly planted on the ground, without moving from my fighting stance, and pulled the sword from the floor.

'You wouldn't miss the opportunity,' I said. 'You love being the centre of attention.'

'Didn't you once tell me I would have been a great vampire?'

I gasped. I had said that, hadn't I? What was worse . . . I had been right.

'You may be flesh and blood now but you're still a murderer,' Justin said. 'You were responsible for Tony's death.'

'You loved Tony,' I said, and I hated it but my voice broke. I looked at the gymnasium floor and the streamers trampled by our feet. Justin's body was turned towards me. I lifted the sword above my head again and as he jumped forward to plunge his dagger into me I stepped left, dodging him.

Justin rounded on me quickly. 'The whole vampire world knows about your ritual,' he said, staring at me. 'Give it to me. I can offer you protection.'

'I'll die first.'

'I should have let Odette catch you long before that day in the art tower. I thought you might have figured it out by then.'

'What are you talking about?' I asked.

We circled each other, round and round, my sword held high, his dagger at the ready. For someone who had no experience of knife work, he was certainly agile. But then . . . his words crept into my mind.

'You, the ritual. Rhode. Why you're alive . . . so whatever you did with that ritual doesn't matter to me. I want . . .'

He had been talking about the ritual all this time. From that night onward.

I clamped my jaw together, biting my words back, but I couldn't help it. I had had no idea Justin had been in league with these vampires for weeks.

'How long?' I asked. 'How long have you been under her control?'

'I knew your true colours, Lenah, the night of your birthday. You think I didn't set this up? I worked it all out. Planned it so you would trust me.'

He was with me that night for the *ritual*?

Behind Justin, one of the other vampires jumped at Vicken. Vicken's back arched as the vampire hit him and he slammed into the ground. Vicken flipped over quickly, dagger still in his hand. I had to stay focused.

Justin broke the rotation and took a step towards me. I was close to him, closer than I needed to be to drive the sword into him. I concentrated on the place just between his arm and chest. I was going to pierce him – to disarm. *Yes . . . right there, right between the arm and the chest.* My right hand gripped the handle tighter.

I leaped at Justin but he was too quick and kicked

me in the stomach, sending me to the ground. My sword clattered against the gymnasium floor. My stomach cramped. I clutched at it in time to see Justin preparing to thrust forward to stab me. I scrabbled over and grabbed for the sword again. At the same time, I kicked upward, knocking Justin's dagger out of his hand. He snarled, lifted his foot and stomped down on my stomach before I could roll out of the way. My hand released the sword and the breath came out of me in a whoosh. I coughed a dry, hacking cough. My throat was already so sore.

Breathe, Lenah. But I couldn't. My chest was tightened. I was on the floor of the gymnasium but then, her words . . . Odette's words from weeks ago in the dressing room came to me.

I can see why he likes you. She had meant Justin! The rune around his neck swung back and forth over my eyes as he towered over me. *Knowledge,* Fire had said. *Knowledge is the key.*

I needed to understand what she meant.

I also needed the sword. I tried to breathe in again. *Breathe, Lenah!* I yelled inside my head.

'Mortal,' he grumbled, and lifted his foot again. 'Give me the ritual!'

An enormous crash brought Justin's and my attention back into the room. An arrow protruded from the chest of one of the vampires in Odette's coven. He collapsed against a set of chairs and the drinks table, bringing them to floor in a heap.

Time seemed to slow even further. By the base of the bleachers, I saw Odette. Her neck craned over Tracy as she fed off her. Tracy's eyes were closed and her mouth lay open and slack, just like I had seen with Claudia. Rhode appeared out of the chaos, kicking Odette away so the blonde beast fell back from Tracy. She grimaced, and before she could assemble herself to lunge at him, before she could reach for the knife I was sure she had, she glanced across the room at Justin. Her anger changed to wide eyes and a menacing sneer.

The pain that spread through from my spine to my arms came in small waves. Justin towered over me again, bringing my eyes back from Odette and Rhode. He brought his beautiful face closer to mine – even more beautiful now that the pores had sealed. In his right hand was my sword; he lifted his arm just high enough to point the blade at my chest. As he lifted his hand to plunge, I rolled away, raising my foot, and kicked him square in the chest with what I hoped was enough power. My foot stung from the force of the impact. Justin stumbled but I was quick, and as I jumped up I lifted my leg again, kicking him in the chest. His arms flew out as he hit the ground, dropping the sword. I snatched it up and held it pointing down at the ground, my fingers resting on its hilt.

I let the weapon hang between us. I saw myself centuries ago, snapping my fingers and commanding hundreds of vampires to murder one helpless Dutch woman. I saw myself drinking goblets filled with blood. Death parties, Nuit Rouge.

'Do it, Lenah!' Vicken screamed behind me as he ran out of the gym after one of the vampires who had fled the building.

A sneer crept across Justin's mouth and he laughed. 'I will get the ritual from you one way or another, Lenah,' he said.

I threw the sword to the ground to confuse him and, just as I hoped, Justin's eyes followed the slide of the sword along the ground.

There, lying against the bare skin of his chest was the rune. The *knowledge rune.*

Of course.

I had no idea how long that rune had been controlling him. Endowed runes, items infused with magic, could control the mind of someone weak, someone grief-stricken, someone with a broken heart.

'Justin, your necklace!' Odette cried, moving fast. 'Protect the rune.'

The evil blonde vampire stood before me. Odette

was using her body as a shield between Justin and me. I needed a clear shot to get the rune from his neck.

It wasn't just bleeding Odette that would weaken her – it was taking the rune.

The rune was the connection between Odette and Justin. She might have summoned super-powerful strength through spells and incantations, but the rune was the key! How blind I had been! The knowledge rune channelled that strength, bound it to her, along with her supernatural speed. She had fuelled herself by feeding off Justin's mind.

Intention is what matters. Intention in the soul, in the mind. Mind over matter, call it what you will. The mind is always more powerful than the body.

The symbol on the rune, the knowledge symbol, worn inverted, can be used in spells of trickery and manipulation.

Knowledge is the key. That's what Fire had said.

An arrow flew through the air and embedded itself in Justin's shoulder. He cried out and fell to the floor, where he thrashed, clutching at the arrow.

Odette grabbed a fistful of my shirt and tried to immobilize me by holding me close to her. She squeezed me tighter whenever I moved; I coughed, struggling to breathe. Something in my chest felt as if it would burst.

I had to get the rune. It was the only way to weaken her. She squeezed me again, sending a tightness up into my chest. Justin lay motionless for a split moment, his hand grasping the arrow. This was it, my only chance.

I stretched my body forward. Just a little further. Then my hand . . . almost there. I reached and my fingers curled around the leather strap. I jerked it from Justin's neck. Immediately Odette released me. I stumbled away, the rune dangling between my fingers. Quickly I spun round. I had to keep my eyes on her.

'I'll destroy it!' I threatened, holding the rune in the air.

Odette lifted a foot, threatened to jump but then stopped. Her eyes darted from the rune to me. A heartbeat passed between us as she seemed to consider her choices. In the time of that heartbeat, the dagger from my boot was in my grasp.

Then Odette sprang through the air at me, scratching her knifelike nails towards my face. I ducked but saw the red talons out of the corner of my eye. *Now or never, Lenah.* She turned to face me again. *This is it.* I lifted my right hand and I did what I had been trained to do by Vicken a hundred and fifty years earlier.

I stabbed my dagger into her dead vampire heart.

'No . . .' she yelled – but it was hollow, animal-like. She fell to the ground, her weight thrown on to one hand.

She looked down at her chest as though she couldn't believe I'd done it. That I'd outsmarted her. She crumpled in on herself down on her knees. She looked up at me, her lips parted. Her fangs descended but they were not scary now, they were sad. She looked like a shattered version of the young woman she once was.

She collapsed on to the ground, lifeless. A beautiful woman, made into a vampire and who died much too young. At the strike of dawn, she would turn to dust. And, I was quite sure, she would join the white light of the Aeris, and would eventually return to the natural course of her life.

And me, I would get my wish. At sunrise, this would all be over and we'd go back to a time before sudden unnatural death and empty sadness. I would return to the medieval world. Relief rolled over me only momentarily, because Justin reached for his neck. He shook his head as though trying to clear his sight and swayed back and forth before me. He had ripped the arrow out of his shoulder. I placed the rune on the floor and knelt before it.

Rhode joined me at my side just as the distinct sounds of sirens wailed in the distance.

'You must break it,' Rhode said. 'His mind is connected to it even in her death.'

He handed me his dagger and we glanced up at Justin one more time. He continued to grab at his now bare neck. I used all the force in my arms to come down and stab that silver rune so hard that it exploded with a bang. A cloud of white smoke came from it. I looked from the rune to Justin, who now held a hand to his head. But his chest was exposed, facing right at me.

I could stab Justin through the heart and end him. End his human life, and end his vampire life. The rune lay broken on the floor.

'Stab him, Lenah!' Vicken called.

The sirens in the distance grew louder, closer. The gym was nearly empty and we had to go.

Justin shook his head as though to focus his eyes. In this world, his eyes would never need to focus again. He was now the undead.

Again Vicken urged me to stab Justin. But I would not. I wouldn't stab the chest where I had once laid my head, not even if everything was going to change come morning.

Because of the Justin that day in the rain when I first got to know him. Because of the Justin in the hall of his parents' house the night I had slept there. Because of his love for life, and how one time, not long ago, he had shown me the way to be human and I had loved him.

Justin blinked in shock at me a few times; those marble green eyes had a strange gaze. His beautiful lashes batted at me; he shook his head again, as if he couldn't quite see straight.

Rhode stood up and together we looked at Justin, who was holding his dagger in his hand. He looked down at it as though he wasn't quite sure what he was doing with such a thing.

'Welcome back,' Rhode said to Justin. The gym was empty now, except for us and Vicken, who had a line of blood running down his temple to his jaw.

'What did you do to me?' Justin asked.

'I freed you from Odette's mind control . . . through that rune,' I explained.

'Rune?' Justin said.

'This thing,' Rhode said, and picked the pieces up. He showed it to Justin, nestling it in the palm of his hand.

'You are a vampire, Justin,' I said, and his eyes jumped to mine.

He reached up to his mouth and felt for the fangs, which came down on command. He pulled his hand back as his fang pierced his index finger and a tiny droplet of blood blossomed.

'Don't waste that,' Rhode said. 'You'll need all the blood you can get, vampire.'

'I know what I am!' Justin yelled, and backed away from us towards the door of the gymnasium. 'I know. You don't need to tell me.'

A common vampire reaction. Hubris. The blatant inability to be wrong. The young vampire does not miss their humanity right away. They have a zest for knowledge. For power. Often, they are excited about their new immortality.

But, really, Justin had not known. He had not known what had happened to him. This was perhaps worse than all our stories. The rune had prevented Justin from realizing what had happened. It not only provided Odette with strength, it clouded Justin's mind. It took him over. It made him someone else.

Justin backed out through the door of the gym. He held his shoulder where Rhode had shot the arrow. He looked to it, checking for blood, but, just as I had suspected, he healed quickly. He kept his eyes on me and then they dropped to the floor, to Odette. After seeing her crumpled body – he turned and he ran.

He would not get away. I ran too.

'Lenah!' Rhode called.

I followed him as fast as I could. But Justin was an athlete and was faster than me. He pressed into the crowds of people and ran on beyond. I was running too, but I got caught up in the crowd.

Lenah!

Are you OK?

From where I stood, near the great oak tree in the centre of the Wickham campus, I turned to look up at the archery field where so long ago Suleen had separated Justin from me by the water shield. Now Justin stood at the base of that hill and turned to me. Our eyes met. Early in vampire life, one can recall happiness and concern. What met my eyes was regret. But it was fleeting. He made for the woods next to the hill and was lost in darkness.

Within moments, I was enveloped by hands and concerned faces still splattered with Halloween paint. A group of people circled me and led me away.

CHAPTER 26

News of Justin spread like hundreds of feathers fluttering through the air.

What happened to him?

Did he join a gang?

Who was he with?

All kinds of questions carried over the quiet campus, massing together like a thousand whispers. How? What? Why? Who? The questions of victims. Questions that would never be answered.

Vicken, Rhode and I sat at the base of a tree, waiting for what? I wasn't sure. Rhode reached for my hand. It surprised me for a moment; I wasn't used to him touching me. Vicken held a bloody T-shirt to his head. We hadn't said much.

'It's going to be OK,' a firefighter said gently. 'It'll be all right.' She was consoling a group of crying girls who sat huddled near Hopper Building. Other firefighters and police officers ran past us in and out of the gymnasium. They went with axes and a hose, guns and stretchers and body bags in their hands. I didn't want to think about it, didn't want to know. The great clock on Hopper Building said it was four thirty in the morning. Only two hours left until sunrise.

I overheard a snippet of a conversation between Ms Williams and a police officer.

'You're sure he is in a gang?' the officer asked, writing in a small notebook.

'Yes. He is most definitely in a gang. A violent gang,' Ms Williams said.

'We're going to need to get these kids inside. Start calling parents,' another officer said, walking by me.

Vicken, Rhode and I met eyes and maintained our silence. A paramedic with a medical bag approached us. He bent over and squinted, examining Vicken's head wound.

'Come with me,' he said. 'That needs to be stitched up.' He removed the T-shirt and a little line of blood ran from Vicken's head down towards his top lip. When it curled over, for the first time in our long history he didn't lick it away.

'Do you mind explaining to me the shape of this head wound, sir?' Vicken asked as he walked after the paramedic.

Rhode and I sat, backs against the tree, our daggers, bow and arrows, and sword hidden around the side of Hopper Building. I leaned my head back against the trunk and looked at Rhode. He was out of his costume now, the only remnant of it the black T-shirt. He was back in his jeans. So modern. And it hit me then . . . he too was ageing. Though I would never see it.

He squeezed my hand and it sent my heart racing. *How right*, I thought as the chaos ensued around us, *that now, after all this, he can make my heart pump so solidly.*

I had waited for it for so long.

'What you did was very brave,' he said. I exhaled, losing myself in the softness of his blue eyes.

'It didn't feel brave. It felt like . . .' I searched for the words. 'The end.'

'How many were there?' The police officer's voice pulled my attention away. He was still interviewing Ms Williams.

'I think four or five,' she answered.

'Do you think, at sunrise,' I whispered, 'that Justin will still be a vampire? I mean, when I go back to the fifteenth century?

'I think Fire will keep her promise,' Rhode replied. He lazily rolled his head to look at me. 'He'll be Justin, I suppose.'

'Where do you think he went?' I asked.

'To find other vampires. It won't take him very long.' Rhode sighed, then said, 'Perhaps your plan is in fact the best thing for everyone.'

He didn't meet my eyes when he said this. He then broke our hands apart to reach into his pocket. He held the broken rune out to me. I did not take it. I didn't want to play the guessing game as to when Odette got to Justin.

'Hey . . .' Rhode said, his eyebrows narrowing. 'Where is your ring?'

I held my hands out before me and spread my fingers wide.

My onyx ring – it was gone.

'It must have fallen off during the fight,' I said in disbelief. I glanced at Hopper Building. 'I'll go and look for it.' I pushed against the tree trunk to stand up.

'Ah, let it go. It's a cursed stone anyway. It makes people linger. Souls too. Connects people to their pasts in a world that may not want them any more.'

I nodded and sat back down, knowing that somewhere on the gym floor my ring, the one that had linked me from life to life, human to vampire to human, was discarded under Halloween decorations and party punch.

Rhode offered me the broken rune again. This time I took it and let the pieces lie in the palm of my hand, cool against my skin. And it came to me then. How easily I had taken Justin's word for it. How easily I had listened to him when he'd said that he wore the rune because he worried for me, because he wanted to understand me. Every time he got me alone, he asked about the ritual. He was so eager to come to watch me do the summoning spell. So interested in power.

'You couldn't have known,' Rhode said.

'When . . . When he and I . . .' I stopped, choosing my words. 'That night. Of my birthday. He told me in the gym . . . he wasn't in his right mind.'

'He was probably captured early. I don't think he did any of this of his own accord.' Rhode sighed. 'Either way, it's over now,' he said quietly.

He leaned forward and tucked a piece of my hair behind my ear. Justin had done that to me, but when Rhode did it, and his fingers grazed my skin, my pulse thudded.

'Remember the story you told? About the Anam Cara?'

Rhode nodded and lovingly held my cheek with his hand.

'Do you think we're like that?' I asked. 'Or is it only reserved for really powerful vampires like Suleen?'

'I think Suleen would say the love between us is even stronger than the love he felt for that woman.'

He didn't remove his hand from my face, and

its warmth reminded me of all the cold moments in my life. During those long years his touch had brought comfort to me. Yes, I was human now and the touch was different; there were nerve endings and senses now involved.

But the love was the same.

'Lenah?' A feeble voice called me.

I twisted to see who was calling my name. Everyone was still in their costumes, their eyes lined in sparkly glitter, lips and noses painted or furry. Beyond the groups of students huddling together on their way to Quartz dorm, two paramedics carried someone on a stretcher. As the stretcher passed by, Tracy turned her head slowly to me.

'Lenah!' She said my name again.

I jumped up from the grass but stopped and groaned as a shooting pain travelled along my arm. I reached up to hold on to my right shoulder; I hadn't needed such arm strength the last time I'd wielded a sword.

I walked past students talking about Justin and his changed appearance. There were dozens of excuses: drugs, an adrenaline junkie, maybe he'd joined a gang. All words and phrases I had learned over this human year. They were just excuses people made to explain what they could not understand.

'Can you wait one moment?' I asked as I

approached Tracy, and the paramedics stopped.

A tear rolled over Tracy's cheek. She wiped it away and looked at me.

'I tried,' she said. 'I brought a small knife but she just kicked it away.'

'I couldn't get to you,' I replied, squatting down to her eye level.

'Is everyone I love going to die?' she asked, and her voice was so shaky. 'I don't want to go home, Lenah, but they're closing the school.'

'Not forever,' I replied.

'Is he going to come back and kill us all?'

'He's a vampire,' I said softly, so only she could hear. 'But I don't think you have to worry about him any more.'

She wiped her eyes.

'What you did. Tonight. It was amazing,' she said.

'It's because of me that you had to see that at all.'

Under the moonlight, I could see her pain so clearly.

I reached out and took her hand. I was so used to embracing Justin or Vicken, young men with strong shoulders and wide backs. But Tracy was just a young woman – like I should have been. She felt frail to me, as if I was holding the hand of a small child.

'I can't believe they're cancelling school,' she

said, and let go of my hand to wipe tears from her cheeks again. The men who carried the stretcher started walking again towards a collection of ambulances in the centre of the green. In front of those ambulances were six bodies. Four vampires including Odette, and two students. Just when I turned away, someone behind me said, 'The news crews are coming.'

'See you soon, Lenah,' Tracy said, and she was carried away into the fray of emergency workers and flashing lights.

'Sure,' I said, though I knew I would not, in fact, see her ever again.

When I turned back to face the chaos on campus, the police were corralling students by class. Everyone was on their cell phones. Ms Williams pointed some students towards the dorms.

I met Rhode's eyes as he joined Vicken by the great oak tree. Vicken had a white bandage wrapped around his head and they talked with quiet confidence. It had been hours since Justin had run off to the woods and only now, with midnight long past, did the police officers and firefighters usher the students back to their dorms. Statements had been made, notes taken – it was time to go inside and try to rest for whatever was left of the night.

I exhaled as a cool wind swept through the

campus, making the leaves shiver. I knew that a shiver was a sign. A familiar knowing feeling swept over me.

I looked past the students, up the archery hill, where at the top finally, *finally*, stood Suleen.

I walked towards Vicken and Rhode. On my way Ms Williams stepped before me. Her mouse nose had worn off. All that was left of her costume were some smears of whiskers over her cheeks.

'I've been waiting to get you alone,' she said.

Her eyes, a blue-grey colour, penetrated mine in that pre-dawn.

'What did you do?' she asked. 'How did you know? You, Vicken and Rhode?'

'Ms Williams, I have to go.'

'Those men. And Justin . . .' she started to say.

I touched her on the shoulder, as she would have done me, like a parent to a child. Because really I was so much older than she would ever be.

'It's over now,' I said, repeating the words Rhode had said to me, and I walked towards the tree.

As I went, I ignored her calls.

'Lenah, wait. I don't understand. I don't . . .'

When I reached the tree, I saw that Vicken's bandage stretched from his eyebrows to his hairline.

'Are you all right?' I asked.

'Nothing but a scratch, love,' he said, and we

shared an exhausted smile. At the top of the hill behind him was the white garb of Suleen. He reminded me of the grey orb that hung over my heart in the onyx ceiling at the house of the Hollow Ones.

I looked back to the crowds of people behind us. No one turned in our direction; no one demanded we go inside. I knew this was Suleen's doing. He made us invisible, to allow us a clear getaway.

It also gave me time for one last look. And I did. I swept over the campus, stopping, of course, on Seeker dorm in the distance. Its brick structure was framed by trees bursting with orange and yellow leaves. My heart pained me.

'It's time to go,' I said to Vicken, and started walking up the hill.

'Go?' Vicken asked. 'Go where?'

'Come on,' I said gently, and took his hand in mine. He looked down at it and then up at me.

'What's going on?' he asked. We climbed the hill. Rhode squeezed my other hand hard as we ascended. He was on one side of me and Vicken on the other. Three generations of murderers walked to their rectification. The reckoning was by my own doing this time. When we crested the top of the hill, Suleen stood ethereal and silent.

I wanted to be angry with him. Wanted to know

why he hadn't come after I'd called him with the summoning spells.

The truth was that I already knew the answer. He didn't come because I didn't deserve it. Because coming to save Rhode wouldn't have solved anything. I would have just found another way to try to break the decree, to do magic that I was specifically asked *not* to do.

As we walked towards Suleen, I drew a breath. The fall was finally upon Wickham campus. As we made it to the top of the hill, huffing and puffing, we could see our breath in the air.

'Suleen,' Vicken said in a breathless wonder. He had never seen the vampire before – not in the flesh. 'You came,' Vicken said. 'We didn't even have to burn any appendages.'

Suleen smiled kindly but then turned his gaze to me.

'I am proud of you,' he said. Rhode stood by my side. Suleen looked to him next. 'And even prouder of what *you* could not give up.'

Rhode nodded once.

'Now for a proper introduction,' Suleen said, and turned away from Rhode and me. 'Vicken Clough of the Twenty-first Regiment,' he said, and Vicken puffed out his chest. Suleen reached out and held Vicken's forearm. Vicken held his in return, a common way for vampires to greet one another; it was a shake that protected the wrist. Vicken's eyes lit up, more than I had ever seen as a mortal. This must have been a very important moment for him.

'He doesn't know,' I said to Suleen.

Suleen stepped back, and it was only then that I realized the sky was no longer black but grey, soon to be lavender, and then the burning orange of the day. The sun – the harbinger of change. The reminder, though this time my chariot.

'Tell me what? What's happening?' Vicken asked.

I threw a glance at Suleen, 'How long do I have?'

'Just a few minutes,' he said softly.

I turned to Vicken and put my hands on his cheeks. I met his look with mine and held it. It seemed hard for him to keep my gaze; his nostrils flared a little. He would cry, though I was not sure if he knew it yet. Or if he was fighting it. I watched his eyes slowly remembering the human reaction when the body cries. I met his brown eyes and said, 'Do you know why I saved you last summer in the gymnasium?'

He shook his head.

'Because when I met you, you danced and sang on tables. You *loved* the world, and I had made you a spectator in it.'

'Lenah?' he said gently.

'You'll be a spectator no more.'

'I don't understand you, love,' he said.

'I'm going back to the fifteenth century,' I said.

'No!' he cried, and I dropped my hands from his face.

'And you to your father's house. At dawn you will return to the night I stole your soul and made you a demon. You will be the navigator I met, with maps tacked to your walls and socks hanging over a wash-tub.'

The sky was purple now and the sun would soon crest the hilltop. The first golden glimmers kissed the plateau.

'Lenah, please, no!' Vicken cried again, but I turned away anyway. 'What does that mean?' he called behind me. 'Suleen, what does that mean?'

I turned back to Rhode, whose eyes were cast to the ground. His arms hung by his sides; he could have been a modern-day statue he was so still.

I walked over to him, stood just as we had for months now, inches apart.

'I'm going kiss you now,' I whispered. Rhode lifted his eyes to mine.

'I was hoping you would say that,' he whispered back, and we both cracked a smile. 'Lenah,' he said, and I could feel his body heat humming off him. 'What will I do without you?'

I shivered as one word travelled through me.

'Live.'

Our lips met . . . the beautiful pressure of his mouth against mine. The heat of his mouth and his taste. I followed the movement of his lips and the soft pressure of his tongue. His hand climbed my back, sending goosebumps over my arms.

It was better than I ever expected. My Rhode kissed gently. He cradled the back of my head and pushed deeper into my mouth. *Don't pull away.*

The apple scent, which had haunted me all year, overwhelmed me again, but this time it was coupled with the familiar white light of the Aeris. The images that came to me now showed thousands of memories from my past with Rhode. A slide show of our years together.

Gold earrings in the rain. Dancing at balls. Laughing under the stars. Rhode and I on a straw bed. By a fireside, Rhode laughing at something I said.

It wasn't all pain and death, was it? It was love.

He pulled away and the air between us was warm even though the early-morning chill bit at my ears. His eyes were fixed on mine.

'Having an adventure?' he whispered with that slight lift of his mouth into an uneven smile. He had said that familiar phrase to me hundreds – no, thousands – of times. It lifted my heart.

'Anam Cara,' I whispered. He gave me a small smile and that was enough for me. I didn't have to explain what I meant. For it was a new world now, one where our histories no longer mattered and we were set free.

'Lenah . . .' Suleen said, and I could see the gold touching the horizon. Perhaps it was because the Aeris had told me, or that I knew the sun was Fire herself, but I knew. I was supposed to walk towards that sunrise. I knew it would take me home.

The blue of Rhode's eyes was so fierce, as always. He loved me. I could return to the fifteenth century knowing that, for once, I had truly loved and been loved. Rhode cupped my face in his hands and gently kissed both my cheeks, my forehead and then brushed his lips over mine.

I backed away from him, chills rushing over my whole body. When I looked to Vicken, tears, large gorgeous tears, ran down his face. He wiped them away and stared at his fingertips, momentarily shocked by the power of a cry for which one has waited more than a hundred years.

Suleen held his hand out and, as I had seen him do the year before, he drew it towards him and held it over his heart. The golden glow of the sun warmed me; my whole body was engulfed in its heat. I was going. The trees behind Rhode, Vicken and Suleen were blurred orange and red smears against the sky.

Last, I looked to Rhode. I wanted him to be the last thing I saw in this world. His lips were barely parted. We could have said any number of things just then. But I was going quickly. I could barely see Vicken any more; he was a white wash of light. I thought I could smell apples.

There was nothing left to say between Rhode and me. No words would ever be enough. So I brought my hand over my breast, where my beating heart lay. He had died for it – for the ability to breath and live. I left it there and didn't break eye contact from the blue of the eyes that I loved more than love could possibly explain.

I love you. I love you. I love you.

The light was all around me now, overtaking me.

This would be a different world. One without Lenah Beaudonte.

And just like that, with the light before me in a wash of gold and silver . . .

I was gone.

Do all our mistakes remain lodged in our hearts? Can we ever really let go? That which is written in stone may be undone. For stone cannot hold sway.

Even stone can be broken.

CHAPTER 27

1418

Apples. Great crimson orbs glisten in the morning sun.

'Lenah!'

Someone is calling my name. Round apples dangle from a branch outside. I know this view. I know this raw smell – the straw of the bed. I am on my family's orchard. The sun filters through the window, washing the wooden floor with yellow light. A roosters crows outside – they wake with the dawn. I remember this!

'Lenah!'

My father! Joy blooms in my chest. 'Sleepy girl! Are you ill!' My father's voice echoes and I have not heard it in so long. I shoot up. Momentarily, I raise a hand to touch the thick glass of a medieval window. The light is more natural than in the modern world – it is real, not made by lamps. It filters through the old glass, thick and imperfect.

I don't care that my sleeping gown is long, covering my feet, I raise it up to run down the stairs, jumping two at a time. There is my father, with his heavy beard and working clothes. My mother is before the fire, with a tub of water and dirty clothing. I can recognize some of my gowns. I remember!

I throw myself around my father's scruffy neck. There is a hint of lavender to his skin; he has just bathed. He pulls back from me.

'Have you stolen the monks' tomatoes again?' he asks.

I kiss his cheeks. 'No,' I say with a smile. 'Give me two secs,' I add, and motion to the stairs.

'What did you say?' my father asks.

Oh. I turn. Secs is a modern word – a measure of time. My family cannot measure time this way. Their routine is governed by the movement of the sun. Instead I say, 'I shall follow.'

'Quickly now,' he calls.

I peek out of the window, with the sounds of my mother's washing behind me. I forgot over my long history how quiet the medieval world was. The harvest has long passed; most of the trees are bare. I look about – I recognize this exact scene. The Medici family has taken most of our crop, and the rest has gone to the monks, whose property we live on. To make cider to drink and for food.

Today is a day of cleaning. After the harvest – we

must clean the rows to prepare for the oncoming winter.

I think I know what this day is but I don't want to believe it – not yet. I will be able to tell this evening – when I watch the sky.

I spend the afternoon in the orchard with my father. I have missed him for so long that I find myself standing behind a bare tree watching him rake the ground, humming. For the barest of moments I long for the easy push of a button. I have seen workers at Wickham use motorized leaf blowers. I think how much easier this would be for my father's weathered hands. I wish we could play some music as well, and of course I think of Wickham and the long fields. The lacrosse practices I watched where they blasted music to help the time pass.

Lacrosse.

I blink the sun from my eyes and pick at the dirt below this bare tree. I hope Justin, wherever he is now that I am gone, is happy. And human.

I wipe the sweat from my brow, watch the sun move across the sky. This world has no cars, no medicine, no rocky-road ice cream. I smile at the memory of Tony's hands running a brush through cerulean paint. I will suffer with the loss not only of my friends and Rhode, but of my new-found love for the modern world.

I want to tell my father everything. But I cannot. There is no way that he could possibly ever understand. I squat at the base of a tree, running my fingers through the rich earth. This routine has come back to me quickly. I remember so well how to prune the branches, how to cut them so the apples will return fragrant and strong.

'Lenah!' my father calls, and he points at the house just as dark bulbous clouds hang over our orchard.

I call back and hold the hem of my dress up to walk more easily. Dirt covers my hands as I follow my father and make my way home.

We are due for church, my mother tells me over dinner. I look forward to this. To seeing Father Simon and hearing him speak of God and religion. Once, so long ago, those services taught me how to live my life – to serve God, to live a life for the afterlife. These were medieval thoughts. I never imagined I would have my own views on religion, on God, on the ether and life before and after death.

My mother smiles at me over our meal.

'You seem happy,' she says.

'The food is good,' I reply.

It's only a simple stew and she says as much. I

remind myself that food here is food you cook yourself. You either catch or kill it, or buy it from someone who does. Food here is made by hand, not created in a factory.

Rhode told me long ago that love was an emotion that existed beyond the confines of the human condition. It could rise to the highest peaks, he said. Even out there in the heavens, love flew, soared and spread between the stars. As I sit here across from my parents, I believe this is true.

'You are so quiet,' Mother says as a crack of thunder vibrates our small house.

'Rain again,' my father says with a sigh.

'Harvest is over. Rejoice,' Mother says, and kisses him on the head.

The oncoming rain is a downpour I know.

As it finally hits, I know this pelting on the roof as well as I knew my soul.

This is the night I died. This night is the night Rhode made me a vampire.

Hours pass and soon the night's fire is almost burned out. My mother's earrings are safe – I did not ask for them today. I did not lose them in an orchard lane.

The Aeris have sent me back to this day to remind me of my choices. I walk to the stairs, to the window that hangs over the eighth stair. It has always been a childish inclination to count, yet I do it anyway.

I place a hand on the cold glass. My fingers warm it, a halo of condensation billowing out from my body heat. So many things I know from my modern life. How science changes, how music changes, that people get to live for many, many years.

I spent five hundred years becoming a monster, feeding off people, making them my misery. But I also saw the way of the world. I focus on the end of the orchard lanes. Though I cannot see that far, once, in a different world, Rhode waited for me there.

There is no Rhode at the end of the orchard lane – I know that. I saved him. He is safe.

I also know I will never meet Justin . . . or Tony.

Wickham will exist hundreds of years from now when I am long gone, gone from the world.

I leave my hand on the glass. My jaw clenches. This hurts, this standing here knowing what I know, aware of how much lies before me with this whole world and all its beauty.

Even though he is not watching me, I do it for history. For the souls that were saved in one moment. I whisper the words:

I will love you forever.

I bring my hand over my heart and the tears well in my eyes. Shivers cover me, head to toe; they roll and soon the tears do too and I say the words only vampires share: 'Go forth in darkness and in light.'

I gulp away the tears, turn from the window and stand in the doorway of my parents' room. They sleep back to back, close together. I wonder if I will live out the rest of my days here in this house. If I will get sick or if the immunity I picked up in the modern world will extend my life. Perhaps I will even settle for a kind man from this world and marry. One thing I know is that this time, I shall meet my sister, Genevieve. I will witness her birth and see her grow.

I lean hard in the doorway, watching my parents for some time. I know the night, the ebbs and flows of the hours; I can feel it passing by. The turn of the dark sky from black, to blue, to a lavender tinged with pink. It is only when I am sure the sun is rising that I dare to lay down in my bed.

No more bloodlust. No more needless death. Only one more thought passes through my mind as I finally drift off . . .

Oh . . . how I will miss him.

EPILOGUE

Dear . . .

I don't even know your name, dear. I cannot write it here on this paper for it escapes me. Every day it sits on the tip of my tongue like a sweet candy. I can taste it for the barest of moments and then it is gone, gone before I can savour it and swallow.

I burn for you.

There is a halo of condensation here on this window that looks out on to a campus barely clinging to summer. Fall will be upon us soon. Yesterday I dreamed of you again. You wore your hair clipped above your ears and a long gown. A gown not found in the modern world. It was corseted to your body and you stood on a great hill that stretched out far into the distance.

You're beginning to haunt me in my day too. Randomly, as people speak to me, your face, with your dark blue eyes and knowing smile, will sift into my mind. Always, always, that knowledge plays on the edge of your lips.

What is your name? Why do you torment me?

Why do I want to tell you that there are students disappearing at this school? Three in total. The first is still missing, his name is Justin. The second, her funeral is today, and the third went missing yesterday morning.

They discovered the body of Jane Hamlin by the beach, two holes in her neck, drained of her blood. Why is it that your face came to my mind when I heard this information?

You, with your porcelain grace and your unnatural skin.

I would scream for you if you would hear me. I would burn this place to the ground if it meant you would see the smoke. I love you – I know this. Yet I cannot recall who you are.

I must go and close the pages of this journal. I sit here in a lounge suit ready to attend the funeral of Jane Hamlin. Someone has already knocked on my door. The whole of Wickham Boarding School is going. Odd. Just now, as I was about to put down my pen, did a phrase come to me as though it were coming to my mind from a very long slumber. I wonder if my parents taught it to me before their deaths, though I was too young to remember.

Evil be he who thinketh evil.

Do you know the meaning of this? Perhaps it is another clue. Another way to find out who you are.

Evil be he who thinketh evil.

Whoever is killing these students should heed this advice.

Until then,
Rhode

Acknowledgements

First, thank you endlessly to: Ruth Alltimes, Emma Young and Jennifer Weis. How can I thank you enough? What words can I choose that could possibly do justice to the support, patience and guidance of this novel? I've enjoyed all of it. The Macmillan family has made me a better writer.

Mollie Traver: Thank you for your guidance and your time. I can't wait to work with you again on book three. (If I ever need an elevator buddy, I'm calling you.)

Rebecca McNally: A keen eye, a wonderful editor, and now at a new home. Thank you so much for your editorial guidance. I feel lucky to have worked with you and hope to do so again soon! Book three won't be the same without you!

A. M. Jenkins: Thank you for that afternoon at the VCFA picnic tables. Your passion and dedication is unparalleled. Working with you made me a better writer. Working with you showed me what it means to be a great teacher. I miss you!

Kirby Kim, my awesome agent: I can't wait to work on book three and dig our heels into this final book.

Matt Hudson: Your guidance from the get-go was always brilliant and always appreciated. I miss our editorial talks and hope we can work together again soon. Next time, the milkshake is on you.

All of the VCFA community, especially the Keepers of the Dancing Stars: Keepers are for keeps!

The CCWs: Laura Backman, Judy Gamble, Gwen Gardner, Maggie Hayes, Mariellen Langworthy, Claire Nicogossian, and Sarah Ziegelmayer. I love our monthly meetings. You add so much joy to my writing life.

Also big thanks to: Franny Billingsley, Josh Corin (a wonderful reader), Amanda Leathers, Monika Bustamante, Heidi Bennett (vampirequeennovels.com), and Cathryn Summerhayes, my wonderful UK agent.

Also thank you to: David Fox, Michael Sugar and Anna Deroy, and all the WME West crew.

And of course my sister, Jennie: You always know what's best. For my writing and for me. I love you.

Mom and Dad: I don't know how else to say thank you for your endless support. 'If you don't try . . . you don't get!'

And last but not least, Kristin Sandoval: Everything I write in this spot seems incomplete. So, simply, thank you. Thank you for reading my novel endless times. For being honest. For having a hawk-like editing eye and showing me the way when I just couldn't see it. For our Skype calls, and for your patience. You are unbelievably talented and giving. This book would not exist without you. I'm so grateful we met. Thank you. Thank you. Thank you.